We Have Been Warned

# We Have Been Warned

*Naomi Mitchison*

With an introduction by
Isobel Murray

K&B
Kennedy & Boyd

Kennedy & Boyd
an imprint of
Zeticula Ltd
The Roan
Kilkerran
KA19 8LS
Scotland.

http://www.kennedyandboyd.co.uk
admin@kennedyandboyd.co.uk

First published by, and reprinted by, Constable in 1935

This Edition first published 2012



ISBN-13 978-1-84921-026-3 Paperback

# Introduction

Half way through writing this Introduction, I went back to the beginning to write this paragraph. Readers will find this a very negative account of the book, and it is. It was a disaster for Mitchison and her literary reputation, and it is so full of faults that they cannot all be considered. But I fully endorse Jenni Calder's summing-up: 'It is not a good novel, but it is an extremely interesting one.' The interest is for all interested in Mitchison in general, but new readers should not start here!

For far too many reasons, *We Have Been Warned*, not reprinted since 1935, is a very unsatisfactory novel. The reasons include the political climate in Europe at the time of writing; the fact that it is Mitchison's first novel set in the present (1931-3) instead of more or less ancient history; the fact that real life and fiction are endlessly blurred, with characters from the first turning up in the second, under their own or fictional names, the fact that, let loose on the twentieth century and her own life and times, she cannot bear to leave anything out. There are plenty more, but these will do for the time being.

Mitchison's Foreword insists that 'the final chapters of the book were written before the events of summer 1933 in Germany, and before the counter-revolutions of 1934 in Austria and Spain'. The reason for this time gap is that she had a two-year struggle to get it published, because people and publishers found it shocking that it included scenes of abortion and rape, discussions about birth control and sexual experience, by no means always only between husband and wife. The warning of the title presages summer in Germany in 1933, when the Nazis engineered that the Communists be blamed for the Reichstag fire six months earlier, and

*Bad for her literature rd*

*Content is not bad structure is*

*Not well written but interesting to read.*

*change from her POV*

*confused character between her life + fiction*

*What need for*

*Reason one it failed to get published. Raises these things were not discussed in novels at the time* the situation she herself witnessed in Austria in 1934, with fascism in the ascendant.[1]

Mitchison was particularly anxious about the rise of fascism in Germany and Italy, as early as 1931. The fear and disgust Hitler and Mussolini roused in her are fairly clear here, but more strongly expressed in a book with the apparently innocuous title *The Home and a Changing Civilisation*, which she wrote in summer 1933 and published in 1934. As early as this she was outspoken among British writers to excoriate fascism, 'this final and peculiarly revolting end-form of capitalism' as 'all kinds of filthiness and oppression' (102,104) [2]

Her own politics, as she explains through her heroine Dione Galton, are in a state of constant flux. She had visited the USSR in 1932, hoping to find a truly brave new world. But as this novel demonstrates it delighted and unnerved her by turns. She was in the habit of using the ancient Greek Sparta as a convenient shorthand for oppressive or fascist states, and repeats in *You May Well Ask* as she leaves Russia, 'a lot of Sparta about this'(188)[3]. She summed it up in retrospect:

> The visit left me, like many of us more or less left-wing socialists who had read our Marx and all that, with a somewhat ambivalent feeling about the Communist Party. This comes out clearly in *We Have Been Warned.* (Y191)

She was also, as the novel makes abundantly clear, unsure whether the Labour Party the writer and her husband were working for would ever form a sufficient barrier to fascism. There was little authoritative guidance for Mitchison and others. 'We disliked our government intensely,' she writes, and

> Neither Dick nor I realised that perhaps the only chance of avoiding war but containing fascism was to . . . ally ourselves firmly, if not forever, with the USSR. (Y193)

This novel is concerned with opposition to fascism above all, but also with the ferment of emotions the very idea arouses in the main characters. She wrote in *You May Well Ask*, 'Even then I knew at the back of my mind that if I got really involved with politics it would be exceedingly bad for my writing'. (Y182)

It is also Mitchison's first novel set in the present day. She was 'sick of the past really', she wrote in a letter, but unconfident of writing about the present:

> I had started two or three modern novels, but as I was completely without direct experience of the emotional or social situations I had got into my plots, they were very bad and the main characters were all versions of myself, a common enough fault in young writers (Y161).

After her very successful historical novels of the ancient world, friends had urged a modern novel. Auden wrote: 'I do wish you would do a contemporary setting sometime. What is this curious psychological sturk of yours against it?' (B120)[4]

'Ferment of emotions' about politics, but not only politics. The novel is a hectic read. The writer includes every aspect of her extraordinary life, in her heroine Dione and her elder sister Phoebe: she needed *two* characters to share her extraordinary love life. Dione is wife to an Oxford academic and would-be MP, who in many, many ways resembles Dick Mitchison, and she has a family of children not unlike the author's own, while sister Phoebe, an artist in woodcuts, is suffering over the end of a long extra-marital affair, broken off suddenly when the lover decided to marry – all oddly like the situation of Mitchison when her longterm lover Theodore Wade Gery did likewise. Interestingly, after writing this novel and before its publication, Mitchison collaborated with artist Wyndham Lewis on *Beyond This Limit*, text plus illustrations, which deals with the heart-broken woman, here called Phoebe, trying to come to terms with her lover's abandoning her. This is a Modernist fantasy set in Paris, London, Oxford, the Gorilla Arts Theatre and the British Museum . I consider this the only successful treatment of the situation, and very well written. I think the fact of collaboration with Lewis helped the writer to achieve the appropriate literary distance – something she all too frequently fails to do in the novel.[5] There is enough emotional material in these emotional affairs to supply a long novel, with no mention of politics. And this could be done without the agonised worrying over whether Dione should initiate Communist Donald MacLean sexually, or the account of her walking alone into a classic rape situation with Welsh Communist Idriss Pritchard.

It is surely hard to achieve and maintain what I have called the writer's appropriate literary distance from her characters and her heroine's thoughts in a book so nearly describable as autobiography. It is only making life and the literary experience more perplexing to dedicate the book at the start to a page-long list of 'comrades', some well known, and follow with two and a bit pages of characters in the book, many clearly the same people. When the author is passionately involved in world affairs and at rather a loss what if anything to do about them, and just as passionately emotionally involved with love affairs and different men, in birth control and whether it is justifiable to have another child while the world is in such danger, appropriate literary distance may be an unreal quality to look for.

Her first biographer, Jill Benton, is as kind as possible:

> Her brave political novel, *We Have Been Warned,* identified the contradictions which plagued the uneasy upper-middle class alliance of communism, socialism and feminism. It was the only work of its kind.(B xv)

And again: 'She had invented a female hero who was adventuring into the world, questing fully within a historically specific moment, even though that moment was not propitious for free women.'(B94). Benton says the novel contains exquisitely written passages, and it is an invaluable first-hand description of British politics and mores in 1932: I find it hard to disagree with this. 'But as a novel, it does not quite hold together': no indeed. She also stresses the aftermath: 'few reviews, none favourable.' Reviewers were shocked: 'the book was a disaster for Naomi; it went to only one printing. Her Left politics had already limited her readership, and now she had alienated those who remained. Naomi never recovered her literary reputation in England'. (B106)

Her official biographer, Jenni Calder, in *The Nine Lives of Naomi Mitchison* (1997) is more trenchant. She points to rawness, 'a lack of authorial mediation, which makes it uneven and unsatisfactory in many ways, the melodramatic strains of the plot, the near-naivety with which Tom and Dione discuss their marriage and their feelings for others', and she concludes: 'It is not a good novel, but it is an extremely interesting one' (C122). [6]

At the time of writing, and over the years before it was published, Mitchison herself was very confident about it. She was proud of what was new, and protective in its defence. She wrote to the censorious publisher that it is essentially a woman's book:

> For, of the people who have read it, the women have been much the most enthusiastic. The whole business of contraception is done from the woman's point of view, which is, of course, a new thing in writing. But it's damned important.(B 93)

She refused to modify the vivid Dione:

> You see, I'm more sure about this book than I've ever been about any of the other books. I know that Dione behaves in an odd way, but I'm quite certain of her behaviour. She isn't a completely normal person any more than Erif Der was – or than I am myself. Possibly I am suffering from a complex of sexual obsessions myself – I suspect many people would say so. (B94)

She changed her mind somewhat, late on. When I interviewed her at length in 1984 she was still proud of it, and was expecting Virago to reprint it next. They did not. Any such plans were cancelled. They republished *The Corn King and the Spring Queen*, *The Bull Calves* and *Travel Light*. She complained bitterly about the publisher-enforced cuts, on birth control, contraceptives, sexual matters and rape:

> I've had now to reconstruct it. I've now rewritten it as I think I would have written it then. . . On the other hand, there's a lot of rather turgid writing in it, which I

*blames the lack of success on content of the book not her novel itself* must really leave because it's of its period. I sort of ran away with myself over the descriptions. Adjectives. I used too many adjectives.(S85) [7]

I was nervous of her: it was our first meeting, and I didn't dare to go in for directly negative criticism. I wanted to ask about how she divided herself into the two sisters, and why the book is to my mind overloaded with personal symbolism, from kelpies to elephants. It went like this:

**IM:** And clearly, not only the main female character but also I think her sister are both in some senses you, are parts of you – both Dione and Phoebe. . . .Dione is 'the' central character, 'the' central consciousness.
**NM:** Yes.
**IM:** And I wonder how she is going to go down in the 1980s.
**NM:** Because she's very wuzzy. She doesn't make up her mind.
**IM:** There's no harm in *that*, I think. And she's a feminist, and that's fine, and she's a socialist of a very personal kind, working out very personal dilemmas about what she thinks about it. I wonder, though, about her magic side?
**NM:** Phoebe?
**IM:** Well no, not Phoebe so much here – or Phoebe as well, the magic bits, the Campbell women, the Kelpies.
**NM:** The Kelpies, yes.
**IM:** Do you think that necessarily works?
**NM:**I don't know that it would, you see. It would be very difficult to take out.
**IM:** Oh yes, it would be impossible. I mean, it's a period piece, and I wouldn't want to take it out, but when

you were writing in, I think, *You May Well Ask* about Stella Benson, you said that she was less fashionable now because of an element of fantasy which you said very occasionally verges on whimsy [Y 129]. And I wondered whether. . .
**NM:** Yes. I think this is probably so. But whether one can take it out.
**IM:** No, no, I'm sure not. You wouldn't write it that way now, but she's there. (S85-6)

But clearly something took her back to it, and in 1993 she told Jenni Calder 'what a bad book it is, as far as I have looked at it again' (C124) She disliked the characters, and was embarrassed about it – 'the book seems to have a lot of photographs about myself'.

Here I want to add a bit more negative criticism, which again illustrates a certain lack of authorial control. After the tricksy dedication and list of characters already mentioned, there is to my mind an over-elaborate start to the book, offering the reader unnecessarily hard work. First, each of the seven parts is headed by a reference to Bunyan's *Pilgrim's Progress*. The references are fairly cursory, and I am sure that some readers in 1935, as well as many today will need 'reminding' of the context if it is to add anything to the book. The City of Destruction (Part I) stands for the fallen world and is opposed to the eternal celestial city which is Christian's destination. The Slough of Despond (Part II): consciousness of sin was a recognised preliminary to conversion, and the wicket gate, kept by Christ, represents the conversion experience. In Part III The House of the Interpreter - the instruction of the new convert by the Holy Spirit, and the House Beautiful episode represents church fellowship. Part IV: In the Valley of Humiliation Christian fights Satan the

Destroyer, visits Vanity Fair, where all sorts of earthly values are sold, and is imprisoned in Doubting Castle. Part V: Led astray, assailed by doubts of their election, they are shown pilgrims dashed to pieces at the foot of Hill Error, and walk with shepherds on the Delectable Mountains, but are warned not to sleep on the Enchanted Ground. Part VI: the country of Beulah is on the borders of Heaven, and the river (Part VII) is a pleasant place with meadows, trees and fruit. [8]

Interested readers may want to consult Bunyan further, and then conjecture whether the various parts of the novel usefully refer to Dione's progress in socialism, or not.

Each Part of the novel is also prefaced with a piece of poetry, something Mitchison had done since her first novel *The Conquered.* These range from Fabian G D H Cole and Mass Observation's Charles Madge to Belloc, Spender, Auden, Day Lewis and Blake, and generally reflect the Left wing mood . So far, then, so good. But the first chapter spends a lot of time on what seems to be a personal Scottish mythology for Dione and Phoebe. We hear about ancestress Green Jean MacLean on the first page of the chapter, which is set in the sisters' family home in the Highlands, at Auchanarnish. Dione ponders the sisters' 'witch names', and Green Jean's trial for witchcraft, her acquittal, her eventual death with her baby at the hands of the Campbells, and her haunting the castle thereafter. Dione's sympathy for her ancestor includes interest in witchcraft. Soon she associates the murderous Campbells with the modern Campbell Women, 'the cruel, successful people' with modern women at lunch parties, and 'the kelpies, who twisted everything and made it horrible and lonely, full or corners and evil magic'. The reader assumes that this way of thinking will be important in the novel, having taken such a crucial place in the first chapter. Later one suspects that Green Jean's prominance here is chiefly to account for her reappearance some five hundred pages later, to show Dione visions of possible futures. She only recurs infrequently before that. But there is more!

On the very next page there is another account of an ancient mythology adopted by the family, the characters from *The Birds* of Aristophanes. Again, the reader needs to be familiar with at least the outline of that play, and even after rereading it I find it hard to follow the connections the author is making, or to understand what it adds to the mix.

And in any other first chapter less full of hints and guesses, the water imagery would catch our attention and lead us to expect continued and meaningful reference to it. Phoebe repeatedly filled the cans with water for the flowers to decorate the room for the party. She remembers punting with her lost lover on the Cher, and follows a long passage where she contemplates all the rivers flowing toward London. She also thinks about 'another imprisoned river, half imprisoned, the evil Marsh-brook' that flows through slum housing, where in winter 'the houses were flooded three feet deep in brown and filthy-smelling water.' The fourth water she ponders is 'the sea-mist at Helm', where she lives, and which she loves. Next the sea at Auchanarnish, Gare Loch, even (from Phoebe!) a political angle clear now: 'Scotland is not functioning. Because the sea is full of seals and kelpies and dragging currents.' Her personal image is the gules lion which is here 'asleep like any donkey on a bed of thistles':

> And I am left alone with the sea and the kelpies and the Campbell women and poor Green Jean, and Saint Finnegal stands there with a stiff little smile and she is no good at all either. (15)

Phoebe and Dione are rarely clearly distinguished, and it

is Phoebe who here laments the slump and unemployment and has a vision of what she could do for Scotland (but in later chapters there is very little evidence of this!).

> If I could make up my mind about anything except wood-engraving I would be able to do everything. I would be able to wake up the gules lion. I would be able to say Scotland in such a loud and surprising voice that walls would tumble down and sea-waters would part and collapse under the surprised seals. I would say Scotland so startlingly that the clans would gather at Gare Loch head, and we would go down to Clyde bank and drive all the kelpies out of the sea water. (15)

The chapter ends with Phoebe wanting to walk along the sea shore with one of her lovers and see just the beautiful surface colours, 'but to be able to see it without trying to look through the water and behind the rocks in case the kelpies were hiding there.' (17) We have the impression that she is to be the main character, which she certainly is not, or at least that she and Dione are to share the narrative interest.

Thus the first chapter, and all the images, symbols or metaphors started here. But they all belong to the sea and Auchanarnish, and do not transfer very well to the slums or decent working class Sallington, or the Galtons' Oxford. By early Part II the sisters are discussing another figure, the Elephant:

> He's a very big Elephant, and they're quite little people. He's a very respectable Elephant too. He wants you to have a trunk the same as he has, and little bright, prying eyes and a thick skin and rather a limited brain space. Oh yes, and a backbone. The backbone of England.

> And if you aren't just right – well, he picks you up with his trunk and he pulls your arms and legs off. He can be a very nasty Elephant. (121)

The Elephant works rather better than the earlier fey Scottish ones. He represents the Establishment, and respectability. I feel he would work better still if not preceded by the earlier ones, even when we find Auden writing to her asking for an elephant in the book, to interrupt a garden party. She wrote in pencil in her copy of the novel:

> This elephant part is in a way the genesis of the book – Wystan telling me to write a book about an elephant at a garden party. (B 90)

Mitchison duly provides a real elephant at the party, but its escape proves only a sideshow: the real interest of that chapter (Oxford 3) being the Galtons' family conspiracy to help the murderer of a newspaper owner escape justice!

Green Jean may well have been forgotten by now, but she returns at the end of the book. She has come to help, with a warning. She has a magic stone through which one can see possible futures. Dione looks. First she sees a splendid scene of a Labour landslide all over Britain, a Socialist triumph. But Green Jean says: 'The stone, as you will have heard tell, is not a stone of truth but of warning' (536), and she invites Dione to look again. 'Oxford 6' finds devastation – Morag raped, Ken captured, the house smashed up, Phoebe lost, fascist revolution let loose. When she looks again she is to be forced to watch Tom's execution by firing squad. She comes back to consciousness rapidly after this vivid picture, and the novel ends briskly soon after. It more than justifies the title, *We Have Been Warned.*

The main action of the novel centres on Dione, whose Oxford lecturer husband Tom is about to offer himself for a parliamentary seat in Sallington (Birmingham), where a previous Labour candidate has had to retire because of illness. He is a sympathetic but not very central character. The action begins in 1931, and covers Tom's unsuccessful candidacy at a General Election, and the preliminary work he and Dione do in the constituency. A great deal of the writing here is very clear and convincing, as wealthy intellectual Dione encounters the realities of working-class life, and the worst of slum living, and comes face to face with Labour Party workers and with Communists. Indeed she also later meets Hunger Marchers from the north, and is part of a riot in London's Hyde Park.

> Again the crowd heaved violently; Dione, right off her feet this time, was really frightened. People were throwing things, shouting. There was a scream from somewhere, the crash of something breaking; she was horribly near the spiked railings. Then a yell: 'They're charging us!' and above the human voices the primitive whinny of a horse, frightened too. Then to her right the crowd broke and ran. She was knocked down on to her knees, but not right over – she picked herself up extremely indignant and almost under the nose of a police horse. 'Look out, my man!' she said. The rider swerved: 'You clear out, ma'am!' he said, irritated but still respectful. (453)

And much more, clearly an account of a personal experience, plus the thoughts that went with it.

An important sub-plot concerns Dione's distant kinsman Donald MacLean from Auchanarnish, where her mother is 'the Laird' and his parents are employees. Donald has left home to become an embittered unemployed Communist whom Dione encounters and tries to befriend down south. In a moment of desperation he murders a newspaper proprietor, and his escape to the USSR is facilitated by the Galtons. He remains there, and after a somewhat blush-making verbal 'affair' with Dione, meets a girl of his own and starts a family. (Dione has many encounters with different classes, culminating in her rape by a Welsh comrade).

The Mitchisons went to the USSR in 1932 on separate trips, with great hopes for the new Society. Dione and Tom go there too, and the plot requires that they too go on separate trips, so that Tom, with his wife's permission, can enjoy an affair with a Russian girl. If we can ignore the often embarrassing sexual affairs they variously undertake and discuss, the account of the experience of English intellectual Socialists encountering the new Russia is full and engrossing, with both delights and disappointments. This is another part of the book that will be interesting to the historian of the Thirties.

Toward the end of the book Dione returns to Auchanarnish for a break, with Labour schoolmistress Agnes Green, and it is then that she has her momentous close encounter with Green Jean. Throughout the book we are often trapped in Dione's head, along with her wavering political inclinations, her doubts, her anxieties over class and wealth, and even whether a truly socialist woman should sleep with a man just because he is a Comrade, and wants it (while she does not!). Some of this becomes a bit oppressive, and the problem again,I think, is lack of distance – almost of breathing space.

There is no omniscient narrator. Dione is both narrator and major character, and Mitchison ignores any sense of appropriate distance from the reader that she would retain effortlessly in any of her historical novels. Interestingly, this does not occur in her memoirs, her *non*-fiction writings about her past, where she remains poised somewhere between her past self and her later feelings or judgments about it all.

Early in her third memoir, *You May Well Ask* (1979), she writes:

> This book will try to show honestly how I grew up and changed into the woman I was when the next war came. But it will be about a family and the friends and acquaintances, fellow workers and fellow voters who shaped us as we in turn shaped them.. . . It has been hard to write. . . . One is still involved. Bits of it are still powerful to hurt or to recall stupidities and bad judgment and cruelties, perhaps inadvertent or perhaps not. (Y12)

This is quite a different volume, and more like the Mitchison of her best work. *You May Well Ask* is not impersonal, but it could hardly be more different from *We Have Been Warned.*

**Notes**

1 See her *Vienna Diary*, Kennedy and Boyd 2009.
2 *The Home and a Changing Civilisation*, 1934, pp 102, 104.
3 *You May Well Ask: A Memoir 1920-1940*, London 1979. References given in brackets as (Y000).
4 Jill Benton, *Naomi Mitchison: A Biography*, London 1990. References given as (B000).
5 See *Beyond This Limit: Selected Shorter Fiction of Naomi Mitchison* ed Isobel Murray, Kennedy and Boyd 2008, pp xi-xvi.
6 See Jenni Calder, *The Nine Lives of Naomi Mitchison,* London, 1997. References given as (C000).
7 See Isobel Murray, ed, *Scottish Writers Talking 2*, Tuckwell Press, 2002. Mitchison interview pp 67-109, here p 85. References given as (S000).
8 This paragraph is heavily indebted to the apparatus to N H Keeble's edition of *The Pilgrim's Progress,* Oxford World's Classics, 1984..

# FOREWORD

In deference to the intensive criticism which this historical novel about my own times has already received, I wish to state most earnestly that the views on socialism and in general on social morality expressed by the main characters in the story do not represent either the official Labour Party attitude nor the views of any Left-wing or "intelligentsia" group. Nor do they, to the best of my knowledge, represent the views of any person in the dedication of the book.

I must beg my readers to believe that all characters in this book are creatures of my own imagination; both their adventures and their opinions are fictitious. Occasionally real people are introduced under their real names, but they take no part whatsoever in the action of the book. May I add that the final chapters of the book were written before the events of summer 1933 in Germany, and before the counter-revolutions of 1934 in Austria and Spain.

In conclusion, I should like to thank the editors of *The Modern Scot* and *The Oxford Outlook* for permission to reprint two chapters in this book which originally appeared in their papers.

N. M. M.

## TO THE COMRADES

especially

The girl in the train between Odessa and Kiev, *Aeroplane engineer, citizen of the U.S.S.R.*

WYSTAN AUDEN, *Schoolmaster and poet.*

ZITA BAKER, *Explorer.*

BETTIE MELISSA BAXTER, *Working woman.*

TOM BAXTER, *Ex-colliery worker, Labour Party agent.*

LANCE BEALES, *Historian, lecturer at London University.*

DOUGLAS COLE, *Economic historian, lecturer at Oxford University.*

MARGARET COLE, *Historian and writer.*

ARTHUR DAVIES, *Ex-Labour Party agent, cabinet-maker.*

VICTOR GOLLANCZ, *Publisher.*

WALTER GREENWOOD, *Writer, Labour Councillor.*

THEA GRIFFITHS, *Working woman.*

GRAEME HALDANE, *Consulting engineer.*

GERALD HEARD, *Writer.*

AGNES MACCANCE, *Painter and wood-engraver.*

" MAISIE," *Secretary.*

JULIUS MARTI, *Archæologist and Director of the Museum at Kerch, citizen of the U.S.S.R.*

DOROTHY MELENEVSKY, *Working woman and teacher, citizen of the U.S.S.R.*

RUDI MESSEL, *Propagandist, Labour candidate.*

DMITRI MIRSKY, *Writer and historian, citizen of the U.S.S.R.*

DENNY MITCHISON, *Schoolboy.*

DICK MITCHISON, *Barrister, Labour candidate.*

JOHN PILLEY, *Lecturer in Education at Bristol University.*

JOHNNY PRITT, *K.C., Labour candidate.*

LEON THOMPSON, *Analytical chemist.*

JOSEF RANDICH, *Seaman.*

MARGARET WILSON, *Social worker, ex-Labour Councillor.*

and to the memory of

STAN BOYLE, *Ex-Guardsman and public-house keeper.*

# PEOPLE IN THIS BOOK

## THE FAMILY

MRS. FRASER (*née* MacLean), *Landowner.*

Her daughter, ISOBEL DIONE, *Married woman.*

Her elder daughter, ELIZABETH PHŒBE, *Painter and wood-engraver.*

Her son ALEXANDER, *Writer to the Signet.*

Dione's husband, TOM GALTON, *Economist, Historian, Lecturer at Oxford University and Labour candidate.*

Their children, MORAG, KENNETH, IAN and LILIAS.

Phœbe's husband, ROBIN BATHURST, *Landowner and farmer.*

Their children, PETRONELLA, CLEMENCY and BRIAN.

Tom Galton's elder sister, ROSALIND, and her husband, REGINALD COKE-BROWN, *Manufacturer.*

Their children, GEORGE and ELIZABETH.

MARGARET COKE-BROWN, *Ex-student*, married to a nephew of Reginald Coke-Brown.

Tom Galton's younger sister, MURIEL, *Social worker.*

Various relations on all sides, including DANIEL COKE-BROWN, *Newspaper Proprietor.*

## MEMBERS OF THE LABOUR PARTY IN SALLINGTON

STANLEY MASON, *Labour Party agent, ex-factory worker*, and MRS. MASON.

REUBEN GOLDBERG, *Electrical engineer*, and MRS. GOLDBERG.

ALBERT TAYLOR, *Bricklayer*, MRS. TAYLOR, and their child EMMIE.

COUNCILLOR FINCH, *Co-operative Society employee*, and his daughter DOROTHY, and her husband BILL, *Factory worker (Synthex Works), unemployed.*

GEORGE GROVE, *Engineer*, MRS. GROVE, HER SISTER, and their child BILLY.

SAM HALL, *Tram conductor.*

MISS WATERHOUSE, *Social worker.*

MRS. EAST, *Forewoman at laundry.*

GLADYS WILLS, *Typist.*

JO BURRAGE, *Mill-hand (Woollens).*

ED PALMER, *Factory worker.*

JOHN COLLIS, *Branch Secretary of the National Union of Wool Workers.*

And others.

## PEOPLE IN THIS BOOK

### MEMBERS OF THE COMMUNIST PARTY IN SALLINGTON

AGNES GREEN, *School teacher.*
DONALD MACLEAN, *Riveter, out of work.*
IDRIS PRITCHARD, *Skating instructor.*
DORIS, *Mill-hand (Woollens).*
And others.

### MEMBERS OF THE NATIONAL UNEMPLOYED WORKERS' MOVEMENT IN SALLINGTON

HARRY GARDENER, *Lorry and general driver, out of work.*
ADAM WALKER, *Ex-service man with war disability, labourer, out of work.*
And others.

### PEOPLE LIVING NEAR AUCHANARNISH

MR. MACLEAN, *Head gardener*, and MRS. MACLEAN.
ROBERT FINNEY, *Farmer*, MRS. FINNEY, and their children, CHRISSIE and JAMES.
JIMSIE MACKIE, *Garage mechanic.*
MR. ANDERSON, *Farmer;* MRS. ANDERSON, *Dairywoman;* and their children.
MR. MACCALLUM, *Keeper*, and MRS. MACCALLUM.
JOHN MACLEAN OF LERGULIGAN, *Farmer*, and his young sister.
CHRISTINA CAMPBELL, *Waitress at Temperance Hotel.*
WILLIE, *Boatman.*
RED PETER, *Boatman*, and his son.
MR. and MRS. MACKIE, and LADY ANN, *Landowners.*
And many others.

### PEOPLE AT OXFORD

PHILIP BICKERDEN, *Physicist, University Lecturer*, and his wife, MAY BICKERDEN.
DAVID HAWKES, *Undergraduate*, and other of TOM GALTON's pupils.
TEDDY BROOKS, *Biologist and reader at Oxford University.*
*Chaplain of St. Mary's College and other dons.*
DIONE GALTON's *Nurse.*
ALICE, Dione Galton's *Parlourmaid.*
And countless others.

# PEOPLE IN THIS BOOK

## PEOPLE IN LONDON

PUSSY MORGAN, *Painter.*
JOYCE WARD, *Independent means.*
CYNTHIA, *Model.*
VICTOR, *Minor poet.*
Several others.

## PEOPLE GOING ON A TOUR TO THE U.S.S.R.

LADY NANCY ELLIS, *Social worker and Publicist,* and her daughter,
JANE ELLIS, *Schoolgirl.*
FRANK MEDINGLEY, *Barrister.*
JACK LAMBERT, *Journalist.*

## PEOPLE IN MOSCOW

MARFA, *Engineer.*
MARIA, *Engineer and Student.*
NINA, *Electrical Engineer.*
PROFESSOR NIKOLAEVSKY, *Mathematician,* and his wife,
MRS. NIKOLAEVSKY, *Doctor;* his elder daughter,
OKSANA, *Radio Specialist and Student;* his son,
LEON, *Cinema Technician;* and his younger daughter,
NEONILA, *Student of Languages.*
And others.

# CONTENTS

## PART I

### OUT OF THE CITY OF DESTRUCTION



## PART II

### THE SLOUGH OF DESPOND TO THE WICKET GATE



## PART III

### THE HOUSE OF THE INTERPRETER TO THE HOUSE BEAUTIFUL

## PART IV

### THE VALLEY OF HUMILIATION, BY VANITY FAIR, TO DOUBTING CASTLE



## PART V

### HILL ERROR AND DELECTABLE MOUNTAINS TO THE ENCHANTED GROUND



## PART VI

### BEULAH



## PART VII

### THE RIVER

# PART I

## OUT OF THE CITY OF DESTRUCTION

"There is a wall of which the stones
Are lies and bribes and dead men's bones.
And wrongfully this evil wall
Denies what all men made for all,
And shamelessly this wall surrounds
Our homesteads and our native grounds."

H. BELLOC.

## AUCHANARNISH I

HER mind focussed sometimes on to the page and sometimes beyond it. It shifted her in time and space. It shifted her more in time than in space. For in the book the time was middle seventeenth century and the place was Inverary, but out of the book the time was September 1931, but the place was Auchanarnish, only about fifty miles away from Inverary. The shapes of the hills were almost exactly the same, and the shapes of the sea-lochs, and behind the wall-paper, which was about thirty years old, the stone outer walls of the Auchanarnish schoolroom were the same as they had been then. It was only the woman in the book and the woman who was reading it who were different.

Beyond the edge of the small, old-fashioned print was the margin; the margin was pleasantly spaced, but it was yellowing with time, and the paper was growing stiff and brittle. On the margin was the thumb, strong and rather wrinkled—but why not?—and the nail cut unfashionably short. This was page 57, and at the beginning of the book there was a dullish engraved book-plate with a coat of arms, and under it, in solid legible half-childish script, her name, Isobel Dione Fraser, and her sister's name, Elizabeth Phœbe Fraser. Isobel and Elizabeth were their witch names. And Jean was a witch name. If she had another girl she would call her Jean. No, no, she mustn't think that! She knew she mustn't have any more children. Unless the revolution came in time, before she was too old. She mustn't think that either: it was romanticising; it was making personal and little something that was so big and so real that she couldn't think about it properly. What Tom called Realistically. Run away from that, back to Inverary in the seventeenth century.

The book was a volume of criminal trials. The third trial reported in the book was the trial of Jean MacLean, called Green Jean, for witchcraft. She was acquitted then; five years later the Campbells got her. In the family everyone said that of course Jean MacLean had not been a witch; there were no such things as witches. She had been fortunate in finding a moderately enlightened jury. And now this other woman, her descendant, Isobel Dione Galton, re-reading the trial in her old schoolroom after fifteen years, was doubting and criticising the family tradition. On the evidence it seemed to her more than likely that Jean MacLean had been a witch, had belonged to this other, this oppressed secret society, and had probably had dealings with some pre-Celtic and conquered folk. And the jury had acquitted her, not because she was innocent, but because she was the Lady of Auchanarnish. There were no burnings at Inverary for a few years; the secret society had too many members among the rich and powerful. Perhaps Campbells too. But all the same the Campbells had raided Auchanarnish one January night when the men were away over at a gathering, and Green Jean had been thrown out on to the hillside with her baby at her breast. She had wrapped her plaid and her kirtle round the baby, but when the MacLeans came back they found her dead and stiff and the baby dead and the snow seeping down on them. Since then she had walked in Auchanarnish, in her green dress, carrying her baby and mourning; perhaps that was because a witch would rather be burnt and her ashes scattered on the fields. The un-ritual death by cold could not lay Green Jean.

"Nonsense, nonsense!" said Dione, half aloud, "what

would father think of me imagining all that, father who was a Fraser and a sceptic and one of the foremost Scottish archæologists of his day! What would he have thought of Phœbe and me for seeing Green Jean in the nursery corridor? Tom doesn't believe we ever did. But Tom is a lowlander."

She went on reading the book, skipping pages, half listening to the children at the piano in the room beyond. Morag and Petronella singing. "Cut down like a flower is MacLean of Ardgour." And some day Morag would have a beautiful voice; it was nice when one's children did things better than oneself, got further. Now she had come to the evidence; she liked reading what the witches themselves said; at that time torture wasn't being used much up here. The Sabbats sounded very like Labour Socials. First there was a dance, with an M.C. to see it was properly done, and then someone gave a recitation and someone else sang a song, and everyone gave accounts of what they'd been doing, whether they'd done any Party work, got any new members . . . and the Candidate had to talk to everyone and go through all sorts of antics which were no doubt very boring for him . . . "and his tail goes aye wig-wag, wig-wag" . . . and at the end the League of Youth rides off home on broom-sticks and everyone feels it has been a most enjoyable and profitable evening.

But the Church did them in sooner or later; it didn't hold with groups against its own. The Church. And the Campbell Women, the cruel, successful people, the Campbell Women who had helped to drive Jean MacLean out into the snow. Like the Coke-Brown women at lunch parties with her sister-in-law at Sallington. And the kelpies, who twisted everything and made it horrible and lonely, full of corners and evil magic. There was something always going for one, going for the good group and turning it bad. Or was it in the groups themselves, something really wrong with people? She didn't want to think that. She propped her elbow on the open book left lying on her knee, and dropped her chin on her hand, frowning and bothering. In the other room Morag was singing "Linten Lowring." "I'll gang the gait I canna gang, And a better bairnie I will be." Yes, that was it, one was always trying to be a better bairnie, trying to go back the way one can't go and undo all one has done and all that has been done to one. Class, upbringing, education. . . . "Oh, Rynie's work is hard to work, And Rynie's wages are but sma', And Rynie's rules are double strict. . . ." Yes, there seemed to be a solid economic basis about this song! Was that it after all? Just economics, and all this about groups her romanticising again. She sighed and stretched. She would have liked to ask Tom, to be made to look at things plainly and solidly again, but Tom and her brother were out shooting Ardfeochan. They had both of them flatly refused to have anything to do with getting things ready for the dance. And it was about time she and Phœbe did something about that.

She got up and put the book away and went to her room, then she tied one of Tom's big handkerchiefs pirate-fashion over her brown hair. Last week she had seen some white hairs on Phœbe, sudden, irrational white hairs among the brown which was a shade lighter than hers. It had frightened her rather, though she and Phœbe had laughed about it at the time. But then, Phœbe was three years older than she was. Three years. That wasn't much. Three more summer holidays at Auchanarnish. Perhaps it was that Phœbe was always being worried about things. The people she fell in love with. And her work. And the children, especially Brian. And she hadn't got Tom to share things with, only Robin, who never seemed to get well, and who was always being worried about things himself.

No, at present Dione Galton had no white hairs; she looked at herself in the glass, enjoying the Peter Pannish knot on the pirate handkerchief, and hastily rationalised it by saying that the furniture would be dusty. And then grinned at herself, because she knew it wasn't true, and would have annoyed Flora the housemaid very much if she had suspected it. Then she went up to the high drawing-room to get it ready for the dance. Morag was still playing songs to herself.

"Aren't you going to get me the flowers for the dance?" said Dione, looking in on the way.

"All right, mother," Morag said, getting up rather reluctantly and leaving the piano open, "I will if Ken will."

"Tell him from me he's got to," said Dione, "he's been at the smithy all morning interrupting Black John, and he can do a spot of work now. Besides, you'll both like it! I'm sure Petronella and Clemency will help, and I expect George will if you ask him nicely."

"Oh, bother George!"

"Well, you'll find two pairs of scissors in the scissor drawer, and if you don't, you must make Ken remember where he lost them last. Cut along."

For a time Dione was pleasantly busy, shoving furniture about and rolling up the rugs. But when it came to the china cupboards, which had to be moved out of harm's way, because of the country dances and reels, she shouted down over the stairs for her sister to come and help.

"Can't we leave them where they are?" said Phœbe, standing in the doorway, glaring balefully at the Crown Derby. "I'd love to see some of that junk get smashed up!"

"Nonsense!" said Dione, and then: "What's biting you, Phœbe? That young man of yours? Or is it work? Come on, Phœbe, you goose! let's get Odd Bits into the corner. You take the far end: now it'll slide. Push it straight! There."

They settled the Odd Bits cupboard into the corner by the fireplace, with a sofa across it, then pushed the rest of the furniture against the walls, and wiped over the floor; they didn't want it too slippery for country dancing. They planned where to put the flowers, swags over the lamp brackets and big jars with trailers coming down from them on the tops of things. They would have a great spiky jar with agapanthus and red-hot pokers and spiræa on the top of Odd Bits. It would look rather well, for the cupboard itself was a fine bit of Scottish Adams. Most of the Odd Bits inside the cupboard were completely worthless, and some had vague associational value; but there were a few good attic vase fragments, and one red-figure cup nearly complete. In the middle of the cup was a man with a short black beard, a determined and enquiring grin, a wide-brimmed hat, and a travelling-cloak and staff; round the outer edge of the cup there were various rather shapeless birds. Mr. Fraser had brought them all back from Greece in his young days; he had married late and settled down to comfort and folklore controversy. He used to show this cup to the girls and tell them that the enquiring man was Peisthetairos, the Persuader, who met a Talking Crow which guided him to Cloud Cuckoo Borough, the house of King Hoopoe and the Parliament of the Birds, and in the end he married Basileia, the Queen of the Fairies.

But later on Phœbe and Dione had seen that Peisthetairos, that determined and persuasive man, was Intellect and Imagination applied to life, and especially to dealings with people: that the Talking Crow was the Dæmon—the voice of reality that one has to follow: and that Basileia was Power or Grace or conscious Happiness, or whatever combination of the three it is that comes suddenly to those people who have used Intellect and Imagination for the good of life, of the Birds, for the citizens of Cloud Cuckoo Borough. But Phœbe's identification of the Hoopoe with the Scientific Intellect was accidental, and in some way connected with Phil Bickerden, who was a physicist: Phil Bickerden with his bright eyes like a bird's: Phil who had been kind and aware and happy-making, who had walked and talked with Phœbe on Sunday mornings of summer term: Phil who had suddenly got married and was now in process of living happily ever after in North Oxford. Phil the King Hoopoe with his sharp bird-dart at a fact, gobbling it down, Phil with his crest feathers up. She had painted Summer Island for Phil, but hoopoes don't like pictures much. Or perhaps it was because he'd just decided to marry May. Anyway, Summer Island was a good picture. Old Eumorphopulos wouldn't have bought it if it hadn't been!

Dione saw Phœbe glaring at Odd Bits, and knew from her glare that she was thinking away from Auchanarnish and the dance. Which of the many things was she glaring at? There was nothing to be done about any of them. The lunch-gong roared throatily at them from below; it became a question of seeing that the children were all collected and washed.

In the afternoon they did the decorating. The children brought up the baskets. Dione and Phœbe arranged the flowers. Some of the baskets were full of sweet-peas, cold and delicate and autumnish, from the back of the long border. Some were full of montbretia and fern, or phlox and snapdragon, or branches of the little half-wild fuchsias, that don't last but are good for a day or two; and Morag's flat basket had blue and white agapanthus, and hydrangeas, and great stiff gladiolus, and tree pæony, and late powder-blue ceanothus, and branches of ramblers from the north walk. When Dione looked out of the window she could see all the children, small and scurrying, still picking in the square garden, and hear the faint shrilling of their voices, air-dimmed between the lawns and paths and the window-ledge of the high drawing-room.

Phœbe filled the cans with water. Then she filled all the flower-jars for the house, the pottery milk-jars, and the Breton and Italian and Dutch jars, spoil of their Europe-trotting father forty years ago, and the pair of green vases from Jenner's, which she used to like as a child and had forgotten to stop liking, and the copper bottling-pans from the kitchen. Dione was making the swags to hang over the lamp brackets out of the flowers that lasted best, the asters and the faintly disagreeable-smelling phlox. She knew MacLean thought they were just a waste; he would really have preferred never to have his flowers picked at all, especially by the children. But Dione could manage him, and anyhow he would be so excited at being M.C. this evening that he would scarcely notice.

But Phœbe refilled the cans and went on pouring water into the flower-jars. She dipped her hands into the copper pan that was going to be filled with iron-blue hydrangeas. The water struck chilly at her wrists, over the pulse. Once she had trailed her hands over the side of the punt high up the river towards Islip, and Phil had discussed relativity and she had understood. But it was not Phil she was thinking about. Take him away, wring that Hoopoe's neck, stop him pecking! For then there was, more strongly than relativity, the feel of the Cher water on her wrists. It was at the beginning of the Michaelmas term, the most stilled and magic time; the water was deep green and so smooth that she had to insert her hands deftly and quietly so as not to ripple it. On the surface there were golden poplar leaves ; when she leaned down towards it she became dizzy with the breathing out of cold autumn-sweet air from that clay-bedded river, from that water that had soaked through ripening bramble hedges and down the aged boles of thorn trees, and crept across cowy pastures under moonlight or dawn, and now enclosed and gently, sweetly, rotted the stems of water-lilies and flowering rush and arrow-head and tall water-docks, and would in time slither down, looping south to Oxford past flat meadows and osiers and boat-houses, that would in time reflect Magdalen tower and Magdalen bridge and the steep brick sides of the Botanical Gardens, and the great chestnut tree that one floats under to Eights, that would in time go down to the Thames and the locks and the busy traffic and Henley Bridge and Maidenhead Bridge and Staines Bridge, and all the bridges of London stamping and striding across.

And she moved her finger-tips in the water over the copper bottom of the pan, and under London there were rivers, the Tyburn and the Fleet boxed up and silent in hollow culverts below the 'buses and the lorries and the offices and the studio parties. The parties went on almost all the time and people talked and got drunk and made love, and sometimes they wrote or painted, and sometimes they were at the London School of Economics, and sometimes they were architects, but they were always the same people and Basileia was not among them. The Talking Crow said to come away. But under Bloomsbury and under Chelsea and under Hammersmith the dark imprisoned streams of London went on, voiceless and sullen.

There was another imprisoned river, half imprisoned, the evil Marsh-brook, rising out of a chain of ponds where the Barton's End children sailed boats in summer, and dipping into the channel that had been dug and faced for it by afraid people, and sometimes allowing itself to be bricked over, but not for long. In winter the Marsh-brook hunched itself and hunched itself and burst up through manholes and drain-pipes, and quietly and successfully flooded the houses in Carisbrook Road. The houses were flooded three feet deep in brown and filthy-smelling water. Dead kittens and sticks and bottles floated about in the corners, and the children got sore throats, and the old people died off. But the men and women in Carisbrook Road did not complain much. They did not insist. They did not think they had any rights against the Marsh-brook which had flooded houses in Marshbrook Bridge ever since some speculative builder towards the end of last century had built Carisbrook Road and all the other little streets of houses which got flooded, and then the houses had been let and sub-let and sub-sub-let, and there had been lodgers as well, so that the Marsh-brook had plenty of opportunity there, before it flowed down into the dark, sluggish Sall, slimy with all the muck of a hundred factories, and forgot the innocent green ponds up beyond Barton's End and the new council estates.

Although I have never dipped my hands in the Marsh-brook and nor, I think, has Dione, that is three kinds of water. And then there is the sea-mist at Helm. There is waking in the morning and finding the house wrapped in white, moving mists, more luminous than noon-day because of the sun behind. When there is a mist like that, a sea-mist over Vectis, it becomes imperative to run into it, bare-foot and bare-headed, to become damp and clinging like something under water, something mysterious, and the magnolia leaves and the vine leaves and the leaves of the passion-flower are wet and dripping with the sea-mist, and the flanks of the cows are damp and sticky to touch and it is impossible to hear from just which tree the birds are singing. In summer we would wake at Helm morning after morning and find the sea-mist wreathed about the house, and I ran out, I jumped out of the dining-room window, I vaulted out and I ran on the lawn, and the children came squealing and scuttering out, and sometimes Robin used to run out. But not last summer or the summer before and only once the summer before that. So I will not think about any unkind things which Robin may have said about the sea-mist which I love ; and I will pull apart the tangles of the sweet-peas and the thinness of their frilled pink standards will cling to my damp hands.

And I will fill the large crock with this Auchanarnish water which is faintly tinged and faintly scented with peat and beech leaves, since it rises high in the peat and comes down brown or blinking under birches and rowans and then under beeches to the catch-pool. But the drinking water, which is really Saint Finnigal's well, comes straight out of the rock, and you would know the taste of it if you drank it in your sleep. Saint Finnigal wears a white dress all over Celtic patterns like the fireplace in the smoking-room, and she has long, tidy hair, and she is all part of Highland folklore in grey cloth with gilt lettering out of the best book-case, so she is not quite alive or quite solid. But all the same it is probable that the kelpies are sometimes afraid of her.

Both the kinds of fresh water go away quickly, after only a little time on land, through the water garden under the fern leaves and the mealy leaves of the giant primulas, and across the lowest field and through a thicket of buck-thorn, and down into Auchanarnish loch and the salt water. And the salt water goes on past Eileann Dubh and the ruined house, till it becomes strange and ruffled and fierce with tides and currents tugging in and out among the islands, thickening and strengthening the stems of the kelp. The currents and the tides enclose and net the islands, swinging and hurrying for ever under the Paps of Jura, under the steeps of Islay, twisting out beyond Colonsay and Oronsay and the Outer Islands, forced in saw-toothed fierce tide-ripples through the Sounds and south along Kintyre, places of deer and birds, tiny bays with one or two fishing-boats and maybe a cow licking up the salty grass and a wee ragged lad playing with sticks at the tide edge. The sea water goes by all these lonely places, and wherever they like the seals go with it, diving and wriggling through the currents, and they hump themselves out on to the rocks, or look all together in one direction with their sleek black rubber bathing-caps, and jump their dripping shoulders out of the water and cough angrily when they ask questions. Seals land on the rocks all down to the Mull and the rocks smell musty for weeks after they have been.

But by and bye the tides begin to set a new way, up, up, past Arran, past Bute, up into the mouth of the Clyde, and great huge ships are going about in the tides, not minding them, and there between hills is the Gare Loch, full of ships, the lowland ships, the Glasgow ships, the Greenock ships wedged into the highlands. That is the meeting-place, the gathering-place. When I say Scotland I mean the Gare Loch, I mean the coming together of Highland and Lowland with sparking and flaring and building of great ships full of engines, propellers turning slowly and then faster and faster and faster. Only they are not turning and building now. Because of the slump. Because Scotland is not functioning. Because the sea is full of seals and kelpies and dragging currents, and no one can say Scotland loud enough to start it all off, to gather the clans. The islands feel the sea all round them, threatening them, and the people in the islands are frightened and come crowding away from the sea. It is no use saying Scotland to them so long as they are frightened. The kelpies can't be kept away any longer.

I will put fronds of male fern and lady fern in with the fuchsia and stiff fronds of broad buckler fern. My tartan is beautiful in autumn; my badge is the dark, dark yew. But what is the good of all that? The gules lion is asleep like any donkey on a bed of thistles and I am left alone with the sea and the kelpies and the Campbell women and poor Green Jean, and Saint Finnigal stands there with a stiff little smile and she is no good at all either. And the men of Morven think of Hollywood maidens and the maidens of Morven think of Rudolph Valentino, who is still alive in their hearts, and it is cold in the bothy, cold under the plaid, and my sister Dione is not thinking about Scotland. Dione is thinking about Tom and Sallington and the Labour Party. And I am not really thinking about Scotland. I am pitying myself; I am thinking about how to draw seals. I am not even thinking about that properly. I am thinking about Phil and I am thinking about Pussy, who are both English. I know I am in love with them, but I don't even know if I want to sleep with either of them. If I could make up my mind about anything except wood-engraving I would be able to do everything. I would be able to wake up the gules lion. I would be able to say Scotland in such a loud and surprising voice that walls would tumble down and sea-waters would part and collapse under the surprised seals. I would say Scotland so startlingly that the clans would gather at Gare Loch head, and we would go down to Clyde bank and drive all the kelpies out of the sea-water.

Dione said: "Phœbe, love, you're wool-gathering. Let's do the rest of the sweet-peas."

Phœbe said, looking round her in a bothered kind of

way: "Where are the others? Did they go to look at the seals?"

Dione said: "No, why should they? Tom and Alex are shooting Ardfeochan and the others have gone into Oban to get drinks for to-night."

"I thought Pussy might have been going to stay and help with the flowers."

"It's no use expecting anything from Pussy. He's flirting with Joyce now, just to annoy you, Phœbe. Can't you see? You let him know you were that much in his power, and of course he enjoys that, damn his silly little eyes. Why have you got to go and fall for a man like that, Phœbe?"

"I can't help it. Lots of people do."

"Everybody told you what sort of a lad he was. I wouldn't have had him to stay if I'd thought you were going to be such an ass. He paints so badly, too! And you paint so well."

"I suppose I was bound to fall in love with someone. I was feeling so empty after Phil."

"Can't it ever be Robin again? It would be so—convenient. And he's really such a dear."

"I know. That's what's so stupid. I'm so awfully fond of him, Dione, and we've got so much in common. I do love him, you know, only I'm not in love with him. But, oh dear, there it is; I'm afraid I'm a polygamist and a very unsuccessful one at that."

"You ought to join the Labour Party."

"I know I ought. At least I think I possibly ought. But that wouldn't make me a monogamist, though no doubt most good party members are!"

"It would give you something else to think about besides the emotions. And kelpies."

"I wasn't thinking about kelpies!"

"Yes, you were. And Green Jean. So boo. I shall wear my red velvet to-night. Then I can have flat heels for the country dances."

"Pussy doesn't like the country dances."

"Nor does Tom. But who cares? You and I danced Strip the Willow and Petronella long before there was either of them! I wish young John from Lerguligan will dance with me to-night. I wish he'll dance the Foursome."

But Phœbe looked out of the window because she thought she had heard the car coming back from Oban. Not that it could be, yet. But she wanted the car and Pussy to come back. She wanted to walk again along the edge of the sea with Pussy, and to look at it and know it was beautiful and notice the colour of the headlands and islands, but to be able to see it without trying to look through the water and behind the rocks in case the kelpies were hiding there.

## AUCHANARNISH 2

Five of the children stayed up for the dance. Not, of course, that George Coke-Brown counted himself as a child, but, annoyingly enough, the grown-ups did. The other children definitely didn't want him as one of themselves. He spoiled games. He condescended. And he didn't play tennis any better than Petronella or climb trees as well as Kenneth or Clemency. He certainly did not dance as well as Kenneth, not the real dances—jumpy dances that made you sweat and laugh!—only his silly sort of London dancing when you squash up against someone and walk. George was sixteen; he was Rosalind's boy. Rosalind was Tom Galton's eldest sister. And Tom Galton was Dione's husband. Rosalind did not care much for Auchanarnish herself, nor for the society of her in-laws, but she sent George up to stay with his cousins. At the beginning of the holidays his younger sister Elizabeth had been staying too. But now she had gone back to Sallington; she was going to be a bridesmaid at the beginning of November and she had told Petronella and Morag all about the frock she was going to wear and how important she was going to be.

Morag was staying up; she was ten years old, thick and dark and competent; she was not afraid of kelpies. Her next younger brother, Kenneth, was more likely to be afraid, but he had to keep up his prestige with the rest of the family. The two smallest ones, Ian and Lilias, were too young even to protest at being sent to bed. Phœbe's two elders were allowed up too: Petronella, who was thirteen, danced beautifully and hated reading, and Clemency, who was eleven, and read everything she could lay hands on. But Brian had been sick after tea and gone straight to bed. He was very apt to be sick at Auchanarnish just because he enjoyed it all so violently. But the other children were used to him and didn't bother.

The ones who were staying up dressed for the dance, in and out of each other's rooms—except George. Kenneth remembered to brush his finger-nails. It was worth it, he thought, to wear the sgian dhu in his stocking top, as he was allowed to with the kilt on grand occasions. Morag wore the Fraser tartan too, a green silk bodice with white collar and a silk tartan skirt, full all round. Petronella and Clemency wore block-printed stiff muslin got from some high-brow place of their mother's and made up at home, and painted ribbons from Munich in their brown hair.

The grown-ups changed too, after the usual scramble for baths. Alex, Dione's younger brother, wore the kilt, and a jacket with silver buttons, and sporran of seal skin. But the other two men wore ordinary English clothes. Dione and Tom shared a bath and talked to one another all the time they were dressing and hair-brushing. Dione's hair was long and brown and its two plaits went right round her head; but Phœbe had cut hers and would never grow it again. Dione sat on the bed brushing hers out slowly so that Tom could enjoy seeing it and taking it in his hands while they talked. He was only up at Auchanarnish for the week-end; he had meant to come for most of the holidays, but things in England were moving too fast. The makeshift National Government was beginning to break up; a General Election looked likely. He was going down to his constituency on Monday to talk things over with Mason, the Party agent, and the D.L.P. executive. But to-day, to clear his head, he had gone off shooting with Alex in the high air of Ardfeochan; they had brought back three brace of grouse besides a hare and two rabbits for the pot. Old MacCallum said to himself that Mr. Galton was shooting well.

But now he was turning towards Marshbrook Bridge and the Midlands, and his wife knew that to-morrow he would be thinking of nothing else, breaking the Scottish Sabbath. He was thinking of his constituency and also of his sister. The thing was this: Marshbrook Bridge—the old village and all the new industrial and residential districts down as far as the River Sall—was the westernmost of the Sallington divisions, and Sallington was the city where his brother-in-law, Reginald Coke-Brown, and all the clan of Coke-Browns ruled and had honour. Except from Labour. Reginald and Rosalind didn't, of course, live in Marshbrook Bridge—it was the wrong side of the city; they lived in Barstone, the big southern suburb, on the edge of the hills whose breezes blew back industrial stinks. But many of the workers in brother-in-law Reginald's several factories lived in Marshbrook Bridge and came in and out by tram.

Rosalind Coke-Brown had been very cross and hurt when her brother, Tom, had come up and contested Marshbrook Bridge right under her nose in the 1929 Election. It had been very awkward for her in the shining drawing-rooms of Barstone; her friends had felt so sorry for her, but at the same time rather uncomfortable, as though she'd had measles in the house! And of course Marshbrook Bridge had been a safe Conservative seat in those days; that nice old Colonel Merrill with his pretty daughter. But now? There was no denying that Marshbrook Bridge had grown. The Synthex works had made a great difference, and there were several other new factories, whose workers had to be housed either in the tight, grubby Victorian rows or in neat new housing estates.

But the new Labour candidate had been going about Marshbrook Bridge, along the new streets and through the crumbling, propped-up slum tenements along the river, at street corners and factory gates, talking elementary economics and elementary social morality; and so still more had Mason, the agent, and so had George Grove and Miss Waterhouse and Sam Hall and Mr. and Mrs. East and Reuben Goldberg and John Collis of the N.U.W.W. and Councillor Finch and Edna Boffin and Jo Burrage and the rather fluctuating League of Youth. And so, less often and with considerably more reluctance, had Dione, carefully impersonating Candidate's wife. So that by 1931 Marshbrook Bridge was not really a safe seat for anybody.

Tom had joined the Labour Party ten years ago for no elaborate economic reasons, although he was an historian and economist, but just because he hated other people to be overworked and underfed and not to have so much leisure or such a good time as he had. And now he was on no account going with Ramsay MacDonald and Snowden on any devious transactions with the powers of gold. He stuck to the Party; to those thousands and thousands of men and women, trade unionists and co-operators, the workers, the people he respected deeply and without whom nothing worth doing could be done. Dione, on the other hand, was simply thinking that it would be rather fun to have a situation with Rosalind!

They had dinner early and rapidly, so that it could be cleared. Tom and Dione were still discussing immediate politics at their end of the table, and Clemency listened and felt that destiny was being made. Old Mrs. Fraser was magnificent in family lace, but occasionally mixed the children's names. There were two Fraser cousins and one MacLean, the MacLean and the Fraser boy—rather a bore, but a good dancer—in kilts. The Fraser girl tried to talk

London amusements; she would much rather have been going to a London dance! She asked Phœbe about her husband, and Phœbe explained that Robin was in England, trying another cure; his leg had been bothering him again, there was probably still a tiny piece of shell in it, evading the X-rays—just enough to set up a kind of mild general poisoning from time to time. She was going south again to join him as soon as the children went back to school.

It worried Phœbe to talk about Robin when Pussy could overhear; for Pussy didn't like Robin—not only didn't like Robin but told her so, and she couldn't bear it! Phil had always been so sweet to Robin, so considerate. Pussy was on her other side now, between her and Morag. When she talked about Robin, Pussy turned half round and grinned a little. And suddenly out from behind the screen came one of the Campbell women, and stood behind him and grinned at Phœbe, too! The narrow, cruel, arrogant Highland face, the twisted lips, the thin overbred hands quick to twist and pinch! She looked again, and, of course, there was no Campbell woman, only Morag, her niece, so dear and kind and helpful. And then Pussy turned further round towards her and smiled at her with his eyes, excluding the Fraser cousin, and suddenly she had those odd shooting feelings all down her body, like smelling roses in mid-winter.

The piper came and paid his respects; he had curly iron-grey hair and wandering blue eyes, and a complimentary sprig of yew in the silver brooch of his plaid, which no doubt he had broken off the big yew tree at the corner of the drive. "And there will be Miss Morag again, the flower of the hillside," he said, in compliment to Dione who had been Fraser. Morag blushed between her dark curtains of hair and slipped a hand into his and felt like Flora

MacDonald. She wished it would all begin. She wished the fiddler would come, too.

Dione and Phœbe went upstairs to the big drawing-room to receive. First came MacLean, the gardener, Master of Ceremonies, and Mrs. MacLean in stiff black silk ; and then came the Andersons from the home farm, and the two Misses Anderson, one in pink net and the other in yellow net ; and MacCallum, the keeper, and Mrs. MacCallum, a gaunt, nervous, childless woman, her skin over the high cheek bones finely netted with red veins, beaten to the surface by days and nights of cold air and rain and heights. And then they came all in a rush, fathers and mothers, boys and girls from the farms, eager and aglow, young house-maids and kitchenmaids from the big houses, the postman and the carrier and the gilly from Ardfeochan, a boatload of islanders, MacLeans and McIntyres, the girls in light-coloured dresses with roses at their breasts or shoulders half crushed by heavy oilskins they'd worn for the crossing. There was Jimsie from the garage, amazingly clean and respectable in his blacks, and Christina Campbell from the Temperance Hotel, more beautiful than a barmaid, with pure gold hair, and Red Peter and Willie, the boatmen, whispering sardonically to one another in Gaelic. Some of the boys wore the kilt, but very few ; most were in their best Sunday suits from Oban or Inverary, with a corner of coloured handkerchief showing.

Then Dione's nurse came in, living up to the occasion in green and white, and her friend, the shepherd's wife. The children were all there now, all saying how-do-you-do, and the fiddler and the melodeon player had come and were tuning gently. Alex was talking to Mrs. Campbell from the high farm, who was quite enormous and wore two silver crosses and a portrait of her son in New Zealand. Tom was talking to the Finneys, Fifeshire folk who had lately come to Carse of Easland; Mr. Finney had suddenly said: "I was reading an article of yours in the *Daily Herald*, Mr. Galton, fine and powerful it was. Could you tell me what will happen to the pound now?" Mrs. Finney smiled and nodded to show she had read it, too. That was, somehow, rather surprising. Tom was always shy of talking politics here; they were all such good Tories, so solidly out of reach of argument.

Old Mrs. Fraser was sitting in her arm-chair; Kenneth and Clemency were bringing people up to be presented to her. There was a battle going on at the moment about the flower show and fête; undercurrents of it appeared in the conversation; Mrs. Fraser twinkled comprehension and refused to take sides. The rest of the maids had now come up, and Mrs. Cook. Men were standing at one side of the room, women on the other. The gentry were talking and flirting with one another. Joyce's dress was long and diaphanous, orchid-coloured, slim over the hips and frilly below; she was being regarded covertly by the other girls, who were still almost all wearing short dresses in the style of the last few years, with light-coloured art-silk stockings. Pussy put an arm round Joyce and whispered. It meant nothing, of course, but had Phœbe seen?

Then John MacLean of Lerguligan came in and Dione began delightedly looking forward to dancing with him, for his crisp hair stood up from his forehead in strong and glinting corn-brown, and he stepped like a spring lamb.

And then MacLean, the M.C., nodded to the fiddler, and cast a look round the expectant room, and came forward and bowed to Phœbe, and led her out to be first couple in the Circassian Circle. Tom, instructed before dinner, bowed to Mrs. MacLean, and there was a general rush over from the men's side of the room to the women's, and old Mrs. Fraser beamed approval. MacCallum, the keeper, took

Dione's arm and Alex cleverly captured Christina Campbell, and young John of Lerguligan smiled at Petronella and she bobbed after him like a leaf, and Pussy bowed to one of the island girls, who blushed, nervous of her English, and Morag and the postman made one couple, and Kenneth, who was rather shy, danced with the under-housemaid, and Red Peter paired with Mrs. Cook, and Willie with young Jean Anderson, everyone was paired off and stood round the sides of the room in couples ; MacLean cast an eye over them ; the feet waited and the hands and the laughter, and the sweet-peas and the phlox and the roses ; and then the fiddle and the melodeon struck up, and the Circle began crossing and turning and meeting, and all the men danced with all the women, in the continuous weaving in and out of the tune and the pattern, and the dance at Auchanarnish had really begun.

*First Set of Quadrilles* MORAG GALTON

This is the end of the first figure. The tune is going to change. We bow. The second figure begins. I can remember all the figures. I have them all in my mind like things in geometry. Petronella has them in her feet. She doesn't have to remember. I remember the tunes, but I forget the figures. Cross over. I nearly didn't ! If I had a puppy it would nuzzle. I would drop down my left hand when I was doing geometry and the puppy would push his warm wet nose into the palm of my hand. I am a lady in a high wig and an embroidered taffeta crinoline dancing quadrilles in the middle of the eighteenth century. I set to my partner. How elegantly I sway in my buckle shoes ! My partner is the Duke of Bonaventura. Lud, sir Duke, 'tis a distinguished melody. Rot, it's only Jimsie from the garage ! I say, Jimsie, what about my bike ?

*One-step* DIONE GALTON

I'm coming alive. My blood is coming quicker already. I like dancing with these men better than dancing with high-brows; their breath isn't nasty. Because they can't afford constant alcohol and tobacco and meat twice a day. And round we go, and down to the fiddle! If this were a London foxtrot it would be all slurred and dragging, slowing the blood. Now it's quickened. It's mixed with something Highland. It's in time, in time, in time! Clear on the beat, picking one's feet up, not keeping them tied to the floor. Oh, I do like this. Oh, my lovely, lovely swags, the shining of the petals! I don't care if Murdoch McIntyre is a high Tory, he gets me round and along; he dances the quick one-step with his clever legs; he fishes lobsters and sells them to the English. The faces go round and round. Fiddle, keep time, keep time to the quick one-step!

*First Eightsome Reel* PHŒBE BATHURST

I wait. I wait. In a moment the pipes will start. I will be swept, be lifted—there! And chain, and chain, and chain. The pipe music carries me, the noise of the eight-some. Hands in mine, round we go, hard hands gripping, grip me, leap to the pipe noise! The island girl dances in the ring, the proud girl, upright, tossing her head, pointing her breasts, her young, her hard young breasts pointing at the men. And in and out she goes and away. Rough hands, strong arms, plowmen, all the rings, all the reel rings, are going, turning, whirling on the blast. Eight eightsomes, sixty-four dancers. The floor leaps under us. I leap, round goes the ring, leap to my partner, sweep round back to back, air all round us, pipe-filled air. Now all the rings, eight eightsomes, the lights shake on the walls, the petals shake away, but hang suspent in the thick, shuddering, solid air, the whole room filled with the noise of the pipes. Men dance in the rings now; to the pipes. Dance, the Frasers! High, high, leap, shout! Gules lion, wake, lion of Scotland.

*Petronella* PETRONELLA BATHURST

We dance Petronella. It is called after me. I told Brian it was, so it is! It is such a dancy dance. Setting and waltzing and setting and waltzing all down the line. Anderson goes jiggeting round, he is quite round himself; he has been wound up and he goes on jiggeting round. That silly Joyce is making a muddle of it. How can she be so stupid when the tune makes you dance right. They aren't listening to the tune, they don't belong. I belong because I am Petronella. George is muddling it, too! Hooray, I told him so! Elizabeth is going to be a bridesmaid next month; she's been a bridesmaid three times and I never have. It's not fair! A blue chiffon dress from Jay's, looped up over rose. Damn, I shan't ever be a bridesmaid; mother can't afford it, I don't expect. Well, I don't care, who wants to go to church and be married by a silly old parson anyway? Oh, my turn, and I go setting and waltzing, setting and waltzing in Petronella. I am light, I am light on my partner's hands, I am light on my feet. But it will be over. Oh, why need it ever be over, my dancing, my dancing of my own dance?

*Highland Schottische* KENNETH GALTON

Right in front, right behind, left in front, left behind, Tah de dee and diddle de dee and diddle de dee and diddle de dee. Oh, I can dance it, my feet are dancing it all by themselves! This is the Highland Scottish. I *will* call it that. That is its name. I am half Highland Scottish. Father is half Lowland and half English. I am a quarter English, I can play Rugger. Nurse dances jolly well. Brian is in bed. Brian is a baby. Oh sucks, oh sucks on Brian.

*Waltz* TOM GALTON

Dione has been pounced on by her ass of a cousin. Will you dance this with me, Phœbe ? Oh well, if old Charlie's going to buzz you round—— ! Suppose I've got to dance this with someone. Hell, why not Mrs. Cook. May I have the pleasure ? Over the top with us. She doesn't go too badly, either. Anyway, I haven't got to talk.

Ought I to be here ? Ought I to have drunk '23 Burgundy and eaten roast grouse with chipped potatoes, and black-currant meringue made by Mrs. Cook, when men and women in Sallington haven't got enough to eat ? Ought I to go shooting while men and women in Sallington are unemployed ? Ought I to have a holiday at all ? Ought I to be a don at Oxford and talk to other dons about the authenticity of Halévy's conclusions ? Ought I to drink College port ? Ought I to have let Dione bear me four children ? Christ, what a bump !—Sorry, Mrs. Cook, not our fault, was it ? I believe it is not wrong so long as I understand that all this is only temporary, so long as I do not let these pleasures and these possessions influence me. So long as I go on steadily working for the economic liberty of the men and women of England and Scotland and the world, I can in the meantime use my own leisure my own way. But can I stop it influencing me ? Isn't it influencing me to think this ? Hell, of course it is. I know that much. There go Ken and Morag dancing together ; they are jolly little blighters. But I wish I was dancing with Dione instead of Mrs. Cook.

*Lancers* ROBERT FINNEY

I doubt it will be best for me to dance this with Miss McIntyre of the Grocery. Aye, it will be best. They should have co-operatives up here ; but these Highlanders have no sense of realities. Mr. Galton would do well to try to put some sense into them. It is hard enough for me to get my *Herald*, even. These Highlanders with all their haverings and pride and ignorance ! . . . I am never just sure of this figure of the dance . . . a good Fifeish dance . . . Mr. Galton is a Lowlander too, he is an educated man. My James will surely go to the University when he is grown. He will get scholarships. No man will ever have the right to look down on him. Maybe my Chrissie will go to the University, too. She is a clever one with her figures. Education is the key . . . in Russia they understand that. Red Universities, in Scotland. . . . The English have little education. The *Herald* has little education. It is full of English actresses and boxers and gentry-pups . . . English and Highlanders ! . . . I would thank them for a strong authoritative article on the Gold Standard.

*Foxtrot* " PUSSY " MORGAN

Phœbe is looking at me. I won't have it ! She is a good wood-engraver and a good painter ; she painted Summer Island ; she is a damned good wood-engraver, but she shan't get me ! She's got a soft skin, haze-blue eyes, soft, clinging lips. Oh, clinging of women—knock them off ! Keep free, integrity of personal relationships. Come on, Joyce, my pet, let's dance this. I keep my male unity, I will not let it be broken into by any woman. I won't have Phœbe breaking my fine edges ! I will paint a great canvas of water-light she-women like bubbles, breakable like bubbles, like big buds of flowers. Petally flower, Joyce, her neck sinking down to her bud-breasts. Her legs talking to mine in the foxtrot. Why the devil do these Scotch play so jerkily? Glide, damn you, glide, I want to glide with Joyce! Jumping peasants in layers of flannel. Phœbe dancing with a jumping peasant. Oh, to hell with her, looking at me, getting at me. Women should wait, wait for the dark-bright stallion. She's too old for me anyway. Old and used. Flaccid petals, drooping. Bearing children to that man, going on living with him, sleeping with him. No integrity. Women have no integrity. Only bodies. Faces. Lips. Soft lips. Let her come to me, then! I'd show her. God, I would.

*Foursome Reel* PHŒBE BATHURST

I don't want to dance. Why should he hurt me so? Why should he hurt me in my own house? Green Jean, you were hurt, you too died. Why? What have I done? God, what have I done for Pussy to hurt me so? Help me, God! God! Oh, Phil, Phil, my gentle Phil. . . . But I haven't danced a Foursome for years, MacLean! Well, you'll just need to put me through it some way. . . . And I must stand here and wait while they line up. They are all gay, all laughing, and I am separate and hurt. They will be able to see how unhappy I am. Oh, Basileia, Queen Basileia, why have you gone so far from me? Where is the Talking Crow to bring me to Cloud Cuckoo Borough, to the house of the Hoopoe, and Queen Basileia carrying Peace in her arms? Oh, why can't they start dancing? Why must I wait? Father, do you remember telling me the story of the Birds? When I was little I climbed hills with Basileia, over at Ardfeochan I climbed, and the heather was bright, bright, drunken waves, honey-sweet bright purple, humming with bees. The Campbell Women couldn't come near us, we left the kelpies in the sea. But now Basileia has left me and the dance is full of Campbell Women and kelpies! Oh, Pussy, Pussy, Pussy, you can be so sweet, why have you got to be cruel, why listen to the Campbell Women?

There. The line's waiting. I've got to dance. Oh, oh, the pipes, blare, flare, flame, the broad twisting flame is carrying me! I am a wisp twisting with the flame in the right-handed figure of eight. I can't not dance when the whole line is dancing and twisting and flaming. Dione is dancing with an islander. Petronella is dancing beautifully, leaping like a little flame. Clemency and Morag and Kenneth are dancing. Only the English can't dance this, the dull, stupid English like Phil and Pussy. I dance on them. I dance, I flame over their hearts. Toe and heel I dance to the pipe tune, dancing on the hearts of the English. Now, now it changes: the reel of Tulloch! The quick reel, the quick, quick, bonfire flames—Oh, I am with you, I am part of you, hoich, hoich, up with the flame, the reel, the pipes, wake Lion! Oh, this will go on for ever and I will never die!

*Interval*

While the room was clearing, Dione sat on the end of the sofa, talking with Joyce who had flopped down into it; Joyce hadn't really wanted to dance the last reel at all, but MacLean had firmly found her a partner, who had pushed her through. She felt that the Scotch took their pleasures hardly! Still, it was being quite a good visit, and Dione Galton was pretty cheerful considering how almost pre-war she really was. Phœbe was rather embarrassing, but Lord, it must be utterly ghastly for her being married to a bundle of nerves like that husband of hers! "Did we ever show you the family cup?" said Dione. Joyce shook her head, breathless still, and Dione reached across the back of the sofa, undid Odd Bits and took out the cup with Peisthetairos and the birds. She felt through her fingers the delicious texture of the clay, like some cold, fairy, entrancing face, like Peisthetairos after he marries Basileia and becomes half a god. While she showed it to Joyce, the story was solid and real in her mind, tangible as the cup.

Dione shared the Birds with Phœbe, though she had an image of her own which she found more satisfying than Basileia, an image of plow-tractors. Whenever she was dispirited and disappointed, impatient with her friends or angry and violent against the world of happenings, she called up the calming image of the tractors, moving slowly and securely across a hillside, either under March sun and blowing wind, or through a pale April mist. She had told her sister about the tractors, hoping that Phœbe would make a picture of them, but Phœbe had rather crossly said that she wouldn't waste her time on slushy propaganda posters, so the picture never got made.

Phœbe, though, had drawn many of the images of their common childhood. One of the first things she had ever drawn was a hard and detailed picture of the Campbell Women, arm in arm, laughing at Green Jean. It had distressed the art mistress at school. Later she had made a wood-engraving of stiff little Saint Finnigal, who is that part of the spirit of Scotland which has come to an end as a living thing. As for the kelpies, if she had managed to draw them adequately, it would have been such a horrid and terrifying drawing that she would have had to burn it at once.

As she grew older Phœbe had begun to realise that none of these images was really private to her sister and herself. Whatever he had chosen to call them, Cocteau had certainly drawn pictures of the Campbell Women, stiff and faceless with cruelty and ignorance. It had given her a deep and unpleasant shock to meet them again in Chirico's pictures; she had gone on discussing technique with Pussy and another painter friend, but what had Chirico meant by his waxen Campbells?

Both the sisters knew about the seals, which were sometimes definitely malevolent and allied with the kelpies, and sometimes just asked questions and even played—there had been days when Phœbe, eight, and Dione, five, had agreed to be friends with the seals—but they were rather a nuisance. What did their own children now think or feel about such things? From outside the children's group it appeared that they did things like wireless and tennis and dominoes and consequences and the murder game in and out of season, or they rowed the dinghy out to one of the small islands and had picnics, or they bathed and explored for sea anemones and star-fish, or they played hide-and-seek in the hay-lofts. Morag milked the cows most evenings; and on wet days played the piano greedily for hours, snapping at the others when they interrupted. Petronella played tennis with anyone; Kenneth and Clemency went fishing on the sea loch at sunset, and brought back baskets full of saithe and lithe, which had to be disposed of somehow. Brian and Ian and Lilias went out with Nurse and played all kinds of games in the gardens or beside the loch. George Coke-Brown was definitely outside the group! But were the kelpies or the Campbell Women or people from Greek cups inside it?

The children attended to the business in hand. During the dance they danced. During the interval they ate ham sandwiches, and chocolate biscuits from Oban, and fruit-drops and jelly. So did all the guests. The women drank lemonade or some horrid pink fizzy stuff out of bottles that made Kenneth feel sick. The older men drank whisky, especially the piper, with whom it was traditional, and some of them drank beer, but many of the young farmers took nothing but lemonade or soda-water. They were rather indignant when two new whisky bottles had to be opened for the older men.

Half-way through the interval, after Dione had put away the family cup and gone down to see that everything was being a success, Pussy wound up the gramophone, and he and Joyce danced in the manner of south England or North America. Then they faded away to the library, where by and bye they were joined by the two Fraser cousins, and from time to time Alex. They talked and played card games desultorily and told faintly indecent stories. Joyce was a little worried because she could see that Phœbe was being hurt; she made attempts to be a good guest and flirt with Alex, as she had obviously been meant to do, but Alex wasn't responsive. She had also torn the bottom frill of her frock.

Clemency and Kenneth were afraid of being sent to bed. They were elusive after the interval, and danced Strip the Willow with one another, in a set which contained no parent or nurse.

*Strip the Willow* AN ISLAND GIRL

Ach, I am glad I came! I was afraid coming over. I was afraid the English would be too fine for me. I was afraid Big Hugh would be looking at the girls here that have been able to read the fashion papers from Oban and have their hair put in waves; I was afraid he would be looking past me at the Campbell girls. But no. Hugh has been watching me; it was not one of the girls from a mainland steading that Hugh chose for the reel! It is not one of the mainland girls that has a better colour than me. Hugh stands in front of me now, on the far side of the line. Big Hugh, tha mo ghaol ort. There are red roses in the bowl behind you ; I would dearly love to see a red rose on your black hair. Old Mistress Fraser is almost sleeping ; I will not grow old ; I will not sleep through the dancing ! There is the fiddle—haste then, haste, or we will miss the tide of return ! Ach, link and catch, link and catch, all down the line and up the line, leaves stripped from the willow, the bonny willow, dance, leaves, in the hard stripping ! Ach, Hugh, it is us ! Go to it, Hugh, link and twirl the girls once each and come again always more and more strongly to link and twirl with me, strip down the willow, but I am the heart of the willow wand, the white, shining heart of it !

*Valetta* TOM GALTON

They dance this at Labour Socials. All over south England and the Midlands. Wonder why it kept on when better ones dropped out. Civil servants folk-dance in London and she dons in Oxford. May Day in the High : all nonsense. Not even William Morris behind it. Dione, can't we have just one, or have you been snapped up ? Good. Liking it ? Yes, so am I in a way. I'm bothered about things. Yes, Sallington. By the way, do you know what happened about the MacLean boy, the black sheep ? I don't like to ask. Gone to England, has he, and doesn't write ? And the old folk are being tough about it and not complaining ? He was an intelligent boy, I thought, though he looked a bit grim at one from under his eye-brows. Educated a bit, I take it ? Oh, for the Ministry, and didn't want to be ! I see. This is the most idiotic dance. It strikes me as possible that he's not such a very black sheep after all. Breaking his mother's heart? Mm. But one can't always help that.

*Flowers of Edinburgh* CLEMENCY BATHURST

Oh yes, I'd love to dance with you! Oh think, oh think, me dancing with the piper. Only one more. After this, Ken and me will have to go to bed. And Granny. Next year I shall stay up for the whole dance! I wish we could stay here always and never have bills. Mother never getting worried by bills and things when she's in the middle of drawing. I do hope I shall dance this properly. Anyway, we're not top couple. How beautiful my partner is! I shall swank to the others to-morrow, specially Morag. Oh, I *shall* swank! . . . It is a nice dance, like threading beads. Elizabeth is going to be a bridesmaid, but not Petronella or me. Perhaps I shall be something else. I like dancing with my beautiful partner the piper, better than being a bridesmaid. He smiles at me such a lot. I like the way his kilt swings round and kicks up at the edge. His is the same tartan as mother's and mine. He is so lovely, but Aunt Dione and Uncle Tom are both going to lead the Revolution. I shall help with the Revolution. I shall carry secret bombs; I shall die on a barricade. Or perhaps I won't. Now it's us! Round and follow. Round outside. Up the middle. Oh, I do like dancing when I'm doing it properly! I shall be able to dream about it all the time till to-morrow morning. Oh, but how lovely, it's so late that it's to-morrow morning now!

*Military Two Step* GEORGE COKE-BROWN

Thank goodness, those two kids have been buzzed off. But, oh Lord, here's another of these idiotic dances. Could

I go downstairs to the others? Or would they turn round and glare at me and stop talking? 'Tisn't as if I couldn't understand their rotten stories! I know some myself. Fellows I know been with girls. Uncle Tom didn't take me to Ardfeochan to-day. These beastly politics. If I don't ask someone to dance, MacLean'll come and shove me off on to some wretched giggling girl. M.C. indeed! It looks easy enough really. Now then. . . . What does Uncle Tom mean anyway, going Socialist? Ruining the country. If only I could explain to him—like Father explained to me. But he always gets round me somehow. I can't understand it. He fought in the War, so he must love the Empire. And how is the Empire to keep going unless we keep going, us with a Sense of Responsibility? The National Government is fine. National! He *can't* go against that! Imperial Preference. Imperial. Like Rome, Sallington stands firm! . . . I say, the old piper's had a drop too much! . . . And Aunt Dione talking about the General Strike all the wrong way round. I can see them being tactful, the beasts, not talking politics when I'm there, but there is such a thing as atmosphere! Thank goodness that's over.

*Second Set of Quadrilles* ALEXANDER FRASER

Would you dance this set with me, Miss Campbell? Yes, a good floor, isn't it? Quite a revival of dancing among the young folk, the traditional dancing. You think so too? The Scottish Renaissance? Mm, to tell you the truth, Miss Campbell, I hadn't just considered that except in Edinburgh. You say, it's coming here too? And—if I may put it this way—not your hotel visitors, but everywhere? On the farms? A result of education? Mhm, maybe it's a better result than some! How's business this year? No, the water's low, I doubt there'll not be much doing till after a spate. We're top couple, I think, Miss Campbell. So . . . And it looks as if Scotland really might wake, not just stay folklore and sentimentalising. Though I like it the way it is. The islands and waters. Windless, soft mornings in Edinburgh, the old beautiful squares soaked in light and gentleness and leisure. Even the office is light, and in winter the heavy stone keeps out wind and cold. The Advocate's Library. Men I know. Talk. Part songs. Dinner parties. And coming here: days up on Ardfeochan, soft purple and gold, the top of the world. The lochs spreading away beyond and below. But suppose it all changed? As Tom wants it to. Good fellow, Tom. Yet perhaps it should change. Not decent. A gentleman can't stand by and see his fellow country folk oppressed. See these manufacturers get it all their own way. We let them go on doing that too long, didn't watch them. Our own fault, serve us right now if—— This last year or two . . . can't help thinking of slums. The old town. The wynds and closes in summer: flies on the food, rats, babies dying and all that. . . . How they do tear up the quadrille, these lads! Jazzing it up. Birl your partner, shoosh your partner! Christina Campbell is too beautiful for shooshing and birling. She has the grand manner. Hands across. So . . .

*Paul Jones* JOHN MACLEAN OF LERGULIGAN

All the girls want to dance with me. All of the grown women want to dance with me. When the tune stops and the rings stop whirling, it will not be me who is left with the broom-stick. There, I have got Katrine McGregor! She is laughing, she is breathless with the whirling of the rings. She laughs into my face. Dance close to me, Katrine, we will laugh and dance while the tune lasts. . . .

The men's ring catches hands and whirls, faster, faster than the women's ring, the laughing, facing ring of girls! The two ladies are in the ring; they are laughing too. They were not laughing all the time, the sisters; the one of them was nearer to crying before the Reel. I am glad they are laughing now; I am glad they have stayed for the whole of the dance. It is not for courtesy they are dancing still, but because they are wanting to. That is good, that is as it should be between Scots. The ring breaks! Dione Galton, I have caught you round the shoulders as you turned, and you turn again to me, quickly glad, laughing, breathless. You with the mad-like, heathen name, laugh and dance with me till the tune stops. . . .

The ring, the ring, I have Red Peter by the one hand and old Charlie the plow-man by the other; they have the drink in them. It is fools they are drinking whisky at the dance of Auchanarnish. They will not get the girls so. They drink whisky and they do not read good books nor make tunes on the melodeon as I do, and in the dance ring they stumble. There, Charlie is out and I have Jean Anderson. Jean, you are douce and smiling, your hair is pale gold like the straw of oats in sunshine, your hair is feathery across my face while we are dancing. . . .

The rings are sweating now, the floor leaps, the petals drop suddenly from the roses. The faces of the young girls shine with sweat and their eyes are all the brighter. The lightest, the lightest to me! I have you, Petronella, young thing, bonny young thing in your braws, you want to dance with me as the grown women want. Dance and laugh then, while the tune goes, and I will laugh too. . . .

And the ring, the ring, keep to it, fiddle, keep up the dance! Once there were dance places through all the Highlands and Islands. They have been taken from us. And my big brother Alan, he went to Canada, and he does not write as often as he used to. And Donald MacLean, my cousin, he went. He went south. And maybe I will go. But I have caught Christina Campbell and she will laugh with me, she with the hot laughing face, and maybe she will kiss me on the way back. Will you so, Christina? Dance with me, dance and laugh in my arms, Christina, till the tune ends. . . .

And the rings catch hands again.

*Second Eightsome Reel* DIONE GALTON

Oh, I am nearly dropping! Where's everyone? It's three in the morning, isn't it? The islanders have all sailed. And to-morrow I've got to think about things again. Sallington. And my poor darling idiot Phœbe. And I'll have to go through the books with Mother. . . . Damn. . . . Yes, Peter, I'll surely dance with you. . . . If one could only go on between dances what one feels at dances! Oh, Phœbe's coming to our set. Hullo, Phœbe! She and the plowman, they'll be top couple. Young John and Christina opposite us.

In a moment—in a moment now—there, the pipes! And my Phœbe drinks the pipe music like the ghosts drinking blood. The chain. How it goes! Now the plowman's in. He is shouting something to Red Peter; I wish I had the Gaelic! Hi and hoich, he's dancing well! Ring, ring, ring! Aie, we are not to dance the figure back to back, but twirling, but caught and whirled! This is—this is—I know what it is about this set, all the men are drunk except young John. Drunk and dancing like drunken fantastic angels! God Dionysos, let's not catapult into the next set! This is—I have it—feudal democracy. Off my feet, Phœbe caught off her feet too! They throw their heads about and shout, drunken, set free. Young John sees I have seen. He looks in my eyes as he sets and leaps, looks as he flings me round. Blue eyes, bright proud hair, gay proud mouth, young John, our pride, pride of Lerguligan, pride of Auchanarnish. The pipes go wilder, louder—spin, leap on the blast, oh I will not ever forget this night or the last reel set!

*Circassian Circle* MRS. MACLEAN

This is the end of the dance. Mr. Alex has me by the hand. It is the grand lad he looks in the kilt. I remember when he was a wee boy for ever after the raspberries. If I do not think at all, I can say to myself that it is Donald's hand I am holding. The dancing begins. Donald is not here. Maybe he will not come back ever at all, not though I am waiting for him, not though I am thinking on him morning and evening. He was angry with his father and with me. He wanted me to side with him, but I must side with MacLean, with his father. I was married to MacLean young. Donald has gone south. First he was with the wild boys at Girvan, at the shipbuilding. He was in a riot. The police came. But he knocked down the police with one hand and he escaped. For he is MacLean too. But now he is gone south, gone south to some English city, and maybe at all kinds of doings there with the wild lads, the Reds. I wish I could see him come dancing towards me now, dancing and crossing and turning in the Circle. Oh Lord, oh Lord, my God, if I could but see him once more. . . .

*End of the dance at Auchanarnish.*

# AUCHANARNISH 3

PHŒBE had gone back three days after the dance with Brian and two brace of grouse, leaving Petronella and Clemency to come back with their cousins, which meant, incidentally, that their grandmother would pay the fares. Brian was called after Brian Bathurst, Robin's younger brother who had been killed on the Somme in 1916. It had been an understood thing between Robin and Phœbe that when they had a boy he was to be called Brian; yet by the time the boy was born that first Brian had faded and become a strengthless ghost. Only now, in moments of horror, it seemed to Phœbe that this ghost, whom she had scarcely known, was sucking blood from her boy. But the doctor said there was nothing wrong with Brian; he was overgrown and nervy; he only needed a good tonic and plenty of rest. That was so, Phœbe agreed, oh yes, that was probably so, and at any rate he managed the journey very well this time and wasn't sick in the train. How Phœbe dreaded that, and the cleaning-up and apologising to strangers! They picked up his father from the cure place, looking rather better, and all went home to Helm—and Brian was sick on the little Isle of Wight ferry-boat, but still it seems more natural to be sick on boats. When they got to the house Brian went straight up to the nursery and took all the things out of the toy cupboards; his sisters were not there to interfere. And Robin had a gloomy interview with his foreman, another ex-Service man, about the autumn prospects for the farm.

But Phœbe, guiltily aware that she should be delighted

to be home again and seeing to everything, womanly aware of all that needed doing about the house, planning with interest, yet evaded the issue with Gladys, the house-parlourmaid, and slunk off across the kitchen garden to her work-room with the big north window, and the canvases with their backs to the wall, and the tidy drawing-desk. I am not a real woman, she said to herself, apologising to some remoteness that was partly Robin and partly all the grown-up people in the world, I am not clever enough to be able to deal with stair-carpets and jam and things, I should be found out—do let me off till to-morrow ! And she shut the work-room door behind her and unlocked the desk and began rummaging slowly and deliciously like some she-animal back in its own lair. It struck damp and chilly at her, for the stove had not yet been lit, but she did not notice that. She wanted again to consider certain æsthetic and technical problems, to see whether while she had been away from them they might not have become soluble. She felt with her fingers at the glossy boxwood blocks ; weighed in her hand the tool roll full of gravers and scorpers, part of her working self ; touched lightly the pencils and the sheets of notes for drawings ; and she took a breath of autumny air and she was aware that here she could chase Basileia, and knew for certain that she was a better artist and also a better technician than Pussy.

He had gone back to his studio, too. He started an oil-painting on a grand scale. Phœbe Bathurst could do little niggling black-and-white she-pictures, could perfect and re-perfect her technique—like so much needlework ! But he had all the man's world of colour, buds and bubbles and bubs and bottoms, all colours, all convex, centrifugal, bounding out from the vortex. And there was also Cynthia who was quite ready for him again, not bothering or criticising, un-self-conscious, bullyable. They went to parties and they went to bed, and he painted his great picture and she mended his socks which had gone into holes at Auchanarnish; she was pink and had thick yellow hair, and she wore different kind of clothes from Phœbe, not arty at all, and she used the right amount of scent, instead of none or too much, like Phœbe; and all that would have been all right, only the picture was *not good enough*. Suddenly Pussy became full of a terrible, devastating respect for Phœbe and hungriness for her, for her advice, for her interfering, for her wanting him, for the conscious, un-Lawrenceish way she walked and thought and made love and made wood-engravings. And he saw her sharply stuck down there in the country, at Helm, stuck with the half-man, Robin Bathurst, and the winter coming, and, because he could not get at Robin Bathurst, he got at Cynthia and made her cry and say she'd leave him again. But she didn't.

George Coke-Brown left Auchanarnish and so did Joyce. And then it was the end of the holidays. Dione took Morag and Kenneth, Petronella and Clemency, into Oban to pack them into the south-bound express where they would have a third sleeper to themselves and their rather miscellaneous luggage. She always rather hated these partings, however cheerful, and drove fast through a golden late afternoon by hill and loch and pass. Kenneth sat beside her and talked about whose form he was likely to be in this term. Dione explained once more that his Aunt Muriel would meet them in London, give them lunch and a hair-cut, send Petronella and Clemency off to the Isle of Wight and take him and his sister up to Oxford. She would be down in three days herself and take over, but she had to settle up everything with Granny first. Kenneth nodded and suddenly discovered a dead mouse in his pocket; he wriggled round and threw it at his cousin Petronella in the back seat; it was important that he should assert his manhood in front of all these females. His mother grinned silently, thinking of Pussy, and hoping Ken would have got over the he-stuff stage before he was grown up and a possible nuisance.

Dione experienced her usual jump of annoyance on getting to Oban. She remembered it so well twenty years ago when it was a self-respecting fishing village with a few small shops, everyone knowing everyone else, and ordinary small town prices. Now it was full of harlotries of one kind and another, devices for attracting the stranger from Glasgow or England, shaming the Highlands. Buy your tartan! Tartan handkerchiefs, every conceivable and inconceivable tartan, Fraser and MacLean among them, her own tartan shown off to strangers like—like her own body. Tartan penknives made in Czechoslovakia. Books of jokes about Scotland—bawbees and whisky! That filthy bawbee joke, as if we hadn't been a horribly poor country, oppressed by the south, as if Burns hadn't died like a dog in atrocious poverty, and now they laugh at us! Joke postcards or sentimental ones, stags and heather, Highlanders with targes and claymores, lassies and sheilings. Oh, sickening! And the prices all away up too, now that the place lived on tourists, honest traders out for their bit of summer dishonesty. The shaming of Scotland!

They had come in after a very early tea, an hour before the train was due to start, as there was shopping to be done. Dione had missed the post at Auchanarnish with to-day's newspapers. They'd be there when she got back. She parked the car by the station and they all spilled out; nothing was explicitly said, but there was a feeling in the air that provisions other than plain sandwiches would be needed on the journey. They walked along the quayside towards the shops, and Oban leered at them. Motor coaches to Glen Coe. . . . Then suddenly Dione saw a newspaper poster, saw one, saw a dozen: "England off the Gold Standard." As her brain took it in she became filled with an extraordinary sense of relief, of elation. Oban was no longer a shame spot, Scotland no longer of great importance, except as the sharer in this. England off the gold standard, England at last going European, doing what the others had done earlier! England refusing to be bullied by America and France! England jumping down off a painful and cramping height. If we go, the rest'll go, she thought, remembering the last few evenings of economic discussion. We'll join with the Scandinavians, all the sensible people. We've called the ramp. Oh, glory, England has done in the bankers! And she ran across to the newsagent and bought all the papers.

She explained it more or less to the children, excited, turning from one paper to another.

"Will there be a revolution?" said Clemency.

"Perhaps," said Dione, almost adding, if you're good. . . . "If there is a revolution, we shall all be uncomfortable for a bit," she said, "but it will be worth it in the end, because afterwards everything will be planned and reasonable, and we shall all want to help with the plan—all the people of good will. We shan't go on being unhappy because most people are miserable and shut off from us and we can't help them; we'll all be friends. That makes up for being uncomfortable."

Morag nodded: "We shall be useful," she said; "school won't go on, of course, but I will go on a farm. The revolution won't be till you're home, mother, will it?"

"There probably won't be one," said Dione, gradually becoming more rational, "and in the meantime you can have some pre-revolutionary chocolate."

She had meant only to get them penny bars, but instead

she got them two big slabs, one plain and one nut-milk, and half a pound of Russian toffee, which sounded somehow appropriate, four bananas and a carton of raisins; they promised not to eat everything to-night. Then she got the Auchanarnish groceries, paying for them—her mother disliked running accounts—with Scottish bank-notes, which had all in a moment become uncertain and fairy stuff. She knew they were likely to go down in value—quite a lot perhaps—and that would be most unpleasant. All the same there was an exhilaration in the uncertainty, like being out in a small boat on big waves.

She left some films to be developed, bought wool and mending for Nurse, some tarred garden string for MacLean, and two books of stamps; she left her mother's spectacles to be mended and Tom's shooting-boots, which could stay up at Auchanarnish till next summer as usual . . . if next summer was going to be as usual. . . . Then it was time for the train. She packed them in and the station master waited tactfully till all good-byes were said before he waved his green flag, and then condoled with Mistress Galton. She waited till the train was out of sight; that was in the ritual of partings. Then, as she turned away, political excitement took her again on its lifting irrational wind and blew her out of Oban on to the homeward road.

She pressed on the accelerator, climbing, and crossed the ridge and came down to water again. It was evening, a golden dusk beginning to be overlaid with purple. She speeded happily. The Talking Crow flew ahead of her, his great wings flapping and lifting. She flew on his wings. He carried her, an un-Greek bird, more like a Highland fairy-tale eagle carrying a princess. Coming off the gold standard was one step nearer Cloud Cuckoo Borough. Her tractors were in gear, they were moving fast across the waste, the thorny land of England and Scotland, the land which had once been under wheat, but had been enclosed, made into parks and deer forests. The beautiful tractors of the revolution! The miles hummed under her. At one time she sang " Jerusalem " at the top of her voice. Sometimes the parcels bumped and rattled. Then the loch lay out under the sunset, fantastically lovely; the islands were semi-transparent, cut out against the last of the sunset, purple-grey, glass islands, fairy islands. There were no kelpies; they had all dived away, skelping and skirling, when they saw the tractors and the Talking Crow flying in front of Dione Galton!

## SALLINGTON I

THE train slowed down, running in to Sallington Central. Tom reached up and swung the suit-cases off the rack. "Mason will be meeting us," he said. Doors banged open at the standstill; Dione picked up the despatch case and her own little typewriter and followed Tom with the suit-cases. The crowd from the train, mostly men, hurried and bumped towards the exits; it was all as usual. Then they were both shaking hands with Mason, the agent; he was big and fair, north-country, in some ways not unlike Tom himself, but with something odd about the mouth, something childish and ironic and defensive. He seized the despatch case and typewriter; Dione walked between the two men, wishing they had left her something to carry, so that she might feel less strange and naked and deprived, part only of the Labour candidate for Marshbrook Bridge.

Outside the station the constituency Ford was waiting. Dione crept in behind with the suit-cases and sat very still. First they left their things at the Grand Hotel in the middle of Sallington; it was not a pretty hotel, she knew it of old. But for a night it was convenient; to-morrow they would be moving into their lodgings, where they would stay over the Election. On one side trams went clanging past the hotel; on the other it looked down into one of the old-fashioned cobbled ways that led to the woollen goods warehouses; even in this slump time the way was half blocked with lorries. They turned and the Ford rattled off along the tram-lines that led for half a mile down the slow, dirty Sall; often their view was blocked by wharf walls, but when they could see the river there was nothing on it but barges, or cabbage leaves and muck drifting out of a broken basket. At the bridge the tram-lines forked, but they kept south of the Sall, past the signpost *Doomington by Marshbrook Bridge*. Every now and then, after a traffic hold-up, the Ford would stop; then either Mason or Tom got out and cranked it.

Driving straight along the Doomington Road they would have come into Marshbrook Bridge by the River Ward, where the older factories were, and the worst housing conditions. But Tom asked Mason to go round by Barton's End, so they turned south again, and for a few minutes ran through a corner of Barstone which she knew well enough. There had been dreadful Barstone afternoons of family reconciliation when she and Tom, each having firmly tidied the other up, had gone over to take tea with Rosalind. And there had usually been a row to end up with! Once or twice when Muriel had been about they'd even gone to lunch, and good old Muriel had tidily averted the row. Well, there wouldn't be any Barstone this time!

From Barstone they took a wide sweep round, through sudden narrow country lanes not yet straightened for villas, and so into rising pasture land which she hardly knew. At one point they stopped and looked down through a gap in a hedge; Mason was pointing out some of the new streets that had been built beyond Little Lumley. Tom questioned and nodded, ticketing it all off in his head. Beside him blackberries were ripening, and haws reddening on the English thorn trees. He looked down across the pasture and the small houses that were eating it up; beyond them to more and more slopes of houses, dotted with green of gardens or allotments, then factory roofs, darker, straight blocks, the Synthex works and the Power Station, chimneys and houses and the lives they made, all still and waiting *under the late September sun, Marshbrook Bridge, tenable* for the man who could take it.

They zigzagged down from that high country past the old village of Babylon Ford, which Dione loved for the sake of its name, but which was no good from the canvassers' point of view: down past Lumley, the Claypits, and Little Lumley, where they waved to a group at a street corner. Now they were at the cross-roads by the Co-op., then on between allotments. To their left were the clay ponds, half surrounded by a tangle of thorns and rushes and hip-bearing briars, where the Marsh-brook rose; to their right was Barton's End, the new housing estate. "We'll have to work this," said Mason, getting out. Tom followed him. Dione was not sure whether she should come or not; it had all suddenly become serious; her soul shrank. Tom smiled at her vaguely, thinking of Barton's End. Understanding she might be in the way, Dione waited, watching the two men walk up a tidy cinder path beside a square plot with vegetables and a few chrysanthemum plants along the edge. They knocked and talked for a minute or two at the door with an oldish man in shirt-sleeves. Tom shook hands heartily and they came back.

"A good man," said Mason.

"A bit down in the mouth over prospects," said Tom.

The agent grunted. "He's been out of work seven weeks. A skilled driver. That's a 12*s*. 6*d*. a week house. His married daughter's helping them."

They stopped at several houses hereabouts. Later, Dione came with them, gradually picking up the thick sense of urgency and nervousness which was beginning to show among the Party workers. It made her shy, not herself, just the wife of all this. She talked to other wives as shy as she was, glancing quickly round the rooms, looking automatically for books and seldom finding them.

The women did not talk politics much, or rather they talked organisation, the women's institute side of things, but the men asked pertinent and intelligent questions and discussed all the local problems, eyeing Tom, wanting him to be up to everything.

From Barton's End they turned north, crossing the Doomington Road again near the goods station and the Synthex works, the corner where you could always be sure of good dinner-hour meetings. On some winds the smell from these works spread almost as far as the borders of Barstone, a sharp, sourish smell like nothing in nature. Then Mason made a detour through three of the quiet, pleasant roads on Morrow Hill, with their semi-modern detached houses, seven- or eight-roomed, with laburnum trees and potting sheds and often a little garage. Mason stuck out his lip at them contemptuously: "No good for us." Safe little houses, dear little, dull little houses, little home-nests, families of two children only, the rest birth-controlled. Too right. But the Council houses had fine chrysanthemums too, and no doubt would soon be having laburnums.

The Ford, warmed up, was going quite well. They slid across the canal bridge. Down to the left now was the River Ward and across it, very near now, the chimneys of the East Midland Power Station. Twice Phœbe had come down with them and made drawings of those chimneys, but that was in another sort of existence. She and Dione had eaten ham and eggs at the little shop at the corner. And beyond was Miss Waterhouse's green front gate and the big drawing-room with the Morris wallpaper and the De Morgan tiles round the fireplace. At the bottom of the slope was Carisbrook Road, where the houses got flooded.

It was getting late; they drew up in a small empty street of 1860 houses, all exactly alike.

" Tea," said Mason shortly, and knocked at a door.

" It's the Groves, isn't it ? " whispered Dione.

Tom nodded, and then a small woman with pale eyes and hair, and a jolly-looking little boy clinging to her, opened the door and asked them in, pleased, then called to her husband : " George, oh, George ! "

He called back from the scullery, saying he'd be along in two ticks.

" He's just washing himself," said Mrs. Grove, " only got back from the works five minutes ago. Come along in, Mrs. Galton ; I've just put the tea on."

It was a small, crowded room : photographs on walls and dresser, a work-basket just shut down but with the tail of a baby's flannel nightgown sticking out of it, and a few books in a hanging shelf, mostly the standard poets, school prizes perhaps, but evidently read, a couple of books on economics, a tattered Shaw, a library copy of Priestley's " Good Companions," and something on children's diet. There was a copy of the *Daily Herald* on the window-ledge, open at the children's page. The table was laid for tea, and Mrs. Grove got out extra cups and plates and put out some biscuits. The cups were hooked up on the dresser and Dione helped her to get them down : she was in a fairly advanced stage of pregnancy. Her husband came in, washed and brushed, a dark, capable-looking man with a very slight squint. They plunged into politics ; he knew Tom's books and apparently disagreed with them all, but that might just have been in the way of conversation. He and Mason were both well up in modern economic theory—fairly modern, at any rate.

The tea was very strong and very sweet ; the little boy had a good deal of milk in his, which he rather resented. Dione sipped at hers and Tom drank his up, though he usually hated it with sugar, but he was quite unaware of anything but the argument, which he was enjoying. Dione and Mrs. Grove talked rather formally, interrupted a good deal by the small boy. The talk turned on the Marshbrook Bridge districts, and Mrs. Grove said they were hoping to get out to Barton's End—their name was down on the housing estate list. She did want a bit of garden for Billy. And the new one, Dione thought, wondering if little Mrs. Grove had wanted very much to have another or whether it had been an unintentional begetting, wondering whether they'd give her chloroform—she looked rather small across the hips—or whether she'd just have to stick it, wondering whether she was frightened, wondering whether she was sick in the mornings, wondering whether she would ever in her life get a real holiday all to herself.

They saw two or three more people before evening and then the Ford took them back to their hotel. "I shan't want you till twelve at the committee rooms," Mason said, "so I got you a permit to see over the Power Station. Young Reuben's there now. Well, so long." He nodded and drove off. They had dinner. Tom was moody and nervous; he hunched himself like a bear over the evening paper. Dione's nerves didn't take her that way. She set herself to watch the Sallingtonians dining. They seemed to do it very thoroughly. She stated them to herself. They were proud; they were ugly; they didn't know they were ugly; they moved badly; they talked about money; they wanted to have things—a step from that, they would be horrible to be made love to by—they wouldn't wait, they'd snatch and grab—yes, grab and be sick afterwards like greedy children. That was it, they weren't adult, not an adult class, as on the whole the intelligent upper classes were adult (adult and dying of old age, poor lambs, sometimes!). These ones were each out for his own, badly behaved children, but all the same they'd got power. A set of children with power! Grumbling and hitting out if anyone tried to control them. There was a party going on at a table near theirs. She watched it carefully, rather afraid that she had met one couple before at her sister-in-law's. They were talking about current events; she couldn't help hearing a few comments; there was something pretty brutal even about the tone of the voice. The women's dresses were tasteless, except for one who might have been a Jewess. They were having champagne and they ordered the waiters about in the most shaming way.

After dinner she typed letters to Tom's dictation; she was disgustingly tired and made type-slips. They went to bed and she successfully short-headed a wool merchant for the bath. The bed looked all right, but the mattress sank in the middle and they kept on rolling into one another in the trough. Tom grunted and swore and went to sleep again, but Dione couldn't sleep much. Early in the morning the heavy traffic began. Trams slammed and rattled, gears screamed, hoofs slipped and clattered, shouts crossed—this was the terrible real world, far and remote from Auchanarnish or Oxford. The world that had to be changed, that had to be struggled against—that one couldn't struggle against—one couldn't even sleep against.

They were both still tired at breakfast. Dione was unreasonably but violently annoyed with Tom because, with the hotel's immense choice of kidneys, fried sole, omelette and so on, he should still unhesitatingly go for bacon and eggs; and she was equally annoyed with the hotel because, although one could apparently have both eggs and fish at the price (and—looking round the room—apparently did), yet they made one pay extra for fruit! After breakfast they got into one of those nasty trams and rattled off again down the Doomington Road. They got off at the Canal Corner and walked across the great lock gate between it and the faintly tidal Sall; the canal water hung heavily against the gates and the mild late September sun shed itself on delicate films of oil and coal-dust across its surface. A few trees still stood by the tow-path, rather broken and barked. They were silly and unimportant here, with the Power Station looming, humming at them. The air smelt of coal-dust from the barges unloading at the Power Station wharf. Now Tom and Dione were within feel of it. It was new and calm, encompassed with great cranes, steel girders, squares and crosses of strength; the four straight chimneys crowned it, joining it to the sky. Here and there steam rose faintly into the still sunlight. The slow water of the Sall was constantly being seized upon, sucked and whirled in through gratings for the condensers and ash troughs and poured out again, warmed and used. Now high iron railings rose in front of them, and barred gates. Tom showed his pass. They were taken through the gates.

Inside, the Power Station hummed and quivered; it was warm with soft movement as a bee-hive is warm. It went on by itself; hardly anyone was there to look to it. The crushed coal was fed mechanically to the furnaces; the flames were hooded and hidden; only a few clock faces showed what was going on inside. The ash was tipped down closed chutes into water, steaming troughs that carried it silently away. A man going by in overalls would watch for a moment. That was all. A shutter pushed aside showed quiet, writhing heat, too intense to gaze at.

Through white-lined, hospital-looking passages they came out into a great humming hall. The men in it were tiny, here and there, unhurried; there were a few coloured lights. The turbine casings were long purring cats. From them there beat out a throbbing through air and concrete and brick, through the bodies of the watchers. But the dark thick steel enclosed them, revealing nothing. The blast of steam tore continually through the massed steel blades, dropped to the condensers. It was all hidden. Tom and Dione were out of reach of the magnetic field. Man had control of the forces. Right at the end of the casing there was a grooved shaft revolving so rapidly that it seemed ice-still. Only the carbon brushes constantly gathered up from it with a faint crackle, a delicate sparking. The note of the humming did not change. All was well.

They passed on from one alternator to the next. There were doors marked "Danger," rows of white insulated plugs. The ventilators sucked and droned. As they went through the white passage again a man came walking quickly towards them, hesitated, and suddenly caught Tom's hand and shook it hard. A word or two, a glance at her, and he hurried on. He was young and dark and bright-eyed, in a linen coat, startlingly small and human after those great dead things. The quick, the quick, thought Dione, and then to Tom: "Who was that?"

"One of our people," Tom said, low, "Reuben Goldberg, an engineer."

They came then to a calm central place, remote from humming, where there were charts and plans on walls and high screens, and a great plan on the further wall which showed Power going out all over Sallington. Here were the names of the districts in blue and red—Marshbrook Bridge, Barstone, Smedbrook, Greenapple, Lamb's Cross, Milford, Sallmouth; if this connection were broken the Synthex works would be silenced, that, and no trams would rattle. A man at the largest desk spoke into a telephone. Peisthetairos, said Dione to herself, satisfied. She was in Cloud Cuckoo Borough.

"That was a nice place," she said to Tom as they went out.

He nodded. "You realise it's part of the Grid? Semi-public. A lot of our people come from there."

They walked back along the tow-path and up the canal. The houses at the other side of the canal did not come right on the top of it, but had narrow strips of garden running down, with michaelmas daisies, late stocks and dahlias, clothes lines and willow arbours. The canal never rose and flooded them. The canal was kind. She couldn't remember now if she had ever seen the fronts of these little houses. How would they vote?

From Canal Corner it was only a few minutes' walk to the Labour Party committee room. It was a big single room divided by match-board partitions, tucked in behind a Wesleyan chapel, off the main road. At the back, one long window which couldn't be opened looked over a wharf on to the Sall. There was no one there but pretty Gladys Wills, the typist, powdering her nose. She said Mason would be there any minute. While Tom looked over the heaps of stuff, old posters, old pamphlets, old polling cards, and a large photograph of Ramsay MacDonald recently taken down and turned on its face, Dione sympathised with Gladys over the office typewriter, which was old and monumental, amazingly different from her own simple little Corona. "Machinery gets out of date quicker than frocks nowadays," she said.

"Yes," said the girl, making a face at it; "looks as if it came out of old King Tut's tomb! I can't get up any speed on it, Mrs. Galton, I can't really, and I can do sixty to the minute on a decent machine." Then she told Dione about her boy-friend who had got the sack from his job at Morney House—the big Sallington drapers—over the slump, and how he couldn't get another place these days though he'd got a splendid character and all, and he'd lost all his spirits and wouldn't come for a walk with her on Sundays.

"But never mind," said the girl, "the election'll buck him up."

"I do hope so!" said Dione, "is he keen on politics too?"

"Not so keen as me," said the girl. "His Dad's an old Tory, a Church of England man—you know."

Dione asked if the Church of England was always Tory.

The girl giggled: "Oh, coo, yes! Don't you know, Mrs. Galton—why, old Merrill" (that was the Conservative sitting Member) "does the Church of England outings and the school treat! My sister was Church of England, but I told her not to be a fool. We've got to stand together, haven't we, Mrs. Galton?"

"We have indeed," said Dione. "By the way, you know, don't you, about Tom's sister?"

"Ooh yes!" said the girl; "we did laugh. Our Mr. Galton'll show old Coke-Brown, I said! I've got a sister-in-law myself." She glanced at Tom. "He'll make a lovely photograph," she said.

Tom was sitting on the edge of the table, swinging his foot and making notes on the edge of a pamphlet. He was certainly very good-looking in his square, northern way, especially after the summer vac., brown and hard from sun and exercise on Ardfeochan. Dione and the girl caught one another's eye and smiled and began to talk about chances.

Mason came in, rather cross and bothered, and threw some letters at the girl to type. They talked about the Municipal Elections at the beginning of November. No one was yet at all certain what date would actually be chosen for the General Election, but they would know in a day or two.

"The longer they put it off the better for us," said Mason.

Tom agreed: "People will see through this National Government stunt. What do you think the chances are, Mason?"

" Pretty fair," said Mason. " This'll be a Labour seat if hard work and keen workers can do it ! "

Dione sat back, one hand out towards the gas-fire, square nails and fingers strong enough from typing and gardening, yes, but a hand unspoilt by scrubbing and cooking and the life of Carisbrook Road. She was watching the two men, loving Tom, liking the other, but herself remote, only a little attached by way of the beautiful Power Station. She had come down to Marshbrook Bridge as a good wife, careful of Tom, trying to stop them from eating him. But now : perhaps he had got to be eaten ? He and Mason were talking of their helpers, men and women they knew and trusted, some for one job, some for another. They talked about the Party finances and Mason for a moment recalled a day five years back, before Tom had come, when there had been an essential bit of printing to be done and no money in the office, and someone had handed over the ten bob saved up in tuppences for the one new pair of boots in the family. They discussed the canvassing arrangements in detail, who would be most competent at what point, who would certainly quarrel, places where Tom was to put in a good word and soothe down vanities. They discussed unemployment, import boards, disarmament. And suddenly, Tom told Mason about that morning fourteen years back, marching into Nœux-les-Mines : the gassed men. The point at which he made up his mind about war : not to go on being one of the voiceless to whom things happened, but to try instead to make things happen, and differently. For a moment he spoke passionately, there in the ugly, battered committee room, as though Mason were a great audience, as though Mason had become the Labour Movement itself. And Mason nodded and approved, slowly. It was to him that Tom belonged, and not to Dione, and not to Oxford, and not even to himself.

## SALLINGTON 2

DIONE looked at her watch. She had been canvassing now for two and a half hours. And the day before, five hours, and the evening meetings . . . and the day before that. . . . She turned down the short-cut by the tow-path, walking fast, talking to herself. As the cold air blew against her shins and up under her skirt, she said to herself that it was time for winter woollies. She talked to herself almost in a half-whisper. Nice to have someone intelligent to talk to at last! Someone who will observe accurately, with judgment, seeing the chrysanthemums reflected in the canal, beginning now to drop into shapelessness, to tip their pink and gold with frosted brown.

For these few minutes, she said consolingly to herself, yes, for this short space between streets, I can relax in my mind. I need not think of screwing myself up to knock at another door which the woman of the house will open frowning, angry with me as I am angry when someone interrupts me. I hate canvassing; I hate the over-simplification, the under-statement; I hate lying, and one has to lie. Some people don't think it's lying; they convince themselves. Sometimes I do that, but it is dangerous for the soul. Tom convinces himself when he is talking; he convinces me; hearing him speak I get hot and angry or cold and dangerous, and so do the others who listen; I resolve to live better. But shall I?

If only one could stay like that between times. If I could be between dances what I am during dances at Auchanarnish, or if I could be between Tom's meetings what I am during Tom's meetings at Sallington, that would be all right. But in the times between I am separate, I am critical, I am not filled with one resolve or one purpose, either the purpose of the dance or the purpose of the Labour Movement. I feel myself separate from these Sallington people, these people I'm working for, lying for. I know I wouldn't choose to live among them between elections. I am a foreigner here, I don't belong, they don't truly admit me.

Where do I belong, then? I think I belong with the young, gay, intelligent people, the girls doing jobs on their own, the writers, the painters, the exact scholars. Those are my friends, my equals, my set of values. I'm betraying them here!

But how can I enjoy all that, how can I be whole-hearted about it when there's Carisbrook Road? I can't be separate from this either. Have I got to be torn, one half of me wanting brotherhood, demanding it as the only sensible thing, and the other half realising the plain fact of intellectual inequality? That means education, of course, equality in the future. But now? The good Labour homes I've stayed in, with their frightful pictures and rugs and art needlework!

That's our fault, though: the people on the top. The owners: even if they've gone highbrow now, like Phœbe and me . . . I'm afraid you can't have æsthetic equality, Dione Galton, till you've got economic equality. And economic equality will be no fun for you. Or for your children: you won't be able to grab things for them then!

Uncomfortable, yes. And the tractors are no use. I think I'm too tired for tractors. And I'm coming to the end of the tow-path, back into River Ward. And now I must sort out my leaflets: our own and these from London, from the Party. Is it likely that anyone even reads them? Is it possible? . . .

I have been canvassing South Street. I have got to 152 and my card has come to an end. I have got rid of nearly two dozen pictures of Tom; not bad. I have made the same joke about giving away my husband on at least one dozen doorsteps. Some of them had him in already, stuck up in the window. I love those houses. I love the houses that are pleased to see me. I hate the houses with Merrill and the Union Jack. I hate the doorsteps and the door-knobs; I hate the privet bushes in front of the parlour. But I have seen so many photographs of Tom that I don't any longer think it is really him. He grins in thousands of Marshbrook Bridge windows, still and grinning; can I have married that grin?

I have been up and down little front paths. I have screwed myself up to knock and have knocked. I have stood and waited, hearing my knocks echo dreadfully in an empty passage inside. Or I have heard steps coming. I have screwed myself up to smile and have smiled. I have been to back-doors; I have tiptoed past perambulators; I have dodged washing and dogs; I have listened to stories of rent and neighbours and gas-stoves; I have known that these are the realities. I have been on my feet the whole time. I don't think I ever knew what it was to be tired before. My legs and back and mind are all aching. And yet me, me somewhere in the middle, doesn't mind, doesn't want not to be tired, doesn't, above all, want to stop. I am going to do this little bit of Spark Lane that is on my polling card. . . . . . .

I am sitting on a very hard chair listening to Councillor Finch introducing Tom. By the end of the meeting the chair will seem very hard indeed. The lights are hard too, unshaded. There isn't a platform, but there is a large desk for Tom and Councillor Finch, and a glass of water and a blue book. And beside the desk is a little hard chair for me. Like the little Wee Bear. Councillor Finch is talking about the Marsh-brook scheme. Hear, hear. This is a classroom, to seat fifty children; and we've got to get those big classes altered! More than fifty in this audience, though; they're packed double-tight. All the old gang. Mason at the back and Sam Hall with the red hair, and Mrs. Rivers in the front row who is rather deaf, and that woman whose name I don't know with false teeth and a green hat, and the man with the beard who asked questions yesterday. They nod to me. I smile back. Tom is getting up to speak. They cheer. I sit a little sideways looking up at Tom. I am part of him, supporting him from the small hard chair, a kind of small flying buttress. Tom frowns, speaking slowly, hitting the table, going over the story of the last two months, gathering up the eyes, the shifting hands, the shuffling feet, the minds constantly twitching back to home or work.

He has got them now. The minds stay hooked on to his voice; they are not twitching back any more, they are all pointing steadily the same way. He is voicing them, saying what they are too tired, too muddled to say for themselves. He makes it clear, a light pathway for their minds to follow; they are content, drugged a little, seeing differently. His voice has become the Talking Crow. It lifts a little, the wings lift, the minds lift. He is telling these English about Pym and Hampden and all the men in England who stood for political liberty. The shining names of Cloud Cuckoo Borough. As now, they must stand for economic liberty. Equality. The wings lift.

When Tom says, like that, the Labour Movement, it makes my heart turn over, it makes me proud and angry. It is that generousness that made me want to marry Tom. It is a laying-open, an acceptance. It is sun and wind on

Ardfeochan. His voice is gathering, gathering. We lean towards him, to be caught in the warmth of acceptance, to give ourselves, to come together, to follow the Crow. Five years ago I heard him speak to a meeting of country labourers, men earning fifteen shillings a week, living in damp cottages, crippled at middle age with rheumatism and asthma. I hated being separate from them, I hated the society that forced me to keep separate, that hid their pains from me. When Tom said, the Labour Movement, five years ago, I who had been hesitating joined the Labour Party. I had been tormented by intellectual doubts; but when I took the step beyond doubt, when I got faith and declared myself, then I was happy. It is sweet, sweet to give up after a struggle, to let oneself be possessed. When Tom is speaking about liberty I am possessed again.

I am running in the dark from the school-house to the car, through darkness like a bird diving, I catch my coat tight against the cold wind. I slam the door, stumbling over a pile of posters and a placard at the back of the car. Mason swears under his breath, rubbing his knuckles barked by the starting-handle. Tom turns to me: "How did that go?" "Well!" The car rattles down dark streets. Tom is talking to Mason; they wonder if Councillor Finch will get in at the Municipals. I sort things in my head. I got this morning ham, sardines, butter, cocoa, fresh eggs, pencils. Morag wrote that she had a fight with another girl about a boy. Kenneth has been moved up in Maths. Incident: a girl in good tweeds came into the office yesterday morning, offered to drive over with canvassers to Babylon Ford and Little Lumley, and to drive on polling day. Sent her off with Edna Boffin and Mrs. Taylor. Must find out who she is. Miss Waterhouse's meeting of professional women. Teachers, clerks, in business. Did I do them right? Lots of questions. Don't mind that sort of speaking. News from nowhere. Propaganda photographs of Russians Five-Year-Planning: grinning at the movie men: lovely teeth: merry peasants. Must go to Russia. Must take Morag.

Ten minutes late for the next meeting—always like that. Running across dark to a lighted door, faces I know—George Grove, Jack North, Ed. Palmer, slapping Tom on the back, pulling off his overcoat. Along a passage up darkish steps on to a light platform—the thread of a very Sallington voice, speaking. The thread snaps for Tom. Cheers. For me too as part of him, part of the Labour Movement. Miss Waterhouse in the chair remembering perhaps Labour meetings twenty years ago when it was still young and fresh, as exciting between elections as it is now during elections. Must there, then, be a growing old of ideas as of women, when the bloom is off them, and they can no longer excite joy or tenderness? I am growing old myself, I am an ordinary woman; I am only special here because I am the Labour candidate's wife; I am only special in Scotland because I was Dione Fraser and my mother is Mrs. Fraser, and was Katherine MacLean of Auchanarnish. I shall die, and Tom will die, and the Labour Movement will die, and so will all the lovely, the young, the virgin ideas which are budding and quickening now in people's minds. And tractors will look as silly as Watt's steam-engine and the Labour Movement will look as silly as the Byzantines fighting over the Athanasian Creed. In a thousand years men and women will be so different from us, so changed, to us now so terrible and shocking, that we dare not assess them or imagine the future. We can only imagine a few years from now; we can only imagine easy things—tidying up the world, making it all as good as the best now. But not better, not different, not strange. That is the strength of the Labour

Movement, it only imagines easy things. The strength and the weakness.

Weakness. I must not imagine that here! Heresy, heresy, shut it away, if that thought got loose what it could kill! They would crush me for having that dangerous thought. Miss Waterhouse and Mason and George Grove would crush me under their capable, their sensible feet. They don't think these things. Who does? Who, except me, is a possible, a secret heretic? Most people have no time to doubt. It is only idlers like me that have these thoughts, idlers, parasites, mensheviks, defeatists. Oh, must women then be defeatists, waiting and watching Tom, watching their men go out so gallantly, earnestly, childishly? No, Miss Waterhouse isn't a defeatist. Nor all those women who have addressed envelopes, canvassed, distributed pamphlets, trotting round with a perambulator, pushing notices of meetings under door-sills. Not Mrs. Rivers or Mrs. East or Mrs. Albert. Not the girl who came and drove for us. Only people like me, with other ideas cutting across the big idea. Other ideas, other questions, the seals, Green Jean. Phœbe and me. Darling Phœbe, you and me in an island of fun among all these damned silly serious politics! Heresy . . . the hunt's up—run, Phœbe!

What am I doing? Must listen. Must think what to say at the cottage meetings to-morrow afternoon, go over the statistics in my head. Tom is talking about disarmament. Spending the war money on houses and schools and health. Miss Waterhouse cranes forward, her old eyes bright. Tom says, the Labour Movement. The hall rises to it, shouting, drowning the whistles and boos at the back. Tom does not hear the whistles and boos, only the shouting. He leans towards it, big enough to burst through any crowd, any danger. But I hear the boos and whistles. I know that for those booing boys the Labour Movement said like that by my Tom means nothing, no light, no dream. They've got another light, another dream, the British Empire, glory, the Union Jack with Merrill's face printed across it! Well, why not, isn't there room in the world for two dreams? No. No. Their dream means war and oppression and owning things and owning people. We've got to smash their dream. Poor kids. Fool, there are twice as many of them, five times as many! All over the world. How be sorry for a dream in power? Fool, fool, wake up, or you'll never be a politician, never any use to Tom or to Carisbrook Road.

Questions. Goodness, Tom smashed that man—and he probably asked it in good faith! That's one of the Junior Imps—Merrill's bright young things. Got him! (The other dream) Import Boards. Oh, damn economics. The unemployed. Poor darlings. Remote. Another dream. Separate. Oh! where did that voice come from? That not separate voice?

## SALLINGTON 3

Tom was apt to be impatient with questioners, with anyone who didn't see, as he did, the beauty and immediacy of the thing he was offering them ; he was apt to forget the time when he himself had been unconverted, the days of his worried liberalism, of the shades of *laisser-faire*. This impatience of his pleased some of his people, Sam Hall sweating with excitement and the two Taylors, and that fanatic, Mrs. Albert from Marl. It pleased the simpler people who came to the meetings partly for the show, but it bothered Mason, and Tom himself realised that he oughtn't to, and tried to get back to his lecturing manner. But these practical questions from the two men who, Miss Waterhouse whispered to him, were the leaders of the local unemployed, were a different thing. He listened carefully, frowning ; it sounded as if there were a bad bit of injustice about ; with one part of himself he disliked that intensely, with the other he was pleased, because he knew that in the class war it must be so. The thick Sallington voice and the harsh, inflected Scottish voice, jarred with reality across the hall. " Wait till after the meeting," Tom spoke across to them, " we'll talk it over then." There were a few other questions, mostly on the economic issues, and then Miss Waterhouse gave out some notices and proposed the vote of thanks. The meeting broke up with cheers and a few cat-calls. Tom jumped down off the platform and waded through the crowd, shaking hands and talking here and there, till he came to the two men who were waiting. Mason introduced them.

The leader of the Unemployed Committee was a youngish man with a three days' crop of blonde bristles on lip and chin ; he smiled one-sidedly, defensively, telling Tom about one of his committee who had been arrested for chalking pavements. Tom took notes and said he'd see the police ; they were usually decent enough ; it was probably a mistake. The man's jersey fitted him closely, much washed and darned ; it came down straight over his belly, and his hip bones jutted it out on either side. " My chaps'll give you a hand with dinner-hour meetings," he said. Tom asked him if he was a Party member. The ironic smile crooked itself on his face ; he shook his head, and Tom remembered, painfully, the penny a week for membership. He would have to talk to Mason about some other way of organising the unemployed. " But we'll vote all right," said the man, " I'm getting the cut—next week. I've got a wife and two kids." This with an eye on Dione who had just come up. She shook hands, thinking quickly, even if he does say it for effect now, it makes it no easier to live on 30*s*. a week. " If you want any drivers on polling day," the man went on, " we've got some skilled drivers in my lot, private work and all. They'd do you a treat."

" We can't pay them on polling day, Harry," said Mason, " not so much as the price of a drink. Rules are rules. Even if old Merrill has the pick of the Rolls-Royces ! "

" Never mind," said Dione, " they'll all be empty ! " It was the sort of mild joke Mason liked. She looked at the other unemployed man, who had stayed quiet, rather behind his friend, thin and watching, no trace of a smile ; she wanted to speak to him, but shyness almost choked her. There was something else about him, a kind of parody of her brother Alex—if Alex hadn't had enough to eat for several years running. Tom was taking notes about the man who had been arrested. Mason had been buttonholed by George Grove, who wanted to know what the arrangements were for the outdoor meeting at Canal Corner. Hardly any of the Labour people were on the telephone, of course, and that made practical difficulties.

"What a shame about your man!" said Dione at last, a little awkwardly, "where was he chalking?"

The man lifted his dark lashes and stared at her; she stood it, smiling back at him. "By the Synthex gates," he said, "they had an eye on him; the police know where their pay comes from."

"They're usually fair, aren't they?" said Dione, "after all—they're getting a ten per cent. cut! They've seemed friendly to me."

"No doubt they are fair to you," said the man, "you will most likely never have been in the other position."

Little Miss Wills, going past, caught Dione by both hands: "That was just lovely!" she said. "I brought my boy; here he is."

Dione was introduced to a rather reluctant-looking young man; she said friendly things, thinking that if little Gladys Wills married him she'd lose that gay, silly, rather joyous enthusiasm. The man waited. Dione turned back to him, eagerly: "You're west coast, aren't you?" Already she knew herself more aware of him than she ever could be of Mason or Gladys Wills or any of the English.

The man answered quietly: "I am." The hall was clearing from round them; he shifted back from her half a step, leaning his weight lightly on one hip: "I am the son of your mother's gardener, Mistress Dione," he said.

Dione blushed violently, felt herself blushing, lifted a hand to her face; she saw that the man was at last beginning to smile a little. "Then you're Donald!" she said, "oh—does your mother know you're here? She's wearying so after you."

" What have I now to do with her ? " said the man, and Dione remembered he had been intended for the Ministry.

" You can't get free so easily," she said, " they have your photograph still between the clock and the vase with the blue roses. I should have recognised you."

" Maybe I'm older," said the man.

" Mmhm."

" And a thought thinner. But you can tell her you have seen me if you choose."

" No other message ? " He shook his head. " What has happened to you, Donald MacLean, since you left Glasgow ? Was it Maxton you were with then ? "

Donald MacLean gave the ghost of an arrogant Highland sniff. " I am a member of the Communist Party," he said.

" Communism seems the only logical thing, sooner or later," Dione agreed, " but I doubt you've less chance of getting things done than the Labour Party."

" What have *they* done, then ? " said Donald MacLean.

" I know ! " said Dione quickly, " but they never had a clear majority ! "

" That's what you folks always say."

" Yes, but—oh, I know fine that half of the Party aren't Socialist ! They just want a nice comfortable little house each, with a nice little wife and the kettle on for tea and a steady job at union rates under the Municipality ! Oh, I know that's not Socialism. But give us a chance, it must come slowly ! "

" Slowly ? " said Donald, smouldering at her. " While folks are starving and growing old and dying ? Slowly ? While your Party is getting the money and the jobs and the respect of their betters ? No wonder you'll prefer it slowly."

" One difficulty is," said Dione, " that the people who

are worst off have all got Merrill's Union Jack stuck up in the window. It seems to them to promise more; it's more —romantic. You know those streets beyond the Power Station? Yes, fine you do! And the clay-pit rows at Babylon Ford?"

"These English!" said Donald suddenly. "It was not like that on the Clyde!"

"Oh well, if *we* ran everything——! Do you think Compton Mackenzie is any use?"

Donald MacLean muttered something under his breath. Miss Waterhouse went past them, a very large umbrella tucked under one arm, a bunch of pamphlets under the other. The lights at the far end of the hall were switched off. "I'm afraid I haven't the Gaelic," said Dione, "what did you mean?"

"I doubt it was not fit for ladies, Mistress Galton."

Dione laughed: "Donald MacLean, I think I might have agreed with you! But don't you think—apart from that kind of maybe artificial thing—there's something in Scottish Nationalism?"

"Not while it's run by ladies and gentlemen," said Donald MacLean; "not with a Burns night, Jacobite, Edinburgh drawing-room ideology! I'd as soon see Scotland dead."

"But," said Dione, "you've got it wrong! The thing's not being plastered on from above. It's coming up from the earth, it's a true cultural nationalism. What about Hugh M'Diarmid? He's a proletarian poet."

"Aye, fine he is, making limited editions and taking all the braws and bits in his vocabulary from Dunbar and Gavin Douglas—a fine lot they know about Clydeside!"

"Mm, yes, but because you've read them and read Hugh M'Diarmid, that shows that you and they are part of the same culture."

" Mistress Galton, I totally disagree with you ! " Each of them at the same moment took a step nearer the other.

And suddenly Mason said : " Come along, Mrs. Galton, we'll have them after us if we don't clear out and let them shut up here. Have you and young Mac been fighting ? "

" Indeed, no," said Donald MacLean, " we have had a very pleasant argument, have we not ? "

" It did me good ! " said Dione. " Will we be meeting again soon ? " She walked out beside him into the dark yard. " You know," she said, " there are times one can believe and times one must just be critical. I doubt I've nearly as many criticisms of the Labour Party as you have, Donald MacLean, and maybe they are fundamentally the same criticisms ; yet if one were always critical, one would get nothing done. One must give one's faith for a time ; that's the only way creation comes."

" It is the only way happiness comes," said Donald MacLean slowly, in the dark.

" The whole end of man. To be lost in the glorification."

" The glorification is not yet," said Donald MacLean, " and not here. Maybe in Russia. I do not know for certain."

As he walked away, Mason said : " Just as well they aren't running a Communist this election. The C.P.'s a damned nuisance down here when it chooses. That young Mac would have been the devil to deal with if they'd had a candidate. As it is he does a bit of heckling."

" It does no harm to keep us awake," said Tom.

" Why can't they come into the Party like the rest of us ? I'm as much a worker as he is ; I did my eight hours a day, all right."

" What's his job ? "

" He's a riveter. He came from Glasgow when there was work going at the docks at Sallmouth ; now he's out.

Why can't these C.P. chaps see they're right out of touch with the workers? It's us in the Movement who've always done everything for the working classes, not them."

"One has a good deal of sympathy with them," said Dione tentatively.

"I haven't," said Mason.

They went along to the committee room; there was always plenty to discuss. On the way Dione asked him who the girl was who had come and driven.

"Don't you know?" said Tom. "That's the girl who's going to marry my nephew-in-law!"

"Not the one Elizabeth's being bridesmaid to?"

"Yes, that's it. Her young man isn't as sound a Tory as he might be, either! But we won't say a word to Rosalind—she mayn't have got the wedding present yet!"

Dione giggled and rubbed her cheek against Tom's, loving him and conspiring deliciously with him. Rosalind had been rather trying. There had been several painful and exhausting hours of argument. Anyhow, she had kept her off Tom. Muriel, the younger sister, had written a very nice letter, but was too completely occupied with her own good works to help, except by occasionally going down to Oxford and looking after the children. Muriel disliked politics, anyhow; she felt that the best ideas always come into politics from outside, and she stayed outside. A good many of Tom's and Dione's friends had turned up, though, and canvassed or spoken; some of them were useful, others needed to be reconciled with Mason and George Grove and Sam and the rest of the locals. Two or three dons had come over from Oxford and spoken; they didn't always go down very well, unless you picked the audience. On the other hand, Laski had been the greatest success, and so were the shock troops from S.S.I.P.

It was cold in the committee room; Mason turned the gas-fire full on. There were five of them there; Dione sat behind the desk in Miss Wills's chair, hoping not to be in the way. There were lengths of cheap red and green ribbon in the drawer, some half made up into rosettes; she picked up the needle and went on with them; the red and green on her own grey jersey gave her an absurd feeling of warmth and pleasure. The men were cheerful, full of excited rumours; they talked and smoked and planned; every now and then the cheap tobacco smoke got violently into her throat. They swapped election stories, or discussed a leaflet; a certain quality of confidence came from them, or rather through them. Mason was planning a raid on the brick-fields at the dinner hour; George Grove quoted the optimistic *Herald;* Sam Hall scratched his red head and laughed. Ed. Palmer had a brother at the Synthex works; he had to keep quiet about his politics, it didn't do to be Labour there. Mason growled at that, and Tom nodded, remembering the Synthex dividends. Little old Miss Tottenham had offered her house for a ward committee room; she would supply seed-cake as usual. The big posters were going well. How many cars could be counted on for the Day?

Someone came running up the steps and bounded in, letting a whirling draught of cold air in with him. It was Reuben Goldberg, bright-eyed, with darting looks and leaning body from one to another of the other men. Dione watched his hands, pointed finger-tips, but a sufficiently square thumb; he brought her into the circle of confidence, asking for her opinion, insisting that she was part of it. Half resisting, she enjoyed it; once she was there the other men accepted her as one of themselves. Reuben Goldberg had a delicious scheme for repainting the Tory posters. When that was sat on, he had another scheme for a procession with torches, but Mason wouldn't have it.

"Cut it out, Reub.," he said; "it might do for Carisbrook Road, but we've got Morrow Hill and Marl to think of."

Reuben agreed gloomily, and Dione suggested a procession of children; they might manage it on the Saturday afternoon, when Morag and Kenneth were coming over. Mason again seemed doubtful, but Reuben was all for it, and Ed. Palmer seemed to think it might catch on at Barton's End; he lived there himself.

"We'll make them sing," suggested Dione.

Sam Hall inevitably suggested Mrs. East and the Labour choir.

"No," said Dione firmly and caught Reuben's eye. She took a pencil and began to scribble on the back of a leaflet. Mason was more impressed; she had already produced the slogan: "Get Galton Going."

"Half a tanner on your rice,
Tuppence on your treacle,
That's the way the Tariffs go,
Pop goes the weasel!"

She hummed it, then produced another verse:

"Up and down the Doomington Road,
Full of pride and glory,
Voters, voters, knock 'em out,
Flop goes the Tory!"

"Tunier than 'England Arise,'" said Sam Hall appreciatively, and she rocked with idiotic delight—we are the music-makers and we are the dreamers of dreams. . . .

Reuben began to talk to her of May-Day pageants in some glorious and faintly possible future. She thought of the Power Station as background, but he of meadows, ideally green and spangled poppy scarlet like the ribbons. No matter, they all fitted into one another.

It was midnight before Tom and Dione could start back to their lodgings, and a full moon. They both felt suddenly tired, saying good-night to the others, and with the tiredness the cold suddenly nipped at their arms and legs. Dione took the wheel; Tom sucked a lozenge; neither of them said anything for a time. Then she felt him staring at her, and half turned, slowing a little.

"How are the chances?" said Tom. "Five to one against? Seven to two?"

"Sometimes I think they're evens," said Dione, "even now, even after Snowden's effort and all the gup that's being drummed in by the papers." She was thinking of the new estates at Barton's End, where she and Miss Waterhouse and Ed. Palmer's little wife had been canvassing: street after street almost solid and rather intelligent Labour.

"I wonder if you're right," said Tom, and then: "God, I do want to get in! I could do something for these people."

"What would College say."

"The Warden would probably break his spectacles again. But I don't care if I never give another lecture. These people trust me; I've just got to help them to get free, and lecturing doesn't do it, however sound my economics are."

"Would being their M.P. do it?"

"Not at once. Not completely. But if the Party gets in with a lot of new blood and the old gang kicked out—Dione, there are two sides to the Labour Movement; one I've always known, the logical side, economics: the means to a good life, the obvious reasons for things. But the other side's this group that we're part of—I know you think in groups!—these people who are giving every minute of their time, every penny of their savings, Mason,

Ed. Palmer, Sam Hall, Mrs. East, Jo. Burrage, George Grove, Councillor Finch, Edna Boffin, Johnson, the Taylors, Reuben Goldberg . . ." He crooned over the names and then coughed.

Dione turned off the main road: "You're in love with them," she said gently. "But it's rather frightening. After all, Tom, you were religious at fifteen, like all nice English public-school boys, but I've never caught it, even as a child; I never had any Old School Chapel, and I can't help feeling rather doubtful of the religious impulse, even here. What's to happen after the election? It will be like —like being cut off from Mass—and they'll all have to go back to work."

"I don't think I can think of after the election yet," said Tom.

Dione smiled; she was thinking of £400 a year, as against the lectureship; still, she had her own income, and he could stay with Muriel in London, and she could easily get a couple of P.G.'s during term; it might be rather fun. She said: "I keep on hearing about works that say they'll close down if Labour gets in. Will they?"

"That might give us a chance of reconstruction and nationalisation," said Tom. "God, I wish I could tackle the Heavy Woollens! I know what's wrong, and none of the fools who run them has the least idea. Look at the questions I get! All the same, Dione, my dear, I haven't got in, and I shall be surprised if a Tory Government doesn't."

"Then the cuts will happen."

"Yes. Poor devils. But the worse things are, the quicker the change-over will be. I suppose the B.B.C. have done us a good deal of harm here. A nice advertisement for a publicly owned industry!"

"You get out, Tom, and I'll run her up to the garage.

No, nonsense, you're tired! And there may be letters. Do your gargle, like an angel, and put a shilling into the gas-meter. I'll make scrambled eggs."

She took the car along to the little garage. A sleepy man let her in, asking sympathetically how things had gone that day. She shut off the engine and got out. At once the frosty night bit at her face. The car looked gay enough with its ribbons; she liked driving royally among the streaming of those bright fairy-tale loops and bows, red and green, the summer colours. They pulled a blanket over the radiator and turned out the light in the garage. But the full moon was so bright that the green ribbon still showed greenish grey, and even the blackened red gave out a dark glow.

There was a short-cut back across a rough field, old pasture already sold to the builders. Earth and grass felt frosty and the air was filled with a wide moon-frost. Scraps of things kept singing through Dione's head, rhymes for Labour, all bad—sabre, neighbour, pipe and tabour. If one could dance things instead of saying them. But how tired her feet were, in the same shoes all day! And how tired Tom was. She thought, only another eight days, and then, shockingly, but if Tom gets in it will be for always! That's what he is offering himself for, to be made tired, to be broken and eaten for the people of Marshbrook Bridge; that's what it must be to be part of the Labour Movement. Then she tried to think out exactly what happened when you sold a pound's worth of goods in France now; more francs, less francs, the seesaw of gold tittered up and down in her mind—she couldn't hold it, though she knew it was quite simple, that Tom saw it without thinking, that Kenneth saw it quite easily. Annoying that women are never taught to think mathematically. The grass smelt of frost; she was hungry; she yawned, feeling that frosty air rush down her throat past her strongly beating heart into her strongly elastic lungs. In a few minutes she would break and beat the fresh eggs, hear the sizzling butter, pour milk into an enamel pan and stir the chocolate flakes to a brown melting sweetness; she would take off her shoes and stretch her toes, have a bath perhaps, undressing by the gas-fire: Tom by the gas-fire stripping and chucking his shirt, his beautiful bare sides rippling and brown with summer muscle; and bed, dropping to sleep almost in a moment, murmuring to one another, touching one another lovingly, closer at Marshbrook Bridge than ever at home. This, she supposed, was happiness—she had caught it by the hair at last!—working at a common cause and eating and sleeping and hoping.

At the corner of the house there was a poster. As she came closer the frost and the moonlight beat on it. She knew that in daylight it would be red, the magic colour. Vote Labour, it said. Vote Labour. And Dione's heart turned over with happiness and a foreknowledge of defeat and a certainty of right.

## SALLINGTON 4

ALL over England, Scotland, Northern Ireland and Wales candidates and their wives hurried about constituencies, anxious and agitated, or anxious and heroic. Wherever they went supporters grew hectic or confident, cheered their cars as they passed, talked about them in quick loud voices. The other side were scornful or else angry that such men should be allowed to exist. Some of the candidates gave out power, others had to be soothed by agents in committee rooms. The women candidates were apt to call up a quite different strain of gallantry among their supporters and of sex-hatred among their enemies. No party had a monopoly of nerves or of heroism. All that could be said was that the supporters of the National Government were most certain of themselves and most apt to joke cheerfully with prominent constituents about the results of the poll. Perhaps the Independent Liberals were least confident, though as a party they probably had a very high average of intelligence. Labour supporters were either encouraged or made particularly sardonic by a wildly optimistic number of the *Herald*. The Tories, having most of the papers, could afford to ignore them more.

Some of the wives of the candidates who were going about with them did it because they wanted to, because they had independent political convictions, which had perhaps even influenced them in their choice of a husband, and had almost certainly influenced the husbands themselves. Others did it because it was their husbands' show, and they were almost inevitably part of it. Some were merely showing off. A few were desperately frightened and hated the whole day. Some couples took sandwiches with them, and perhaps alcohol in some form, though not enough to alienate the temperance sections of their constituencies. Others were fed by friends, and others, whose homes were in their constituencies, would perhaps go home for lunch or tea and even play with the baby for ten minutes—anything to rest the nerves. Many of them had been up early and seen a polling booth formally opened; most had been speaking at high pressure for at least three or four days beforehand. But now they were near the end; soon the strain would relax, the crisis, like other crises, be over, and England would begin thinking of something else.

All morning Tom and Dione had been from one committee room to another, stirring up the Old Village, seeing that Marl had its cars, trying to induce wives to vote early instead of waiting for their husbands, giving advice, disentangling muddles, soothing Miss Batten, who had expected red pencils with blue ends like last time, and had now only got red and blue ones separate. At the edge of Barstone they brushed with other activities, seeing for a moment as they cut across a quiet street the other names on the posters. They chased people off from hanging round the central committee rooms and sent them to help at overworked Carisbrook Road or Barton's End. They scuttled off to east Doomington Road after an S.O.S. for cars, and saw that when the cars came they were properly dressed up.

Several people from Central Sallington had come with cars, mostly two-seaters, including a hitherto unknown parson with a very old Renault and four hard-boiled eggs. The girl Margaret had decided that in view of her future in-laws she had better not come and drive herself, but had lent the little car. Pussy Morgan had come down from London with Cynthia in a really smart Essex they had borrowed from somebody; they got a lot of quiet fun hoisting old ladies in and out, but they would chatter interminably between loads, and Dione, alas! didn't really like Cynthia. Besides, she was afraid Pussy might run over someone. Phœbe had been going to come, but at the last moment Brian didn't seem very well, Robin was in a fuss, and she couldn't manage it. Muriel and Alex had sent telegrams, and Dione had sent them to any of Tom's friends who were standing.

During the morning and early afternoon things went quietly at Sallington and all over the country. You would not have thought there was a crisis. The only thing that seemed to be bothering the early voters was the idea, cleverly put forward at the last minute by one of the Tory papers and perfectly untrue, that if Labour got in the savings in the Post Office Savings Banks would be seized. This had some effect on the women, who were, of course, most directly affected. But, on the whole, people looked in discreetly at the polling booth, deposited a nice unspoilt vote, and hurried away again. A few went proudly, especially some of the older women who had been active in the times when women had not been allowed to go through this rite, and had looked upon it as something wonderful and satisfying; but for most it was a before or after breakfast duty. This was a fidgeting time for all responsible; they had tried to make the thing magic and compelling, and now were heavily conscious of their failure. It seemed to Dione that the streets were full of cars all with new, expensive blue ribbons, cavorting along with Merrill's voters; she longed to throw herself in front of them and appeal to the voters; to make them see that they were going against the future. She thought suddenly of Kenneth and Ian and it seemed as though the Conservative voters were shoving them straight into international wars, into gas and flame, and the smashing of their lovely bodies. It was terrible to be able to do so little. During one wait at a committee room she had suddenly found herself nearly crying, and a woman she did not know had come and petted her, and she had held tight for a moment to the woman's stuffy serge shoulder, and had noticed the ribbed, grimy nails, the work-worn skin of the kind hand that was touching her and giving her back her strength.

Everyone thought of things they hadn't done. Mason thought of whole streets uncanvassed for lack of workers brave enough to tackle the bourgeoisie on Morrow Hill, of the outlying places where nobody had been able to organise anything, of posters nobody had put up, leaflets nobody had distributed; and, instead of thinking warmly of all the men and women in the Marshbrook Bridge Labour Movement he could only think of the people who ought to have backed him up but hadn't, of his old quarrel with Sam Hall over the choir, and how Mrs. Albert once told him he was no Socialist. He glowered at them in the office and snapped at Tom, this mere instrument from outside. If only they had a working man for a candidate, one of themselves! Miss Wills brought in a thick white cup of steaming tea. "Sugar!" he growled. She scurried off for it, and he put in lump after lump, and stirred it viciously and drank it up while it was still very hot. The warmth in his stomach made him feel better; he remembered with satisfaction how his wife had seen the Tory agent looking all to bits the evening before. Perhaps it was as bad for them.

Miss Wills came in again, settling the ribbon favour on the breast of her dress. "You'll have a nice cup of tea, won't you?" she asked, adoringly maternal to Tom and Dione. Tom didn't answer her; he was thinking of speeches where he had failed to make his point or jumped too hard on a questioner; and then he saw Jack North coming in, and was over by him in a couple of strides ; he wanted the news from River Ward. Dione, smiling, refused the tea ; she knew the local brew, and could scarcely manage it at the best of times !

" Come on," said Tom, " we've got to see to Babylon Ford and the Lumleys. Want a lift, Jack ? Mrs. Rivers ? Come along, then." Dione and Mrs. Rivers followed him out and into the car. They started with a jarring of gears ; the driver was tired too. Harry, the leader of the Unemployed Committee, was driving Tom's own Morris—not very well—and another of the unemployed had taken on the Ford. A hired car could not be used for taking voters on polling day, but might for the candidate. There were so few Labour cars available that all which had been lent were taking voters, and Tom's was hired from the friendly garage. The driver had decked it out with red and green himself, and at one of the committee rooms Dione had been given a bunch of red chrysanthemums, which she clung to, fidgeting at the wet stems and scattering petals wherever she went. Tom settled back in the car, breathing more easily, deliberately not thinking of any mistakes he might have made.

They took Mrs. Rivers to her committee room and went in for a few minutes. Men and women were constantly hurrying in and out, bringing in canvassing cards ticked off in blue or red, or with pencilled lists, or names and addresses to hand on to the cars. They were delighted to see Tom and Dione. They shook hands and went off feeling that now things were going better, that the centre of activity and importance was in their own committee room, their own work. They squared their shoulders to take burdens ; they felt like people in historical romances. They felt like Ten Days that Shook the World. Tom shooed them off cheerfully to get the women to the polls now that washing-up was finished, but before the kids were back from school. Someone brought Dione a nice cup of tea.

They started off again, through the traffic, their ribbons flying proudly. They met a dozen Tory cars for one of their own. Was Rosalind's among them? No, probably in the Barstone area; the Labour man in Barstone had no chance, but he'd put up a good fight. There was a Coke-Brown standing against him. Rosalind was certainly being patriotic. She would see that her maids voted right. Oh yes! Dione was wishing they could crash into one of those blue-ribboned cars—one of the shiniest ones covered with Union Jacks and Merrill's superior grins. She peered out eagerly for Tom's posters or photographs in the windows, trying to take omens.

For a moment they were held up at the Goods Station corner, and as they waited the sour smell of the Synthex works drifted in to them. Dione half hated it for what it was and what it stood for, and half liked it because the smell lingered in the hair and clothes of some of their workers. If one lived all one's life in one of these little streets, she thought, one wouldn't notice it. Unless coming back after Easter Monday or Bank Holiday. Living all one's life with that between oneself and roses and mignonette and the sweet warmth of babies. There was no typical smell at the Power Station except the faint, invigorating smell of ozone. And how ghastly the inside of the Carisbrook Road houses smelt even in autumn, when they weren't so firmly shut up as they would be later on!

But by and bye they had dodged out of the dense traffic and down a reach of the broad new road to London and the south. Then sharp to the right and out past the Barton's End ponds. Off this again at a signpost and they were in a narrow, wriggling country lane. No posters. No opposition. No crisis. Only the coloured beech leaves and a few twigs bare already. She had not, she thought, looked at leaves since Auchanarnish. They had been green then. A green Scottish August. Before harvest. Now it was the last still, fair weather before winter. The calm closed over her, making her want to sob. She turned a little towards Tom; he seemed to be rather happy; he sat upright with his hands on his knees, relaxed now, but potentially full of strength. His broad clean nails, the washed pores of his skin, the fair hairs on his wrist. Lots of hot water always, and time to scrub them. Clean neck, a clean collar every day. Chin shaved smooth, nice to touch. He smiled a little, looking straight in front of him. It seemed suddenly to Dione that all this had happened at some earlier time. She half recognised this day of heroic stress, of keeping up for another hour and another hour yet, a return to adolescence, school games. But not quite that.

"What does this remind you of?" she asked Tom.

He answered, "The war, of course; I haven't enjoyed myself so much since then." And suddenly he blushed, catching himself remembering that horrible, that soul-crippling thing for a moment as something completely magnificent, a common effort and common cause, a comradeship—as people had welcomed it right at the beginning.

Upper Lumley. Babylon Ford. The clay-pits. Little Lumley. Driving back between hedges again, under a calm sky, soft, sweet English blue of late September between beech twigs and bramble sprays. They went straight to Sam Hall's committee room. Sam Hall was there, sweating, red in the face, barking at his helpers as they came in, muddling his lists through sheer over-anxiety. He barked at Tom and then was miserable.

Dione said soothingly: "Do let me take on for half an hour. I know what to do."

He hesitated: "I've got to go to the box to 'phone, Mrs. Galton," he said; and then: "I could do with a cup of tea. I could just slip home for five minutes."

"Of course you could," said Dione, "I'll be perfectly all right till you come back. Are these the addresses for the cars? And you're expecting Mrs. Taylor to do Canal Cottages? Right."

"Come on, Hall," said Tom impatiently, "we'll put that call through to Central. Pick you up later, Dione."

She settled down and sorted out the papers. For a time there seemed to be a lull, while everyone in working homes was coming in, washing, having tea, perhaps a kipper, stretching, sitting heavily after work, thinking there was plenty of time yet before they went out into the cold to vote. As it got dark she lighted the gas and found some small coal to put on the fire; it was a narrow, ugly grate which gave little heat, but trickled out smoke into the room. She thought of wood fires at Auchanarnish, split and dry last year's logs that caught at once with a bright crackle. Small boys and girls came clamouring in for papers to distribute. She found some ends of red and green ribbon in her pocket and cut them up small and shared them out. She sent the two cars off to house after house. They would be gone a quarter of an hour or so, and then come back. She hoped Sam would feel better after his tea. Odd, she thought, about drugs. Even they are a class thing. Tannin for the workers and everywhere in the north: caffein for the upper and professional classes, especially in London: alcohol transcends class boundaries, but is seldom used much by working-class women and seldomer still by middle-class women or the older professional and upper-class women: nicotine for men of all classes, and upper and middle class women: aspirin general, but not so widely spread: purgatives mostly for the workers and lower middle classes who can't afford enough fruit and exercise: religion for the middle classes, especially women: cocaine for actors: morphine . . . codeine . . . hashish for the masses. . . . She suddenly realised she was almost asleep, got up, stretched and yawned, poked the fire, looked out of the window between the posters. It was quite dark now; the lights of the trams slid and stopped and slid on again. Her spirits dropped and dropped devastatingly. What was the use of going on hoping now? Obviously the Labour Government was out. Obviously Tom was out. Obviously the whole thing was an utter waste of time and money and energy. England was in for a period of reaction, as after the Napoleonic Wars. All the things she hated were going to win—money, inherited power, bourgeois imperialism, Sallington on the make. She hunted about in her bag and found a nibbled piece of chocolate and finished it. With the sweet taste still in her mouth she touched bottom.

A little later things began to brighten; more Labour votes were polled as the men cheered up after tea and went off to the booths. People began again coming in to the committee room with lists and excitements, and imperceptibly she found herself talking and encouraging them, cheering up the depressed ones, making the room a little centre of life and hope. Sam Hall came back, grateful and refreshed, with a clean collar. Soon after, Tom picked her up again with the car. He had just come from the central committee rooms, and he was excited, flushed a little. "Mason says I'm in," he said. "I said I was out by a thousand, but they wouldn't have it. Oh, Dione——"

After a time he went back there, to the group of men, the priests of his temporary religion. She, at the lodgings, whipped up eggs for an omelette for him when he came in, split and buttered rolls, put her chrysanthemums in water, and stuck up the opened telegrams wishing them luck on the mantel-piece. At half-past eight she had a first instalment of supper herself, mostly coffee. She addressed a postcard to Morag. She started a letter to Phœbe, but couldn't finish it. Ten minutes to nine. She thought how thrilled the children would be if—— She knitted a little at a stocking, dropped a stitch, then another. Three minutes to nine. In three minutes it would all be over. Too late for anyone to change their mind and rush out of the house to give Tom a vote. If only everyone who was going to vote Labour had voted! All Barton's End. All River Ward. She began to do something very like praying. Nine o'clock. Now, for good or for evil, it was all ended. Her heart had been hammering, hurting her; now it quieted. She heard Tom at the door and rushed to gas-stove and frying-pan.

"We ought to be down at the Town Hall by ten," he said.

Sallington again. It was past midnight when they came out of the Town Hall after the count. They were all rather dazed. Defeat! Defeat! There was something almost exhilarating about the string of great names which had gone down with theirs. A kind of dark dazzle. It had been hot in the room under the straight glare of the electric lights, full of the ticking and rustling of ballot papers, oppressed with the triumph of the others. It had been obvious very soon how the votes were going. The tellers went on relentlessly. Mason had gone very white and quiet, and shut up. Miss Waterhouse had suddenly, out of a silence, remarked that the powers of evil were loose. That had been rather startling, intensifying the atmosphere of the room. At the end Tom and Merrill had shaken hands and Dione had shaken hands with Miss Merrill, his daughter, a handsome girl with one of the new little hats perched on one side of her head, a string of what Dione took to be real jade, and a bouquet of roses. Very popular. At any other time, Dione felt, she would have been interested in the girl's mental outlook; she still found it very hard to understand how anyone young could be in the other camp.

The great square of Sallington was cold and open, and strangely roofless. A star or two showed. A cordon of police held back the crowd. Merrill had already gone up to the balcony and been cheered with a wild thunder of voices and hands. Tom and Dione and the five others, the little Labour group, came out by a small door at the side. But the crowd spotted them and yelled. For a moment Dione felt horribly frightened and flinched back towards the warm lighted doorway. Reuben Goldberg took her arm and whispered:

"I won't let them get you!"

She looked round at him then, half touched and half laughing: he was romanticising it all now—had to. She knew so well why one did that! But there was nothing to be frightened of. Tom was not the least bit disturbed by the yelling; he had scarcely noticed it; that sort of thing didn't frighten him. He was talking to Mason already about plans for the next months, and especially for the Municipals, which were coming off so soon. He said he would be down to speak. Are we downhearted? No!

Beyond the cordon of police they came out suddenly into the edge of the crowd. Someone plunged at them, and before she knew if he was friend or enemy a man had seized Dione by both hands:

"Better luck next time!"

And then disappeared into the crowd. She had not time to see his face, only the scrap of red and green in his buttonhole. But now she was ready for anything; if the powers of evil were loose there was something standing against them!

They waited for a time in the crowd which had now forgotten them, watching the results going up on Sallington Town Hall. After a few minutes Tom chuckled, and said:

"I didn't do so badly after all! Some of these majorities are a good bit worse than mine."

As each came out there were waves and cross-waves of cheering and some booing. Half the crowd had flags and were waving them wildly, arms flung back, faces turned up, eagerly open-mouthed towards the results thrown on to the screen above them. The police intervened in fights with a glorious patience and impartiality. Now Dione would have liked to join in a fight! That sudden chilling of the blood at sight of the crowd had warmed into anger. There was a car-load near them, young men and women in evening dress, laughing and yelling with the best. She saw herself creeping in cat-strides towards them, the Campbells, the sharp, secret sgian dhu in her hand, saw the bright gash in the throat—then it cleared; she stood ashamed and tired, holding Tom's hand. She saw he was not angry with anyone; he was already filled with the future.

They watched for half an hour, joined after a time by John Collis and the Barstone Labour candidate who had been hopelessly beaten by a Coke-Brown. Then they went back along the empty roads to the central committee rooms. In the deserted porch of the Wesleyan Chapel the two unemployed leaders were waiting to meet them.

"Well, Harry," said Mason, "no luck this time."

"I've been listening in," said the man, "round at a neighbour's. But I was thinking you'd be along soon. Luck'll change, Mr. Galton. Don't be downhearted." He shook hands with both of them. "Well, we'd best be shoving along, Mac. So long, Mason. See you to-morrow."

"Night, Harry. My respects to the wife."

And they'll get the cuts after all, thought Dione. The American bankers will make the National Government cut his money, his social wages, and they'll be cold all winter. "I hope things won't be—too bad," she said inadequately to Donald MacLean.

He said: "It will be very remarkable if they are not. But this state of affairs cannot be lasting for ever. You have done your best for us, the two of you, according to your lights, and we thank you." He bowed to her in a queer remote way.

She took his hand: "But I will be seeing you again soon!"

"Soon enough, maybe," he said.

"Come on, Mac!" said the other impatiently, and he went off down the street with his pal, and Tom and Dione and Mason went up into the committee room.

There were half a dozen men waiting for them, sitting about, saying nothing, reading listlessly at an old *Herald*, or half doubled up, wrists slack over knees. When Tom came in they most of them got up, coming forward to him to shake hands. They seemed better after that; they straightened up, their voices strengthened, they felt their manhood come back. For the moment Tom Galton had the dæmon in him and could give out the *mana* to them. He knew, and Dione knew, and in a way they all knew, that this would not last, that by the morning even it would have faded. But in the meantime it worked. He made them a small speech—it seemed to be what they wanted—transferring the *mana* from himself to the Labour Movement: where they might always find it, more difficultly perhaps, but also more surely. Again they crowded round and shook hands, and with Dione, his queen, sharer in the *mana*-giving. She wanted to kiss them all, but knew that in England, and in that social environment, it would be shatteringly wrong.

Tom offered to take anyone home. All the trains had stopped running by now and most of them had to go back to work early to-morrow, uncomforted. When they got to Reuben Goldberg's house he asked them to come in and listen to the results coming through on the wireless for a few minutes. His wife and brother-in-law were there too, listening, and came forward eagerly, offering biscuits and the tea that was keeping warm on the hearth. Tom sat down in the big chair, Dione on the arm of it. The others watched them. Tom knew that just for this moment they thought he was honouring their house by being in it; he wished quite desperately, as he had not done since his confirmation in School Chapel, that he was a better man, that he had in any way done anything to deserve this; he was flooded with shame for all the days in his life when he had given no service to the people; he resolved now to be good. And yet he also knew that by to-morrow even he would not be able to keep to his resolve, would not want to. Inevitably he must come off the peak. And the Goldbergs, too, would know that he was not anyone special or magic, would cease to honour him, except as they honoured any man or woman who was in the Movement with them. And that was all right, all as it should be. And now he must remember the other kind of worker he was, the realer kind perhaps, because it was the work he was paid for. He must think of Oxford and the lectures he was to give next week.

It is a fairly long run from Sallington to Oxford; there was a strong wind and sometimes the Morris swerved on the road surface, and always the old ribbons flapped and pulled loose; but Dione could not bear to take them off, not yet. She said to herself that she wanted the children to see, but really she was the remains of Prince Charlie's army after Culloden. As she drove she saw people's disapproving eyes on the ribbons in all the small towns, and she, unhindered, accelerating past them, was glad and proud.

She always picked up people on the road, and half-way to Oxford she saw a couple by the roadside with a handbag and slowed down to offer them a lift. They looked surprised and hesitated; the man glanced from her to the Labour ribbons, but said nothing. "Get in!" she said, "where are you going?"

"Southampton," the man said, "we heard there was work." He got in at the back with his bag, his wife in front.

"What's your job?" Dione asked.

He began to speak, but was caught by a burst of coughing; the wife spoke for him: "He was a collier, ma'am, in Durham. But all the pits is shut down these six months. So we started to walk to Southampton." She was a solid, sensible-looking woman, wearing the remains of a good coat and skirt; she had neat glasses and a wedding ring; the only thing that was dreadfully wrong were the indoor shoes she was wearing, impossible for a long walk; her feet in cotton stockings were swollen and bulging through the sides already: she stooped and felt them. A good country parlourmaid, thought Dione, glancing at her.

The couple didn't want to talk, only to rest, so Dione didn't bother them. Every now and then the man behind coughed painfully. Dione observed him in her driving-mirror: miner's phthisis probably: another two years or so to live; not more. What will she do then? She's fond of him, see her turning to look at him, probably she doesn't know. These decent, innocent people carrying everything they have in that rotten little handbag. People who'd like a home, not gipsies. No room there for more than a change of clothes, still less books, ornaments, memories. Was that all civilisation could let them have?

The Galtons' house was a little outside the main part of Oxford, down a lane off the Banbury road. It had been a seventeenth-century farmhouse, with a barn that made the most glorious playroom or stage. It was built of Cotswold stone, and they had added to it cleverly after Ian was born, with weather-boarding that now had climbing roses nailed all over it. It was a good soil for roses and strawberries and big perennials. There were three fine walnut trees at the end of the garden, with a swing on one, and an orchard of good fruit trees carefully pruned; then meadows, and a narrow path overhung with dog-roses in June, and now with scarlet hips, going down to the river.

As soon as she was nearly in sight of the house, Dione, as usual, began to be desperately anxious in case it had been burnt down while she was away, and put her foot on the accelerator. However, soon she could see the gable at the end of the lane. Then she looked anxiously down the lane to see that neither Dr. Carew Hunt's car nor the ambulance from the Radcliffe was parked there. That was all right, too. She began cautiously to decide that this time the gods had failed to notice. She arrived, remarked that the gate was open, which was either very thoughtful of Muriel or very careless of the children, and told the Durham couple that she could give them supper and somewhere to sleep, but, alas! she had no work for them.

Morag came bounding out, one pigtail undone. "Darling mother," she said, "don't be bothered about the old election! It wasn't your fault! And I fought a boy at school who said——"

"She really is the most awful ass——" began Ken, and then: "Mother, I cut my knee awfully badly—look, it's got sticky plaster——"

Ian (with a drawing-book): "Mother, has a bear got eyebrows?"

Lilias (still cutting that tooth): "Mother, mother, mother—look—me!"

Their tight, pulling hands and soft, sweet-smelling cheeks were all round her. She sat down on the front door-step and they piled over her like hound puppies. For a moment it was intense pleasure, and then she found her brain was switching off already on to the problems of Morag's new frocks, Ken's boots, winter pyjamas—which would do again?—the dentist?—carpentry lessons—new wheel for Lilias's pram—Ian so slow at reading—distemper the bathroom—the swing to be taken down before winter or the ropes will rot—now Muriel, her sister-in-law, was pulling off the outskirts of the pile. Ian, displaced for the moment by Lilias, whom Dione wanted to kiss—whereas she wanted to rush about and shout—hung on to Muriel's sleeve and hopped. Muriel was fair like Tom, but shorter and broader; she was wearing a hand-woven tweed skirt and a rather startling sweater. "Hullo, my child," she said to Dione, "feeling a bit gloomy?"

"No," said Dione, relinquishing Lilias, "just a touch of

home, sweet home! I shall have to see Nurse about a million things this moment and what about the blackberry jam?"

"Don't be so damned domestic," said Muriel, "what does the jam matter? No, Ian, I don't want your worm! What a set of cave children you have, Dione. All except Morag, who is nice, like her aunt; aren't you, angel? Hurry up and change, Dione, the concert's at seven and I've got you a high tea ready."

"What concert?"

"The quartet, mother!" said Morag, rather shocked, "Beethoven!"

"Oh lord, yes. Sorry, Morag. I'd forgotten it."

Muriel and Dione and Morag went to the concert. Muriel offered to drive, but Dione said she would; no, she wasn't one bit tired. And how odd that really is, she thought, when I was up till nearly three at the Goldbergs' last night, and up again at eight to pack, and packing and rushing round and driving ever since! Tom had caught a morning train; he had to give an afternoon lecture, and see about his neglected pupils and generally make up for lost time. College was beginning to clamour. But he wasn't tired either. It was as though both of them had still got the *mana* in them, a queer, drunken feeling. Ever the dentist and the distemper and the blackberry jam couldn't throw her down. She was not yet on earth—still sailing on the crow's back.

"Rosalind," said Muriel, "is very cross. She thinks you've led Tom astray."

Dione laughed. Muriel kissed her ear: "You are an old funny. But I wish—never mind, we'll discuss it to-morrow."

Dione laughed again, just not running into the George Street policeman, skimming round him clumsily but accurately, like a flying crow.

The concert began. Morag sat pressed together, mouse-still, all senses closed but the one. Muriel leaned back, critical, pleased. Dione sat between them, and gradually the music began to break through the magic radiation, the coating of excitement between her and the world. She looked round; she was back in Oxford again; there was everyone, the people she knew, dons' wives and daughters, intelligent on the whole, fairly prosperous, fairly sensitive, with money to spend on extra beauty. You might or mightn't call it luxury; that depended on your standards. But they'd all had tea, and when they got back from the concert they'd probably all have supper. Hot soup. Coffee. Egg salad. Chocolate biscuits. While at Marsh-brook Bridge—

So to-night I sit warmly, listening to music, and you, and you,
Man whose hands I have held in mine, whose eyes I have looked into,
You will go cold and hungry again, wanting things, hating things.
And through the sweet violence, the gypsy sobbing of the strings,
I can hear you wishing us luck, with no luck of your own.
And the crowd waiting in the square for the figures to be shown,
The yelling, cruel mouths of the victors: to the Beasts, to the Beasts with you!
Oh, I can see them still, and their joyful evil voices come piercing through
The solemn or gay pure loveliness of the intent quartet.
Oh the Beasts, my brother, my brothers—but we will save you yet!
For the power of Light is in Beethoven, as I have seen it for sure
In the sweet ironic smiling of you and the very poor.
So you shall have meat, my dear, and you shall have wine,
A steady job, a warm coat, and all these good things of mine;
You shall come into wide, lit rooms from the frost and bitter rain,
And have the rondo with us, to make you a man again.

Tom met them after the concert and they walked back to the parking place near Balliol.

" How's college ? " Dione asked.

" Pretty decent," said Tom, " all saying they were sorry I hadn't got in. Not that they are, but they can afford to say it now. The public-school tradition. My Christ, what a smash it is ! "

" Tired ? "

" Mm. Aren't you ? "

" No ; I—I haven't quite got back yet. I expect I'll get it in the neck to-morrow."

" I had a biggish crowd at my lecture. A lot of girls. Am I a romantic figure, Dione ? Shall I get as many sobbing females as Murray ? I do hope so ! "

" Goose ! "

" You haven't taken the ribbons off the car yet ; you are an old funny, Dione."

" No ; I didn't want to, I will to-morrow. Look, Tom, there are the Bickerdens ! Hullo, May, were you at the concert too ? "

May Bickerden smiled brightly over her seal-coney collar. " Oh yes ; weren't we, Phil ? And so you didn't get in after all, Tom ! Such a shame, it would have been so nice to have a St. Mary's M.P."

Tom looked at May Bickerden with a certain disgust : " The Minister of Public Relations in the National Government is an old St. Mary's man, you know, May. A thoroughly poisonous fellow, I gather. How did you vote ? "

" Oh, we're old-fashioned Liberals ; aren't we, Phil ? But anyhow, we don't know much about politics. They're too difficult for us ! Are you coming to the Bach choir this term, Dione ? We miss you dreadfully ! "

" I don't quite know," Dione answered ; " I shall

have millions of things to catch up with now I'm back."

"Well, do try, you mustn't neglect your music; must she, Phil? What a perfect movement that last was!"

"Come on, old girl," said Tom impatiently, starting the car, "Morag's nearly asleep." He backed out. "Why the hell can't Bickerden speak for himself! That bloody cabbage May is squashing him. He'd have answered me himself in Phœbe's time!"

Tom and Dione slept heavily, the *mana* going out of them. In the morning Tom went off to his pupils, and until lunch time Dione coped with the household, especially one or another problem about the children. Nurse was quite nice to her, but faintly sardonic. She suspected Nurse of not having voted at all, but she was much too shy even to hint at a question. The odd-job man had definitely voted National, but she didn't like to argue with him; it would be so horrible to put any kind of pressure from the fact of being his employer. The amount of delicacies and tact that this capitalist system demanded!

After lunch (at which Kenneth in a moment of excitement broke two plates) she meant to cope with the garden, but found herself so tired and stupid that she couldn't; it was difficult to think that the new rose-bed mattered at all. She contented herself with putting on a pirate handkerchief and gardening gloves, and cutting off a lot of dead stalks in the herbaceous border, and letting Ian stack them for a bonfire. Muriel came out and helped her. They began to talk about polling day. Muriel said: "I was down town, in the crowd, opposite Jones and Sampson's, who were showing the results. There was scarcely any Labour cheering for the seats you held. I cheered myself, of course; I want most of the things the Labour Party stands for to happen—though not all—and I don't in the least mind being in a minority. But it wasn't at all a rich or oppressive crowd. Nor, I think, so very unintelligent. The kind of people who'd look after children properly, read a bit, keep the flies off the milk. The kind who come to my clinic and ask sensible questions and carry out instructions properly."

Dione frowned, stooping, shearing off an armful of dry helenium stalks. "Well?" she said.

Muriel poked a clod of earth off her shoe with the fork. "My dear," she said, "I don't want to be sister-in-lawish, but does your Party really represent the people?"

"Oddly enough," said Dione, "I think it does. But the people always rather hates being set free. It's so—chilly."

"Of course I don't much mind myself about democracy. If one does good works one has to bully people quite a bit. Possibly Tom and I are rather alike."

"I don't think he bullies Marshbrook Bridge."

"Not exactly bullying, perhaps. But, I take it, a candidate has to be either a surprise or a habit. Tom naturally prefers being a surprise."

"Oh, I know. Neither of us ever feel we're properly—the same as them. Friends in a way, because one feels this great affection towards them. Comrades because we're working together (it's a silly word in English!). But not—not what one is with even quite ordinary acquaintances here. It seems to be a matter of—contact. That oughtn't to matter with intelligent people, ought it?—or ought it? But I can't be quite easy with them. There's this house and garden, and not having to cook or wash baby clothes oneself. I'm not sure how much they mind. In fact I think they don't mind because they see it's all rather accidental and unimportant. But—it's bound to make Tom and me feel guilty."

Muriel looked slowly all round the garden ; in this soft late weather it was beautiful with a calm assurance of ever-returning things, the sweeping of leaves and lighting of bonfires and trailing of country smoke. " Do you want to chuck it, then, Dione ? " she asked.

"No ; not yet. But it stops ease between us and them, damn it ! We can't be pals. Instead we've got to be this thing they seem to want us to be : a surprise, if you like. A bit of fantasy. Like movie stars."

Muriel dislodged and trod on a centipede. " My dear, you say '*we*' do things, just as if you were—May Bickerden. What I really wanted to ask you isn't whether Tom bullies his constituents—well, impresses his personality on them—but whether he does it to you. Don't you want not to be just a wife sometimes ? "

Dione wrestled violently with a dandelion root : " Yes, sometimes, of course. On the other hand, I make a reasonably good job out of being one. I like working with Tom. But perhaps I should have liked politics anyway, though I hated it a good deal when he started."

" I knew you did."

" Did you ? I thought I'd kept that to myself ! You're a bright bird, Muriel. You do despise me quite a lot for being married, don't you ? "

" No, I don't. Don't be silly. But you might have been something on your own, instead of just part of a ' we,' and I should like to have seen that. On the other hand, your children are rather adequate, specially Morag. But I don't think I could stand it myself. You wouldn't believe it, Dione, but Rosalind was rather nice once, before she married that nasty man Reginald Coke-Brown. I've seen her being destroyed just through being married to that—manufacturer."

" What a snob you are, Muriel ! "

“ True, all the same. You didn’t know Rosalind before she was married. You’d have liked her. But my esteemed brother-in-law Reginald believes in money and success (though he doesn’t put it as crudely), and, husband and wife being one, that’s killed the Rosalind there would have been otherwise.”

“ Marriage hasn’t got to do that.”

“ No, but it usually does. If the husband’s at all adequate. I expect there’s a lot to be said for it ; all the advantages of a good religion ; you don’t have to think or exist for yourself. But it’s annoying to watch.”

“ It’s horribly difficult. Sometimes one feels one would give anything for a little kudos—a little fame and glory for oneself quite on one’s own ! Phœbe gets that, of course. It’s possible in the arts. Phœbe’s whole-hearted ; but——”

“ Phœbe’s unhappy. Yes. But is it necessary ? Sometimes I’ve no patience with either her or Robin ! Look, Dione, shall I get up this whole lot of nasturtiums ? What hurts is to see a really intelligent girl throw up a career and not even regret it ! Not till it’s too late, anyway. I wonder what Morag will do.”

“ I want her to have both kinds of life. I want her to be tough enough to live two hours to any man’s one ! She will have been warned, anyhow. If only one could be sure things were getting better and better ! Do you really believe in progress, Muriel ? ”

“ Certainly. My job would be unbearable if I didn’t.”

“ Yes. You know, Muriel, I doubt I’d never have been a first-class kind of person even if I hadn’t married rather young. Father decided I was to be a Classic, and a Classic I was, as far as I was anything. But what good was it ? Latin tags are no use nowadays.”

“ I can remember one myself: cras Dione jura dicit——”

"Yes; I know, I used to like that! I used to show off to myself with it. But now I don't think I'm fit to be a law-maker."

She called to Ian and gave him another wheel-barrow full of dry stalks to take over to the bonfire. Ian was pink with pleasure in his work; he talked to the wheel-barrow all the way; it was his own wheel-barrow given to him on his last birthday. It was called Henry. Soon it would be tea-time. Morag and Kenneth would be back from school, more or less ink-stained. Tom would be back from college. All over Oxford that would be happening. And the unmarried dons would be having college teas with hot anchovy toast in metal dishes, and dozens of books to read all over floor or tables, and friends coming in and college gossip and the bee-hive sense of closeness and warmth and business.

In Edinburgh the purple dusk would be falling. They would bring Alex Fraser tea in the office; his clients' affairs would suddenly grow more remote; he would begin to think of the end of the day, talk and music in the evening, perhaps a dance or a small formal dinner with gossip and discussion, Athenian almost. At the week-end he would go to Auchanarnish; the green was off the trees now and there were a few partridges to be got.

At Auchanarnish candles were lighted at tea-time. There would be heather honey and two sorts of scones. The MacKies might come over, or Lady Ann; they would discuss gardening and Celtic archæology. Perhaps farming. Perhaps even the state of the country. Dione and her husband would be thought of kindly, but with disapproval; at any rate, they had lost, so charitable thoughts were quite in order.

At Helm, Robin would have come in gloomily, talking about the rotten prices he was getting for his stock, the way the middle-men took everything, worried about the income tax, rheumatic. And Phœbe would be cutting bread and butter for the children. Quite likely Gladys had given notice; they often did at this time of the year, when the sea mists began coming up in earnest over the Island. Brian didn't like winter either; it would be nice if they could have electric light put in so that you could just turn it on and the nursery at a touch would empty of shadows and shapes.

In London Joyce might be thinking of cocktail time, changing for a party, feeling all gay and relieved now that this wretched crisis was over, knowing that she was a happy-making kind of person, and that everyone would be glad to see her, feeling the delicate tense silk of the stocking draw up over her knee and along the sides of her thigh. And Pussy would have finished work and was perhaps with Cynthia—or with someone else—or temporarily alone at the Café Royal, smoking cigarettes and reading the paper and keeping a look-out for someone to talk to. There was nothing fixed or coherent about Pussy's London. Only when he wrinkled his eyes and laughed a little over the tea-cup or the more interesting little glass people tended to fall in love with him, and up to a point he was usually very nice to them.

And in Marshbrook Bridge Miss Waterhouse would now be giving bread and jam and strong tea to her weaving class, pouring steadily from a beautiful lustre tea-pot, and the Morris curtains would be drawn. The Sallington professional or business people would be having tea; the men of the family might or might not be at home; a few of them were perhaps teaing with typists. But normally it was rather the women's and children's time; picture-books and toys would all be waiting to be played with in the hour before tea. Most of the workers had their teas rather later, because there wouldn't be a three- or four-course dinner for them afterwards, only at best cocoa and bread and butter, or bread and margarine. Donald MacLean had gone to see a friend of his, one Adam Walker, an ex-Service man, with a wonderfully plausible face, considering how much of it had been blown off. It seemed a waste that after spending so much of the nation's best possible surgery on him, his grateful country should then have ceased bothering as to what happened next. He had been out of work for a long time now. There was a souvenir of the Great War at the back of a cupboard, an old Mills bomb, Mark 5, still undetonated. It seemed a handy size for the pocket.

# PART II

## THE SLOUGH OF DESPOND TO THE WICKET GATE

" It's no use turning nasty,
It's no use turning good ;
You're what you are, and nothing you do
Will get you out of the wood,
Out of a world that has had its day."

AUDEN.

The Coke-Brown wedding reception was a very grand affair indeed. It appeared not only in the Sallington papers, but also in the London ones. The bride was extremely pretty and photographable; the groom was young and had a good figure. Among those present were many Coke-Browns, Hatchcocks, Spiffendens, and other local families; Daniel Coke-Brown, who owned the *Sallington News* and was usually supposed to have a controlling interest in one of the big London newspaper groups; also, in a corner, Dione Galton, inclined to be rude. She had half thought she was going to like it. It was, after all, a party. There was something traditional about the word. Dione had been a sociable little girl; she had enjoyed getting into a white muslin frock and blue sash and corals. She had never sulked in a corner behind the Christmas tree like silly Phœbe or baby Alex; no, Dione had led the string of children in oranges and lemons, and lent her shoe for hunt-the-slipper. She had been able to eat twelve ices in one evening without any inconvenient effects. Why weren't parties now like parties then? What magic had gone?

There were plenty of ices at this party, and marrons, and foie gras sandwiches, and bridge rolls stuffed with lobster, and petits fours. There were silver salvers—late Victorian, she noticed spitefully—heaped with slices of wedding cake, brought round to the guests by footmen. As they offered her the cake she tried to look at them, to see into their eyes as she had seen lately into the eyes of—the lower classes, But, in the authentic footman's bow, holding a salver in gloved hands, the eyes are cast down, the revealing fingers and thumb are covered.

Tom had not come to the party; he was not much given to weddings anyway, and in the thick of work, trying to make up for lost time. He had another book on hand; Dione was typing it for him in the evenings, unstiffening it when it had got too academic after a college incubation. Dione had come partly because of the bride and partly in sheer defiance of the Coke-Browns. Rosalind had rather chillily asked her to stay, but she did not feel like facing Rosalind, especially without Tom, especially untriumphant. So she was staying with Miss Waterhouse in an austere bedroom with photographs of Burne-Jones's and the chaster Rossettis.

She had decided it would be warm enough at the party if she wore her best summer dress, a French printed stuff which Phœbe had got for her in Paris, and which had been made up at home. She had got a little hat with a feather to go with it, a good little un-Oxford hat. It had all seemed very grand when she packed and there were no visible darns in her silk stockings. Miss Waterhouse had probably liked it—at any rate she had given Dione a kiss and she would certainly have said if she had disapproved. Yet now at the Coke-Brown party it was not a grand frock at all, and was refusing to help Dione to be gay and defiant.

People made speeches; healths were drunk. Dione kept on wondering whether the young Coke-Brown and his girl could possibly escape from it all or whether money would get them down in a few years, shaping them in spite of themselves, altering them as it had altered Rosalind Galton. So far she had dodged her sister-in-law. Elizabeth had rushed about in her bridesmaid's dress, with a giggling gang of other bridesmaids. Dione felt an obscure jealousy, thinking how much nicer Morag would have looked in that really rather beautiful colour. If only there had been someone else in the rooms anywhere, who'd be her friend and ally and fellow-worker—surely there must be someone! Daniel Coke-Brown went by with another Sallington owner, talking about what ought to be done to the unemployed. Starve 'em a bit. Clear out the Unions. Dione wondered whether he'd said that deliberately for her to hear—he probably knew her by sight—and scolded herself for not having the courage to jump up and contradict him—smack his face—murder him! Beastly to hate anyone like that—to be made to hate. Even the marrons tasted wrong. She knew that in a minute she would get so paralysed with hate and shyness that she wouldn't be able to move. She went in time. She jumped into a tram, and so back quickly to Miss Waterhouse's, and there she tugged that dress off, breaking a stitch in one seam and kicked the little hat with the feather under the dressing-table. They hadn't helped!

She wanted badly to be put right, to be looked at with friendly eyes. Since the election they had been up again once for the municipals, but that had been a hectic, impersonal time. The only personal thing had been Councillor Finch crying after his defeat by a rather surprised Tory. Now Dione thought she would go and see little Mrs. Grove. The baby was about due; perhaps it had just been born. It would be nice to find a small, new, ugly, cuddly baby. She changed into a coat and skirt and walked down towards the river.

It was odd to be walking without urgency, with only a vague good will instead of that tremendous sense of importance that had put springs under her tired shoe soles before. Personal problems began to lift their heads again: Phœbe. Ought she to get hold of Phil Bickerden and talk to him?—tell him it was only cowardice that was stopping him from writing to Phœbe; if he'd just be a little brave, a little kind, it would put the lid on that wretched Pussy, who wasn't worth it on any possible hedonistic calculus, who was only a substitute for him. But how could one get hold of Phil Bickerden these days? May was always there, great thick-wristed blonde cow of a woman! What the devil had he wanted with her? Had she any merits? She didn't understand physics any better than Phœbe had! Not that she supposed he wanted a woman to understand his work. Intelligent women mostly want to share their work with their husbands; intelligent men like marrying cows. Oxford full of women like May. All going down the same tram-lines, deliberately insensitive outside them. No, she was damned if she was going to join the Bach choir again; they put their beastly cows' hoofs into music too. A lot of things she used to care for seemed to be going dead on her now. Music. Books. The arts in general. Her old friends. She was uncomfortable talking to them; she had got outside their group. Had Jean MacLean, the witch, ever felt that talking to Catholic MacLeans? Or had she smiled and pretended? Perhaps the witch group, the coven, was stronger than the Labour Group. She wanted to feel the strength of the Labour Group again. Perhaps at the Groves' some of the others might come in after work, as they used during the election, Ed. Palmer or Mrs. East or Sam Hall or the Taylors. She got to the corner of the little street.

She did not see until she was a few doors off that blinds were down in the front windows. She hesitated, gripping and twisting the handle of her bag. The door of the Groves' house opened, and a bare-headed woman in an apron looked out, stared at her and went in again. She stood quite still, terribly afraid of who might be coming out next. It was George Grove in his Sunday clothes, not very well shaved. He came up to her and took her by the hand; she was dumb, waiting for confirmation of what she guessed. He said: "It's good of you to come, Mrs. Galton. I appreciate it, I do indeed. That's her sister." He nodded at the woman in the apron, who rubbed her fingers on it before offering to shake hands, a little doubtfully.

"It's hard," the woman said, and Dione saw now how red her eyes were, "it's hard losing a sister. Like that. I did think I'd be the first to go. And George here always so good to her."

Dione knew for certain now. That small, gallant woman with her sewing and tea-cups and library books. And she never got out to a new house at Barton's End, never got her holiday. "My dear," said Dione, with a hand of each, "my dears."

"And there's poor little Billy," the woman said; "you come on here, lovey. Say good afternoon to the lady, Billy. She's come to tell us she's sorry about poor Mum." Billy began to sob, burrowing his head in his aunt's black skirt; she put a hand in her pocket and reached out a stick of toffee to him. "There you are, lovey; you stop snivelling." He grabbed on to the toffee, but the sobs didn't stop.

Dione felt her own eyes beginning to fill. "How did it happen?" she said, and then: "Oh no, not in front of them!"

"Why, bless your heart, they know," said the woman, looking from the child to the man. "You see, it all came on sudden-like, a week before she was expecting, and while George was away getting the doctor she had a flooding, and then——"

"Oh, I see, I see," said Dione, covering her face, "and the—and her——"

"Oh, there's nothing wrong with him," said the woman; "a ten-pound boy, isn't he, George? I'm going to take him, Mrs. Galton; I've got five of my own already, so one more doesn't matter, poor innocent. And his Granny's going to take Billy."

"We've got a lot of beautiful flowers," George Grove said suddenly; "you'd like to see them, wouldn't you, Mrs. Galton?"

"Oh," she said, "oh, thank you." They took her in. It was white chrysanthemums mostly; one got more of them for the money at this time of year.

"You'ld like to see *her*, wouldn't you, Mrs. Galton?" said George Grove; "she looks a picture."

Dione, assenting faintly, was brought through into the back room, the room where they'd had tea. She was blind with tears before she had fully seen little Mrs. Grove laid out, clean and pale and ready. Her hand, groping instinctively for support, felt with horror that the little boy was there too; knew he was staring, with every moment identifying more and more certainly for the rest of his life this dead, unreal thing with the live, real person who had been his mother.

"Don't you take on so, Mrs. Galton," said the woman kindly; "it's the common lot. We all come to it. Only it was hard her being so young and all. Did you ever lose any loved ones?"

"Not—not lately," said Dione, gulping.

"Ah, then it comes of a shock to you," said the woman satisfied. Then: "The works gave George three days off."

"And a nice wreath from the machine shop," added George—"evergreens, it was."

After a time Dione got away; she went straight to a flower shop and sent a wreath too: yellow and white jonquils, at least a little hope in the spring flowers. Billy might see that. She took the tram along to Mason's house. She knocked; he opened the door himself in shirt-sleeves.

" Come on in, Mrs. Galton. The wife's down at the Co-op. and I'm making out the election expenses."

" Oh," she said, clinging to his arm, " oh, Mrs. Grove's dead."

" Yes ; I know, poor soul. Left George with two kiddies. But we'll see they're all right."

" Yes, but—but her—she did so want to move to a nice house, and—and have a chance——"

" Now, don't you go making things out worse than they are. She isn't fussing about any new houses now, poor woman."

" But *he'll* think he can never give her what she wanted now——"

" What, George ? He's got plenty to think of without that. We haven't time for these fancy notions, Mrs. Galton."

She let go his arm, feeling small, rebuked. Perhaps he was right. He knew. She didn't. She was silly, full of silly fancies that came of having too much leisure.

Mason put her into a chair and then put the kettle on. " What you need, Mrs. Galton, is a nice cup of tea." She watched him poke up the fire. " Now," he said, " what about the Christmas social ? We're expecting you and Mr. Galton. Our people'll want a bit of cheering up. Mrs. Taylor's going to do refreshments, and we'll have some nice songs."

She discussed dates with him, made notes of various things she was to speak to Tom about. It became all very businesslike. Some of the unemployed had been in trouble again. She asked what the Communist Party were doing. Mason said there were a few in the River Ward, and a fairly strong branch in Sallington itself, and another in Sallmouth, where the docks were. He seemed to dislike the Communist Party very much. " It's all very well your talking,

Mrs. Galton," he said, " but when you've been in the Movement as long as I have you'll know the C.P. are a set of twisters."

" But surely," said Dione, " that's not so. I've met some of them at Oxford, at the October Club and so on, and I should have thought they were almost too sincere."

" Oh, the high-brow ones at Oxford!" said Mason, and his lips cocked ironically at the idea; " they think they know everything, but I've read my Marx just as much as they have. And so've you, I'll be bound, but you've let them put it across you, just because they go saying they're working class and you're not. You stand up to them a bit, tell them you're part of the real working-class movement in England. We've got to defend ourselves on both sides."

" I'm afraid I'm not very good at that," said Dione.

" No," said Mason, " you aren't! But don't you worry, we'll teach you at Marshbrook Bridge. And don't you go letting the C.P. kid you that they've got the goods. They haven't. We'll get Socialism before they do. As to the Communists here, half of them are just on the make; they haven't got the loyalty our people have. Young Mac's all right, but he's a mad Clydesider. Sorry, Mrs. Galton; you're Scotch, aren't you? But half of them—why, I could tell you some funny stories about the goings on in Sallington. They aren't honest."

" Probably they haven't handled money much——"

" It isn't only money," said Mason, then: " They aren't honest with their wives."

" That's all pretty silly, isn't it?" said Dione, rather annoyed. " One can never really tell about other people's private lives."

" I can tell when a man gives half his wages to a fancy girl instead of his wife," said Mason.

Again Dione felt rebuked. It seemed different put that

way. Suppose Phil Bickerden wanted to give half his lecture fees to Phœbe! Again she felt she was living in an artificial world. Yet she must defend some of its newer standards and values. Only how exactly to put what she had to say? Muriel would have done it better. Mason went to the cupboard and got out some Co-op. biscuits with pink and yellow sugar squiggles on the top. She looked at her notes. This social, various meetings, and later on the bazaar. She could never get out of her head the first social she had ever been to, when they had made her, choking and dizzy with shyness, say a few words, and someone had told her she was a brave little woman. No, she didn't really like socials. Mason made tea. "Not too strong, please," said Dione.

"You drink it up," said Mason, "it won't do you any good unless it's strong."

She obeyed meekly. She suddenly felt that, though she liked Mason really rather a lot—and George Grove—and all of them—yet the one thing she wanted now was to get away from Marshbrook Bridge and back to Oxford. And leave them behind, stuck in the edge of ugly, dirty Sallington . . . not able to follow her.

Tom met her at Oxford station, saying that Phœbe had turned up. "She doesn't talk about Bickerden," he said, "but I'm not such a fool that I can't tell what she's thinking about. She'd much better not come to Oxford at all till she's got it over. Well, how was the wedding?"

"Pretty bloody."

"And Marshbrook Bridge?"

"Pretty bloody, too. It's got the between-times feeling now. Mrs. Grove is dead. In childbirth."

"Oh, lord. Is he fearfully cut about it, poor chap?"

"I don't know. They're all so matter of fact. They make me feel as if I was another race, full of elaborate hot-house, high-brow feelings. Are we as bad as that ? "

" The Two Worlds. People like you have been bothered about that for the last hundred years. Yes, a lot of our fine feelings are just a very unimportant by-product of too much money. That's why I can't stand all these novels and poems about them."

" Mason went for the C.P. pretty hard."

" Oh, the C.P.'s all right in its way," said Tom, " but they make it so damned difficult for us to work with them over anything. The dialectic's all right too, but they *will* use it like a penny-in-the-slot machine ! Look, Dione, if I can get this book finished during the Easter vac., I can get my advance on it by June, and I think it can be made to stretch to us going to Russia in summer, if you can square your mother to take the children."

" Oh, Tom," she said, " oh, Tom ! If only one of them doesn't go and get measles just before ! "

Phœbe was in the barn, drawing and occasionally giving good advice to Ian, who was under the table, drawing too. " What are you on ? " said Dione.

" I've got a nice new job," said Phœbe, " illustrating a fine edition of Hans Andersen for the Golden Cockerel Press. The first time I've got off with Gibbings. I'm trying to rough out Kay and Gerda. I want to do the Ice Queen as pure intellect—she is, you know, in the story, a kind of queen to King Hoopoe. She's always teasing Kay, she's an abstract and teasing mathematics. I can't *see* the picture yet, but I've got the idea of it in terms of planes, mathematically linked, sliding over one another like—like the molecular sliding in graphite or something. I want the ice-block-puzzle crystalline, a crystal lattice, a moment of atomic cohesion. But I can't get it right," she said, and drummed with her fingers on the table, " and I know—I know if I could get hold of Phil for ten minutes he could show me what I need. Then I could see it. It's hard enough having one's heart broken, but when it interferes with work it's the bloody limit."

"Is that why you came here?" Dione asked.

After a pause Phœbe said, "Yes."

"But you can't. It's no good."

"If someone let him know I was here," said Phœbe, "perhaps he'd telephone. No? Oh, it's so silly, so *silly*, that I can't see him, even about work!"

"Let's have a look at the drawings," said Dione. "Hullo, what's this?"

"That," said Phœbe, "is a bribe to you to ring up Phil. But if you won't, it's a present for you all the same."

"What a beastly picture. It's—it's a kelpie. What is it, anyway? It's damned good."

"It's Goya on the Labour Party."

"Idiot. What does the Spanish mean?"

"It means 'Other Laws for the People.' You see, those little men in the corner had some good ideas and they're showing them to the Elephant. But they're frightened of him. He's a very big Elephant. and they're quite little people. He's a very respectable Elephant, too. He wants you to have a trunk the same as he has, and little bright, prying eyes and a thick skin and rather a limited brain space. Oh yes, and a backbone. The backbone of England. And if you aren't just right—well, he picks you up with his trunk and he pulls your arms and legs off. He can be a very nasty Elephant. And you see, Dione, the little people are telling the Elephant to read Marx and Lenin, not to speak of G. D. H. Cole, T. E. Galton, H. N. Brailsford, and the *New Statesman.* And he's reading them, but it hasn't changed his elephantishness, and if he decides they aren't quite nice, he'll reach out his trunk, and that'll be the end of you. Oh yes, the elephant joined the Labour Party when it got respectable and took over from the non-conformists."

"Oh, lord," Dione said; "I thought Mason looked rather like an Elephant when he was telling me about the morals of the C.P.!"

"I expect there's a Communist Elephant, too," said Phœbe, "but the Oxford Elephant's a real fruity one. Boar's Hill is my washpot, over Summertown have I cast out my shoe. That Elephant's humped himself between me and Phil, so that we can't even see one another, and if I try to dodge round him, his nasty little eyes'll turn red, his ears'll begin to flap, and his trunk'll reach out for me. Oh, lovely!" She stood there by her drawings, and her forehead twisted and her eyes looked through Dione at something which was no longer there.

Dione caught hard at some fact to break through, some other, bitterer pain. "How's unemployment in the Island?" she said, "any meetings of unemployed?"

Phœbe woke up; she made a face of deeper and guiltier discomfort. "Poor devils, those who're at work scarcely get a living wage. The land's in a bad way, and I don't see your party tackling it. The labourers won't even organise."

"We've had several meetings at Marshbrook Bridge," Dione said. "There was one—oh, it was frightfully cold, and I'd got a thick coat and stockings and I was so ashamed! The man they call Harry was speaking, and—oh, Phœbe, have I told you——"

"About Donald MacLean? Three times at least. You have fallen for him, haven't you?"

"I haven't lost my heart," said Dione, "maybe just a wee bit of my head. There's something pretty exciting about anyone who's so much in earnest. I wouldn't be surprised if he were to throw a bomb at someone some day. What's more, he'd hit."

The bell rang for tea, and across the barn a wing-flap carried the Talking Crow with the dark eyes and grey fierce face of a Highland hoodie. The gules lion shook himself, only half asleep. If ever the lion wakes entirely he will not be afraid of anything; the lion will laugh a fanged and flame-tongued lion laugh about the Elephant and wither him up. But the lion is not yet awake and the Elephant has it all his own way.

Ian came out from under the table; fragments of talk had dripped down to him. He said: "I will tell you a sad, sad story about an Elephant that killed another Elephant——"

"That's it," said Phœbe, "there's always another Elephant. If you go to Russia, Dione, you're sure to find a Bolshevik Elephant there—oh, a *big* one—and red——"

"I will tell you a story about a big red Elephant," said Ian.

Dione and Tom managed to persuade Phœbe that there was nothing to be done about Phil. They discussed instead the possibility of Brian coming to stay in autumn and having a term of school. It might be good for him, and if he liked it they could arrange for him to stay on. In the barn Phœbe worked and Dione typed Tom's book, encouraging him about it, thinking it would mean Leningrad and Moscow. It was getting near Christmas; Woolworth's was beginning to be crowded already. She had to see about the Christmas tree and stocking things, and make out elaborate lists of what the children wanted to give to one another and Tom; they all stirred the Christmas puddings. She hoped to get up to Scotland for New Year, but wasn't sure if it could be managed.

Then it was the week-end of the social. Dione looked

over her dresses: which would the Marshbrook Bridge elephant approve of? It had to be bright but wifely. This time they were going to stay with the Taylors, who had a spare room where they took lodgers whenever lodgers were to be had. Mrs. Taylor was a thin, cheerful woman with one little girl; her husband was a foreman bricklayer, regularly employed by a decent firm of builders and decorators, earning pretty good wages when he was in work, but liable at the best of times to be out in winter. They spent whole days then doing the *Daily Herald* cross-word and planning what they would spend the prize money on if they got it. Some of it always went to building a real Labour hall for the ward, designed by Mr. Taylor himself, with central heating and an asbestos roof. When the Galtons arrived, Mrs. Taylor and Emmie, the little girl, were still making the last of the coloured-paper decorations for the social. Dione went along with them to the hall and helped to hang them up.

The social was a success. Tom, ex-Councillor Finch, and others made short speeches, explaining away the election results and talking about the future. The speeches were designed to make people confident and cheerful, but at the same time full of the will to work. Several romantic part-songs were sung. The workers of River Ward were specially commended; Marl was encouraged; it was decided to form a woman's section in Little Lumley. Tom and Dione went round talking to everybody, too busy to think. There was dancing, and then sweet, strong tea was served in thick cups, and Co-op. cakes and tinned salmon sandwiches. A good deal of business was done quietly; Mason would take Tom aside and whisper, and then Tom would go about from one group to another. "And his tail goes aye wig-wag, wig-wag."

At about 10.30 it broke up. They sang "Auld Lang

Syne" and the "Red Flag." Suddenly, during the singing of the "Red Flag," Dione came clear of her daze of business and wifeliness. A good many had gone out after "Auld Lang Syne," but those who were left sang this in deadly earnest. She saw Mason with his head up and eyes in some other place.

> "Come dungeon dark and gallows grim,
> This song shall be our parting hymn."

Mason would do that really. Mason would die for his beliefs. And she—would she face gallows? Wouldn't she—somehow—compromise? Wouldn't she and Tom somehow get out of it and be found safe in North Oxford when it was all over? "Though cowards flinch——" Yes, yes, her flesh flinched horribly in cowardice and separation. In spite of their ridiculous paper decorations and Sunday-school tea—in spite, even, of the Elephant—they in that hall would keep the Red Flag flying, while she, Dione Galton, was flinching and sneering.

They went out. It was raining a little. Tom had still a lot to talk over with Mason and decided to go back with him to his house. He asked Dione if she could find her way all right alone; the Taylors had gone rather early with the little girl.

"Of course," Dione said, rather depressed all the same, for she was very tired, and would have liked at least a little company on her way. Outside the hall there were still several bunches of men arguing and planning. Behind them in the wet the trams went by, each one a moving island of lights and rattle. Under the lamp she saw a man selling papers. She saw it was Donald MacLean and he was selling *Daily Workers*. She saw he had no overcoat. A few of the men bought copies, ragging him a little as they did so. Tom and Mason had gone off. Dione went up to him and said: "Good evening, Donald MacLean, I'd like a paper." He nodded to her and handed it over; he kept them under his coat where they wouldn't get wet, but his hands and face were streaky with rain, and he was shivering a little.

"You're horribly cold, aren't you?" she said.

"There is plenty colder than I," he answered her.

"Where are you living?" He pointed across the tram-lines and asked a man who was passing to buy. "What, somewhere near the 'Green Man'? I'm going home that way now. Will you walk back with me?"

"No," said Donald MacLean, "I am going to sell my papers before I go home."

"How many more have you?"

He looked: "Two dozen."

"Well, I'll buy the lot."

"That is not the way I choose to sell the *Daily Worker*."

"Oh, come along," she said, "everyone's gone, and you won't sell any more. I tell you what I'll do, I'll give them to people in the train on my way back on Monday. Will that do?"

He hesitated.

"I will, surely," she said, "here's two shillings. And—and—have you no overcoat?" He shook his head. They crossed the tram-lines and started walking. "If I gave you the money would you get yourself one? It's for your mother's sake."

"You can tell my mother, and you had best know yourself, Mistress Galton, I'm not wanting any overcoats! I am a Party member. What for would I be wanting overcoats when there are comrades' children going barefoot? If you in the Labour Party have that much money to throw away there's plenty strike funds you can send it to!"

"I really haven't got it to throw away," said Dione, "I wanted you to have it because you're a MacLean."

"The sooner you learn to think in terms of mankind and not of this nationalist foolery, the sooner you'll see the beginnings of reality!"

"But, all the same, you and I would be MacLeans and somehow cousins."

"Cousins!"

"You're always talking about brothers. Why not cousins too? Tell me—how's the Unemployed Committee?"

"Ach, it's bad, bad!" said Donald; "there's not ten per cent. of the unemployed who are class-conscious."

"I suppose you find, like we do, that the worst off are the most ignorant and the most easily taken in by the Tory papers."

"Aye, or by the *Daily Herald!*" said Donald MacLean fiercely. "Tories and Liberals and Labour, they are all alike, the three bourgeois parties. You Labour folk, with your money and your socials and your fine speakers, you take in the workers as bad—aye, worse than the rest of them!"

"Oh, I wish you wouldn't!" said Dione sharply, and stopped under a lamp-post; she had been quite calm, liking him and sorry that he felt like that, but then it had suddenly seemed as if he was attacking her group, her Tom—she wanted to hit him, but knew this was only her tiredness getting at her.

He looked at her and saw tears in her eyes and was angry with her and himself. "I am sorry, Mistress Galton," he said elaborately. "I should not have said such things before a lady."

"Oh, don't be *stupid!*" she said and stamped. "I won't be called a lady. If you enjoy being nasty about the

Labour Party, go on, but surely a good Communist needn't insult a Socialist by calling her a lady ! "

" It was you, I think," said Donald, " who insulted me by offering me your money for an overcoat."

" You know fine it wasn't meant that way ! " Dione said.

" Well, then " said he with a kind of fierce soft sarcasm, " I apologise."

For a time they walked in silence. Then Dione said : " Shall I tell you about the Elephant ? "

" Aye," he said.

Dione explained ' Other Laws for the People.' " What do you think of it ? " she said at the end.

" Blethers," he said shortly, " decent folks stay decent."

" Have you ever read any Lawrence ? "

" No. What would I do, wasting my time on a parcel of filth ? "

" What do you read ? " she said.

He began eagerly then, pouring out names of books, Communist theory and economics, Lenin, Bukharin, Dutt, Emile Burns, Pollitt, McShane, Saklatvala, conditions in America, Upton Sinclair—yes, and Gorki, and now the new Russia. " If only I could somehow go there ! " he said. " I am longing after it."

" Perhaps you will," said Dione, uncomfortably aware that she and Tom were probably going there in the summer, but didn't want to nearly as much as he did. After a time she said : " I'm probably going to Auchanarnish at New Year. Would you give me your address for your father and mother to write to you ? "

" No," he said, " I have gone another way from theirs. I will not have them writing to me. I will not have them dragging at me to get me back. I would give you the address for yourself, Mistress Galton," he added, " but you would never have the heart to keep it from them ! "

He laughed a little; it was the first real friendliness of the evening, and now they had come to the corner of her street.

"Good-night," she said, "and good luck."

"Good-night," he said.

THERE was no snow at Oxford that winter, just a general damp chilliness and a 'flu epidemic beginning. Hopefully Kenneth and Morag would go off down the river path, but the Cher water still flowed grey-green and opaque with mud, no sign of even the first delicate crinkly ice forming round the sticks and old rushes in the stillest side-pools. Once or twice Dione had taken them to the ice rink, but Ken's ankles were still wobbly, though Morag was beginning to be able to do edges. There had been a good children's party in college, with jellies, and two other parties, and their own Christmas-tree party. Petronella and Clemency had stayed for the first week of the holidays. Lilias was beginning to talk quite a lot and was rather fun. The only really important Christmas present, though a lot of the things were pretty decent and what they'd been wanting to have, was Morag's puppy. He was going to be a Highland terrier, but Morag called him Bran, because he felt to her like at least a wolf-hound. At present she was rather jealous about him and wouldn't let Kenneth give him his breakfast. On the evening of December 27th Dione, Morag, Kenneth, and Bran started off for Scotland.

Morag woke in the middle of the night and smelt snow and peeped out of the window, and saw Cumberland lying white in the moonlight; at Beatock Kenneth woke her and said in a whisper that the snow was so thick that he knew for certain there must be a snow-plow on the front of the engine. There was some at Dalmally, but not enough to count at Oban; their feet just walked through it on to the platform. Alex met them and was suitably enthusiastic over Bran. It was going to be a very small New Year party this year. Phœbe had said she couldn't afford to come and was anyway working too hard. Still, there'd be various cousins and as many parties as they wanted to go to. They'd been asked to go over and shoot by Lady Ann.

"I'm awfully out of practice," said Dione; "I never seem to manage to go out in September when all the children are here. I won't shoot rabbits because I mightn't kill them, and woodcock are the devil. But it'll be fun going over, all the same. They're the loveliest woods in the world."

"I shan't mind seeing a little of you for a change," said Alex, "without all these husbands and children and things!"

"Yes," said Dione, "and while I'm here I swear I'm going to have a holiday; I'm not going to think about Marshbrook Bridge or Tom's book, or anything. I shan't read any paper except the *Scotsman*, and one can't read that! Oh, Alex, look what a colour the loch is; where does it manage to get it all from?"

But it wasn't as easy as she thought it would be, forgetting about things. In the afternoon she walked across the garden to the MacLeans' cottage. There were still all kinds of little flowers out, odds and ends in the rock-garden, and a Christmas thorn. Some of the rarer plants had sacking wrapped round them, but the tree ferns and palms looked quite happy. MacLean had a blazing, aniline-purple cineraria in a blue pot in his front-room. She knocked and Mrs. MacLean came to the door. After the welcomes were over and Dione had produced her New Year present, she said: "Mrs. MacLean, I've been seeing Donald."

Mrs. MacLean stood up suddenly and passed her hands over her face; then she sat down again and composed her mouth. "Indeed, Mistress Dione," she said, "and is he keeping well?"

"He looks wonderfully well—considering," said Dione. "He's out of work just now, but he has friends, and plenty to occupy him; he seems to be reading any amount."

"Aye," said Mrs. MacLean, "he was always the great reader. He is not thinking of continuing his—education?"

Dione shook her head: "He'll never go back to the Ministry, Mrs. MacLean, but no doubt the teaching he got for it is not lost. But—you see, he has taken all the world for his parish now. He believes in the brotherhood of mankind."

"But is it not the politics he is doing now?"

"Yes."

"I doubt there's no' much brotherhood there, Mistress Dione, for all I know you are in the politics too. It is anger and uncharitableness and a smiting of tongues. Will you tell me now—had he any messages for his father and me?"

"He sent you his love," said Dione, lying firmly.

"Aye, he would. My bonny lad. Will he no' come home again just for a wee while? I—his father would like fine to see him."

"I don't think so, Mrs. MacLean. You see—he is thinking so much about his politics that nothing else seems quite real. You see what I mean?"

"Aye; but my love of him is right real."

"It's—oh, it's as if he were a missionary somewhere in the South Seas. He can't think of anything but that. And—he has that look in his eyes."

"I would sooner he were with black savages than with the Reds. For it must be the Reds he is with still?"

"Yes; he's with one sort of Red. But you know, Mrs. MacLean, I'm a Red too. I want most of the things he wants, only I think I know a better way of getting them. But I'm proud to be a Red."

"Ach, a bhroin bheag-gheal! You're my bonnie flower, and I'll just be making you a good cup of tea."

On the 30th Dione took the children over to a big party at the MacKies', but neither she nor they enjoyed it much. Everyone seemed very well dressed; complexions and hair were just right. Most of the little boys wore elaborate, silver-buttoned dress-jackets with their kilts instead of a plain tweed coat like Kenneth; some of them even had plaids and cairn-gorm brooches; the two or three English were in Eton suits. Even the cars had their appropriate tartan rugs! It all reminded Dione rather of the noble Englishman dressing for dinner in the midst of jungles. She saw that to many of these people, almost all of whom were landowners, either actually or by birth (as she was), the world was a jungle, full of tigers and savages called Bolshevism and Atheism and Pacifism and Mischief-making Demagogues; just round the corner Communist cannibals were feasting; and they themselves were the Lone White Men, the sahibs, representing something great and good and wonderful, something they couldn't quite explain, but clearly what they meant by civilisation; and they would arm themselves and their children with every possible kind of difference, in clothes and voice and manners, in the hope that the tigers would be frightened and that, at least, the children would never go native.

She knew a good many of the parents there, and, what was more, she had noticed the Campbell Women out of the tail of her eye; they were cleverly disguised as moderns and no one suspected them but Dione. In general, she was rather out of the conversations; after all, she had gone to live in the south, and a few people realised that not only was her husband half-English, but also that he was allied with the jungle. Once or twice it appeared to her that a political conversation had been tactfully deflected by her arrival in a group. She overheard that several of the richer people there were staying at home this winter for patriotic reasons instead of going abroad. Economies were in the air, cutting down staffs and wages. The King was spoken of with approval. But surely, thought Dione, it usedn't to be as bad as this ? Or have I changed ? On the way back the children were silent or cross, and said they didn't want to go to any more parties.

However, they decided to go over with Dione and skate, the next day, on one of the small lochs further inland, out of reach of the Gulf Stream that kept Auchanarnish from freezing. Bran went with them, and when Morag discovered that he was terrified of the ice she gave up skating so as to stay with him on land. On the ice Dione was really free ; every problem was swept out of her mind by the keen wind of her going. The few skaters passed one another on long easy swoops, called a greeting perhaps and were gone ; no longer need Dione feel envious of sea-gulls. For a time she occupied herself in doing figures in the middle of the loch ; remote the hillside ; nothing mattered but the accuracy, the timing and swinging of these curves, which, better than the sea-gulls, left their durable marks on the blue roof of the salmon's house. Yes, that was all right ; the Campbell Women were unable to skate, naturally, and the ice roof was solid between her and the kelpies. Basileia also, the daughter of the gods, the fairy queen, could move with just such strength and swiftness.

They came back in the mid-afternoon dusk of Scotland's winter, and now it was New Year's Eve, and in spite of themselves they felt solemn. After dinner, as always by family tradition, Mrs. Fraser read aloud to her children and grandchildren. She read from the Victorian poets, Tennyson and Browning. She herself preferred Tennyson, but because Dione, at sixteen or so, had so much preferred Browning and had always clamoured for him, she now read mostly Browning, and did not realise how it made the grown-up Dione squirm. All this hearty optimism, apparently unable to help breaking through: years of England's commercial greatness and success! After a time Mrs. Fraser's voice began to fail, so Dione suggested she should stop for a time, and her mother agreed, though she was distressed about it, remembering her ancient powers of reading aloud, when the longest evening never tired her. Dione and Alex and the two children played a game of four-handed halma, and then the children had the halma board to themselves; if they went to sleep, Dione promised to wake them in time to see the New Year in.

The house was oddly silent. Dione went to the green baize door on to the back stairs and listened; there seemed to be no one about. "Where do you think they all are?" she asked Alex, as he set out the ivory chess-men for a game.

Alex shook his head: "They always go off and do their own stunts on New Year's Eve. Always have, I suppose."

"I know they used to," Dione said. "Do you remember, Alex, when we were little, and everyone was here, and father did family prayers just because his father used to, and told Something-not-ourselves-which-makes-for-righteousness all about the doings of the Frasers and MacLeans, there never seemed to be anyone but ourselves in the house? And we never knew what they used to do, and we were never allowed to go with them. But I didn't think it would be going on still."

"Lord, yes," said Alex; "I think there's a bonfire and dancing or fighting or dressing-up or something."

"I wish we could go."

"They wouldn't like us to. It would make them feel awkward. As if they were being investigated. One's not one of them."

"Even though we're MacLeans and half of them are MacLeans too?"

"That's all rather knocked on the head now. A hundred years ago, yes. But now we're not much better than Sassenach over the things that really count."

"What a nuisance all that is, Alex. Which hand? . . . You're white."

"It's our own fault really. We let our standard of living go up too much. We didn't like people to think we were nasty, lousy Highlanders. I expect, you know, that was the real objection to the kilt—look how they'd nestle in the seams!"

"Pig, Alex! Then you do agree with me that these class distinctions are getting worse and worse?—what I said about the McKies' party?"

"Yes; they've gone too far. Nothing to be done about it now."

They were talking to one another slowly, between moves, in the delicious leisure of being brother and sister. Dione thought away from Scotland to Marshbrook Bridge and Tom: "Except what *we*'re doing."

"Maybe. But—I ask you, Dione: do you see the McKies and Lady Ann and everyone here calmly accepting a Socialist State that you've decided on in London?"

"I suppose it's a matter of education," said Dione. "Did you *mean* to make that move with your knight. Alex? No, I thought you didn't. Look, Kenneth's asleep."

" Education be damned," said Alex; " their children are getting just what they got, if possible more so. They'll be no different."

" But if it isn't education," said Dione, " then it must be—revolution."

" Exactly. Are you prepared for that ? "

" Not really, I suppose. You don't see any other alternative, do you ? Even for Scotland ? Check, Alex. You're playing badly to-night."

" Except marrying Christina Campbell or something of that sort. But that mightn't work either."

" Alex. Are you thinking of that ? "

" Not really. Half. I'm rather bored with all these girls I meet in Edinburgh. They seem kind of—paper-thin one would go through them like paper."

" Obscene thoughts for New Year's Eve : No. 1."

" No, shut up, Dione. But I wish I could get away."

" Look here, Alex, why don't you come to Russia with Tom and me in summer ? You could arrange to get away all right. We shall be going with one of these parties. Oh do, Alex ! "

" What an idea," said Alex; " I think I will. And see what Christina looks like after that. Now, I've got to get out of check. Stop talking for a moment." He sat for a minute or two, frowning and concentrating, his chin pinched between finger and thumb. The candle on the chess table, half burnt down, lighted him in front and from below, heightening the shadow by cheek bones and temple. Again it occurred to his sister how like he was to Donald MacLean ; she wondered what it would be like to sit and play chess with Donald MacLean ; she wondered if he played. A good thing to bring a pocket chess-set to Russia. . . .

Half-past eleven. Mrs. Fraser looked up and saw that

the game was over. " Shall I read some more, children ? " she asked.

" Read *Now Sleeps the Crimson Petal*, Mother." Mrs. Fraser found her spectacles and hunted it out of 'The Princess.'

" It's a good poem," said Dione at the end, " Lawrence might have written it."

Mrs. Fraser frowned a little and went on to read *Home They Brought her Warrior Dead.* Dione wondered a little grimly what Muriel would say to that ; it seemed to embody a good deal of anti-feminism.

A quarter to twelve : time to wake the children. " Thank goodness," said Dione, " the hills cut us off from the wireless stations here. Poor Phœbe will have to listen to the New Year's Eve Message on Clemency's new set—unless it's gone wrong."

" I take it that's the only reason why people here still play fiddles and pipes and so on, and sing as well as they do—they aren't getting it nicely packed up and sent out to them by the Glasgow transmitting station."

" Yes," said Dione, " the wireless would do in bonfires and dancing and working spells or whatever they're doing, in a very few years. And no doubt they'll soon have invented some way of getting the beastly stuff sent through the hills. Wake up, Morag, my lamb, wake up."

Alex went down and got a bottle of hock and poured it out into thistle glasses. They all stood, waiting for the clock. It was ridiculous to feel moved by a thing like this ! They all drank, to the New Year, and to Phœbe Bathurst. Phœbe at Helm would know they were drinking to her. Alex added Tom. Dione suddenly thought of Lilias asleep and pink, her delicate, tumbled brown hair. The baby New Year, always one's own baby. Must Lilias be her last baby ? The New Year when Morag was a baby. Everyone still so thankful for peace, not seeing what kind of a peace it was.

Three days later Dione and Alex drove over to Lady Ann's for the shooting. The two guns were in the back of the car, and cartridges for each of them: Dione's was a sixteen-bore. When they started it was a lovely calm morning, the faintest touch of sunrise pink still in the sky. It was an hour's drive over, and after they had crossed the pass the road began to be powdered with snow. The castle, too, was set romantically in snow that glittered under the sun, but was not heavy enough to make walking difficult, and in the woods they were going to shoot, which sloped south-west towards the loch, there was scarcely any snow at all. The shooters walked together up the drive, and then along a ride between great Douglas firs; there were eight men and three women, besides the rather alarming elderly keeper, who ordered them about, and the gillies. Someone said there might be some wild geese coming in; the keeper told them to shoot all roe they saw. At the end of the ride they split up, taking one or another of the moss-green paths between young firs and rhododendron. Soon the shots began, one or two, or several together. Dione looked about her happily, watching for something to happen. She let a couple of rabbits go by, unwilling to risk wounding them; then, at a shout, a woodcock came bundling out of the firs into the open space between the trees ahead of her. She lifted her gun and shot, and down he tumbled, the bright feather ball, more delicious to eat than any other game bird. After that she missed one, let a hare go by, and nearly disgraced herself by shooting a blackcock. Still, she had something to show. She rejoined Alex at the end of the path where it opened out on to a cleared stretch which in summer would be one mass of rhododendron and heather. Underfoot the thick moss was crisp with frost; the air smelt of frost and pine-needles and an enlivening whiff of gunpowder. The gun snuggled comfortably under her arm ; her pockets were heavy with good cartridges.

The next beat was close to the loch, and Alex got a snipe ; it was exciting seeing him get it, firing quick and low over a ridge tufted with bog cotton, knowing just how to get the zigzagging kind of toy thing it was. Then, walking through woods again, and one more woodcock for Dione. And then sandwiches by a gay, tiny burn, everyone hungry and pleased, rough claret in mugs, cigarettes and an extremely handsome young man, who could do the silliest tricks with matches, to flirt just the right amount with Dione. Moving off after lunch, to be placed in various corners. It was to be a beat towards them this time.

Pleasant to be standing by oneself in a beautiful pine forest in delicious stillness, so still that tiny, friendly tits came hopping out of darkness into sunlight, cocking their heads from twigs. Elegant little Christmas trees, blue sky, half a dozen different and all lovely mosses round her feet. Then, as the noises of the beaters began to come nearer, she loaded and watched, the mere fact of this extra concentration heightening the colours, sharpening the shapes. From where she stood she could see clear between pines to a bank of rhododendron about ten yards away. She watched here and along the ride.

A roe-deer came trotting between the pines, unquiet, questioning, but not yet frightened. It was a splendid shot against the rhododendrons ; perhaps none of the men would get a chance of one, she couldn't miss ! She aimed and the roe-deer turned its head and looked at her, the little, the fairy deer, and she couldn't kill it, and the roe-deer slid away through the rhododendrons, and a moment afterwards Dione missed an easy shot at a pheasant.

When they were all together again the keeper asked if

anyone had seen a roe ; he suspected there'd been one or two about, and they were mischievous little brutes, eating everything, getting into the farmers' corn. Nobody had seen a roe. Dione Galton was engaged in a conspiracy with the roe-deer against the keeper, against the killers.

She shot nothing more after that, though once or twice she fired. They came back to tea with Lady Ann, after frost and sunshine, to almost equally brilliant Georgian silver, faint steam from straw-coloured china tea, butter, new combs of honey, shortbread, Scotch bun for the shooters, heavy with almonds and whisky, chocolates in a plain, aristocratic two-pound box from London : inherited Raeburns on the walls, a red setter and a deer-hound wagging friendly tails. But something had happened to Dione Galton ; her lunch-time flirt put it down to tiredness, and thought it a pity for ladies to shoot more than half the day. It was as though she were being pulled backwards, half reluctant and half eager, back from the glitter of snow or silver, back from the blue lochs and the clear air of Scotland to somewhere that had become in a way closer to her, back to the factories and the little rows of ugly houses, back to stale bread and margarine and the Taylors and Mason and George Grove and Reuben Goldberg and Miss Waterhouse and Mrs. East and Sam Hall and the Labour Movement at Marshbrook Bridge. She wondered if she had betrayed them : not badly, she thought, but if I had shot the roe-deer its blood would have got on to the Red Flag. I don't think I mind a bit, she said to herself, if I never shoot again ; she felt no friendliness towards the comfortable gun or the good cartridges. Saint Finnigal let her go from Scotland ; what else was to be done ? Saint Finnigal and Scotland could not give her what she needed any longer. The kelpies belonged to the other people, Mrs. Cook and the Andersons and the MacLeans and the

MacCallums and the Islanders and Red Peter and Willie and perhaps even the Finneys, and perhaps even Christina Campbell, who did things at Hogmanay that she and Alex might not share. And Green Jean was on the side of the roe-deer and Marshbrook Bridge and against the owners and the killers and the keeper whom they paid.

## OXFORD 2

Tom and Dione thought they were catching colds. This was a sufficiently good excuse for going to bed early and drinking hot lemonade. It was a nice room; the ceiling had pleasing angles. There were striped linen curtains drawn now across the window, but later in the year you could lie in bed and look out of it on to the rounded tower of a blossoming pear tree. The wood fire had warmed the room, and now the burnt-through logs were glowing and even flaming a little before collapsing into lovely ashes. Dione was still sitting up in bed, sipping the remains of her lemonade; Tom had finished his, and lay back on the pillows with one arm round her hips. He was wearing the blue silk pyjamas she had given him for Christmas. He said: "It's very odd, this habit one gets into of going to bed with the same woman for years and years and years."

"It's a nice habit," said Dione, smiling down at him; "I like it."

"I like it too," he said, "but I can't imagine I would with anyone but you."

"That's lucky, isn't it!" Dione said, ruffling up his hair, "but I agree with you, it is absurd. I wonder how much longer you'll go on."

"I see no reason why I shouldn't end up as a doddering old professor without ever having slept with anyone but you, Dione."

"What a horrid idea!" she said. "You know, you ought to do something about it. But you won't end up as a doddering old professor anyway, because the revolution will have come before that."

Tom twitched his head away from her hand, rather crossly. " Your difficulty," he said, " is that you talk about the revolution as if it were some nice, magic hey-presto. Press the button and a new England comes out of the hat, complete with nationalised industries, the classless society, bankers and bricklayers playing ring-a-ring-of-roses round the may-pole on May Day. Comes of your being a Highlander, I suppose; nothing to be done about it. But there won't be a nice revolution like that, my dear, only a lot of bloody hard work and damn-all to show for it in the end, and being kicked by the young men for being a reformist, as likely as not. Or, if there is a revolution, it won't be all nice and magic; it'll be nasty and messy and uncomfortable, and one'll spend all one's time in telephone boxes trying to get connected to a number that somebody gave one wrong. And you'll probably manage to lose the children or something, and then, my dear, you won't care in the least what happens to the revolution till you've found them. However, I shall be well out of it, in college probably, where they will make suitable jokes about it in Hall, because I'm never going to get in at Marshbrook Bridge."

" Oh, Tom," Dione said, " you are! What rot; they like you!"

" They liked me all right at the election, but now they're beginning to see through me."

" Why do you say that, Tom?"

" They'd be fools if they didn't. And they aren't fools. What have I got to give them except words?"

" Well, what has any candidate?"

" Some of them have done something. Oh hell, Dione, what's the good of it all? One'll go on and go on and nothing will ever happen, nothing will ever get done. I can't even get to know them. They'll never be themselves with me because I'm the candidate, just as my pupils never are because I'm a don. There's always something between oneself and other people. One can't ever get so near that one can really trust them."

"There's always me," said Dione, one hand on his forehead.

"It's between me and you, too. I'm your husband. Would you be as nice to me as you are if I were just—some chap?"

"I've no idea. You wouldn't be you if you were different. All I mind about are these beastly contraceptives."

"Yes, you'd like to be the Mother of the Gracchi, wouldn't you! Or Diana of the Ephesians. Well, Dione, you know if I went to an American University and talked respectable calming economics there, they'd probably pay me a salary you could have triplets on. Anyway, Lilias is only two."

"Oh, that's all right. Have an aspirin. I'm going to."

"This curious sacrament of aspirin and lemonade. I must talk to our dear Chaplain about it; so much better for the undergraduates than all that nasty wine. But seriously, my dear; I don't think I've much chance of getting in next time at Marshbrook Bridge, and I'm getting on for forty, and I've never done anything worth doing."

"The war knocked you out intellectually for a good long time."

"My generation are about due to stop making the war an excuse for everything they do badly. The fact remains, what have I done?"

"Your books——"

"Yes, everyone says, your books, your books, as if anyone couldn't write a book and persuade some fool of a publisher to swallow it. What do they amount to? Bits of other and better historians chopped up and flavoured with a little Marx, but not too much or they wouldn't sell. Hash; that's what they are. Monday's mutton."

"Sure you haven't got a temperature?" Dione said.

Tom sat up in bed: "My God, Dione," he said, "if there is a time when I really dislike you it's when you're being a Good Wife!"

The next morning Dione's cold had disappeared, but Tom's had become a mild snuffle, not enough to keep him away from work. On early lecture mornings he drove the children in to school; Dione gave them formamints to suck, hoping the snuffles wouldn't spread. Then she and cook measured the kitchen windows for the new curtain stuff from Elliston's sale. Tom's book was rather in abeyance during term, so there was no typing that had to be done. Dione began writing her bi-weekly letter to Auchanarnish. It was all right about the children going to stay there in summer, though when she and Alex broke it to their mother that they were going to Russia, Mrs. Fraser was pained.

Tom gave his lecture; a few of the undergraduates wanted to ask questions afterwards, but he was rather cross with them; his handkerchief was giving out, and he had forgotten to bring another. He was annoyed with Dione for not having reminded him. He rushed out and bought half a dozen, thinking what a rotten school Modern Greats was, and on his way back met a colleague who normally amused him, but whom he now felt was hateful. The colleague was all thrilled about an emendation to Alcæus. "——!" said Tom rudely. "Who cares if it's a phi or a lambda! Æolic Syntax! What I object to is your teaching moderately intelligent young men and women that this kind of thing is important. What happens to undergraduates when they're through with Greats? They're fit for nothing but to lead a leisured and cultured existence in a Palladian country house with a gentleman's library and occasional horse exercise for the liver like the Parthenon frieze! Then the poor devils have to become chartered accountants and bank clerks. No wonder they go and commit suicide!"

The colleague, supposing this to be a reference to a brilliant young pupil of his who had actually shot himself, was bitterly hurt and walked into Blackwell's without answering. Tom, as a matter of fact, hadn't even heard of the suicide, because it had happened at the beginning of autumn term, when he was down at Marshbrook Bridge. But for nearly a year after this the colleague would not speak to him, and the developments of the feud became one of the most amusing pieces of academic tittle-tattle in a dozen senior common rooms.

After that, Tom met G. D. H. Cole, just finished with a lecture too, and they discussed the activities of S.S.I.P. for a few minutes. Then he met Zita Baker, also with a cold, who gave him a message for Dione which he forgot to give her that evening. Then he met Mr. Carritt, very much worried about the impact of Marxism on æsthetics and about his son in America. Then it began to rain. Then he met Harry Weldon, who said it was a nice morning for the Buchmanites. Then he met Lady Mary in a hurry. Then he met Maurice Bowra taking notes for another chapter of his autobiography. Then he went back to college and began on a pile of essays, reading them, commenting in red and blue pencil, trying to see which if any showed originality or intelligence. Every now and then he ground his teeth a little. He wished they would occasionally choose rather different models.

Then he read the *Manchester Guardian* and cut out two or

three bits ; he was trying to make out what was really happening to commodity prices. In the afternoon he gave another lecture ; this time his audience were almost all specialists. An ugly lot, he thought, looking across at them from his desk, few more than twenty-two or twenty-three years old, but how many already marked with frowns and small miseries ! Would a Greats or English audience be as bad ? Had he and his friends looked like that in February, 1914 ? Surely not. Many wore spectacles. There was that man from Ruskin who always asked questions, avid for his money's worth at Oxford. The girls were rather less unattractive, but terribly earnest too ; that German girl with the *modern-kunst* necklace, the one in red who was said to write good verse. As he went on with his lecture, speaking from notes (he wondered if the front row were all going to catch his cold), he was half aware of what they were thinking, which took it all in like sponges, which were critical. Those were October Club, that lad with the black hair had been to Russia—and never let you forget it. October Club. Labour Club. All so keen and clever and hopeful. But what was the good of it all ? They'd been caught already. They could do just exactly nothing.

He came away from the lecture depressed ; he had pupils beginning at five o'clock. He must have tea first, something hot. He met Phil Bickerden, standing outside the porter's lodge, looking through the index of Darwin's book on Physics. He handed it over to Tom.

"You ought to look through this, Galton. It over-simplifies, of course. The thing's *not* simple. But still, it does nicely for non-scientists. I am recommending it to my first-year men."

Tom looked at it and said : "There seems to be a spot of higher mathematics."

"Not *higher*," said Phil, pained, "oh no, not higher.

Simplicity itself, really. Nothing an economist should find hard."

" You mistake us," said Tom, " we practically count on our fingers, most of us. Statistics is a baby science so far. We're still all romantic and Eddingtonian."

" Eddington . . ." said Phil expressively, " in all the Oxford bookshops. There should be a censorship. We are, after all, supposed to be educating people, not trying to give them religion ! "

" You pure-hearted physicists ! " said Tom. " Had tea, Bickerden ? Come and have it with me."

" No, I can't," said Phil, " I'm waiting for May ; she's been shopping or something. We're thinking, you know, of launching out into a little car. May drives. I find it too distracting. We were going to see it."

" Oh," said Tom. Then : " What did you get married for, Bickerden ? To have someone to drive your car—or what ? "

Phil Bickerden scratched his head : " One does get married," he said vaguely.

" It all depends who to," said Tom. " Here—I haven't time for Darwin now ; I might next vac."

" You wouldn't like to come and see the car with us ? "

" No," said Tom, and shouldered off, looking for tea.

His first pupil was called Hawkes ; he was a young man of considerable possessions, and he was worried. His father, who had not had the benefits of a University education, had encouraged him to take economics, as he thought it would be useful in the firm. But now David Hawkes had joined the Labour Club, and was going through the most painful kind of mental hoops about his political development. Tom sighed ; he knew he would have to hear it all over again, and he lingered rather over the essay, which was not bad, but had come down over a whole series of small facts. Then Hawkes began on his difficulties. " You are the only man I trust," he said.

" I really can't imagine why you should, and I advise you not to," said Tom. " You've got to make up your own mind. That's what we're supposed to be educating you for."

" I don't know what to do," said young Hawkes, disregarding this; " you see, father wants me to go into the firm, but how can I, with my convictions ? "

" What are your alternatives ? "

" Well, I might write."

" Don't."

" Yes, I suppose, unless one is utterly first-class—but, there's politics."

" Well," said Tom, lighting his pipe, " if you care to be a young Tory, I expect you could go straight into it from Oxford, in the grand Victorian manner. You've got an independent income and they're short of brains. Most young Liberals do a little something first—a call to the Bar, or a book (that would be your chance to write), or even a visit to one of our remoter dependencies. Or you might be a Mosleyite or a British Fascist—I'm not sure how that's done, but I should think you might start on it straightaway."

" But, you *know* I don't want to be a Liberal or a Tory," said the young man, hurt.

" I wonder what you do want," said Tom. Then: " You see, Hawkes, you can join your local branch of the Labour Party if you like, and on the whole I advise you to, but you can't become a leader all of a sudden. They won't give you any kind of responsibility or power. It won't do you any good having been at Oxford and all that, not even if you get a decent degree ; it may tickle the snob in a few of them, but not many. Your accent will be against you.

What they want from you is not a class education, but work, party work, something they can appreciate. You see they'd naturally distrust you for your origin and upbringing. They're right. You aren't part of a working-class movement—*are* you?"

"I suppose not."

"The Communist Party would be the same, only more so. I doubt if they'd have you, certainly not at once, and even if you managed to prove yourself to them somehow, they'd make you sell *Daily Workers* on the street corner. They wouldn't give you power either."

"But I don't think I want power," said the young man.

"Don't you? Are you sure? Don't your friends expect it of you? Don't you want a career?"

"Well, a career——"

"You won't get a career in Socialism. That's not what it's for. If you're going to be a good Socialist one of the first things you must chuck is personal ambition."

"Have *you* done that?"

"I wish to God I could say I had. But I'm not a good Socialist. I started too late. No; why should I make excuses for myself? But I can tell you what a Socialist ought to be. Suppose you were to try, during the next week or so, and think out what being a good Socialist entails. You might do me an essay on it."

"Do you mean—economic policy?"

"No, no, in your own life. The way you act."

"But what am I to say to Father? He wants me to decide."

"Why not go into the firm and try being a good Socialist there? You'd be more use that way than writing books or making speeches. Also, of course, it would be much more difficult. You'd almost certainly fail."

"But you think I ought to try?"

"Make up your own mind." Tom knocked out his pipe and walked across to the bookshelf.

The young man Hawkes sat crouched up, staring into the fire, holding his essay. At last he said: "It's not a very cheerful prospect, is it?"

"No," said Tom, "it isn't. Not for anyone, just now. But, frankly, it's worse for a good many people than it is for you. Things may be better in a hundred years."

"I want to make them better now!" said Hawkes lamentably.

"You want to. You. You. It's no good saying 'I want.' But if you find me too gloomy, go and get cheered up by someone else. Very likely I'm all wrong. You'll find plenty of eminent Oxford persons who'll say so."

There was a knock at the door: another pupil. Young Hawkes rose gloomily to say good-bye, and went out. The next pupil came in: she was a girl from Ruskin, rather older than most undergraduates, with brown eyes and a dark bob, one of his most hopeful pupils.

"You have got a nasty cold, Mr. Galton!" she said at once, and offered him a lozenge out of her bag. When he had gone through the essay with her, she stretched out a hand with a new ring: "Look, Mr. Galton, I'm engaged."

"Happy?" She nodded. "Who to?"

"He's a boy at home; I've known him years. He's an engineer: electrical spare parts. He's in the Labour Movement."

"Getting good wages?"

"Fair. But we shan't have a grand wedding. And then I'll be keeping house for him. I can cook a bit."

"Are you going to chuck—all this?" He put his hand down on a pile of text-books.

"Yes, I've got to."

" Are you sure you've got to? You're sure you won't regret it later? Do you mean to have children?"

" Well, perhaps not at first. I—I—we——" She looked down, blushing, fidgeting at the corners of her essay.

Tom wondered whether he dared, as an Oxford tutor, say what he now wanted to say. However, he did: " My sister, among her many activities, runs a birth-control clinic in London. I believe you'd get the best possible advice there."

" Oh, Mr. Galton——"

" Here's the address." He scribbled it. " I'll send her a line. If you want to go, ask for Miss Galton and say who you are. Now, don't you think, after you're married, you'll be able to keep up with a certain amount of work?"

" I'll be in the Party," said the girl, " it'll all come in. But I'm a working woman, Mr. Galton, and I know what it's like. I know how much time Mum had. I'm not going to kid myself about it."

Tom was silent for a moment; he was remembering what he had said to young Hawkes about renouncing personal ambition. Here was this girl doing it, and he wanted to dissuade her. Why was it different? He said: " You really think this is your best way of helping to build a new world?"

She said: " Yes." Then she said: " You know, Mr. Galton, sometimes since I've been up I've met boys I like, you know, at the Labour Club. Not serious, you know, but I liked talking to them and dancing and—oh, p'raps a kiss now and again. Only I'm glad I'm not marrying one of them. I'm glad I'm marrying a working man. I'm glad—oh, I'm glad I wasn't got at here in Oxford, so as to despise him! He thought I might have been."

" But you weren't. I'm glad someone hasn't been. Oxford gets at us all badly. It gets at me. Well, I hope you'll find that being married is as good as you think. Next Tuesday, then."

She went out. Tom got another handkerchief from the parcel and looked at his watch. The next pupil was late. Tom took his essay out of the pile; it was a much red-pencilled one. At last he heard him come running up the stairs, and in, a nice lad, youngish, with an armful of books. "Sorry," he said, "it was the play-reading society."

"All right. What were you reading?"

"'Lady Windermere's Fan.'"

"What, Wilde? Why on earth?"

"Oh, but the Victorians are frightfully brilliant; don't you think so?"

"No, I don't. I haven't since I was sixteen. You'll be saying you like the 'Idylls of the King' next."

"Oh, but I do. They're so deliciously period. I suppose you remember last century?"

Tom grinned, realising that his pupil was trying to put off the evil moment. "Not very accurately. You see, it went and ended when I was seven."

"But you remember the European War?"

"Quite definitely. Especially in wet weather."

"Why?"

"My wound begins to play tricks then. Now, what about this essay?"

"But I didn't know you'd been wounded! It must have been a marvellous time."

"Marvellous? Haven't you read any war books?"

"Oh yes. I adore them. You know that superb scene in 'All Quiet on the Western Front,' the men sitting on boxes in the mud and——"

"I didn't know the younger generation had such a passion for open-air latrines; perhaps college could arrange something. Well, never mind, if the National Government goes on as it's doing at present there'll probably be another war in your time. Now, look here: this essay of yours shows a bad falling off from your usual standard. What were you thinking about?"

"Too stupid of me," murmured the young man. They got to work.

After this Tom felt very shivery. It was raining. The self-starter had gone again, and he knew he'd have to crank the car. He wondered whether he'd dine and stop the night in college; he could ring Dione up. He went down to the Senior Common Room; it was a beautifully proportioned room with Queen Anne panelling, painted an egg-green. There was a blazing fire in the wide hearth, reflected in polished brass fire-dogs. There was something of the same excellence, he thought, in college fires and college lawns; they were immensely good of their kind. College had been able to pay people to make them so for several hundred years. There were two of his colleagues sitting by the fire, reading weeklies, the Chaplain and an oldish mediæval historian. For once Tom did not feel like teasing the Chaplain. Instead, he drew up a chair, and, when the other two turned round, saying, "'Evening, Galton," he remarked at large: "Well, what about the young men? Are they getting their money's worth out of us?"

The mediæval historian grunted and settled into his paper again; this question was not covered by his period. However, the Chaplain answered: "But Oxford means so much more to them than just pure education."

"I know. That's the worst of it. Ought it to?"

"Oh, surely, Galton! What they get is something—a point of view—a way of life. The effect, perhaps, of living with beauty."

"But is that what we should be giving them? We're

supposed to be technicians, teaching them sets of facts, aren't we ? "

" Not altogether, surely."

" But then, what else ? How can we find anything objective to put before them, any valid concept of action ? "

" I don't find it very difficult," the Chaplain answered, a little self-consciously.

" No, you've got a set pattern. Though how you manage to square it, year after year, with the world, the flesh and the devil, which all count quite a lot in the Oxford way of life, beats me ! But are you satisfied that on the whole they go down better kind of people than when they came up ? "

" Oh, quite."

" Nice for you."

Someone else came into the room. " Hullo, Teddy," said Tom.

It was one of their younger Fellows, a biologist. " Hullo, Tom. D'you know, Wallace is going to be in the Boat after all."

" Good thing, I take it. He'd have been upset if they turned him down. Teddy, we were discussing education."

" How quaint ! " said Teddy. " But I shouldn't worry about the lads, my dear Tom, most of them have been spoilt before they got here, and we can't make them any worse than they are."

" I can't agree with you that they've been spoilt," the Chaplain said. " They're far more serious than they used to be."

" Yes," said Teddy, " that's what's so disgusting. They aren't even barbarians—except some of the Rhodes scholars, and even they take the jolly old Empire hellishly seriously. They've got nasty little liver-flukes in their consciences. They don't even have fun. They come up here from

Winchester and Marlborough and all those nice healthy English places, completely done in, poor geese, and not knowing it. Thinking they're IT. We can't help them."

"We've been done in ourselves," said Tom.

"Yes," said Teddy cheerfully, "the only thing left is to avoid constipation and find a nice girl."

Tom got up; he felt more miserable than when he had first come into the room. He couldn't face dinner in college. Everything seemed to be failing him; he was overwhelmed with the sense of always having to make reservations with any group one is talking with. Certain subjects one avoids. Certain formulæ one agrees to. And never—never—that complete freedom, the rest, stopping of the time-clock ticking away in one's brain, that release from the Wheel, the Kingdom of Heaven. Gosh, he thought, I'm going religious, I think I must be in for 'flu. Hope I'm fit to drive! And it occurred to him that with any luck he would have a temperature the next morning and be able to spend the day with a clear conscience in bed.

## HELM I

PHOEBE had been dreaming; it was something she liked dreaming; she couldn't remember; it was gone. Reluctantly, stickily, she came awake, losing her dream. It was light, there were birds singing; the air was cool and salt-sticky; the mist was spinning away under the sun. It was April, Avril; she thought of it as ripples and leaves, the small wild leaves of the wood laurel. *Les lauriers sont fanés.* She lay in bed for a few minutes longer, her hands crossed under her neck. In the bed beside hers Robin was still asleep; he had been sleeping badly again; he would have to start taking that stuff from London that he hated taking. If only she could tell when he was having nightmares, she could wake him in time; but his face didn't show when he was dreaming about those tattered Things caught on the barbed wire that he told her about sometimes.

She thought of dressing and going down to breakfast; the postman would knock and her heart would bump and turn over like a fish in a pool too small for it, a pool the tide had ebbed from. She began to play saying to herself what the postman would bring that morning, saying to herself that she knew well it was only a game, she couldn't anyhow make it happen. On the top, she thought, there will be a letter from Pussy like the letter he wrote last summer, before Auchanarnish, full of flattery for me as an artist, flattery so careful, so technical, that I can half believe it, that it will make me work better; and he will ask me to come up to London and go to a play with him, and wear my green dress. She did over the phrases in her mind, seeing quite clearly his signature at the end of it. And then there will be a letter from Gibbings saying he likes my first lot of blocks so much that he wants me to do a Faerie Queen for him : work for the next six months. And a letter from Redfern's saying they have sold a whole set of my Polar Images, and enclosing cheque with a few nice phrases. And a letter from an unknown millionaire saying he is building a house in Yucatan and can I come out and decorate it for him. And a letter from Black's saying I paid that plumbing bill after all—I know I have, only the receipt has gone and got lost! And a letter from Dione saying Tom has been made the Leader of the Labour Party or something, whatever it is people do get made, and she will be able to have another baby. And then, right at the bottom there will be Phil's letter, which I won't see till the very end, and it will say it has all been a mistake and he has been terribly unhappy without me, but now May has run away with a commercial traveller and he is coming to me, he will be crossing by the morning ferry-boat, and will I go and meet him. And then, instead of porridge and fried bread and tomatoes for breakfast, there will somehow be kidneys, great squishy hot buttery kidneys . . .

She jumped violently out of bed. She washed in cold water to drive all that out of her head and scrubbed her teeth hard, hard, so to make the gums bleed. Her body was still pale from winter, not sun-touched yet, her breasts were beginning to sag. Her stockings were all darned; her dress was boring; her hair-brush was moulting at the side. She wanted to go to Paris. She wanted to go to New York. She wanted to run away to sea.

She went along and brushed the girls' hair for them, and reminded Brian of those toilet minutiæ which he was likely to have forgotten. At breakfast the porridge was rather lumpy, the new girl—she couldn't get it right somehow! Brian said it made him feel sick. The postman knocked and Clemency ran out to get the letters. For half a minute her heart played those nasty tricks she knew it would play, while her mind said no, there won't be—there won't be—there can't be—and at last, there, I told you there wouldn't be. There was that wretched bill from Black's coming again, and another bill, and some catalogues, and a post-card from Mrs. Fraser for Petronella. Then she got up, to face the business of winding up the house, ordering food, talking propitiatingly to Gladys and the new girl. Clemency asked if they could have baked apples for dinner, and she remembered with a start that she'd forgotten to order apples yesterday. When she apologised they all clamoured that it didn't matter *a bit*, which made it somehow worse. "When I've finished doing household," she said, "I'm going to work. I've got to get this job finished, so will you be angels and try not to let anyone disturb me till lunch? Specially not father. He's asleep. Yes, Clemency love, if you can possibly manage it. Yes, you can go along to the quarry if you like, but don't let Brian get tired."

She went straight to the kitchen with a pencil and paper and dealt with her house, trying to concentrate on it and not keep on pulling towards the work she wanted to do. There seemed to be something wrong with the flue again, but perhaps the foreman on the farm could deal with that; she would ask Robin; she tied a knot in her handkerchief so as to remember. The new girl, she thought, seemed quite kind, hadn't started bullying her yet.

Then she escaped; she let herself quietly out of the side door and quietly walked across the garden, past what would be the croquet lawn if anyone ever attended to it. She was out of sight of the house; she ran, she bolted into her workroom and shut the door. Calm began to surround her again, the working peace of the craftsman. She sat down in front of her table; the tangles and worries began to sink down through her mind like sea-sodden tangles of rope through deep water, down to the bottom-most sand; they were silted over, they were forgotten, they were only shapeless lumps and above them the waters of her mind were clear and quiet for her eyes to see through.

She had already sent off the blocks for the "Little Mermaiden," "Clever Hans" and the "Tin Soldier"; she had finished the designs for the "Flying Carpet." Would she start on the block for that, or get down to the thing which was worrying her so much, the designs for "Kay and Gerda"? She looked at the sketches she had already made and frowned at them; they weren't right. Suddenly she wished she could have done plain, simple, childish drawings full of detail, the kind of thing a child would like. But of course fine editions, even of fairy tales, don't get into the hands of children! For a time that worried her and she occupied herself in sharpening pencils. No, she didn't feel like doing the ice-block puzzle yet. Perhaps it would be fun to put some mathematical formulæ into it. Those squiggles that mean square root or infinity or go back to where you started from; only she'd be sure to get them wrong. Suppose she got someone else to write to Phil about it. If Robin did, then the answer would come to the house, she'd see his writing. . . . Oh, stop it! she said to herself, I've got to get on with the job. When I'm paid it'll mean school fees, Brian's doctor, a leather jacket with a zip-fastener for Robin, a week in London—perhaps Clare Leighton would have me to stay and we'd talk shop. Now then, get on with it.

She fidgeted away another half-hour. She started on the "Flying Carpet" block, at first pleased with the mere physical feel of the tools, the handle of the graver in the hollow of her hand, her fingers pressing tensely down on it, the ball of her thumb touching the boxwood surface. Then she felt there was something wrong with the design; she couldn't tell what; it had seemed all right yesterday. This was maddening. Half-past ten. Lunch at one. She yawned and stretched and wished someone would bring her coffee, coffee in a glass like in France, when you can see the sugar melting at the bottom of it. Perhaps it was just that she was tired; she'd been awake the earlier part of the night because of Robin; it had been like that, on and off, two or three nights a week, ever since Christmas. She'd been a fool not to go up to Auchanarnish at New Year; it would have been worth it, to freshen her up for work.

She put the tools and the block back in the drawer and began again on "Kay and Gerda." She could do the boat anyway. When she'd been in Ryde ordering things yesterday, she'd seen exactly how it was to go; if she'd had a note-book with her, then she could have done it. But she hadn't had anything but her shopping bag; and she'd forgotten the apples. Still, she thought she'd kept it in her head; she'd been looking forward to this drawing: Gerda in her boat going away from the house of forgetfulness. She had planned the garden of the witch full of dream stuff, and then the sharp boat coming straight at you, coming awake, Gerda's knuckles hard on the thwarts. Perhaps she had thought it out too much; now she felt as though she couldn't do it, as though it were a weight she had to lift and couldn't.

Was this depression purely physical? If she went for a walk now, would she be able to do it in the afternoon? Nonsense, get on with it, you probably won't be able to work in the afternoon; someone will want you for something! She took a ruler and measured out her exact space and began to draw. If the boat was there, then the lines of the water must go so. And that was the balancing line across of the shore. And what was this line? It must be something, because obviously there had to be a line there to hold down the curves. The slope of the boat, then, must go so; it had to be solider than anything else in the picture, the real thing for Gerda after all those dreams and fantasies. All the dream things in the witch's garden, the narcissus, the snowdrop, the tiger lily, the talking crow, the gules lion, only not the rose because she'd lost Phil, no Kay, and when the rose bush came up she was so frightened of all the things that came up with it, that came at her from all sides of the witch's garden, the kelpies out of the earth and the Campbell Women walking quickly along behind the lilies to cut her off and the Elephant lumbering quickly from among the cabbages, that Gerda ran and ran and jumped into the boat. That then is the prow line, the central thing in the picture that everything else has to come from, the diamonded angles of the water so, and there Gerda's hands.

It had been frightening suddenly thinking of the witch's garden like that, in her own terms. Silly of her. The story after all had very little to do with her drawing; it wasn't going too badly now. But she was still frightened. She had evoked those things somehow and she hadn't got a boat to escape on. Eleven o'clock. How can one be frightened in the middle of an April morning? What was she being frightened of, anyway? She set herself to consider, all senses alert till she found which one had sent the warning, had tugged at the vagus nerve and sent her heart pealing like a bell, like a fire-bell, a tocsin. It was not sight, not touch; it was a noise, a fingering along the wall; she leaned forward to the window and as her face neared it on one side of the glass, the faces of the Campbell Women looked in and nodded to her from the other.

The moment for decisive action. While they were at the window she would escape by the door. Quietly she laid down her drawing things, quietly she opened the door and fled back along the path to the house. She did not need to look over her shoulder to know they were chasing her. If they touched her they would get her, freeze her, their fingers would reach into her and squeeze up her heart. She thought rapidly ; the children would be down in the quarry, no danger to them, and Robin didn't believe in the Campbell Women, so if she got to him they would disappear. She tore past the croquet lawn and into the side door, and bolted it ; she heard their fingers scrabble behind the panels. Robin ? Not in his study, not in the dining-room, not in their bedroom. She daren't yell. Or would it be better ? Failing Robin, Gladys or the cook. Down the back stairs, kitchen, scullery, no one. Any minute they might come in, gliding stiffly. She was in the dining-room ; she glanced up at the mirror over the mantelpiece ; in it she saw Gladys clearing the table. But the table had nothing on it. It was just a table, empty, like a sketch for a table. Then she heard them coming into the house, the hollow slam of the front door. She took the stairs again, three at a time, she was in her own bedroom ; surely, surely, there she must be safe. For reassurance, she picked up her hair-brush that was moulting ; there was still that little smear of face-cream on the dressing-table. Then she noticed in the dressing-table mirror that Robin was still in bed ; he turned over in bed, he looked at the dressing-table, he didn't see her, she couldn't meet his eyes in the mirror. And when she turned the bed was empty, flat, the sheets coldly folded, a sketch for a bed. It became immediately clear that all this was not really her house, but its mirror image. She was stuck behind the mirror, in the image, as also no doubt inside herself. The Campbell Women came up the stairs, with stiff, waxen smiles, into Phœbe's room, smiling that they had caught her. She was standing by the dressing-table in the window bay opposite the door. She jumped out of the window ; it was the only thing to be done.

Even when she was falling she said to herself: people who jump out of windows get into the Debatable Land. The land between here and fairyland. I must look out for trouble. She ran between bushes of fading wild laurel ; the stems had been cut through, *les lauriers sont coupés*. She saw between them the gules lion asleep, lying on a thistle bed, and Saint Finnigal asleep, standing, with her eyes open but blank. For a time she swam in a sea full of seals, coughing at her with musty breath, the smell of the seal islands off Jura. The seals asked her questions, mocked at her for never having waked the lion, never having tied by the leg the Talking Crow, never having held Basileia so tight that they had become one for ever, and for ever lived on high among the shining names of Cloud Cuckoo Borough. Women, said the seals, can't catch Basileia ; she needs a man to marry her. No women in Cloud Cuckoo Borough, only shadows, only wives, only the shadow-nightingale for King Hoopoe ! No, no, said Phœbe, battling with the bobbing heads of seals, there is Sappho. Sappho, said the seals, oh, Sappho lost Phil and jumped over a cliff into the Debatable Land. Cleopatra lost Phil and went the asp's way into the Debatable Land. Joan of Arc was a witch, and when her time came she had to go to the Debatable Land, too. Elizabeth of England, she lost Phil, she lost all her Phils. Oh no ; oh no, Phœbe Bathurst, said the coughing jumping seals, you will never get to Cloud Cuckoo Borough. There are moderns, said Phœbe, desperately splashing, trying to keep the seals arguing, for so long as there were seals the kelpies might not come. In my own job ! said Phœbe, crying against the seals, painters, sculptors, writers, musicians, historians, scientists, Madame Curie, Selma Lagerlof, that Kollontai woman—oh, who did Tom tell me, Rosa Luxemburg, Maria Spiridonova shot in red November! Seals, seals, stop laughing, there is Greta Garbo and Anna May Wong. Anna May Wong dived down among the seals with her black sleek seal head; did she want to go to Cloud Cuckoo Borough? No way of asking her; no common language.

The seals dived away from her, streakily, sleekly, a humping of shoulders and flipping of seal tails, salt seal-smelling water splashed over Phœbe, blinding her, and oh, oh, the arms of the kelpies feeling up for her through deep water, hooking on to her ankles! Oh, close the shore, the dark, weed-hung rocks of Jura, and on shore, smiling, waiting for her, the Campbell Women.

Now for a year, for two years, for how long she did not know, but if there had been a mirror she would have seen not only a few but every hair on her head turned white, she had been imprisoned in the Tower. She and Green Jean were together imprisoned in the Tower, but so complex were its windings that never had they been able to come at one another, to stand together against their gaolers. The Campbell Women came up the Tower; they swarmed up the Tower from the ground, their faces whitish in the dusk, getting bigger and bigger as they came nearer. They came squeezing in through the slot windows; they touched her. She could not remember the touch, only the moment before. That recurred again and again for seven years, for seven times seven years. If she had some weapon she could keep them away from her. A pencil for a sword and a drawing-book for a shield. It was no good; she had left them behind on the desk in the workroom. Gibbings had found someone else to do her work. What did it matter? There are plenty of wood-engravers, plenty as good as she. The children had forgotten her. The children were grown up. If they passed by under the Tower she would not know them.

At the gates of the Debatable Land lists were put up by those persons whose duty it was, showing the names and whereabouts of those who were to be rescued. Pussy came riding by in armour and planned to rescue her by poisoning the Campbell Women. He did not know that the Campbell Women could not be poisoned. It was very awkward; Cynthia came and warned Pussy that they had drunk the poison and were after him. Pussy rode away very quickly; he did not even turn and wave to her.

Phil came riding by in armour; he had a clever plan to rescue Phœbe; he was going to dig a passage right under the root of minus one and come out into the middle of the Tower. He had made such a long equation that it would turn into a ladder and she could creep down on it. But he dug and dug, and there was no way under the root. He called to her what to do; she was to make a vacuum in a tube and put a current through it; she was to creep in at the cathode point and be whirled through with the electrons to the anode; he would be there to catch her at the end. But, she cried down to him, I have no glass tubes, no mercury, no wire, no batteries; oh Phil, don't you understand, a woman never has the materials for doing anything important! But he didn't understand that, he couldn't hear, and then it was night, and in the morning he was gone.

If you looked up through the slot-window there was nothing but grey sky, no sign of a crow flying, and if you looked down there was only the forest floor far below and a movement among the cut laurels that might have been kelpies. Then a long way off there was something coming across, slowly towards her. She knew what it was; it was a plow tractor making a furrow through the forest, a furrow for sowing fern seed. Dione was driving the tractor, Dione with her hair flying behind her; of course, she hadn't put it up yet, wasn't going to for another three years. But it was 1914 already, so what was the use anyhow? Dione was driving the tractor, but would she notice Phœbe in the dark Tower? Was she not too intent on her furrow, on Tom, on Marshbrook Bridge? No, no, because this was before Tom and before Marshbrook Bridge, though already the houses in Carisbrook Road, waiting also to be rescued, had been flooded twenty-four times in successive winters, since the year of their building.

Dione looked up and waved her hand and turned the tractor towards the Tower. Look out, yelled Phœbe at her, look out, the Campbell Women are coming! But Dione didn't mind; they couldn't get past the iron plowshares, the steel pistons of the tractor. Dione turned the tractor on to the Tower, and crash and smash went the sides of the Tower, splitting neatly in two as the furrow went through it, and Phœbe fell into the seat of the tractor beside her sister, and behind them the furrow opened and parted like a wave.

Dione rescued Phœbe on the tractor and they got past the seals' loch and the place where the gules lion and Saint Finnigal were still asleep, and they came to the assembly of the Birds, and Phœbe began to state her case. Then the King Hoopoe was brave, his crest feathers rose like flame, his barred wings double-flashed, he said that he would protect Phœbe Bathurst from the Campbell Women. And the Nightingale was kind, she was his Queen, she welcomed Phœbe: her other name was not May. Phœbe loved the Nightingale; she and King Hoopoe and Queen Nightingale danced through the water-meadows, and along the Cher under golden falling dancing willow leaves; they danced into Summer Island, and everything was going to be all right for ever and ever.

And then what happened? Then into the august and lovely assembly of the Birds came the humping, hunching Elephant, and his little pig-eyes glowed and he reached out his trunk and seized upon one or another of the Birds and wrung its neck. The thick, slug-coloured Elephant scattered to destruction the bright feathers of the Birds, trampled on them, trumpeted hugely! The brave Birds tried to protest, they made speeches to the Elephant, they gave him books to read. But what was the use of that? The Elephant destroyed the Birds, leaving nothing behind him but plucked, bleeding bodies. The Elephant raised his trunk against Phœbe. And again Phœbe fled from him. And again she ran and ran until she came to a river. The river flowed swift and silent, swifter than the Cher in flood time, than ebb tide down the Thames, swift and twisted like the currents between the islands, past Jura, past Islay and Colonsay and the Outer Islands; the river was going over a fall, the water swept to the fall as the salt water sweeps past Jura to Corryvrechan. The Elephant was behind Phœbe, reaching out for her. Moored to the bank was Gerda's boat; Phœbe jumped into it, she loosed the tow-rope—who but she, who had drawn it, knew the knot it was tied in?—she cast off, out of reach of the Elephant. In Gerda's boat, her knuckles white on the thwarts as Gerda's had been, Phœbe went over the falls.

It was nearly one o'clock and in a moment she would have to go in to lunch. She had a headache from her eyes to the base of her skull, perhaps she ought to wear spectacles; she hated the idea of that, it was like white hairs. But how could she work when she got headaches like this? She'd done so little that morning, and now she was tired out as though she'd run for miles. Why? She'd been worrying about these blocks, and, after all, the dreadful thing was they weren't so very important. It didn't really matter whether Hans Andersen had a fresh set of illustrations or not. These books were only being made because a few rich people had thought of a new way of spending their money.

It was an unsatisfactory business being an artist on one's own, trying to work out problems and patterns, engaged with this matter of technique, which was so interesting and yet so little thirst-quenching. As pants the heart for cooling springs. But where were the springs, what were the springs? Would it be better to be working in London or Paris or some other place where there was a group of artists, where they would be kind to one another, where there was sure always to be at least one in the full current of creation, able to give a sense of worth-while-ness to the others? She'd never be able to do that, though. She was a married woman. Robin would never be happy living in a town. Besides, Helm did pay more or less. Rather less than more, but still it provided them with a home and plenty of fresh air and lovely country for the children, their own butter and eggs and milk and vegetables. Suppose they lived in a town and she were working full time, encouraged by other painters, would she ever earn enough to make up for Helm? Probably not, as things looked now, with all the prospective buyers economising, especially on things like pictures! Anyway, it was no good thinking of that: Robin wouldn't like it. Robin wanted to feel he was head of the family, and he could do it here, on the land. Poor darling, wasn't that the least she could do for him, after the war, after all his pains?

But still—oh, she was bored with Kay and Gerda! It wasn't really interesting. It wouldn't last, wouldn't say anything to other people in a hundred years, as Goya's elephant said things. That Elephant. What had she been thinking about that Elephant just now? She couldn't remember. She would remember some time. There was Clemency coming down the path towards her. Lunch time. A morning. Three hours. A hundred and eighty minutes. A perceptible fragment ot a year, of a lifetime, and nothing done. She struck her pencil across the smudged drawing and turned over the page of her drawing-book, ready for the next try-out. Perhaps this wasn't quite wasted, perhaps she would get some ideas from it for her next. At least it was something to know when she had got it wrong.

## SALLINGTON 6

In Oxford on May morning, dons and their young or middle-aged wives, undergraduates of all sexes, and American tourists, mostly female, climb up Magdalen tower and pack into the square top of it, while choir boys sing a Latin hymn. Those who are near the sides can feel the Cotswold stone vibrating and crumbling a little from the hard pealing of the May bells, and the tower itself swings perceptibly against a pale blue, or commonly rather cloudy sky. Below in the High there is Morris dancing. Then all adjourn to large breakfasts and tend to be cross during the rest of the morning unless they go to sleep again.

In Moscow and in all cities of the Union of Soviet Republics on May Day there are great processions, banners and flowers, and everywhere, carried by the marchers or set out in the streets and squares, the heart-stirring triumph and splendour of the workers and peasants made solid by painters and sculptors of the State, who do for Red May Day, fresh and fresh every year, what Pheidias did once and for all for the State procession of Athens. There are songs and speeches, and marching by the Red Army. Men, women and children are all in it, all out for their own May Day that they made with their own revolution.

In Paris and Berlin and London, and presumably also New York and Tokio, as well as most other capital cities of the non-Socialist world, there are also May Day processions and demonstrations by the workers ; these are made partly by the Communist Party members and their sympathisers, and partly by other branches of organised labour. The demonstrators are usually angry and underfed, their banners home-made and only fairly impressive. Usually there is some conflict with the police or other State forces; occasionally people are killed. But it is quite possible, and indeed usual, for the great mass of inhabitants of these cities to ignore such doings altogether; this can easily be done, as the demonstrations only take place in a limited number of streets, parks, etc., in the central areas. Joyce Ward, for instance, was completely unaware of its being May Day, even though she happened to be in town for that particular week-end. And Pussy only knew because an acquaintance of his, a painter who called himself a Communist, perhaps because he liked wearing a red shirt, had taken the opportunity of toasting the revolution and getting very drunk.

In the English countryside, in general, little happens on May Day now, unless there has been some kind of revival of whatever those interested in such things and able to pay for them consider to have been the local customs. Presumably a certain amount also happens, about which the upper and middle classes and the town proletariat know nothing. But it was May Eve, not May Day, which used to be the important time. It was on May Eve that Jean MacLean went with her coven to the Sabbat.

In 1932 May Day fell on a Sunday, which was very convenient. Dione helped Mrs. Taylor to lay the table for breakfast. She was beginning to know Mrs. Taylor a little, not only as a Labour woman, but as a person. It wasn't anything she could count on yet, but perhaps it was the beginning of something. Tom and Mr. Taylor both came down rather later, when the tea was on the table. Tom was distressed and rather embarrassed because Mr. Taylor had taken his shoes away and cleaned them for him. But that didn't bother Bert Taylor; he was used to doing his own—why not a second pair?

The Taylors were cheerful about its being May Day; they had helped to arrange the tableaux for the procession; Emmie in her oldest frock was going to be a starving child in the one about the Means Test. As it was Sunday there was no *Herald*. Many Labour households took *Reynolds*, the Co-op. paper, but in Sallington many of them took the *Sallington Sunday Press*, Daniel Coke-Brown's other local success. Certainly it had all the news of Sallington; it could usually be trusted to find a Sallington mystery of some kind, in which blood, or sex, or both were involved—something to make you exclaim with delighted horror, for, if it wasn't actually in the street next yours, at any rate you'd seen trams which went just along there! It had plenty of photos too, a lot of general news under good splashy headlines, pages for women and children and movie fans, a crossword—which always delighted the Taylors—a serial, and always one political article, which was generally supposed to be written by Daniel Coke-Brown himself. Labour and good Liberals could avoid reading it, but, of course, the whole paper was propagandist; it couldn't help being.

Mr. Taylor handed the *Sallington Sunday Press* to Tom, who grunted with anger, reading its account of the Japanese attack on China. "But surely the League will do something!" Dione said; she had been a very keen member of the League of Nations Union in its early years.

"It's not a League of Nations," said Tom; "it's a League of Coke-Browns!"

"We did hope so much of it at first," said Mrs. Taylor. "I feel—oh, like it was my own boy gone wrong."

"You know," said Tom, "I met this chap once at my sister's; he's a first-cousin of her husband."

"Very awkward for you, Mr. Galton!" said Taylor, grinning a little.

" The worst of it is," said Tom, " that he's the sort of chap half Sallington would like to be themselves."

" He gave the land for the Upper Park—where the procession's going to-day," said Mrs. Taylor meditatively.

" He can afford it," said Tom. And then : " You've got to weigh up the physical good that park does—and Sallington ought to be able to take and make its own parks for its own citizens instead of waiting with its cap in its hand to get them given it !—against the mental harm that's done by these papers of his. The balance would be against him, Mrs. Taylor; the judge would put on his black cap."

" No, Mr. Galton, don't say that ! " said Mrs. Taylor. " I can't bear the thought of capital punishment, you've no idea the petitions we've signed, Taylor and I have ! He was a C.O. in the war, you know; he was two years in prison. We wouldn't shed human blood, not even Daniel Coke-Brown's."

" You won't have the chance," said Tom; " he'll die in his bed with all the specialists in England making money out of him."

" I'd sooner be shot than die of most diseases; wouldn't you, Mrs. Taylor ? " Dione said.

" No, I wouldn't," said Mrs. Taylor firmly; " I like things done the proper way. Now, Mrs. Galton, you stay where you are. I can do my own washing-up. Well—you can put the things in the larder if you like. There now, if it isn't clouding over and my Emmie to go in her old cotton with her stockings all in holes ! "

The four of them and Emmie took the tram from River Ward down the Sall and past the turning by the Art Gallery to the old Market Square, where the procession was to form up. On the way Tom and Taylor talked local politics, in which the tram conductor occasionally joined, between taking fares; he was pleased at having the candidate in his tram! A good deal of Tom's work at Marshbrook Bridge was smoothing out and disentangling quarrels and misunderstandings. Sometimes they were real enough—there were difficult people in the movement, men who liked nothing but the sound of their own voices, women who took offence if a committee started without them. But half of it was due to people being tired and in a hurry and having indigestion. Leisured people, eating good food and getting enough sleep and not being worried about money for meals and rent and the children's boots, would not have quarrelled; they would have tried to understand one another. Good food was only a very recent thing, thought Tom. For millions of years man has eaten what he could scrape together and taken the consequences. The Greeks had leisure and sleep, but their literature is full of reference to violent purgatives. Merry England in the Middle Ages lived half the year on salt meat, salt fish, hardly any fruit or vegetables and little enough sweetening. Porridge in Scotland probably killed off all but those with a well-adapted alimentary canal. Yes, he thought, it's only for about a generation that we've interfered with the survival of only the digestively fittest.

They came to the Market Square; in the middle was the old market cross, tastefully decorated with iron railings and in any case usually half hidden by trams, as it was a main tram stop. In front of it a statue of Queen Victoria marched forward to victory. The contingents from the Divisional Labour Parties were forming up under amiable police supervision. The Sallington Party agent was there in his bowler, and John Collis. The Barstone Labour candidate had brought his little boy. Some of the Marshbrook Bridge people were there already, and more were getting out of each of the west-side trams. Tom and Dione were shaking hands, talking to one friend after another, all cheerful and most wearing their Party badges or ribbons. The great Co-op. lorries were drawn up at the opposite side from the trams, the horses proud-necked and glossy, their tails and manes plaited by their drivers with the red and green ribbons. Most of the lorries were to have scenes on them —propaganda tableaux of some kind, protests against armaments, against the Means Test, against tariff walls, release the Class War prisoners, Hands off Russia, or emblems of Labour solidarity. Several of them had speakers; one had children dressed in green and red paper that firmly showed winter woollies underneath, and carrying Woolworth garlands of poppies and roses. Two of them had choirs. There were cheery men with collecting boxes either in their hands or on poles to reach the windows. There were banners of the Divisional and Ward Labour Parties, as well as Trade Union and Co-op. banners, some new, with up-to-date slogans in scarlet, but others venerable, with Victorian mottoes and honest, virtuous Victorian working men painted or embroidered on them, and great gold and crimson tassels like the ones belonging to the best bedroom curtains at Auchanarnish.

Looking round at them, Dione suddenly saw a small high banner, plain red with the black hammer and sickle on it, and then a cut-out cardboard hammer and sickle on the end of a pole; she began to edge towards them; there was another twenty minutes before they needed to start. She evaded Mrs. East for the moment, smiled and waved to Edna Boffin, and came to the edge of the Communist Group. She felt very friendly, but they looked without favour at her red and green ribbons. For a moment she thought of pulling her coat across them, then shook the thought off, angry with herself. She caught the eye of a woman about her own age, in a coat and skirt, but the woman was busy with one of the banners. Then she saw Harry, the leader of the Unemployed Committee. "Hullo," she said, shaking hands, "how are you? Had any luck lately?"

"Just an odd week, Mrs. Galton. It don't look like my getting a steady job this side kingdom come!"

"Have you definitely joined—here?" She slanted her head towards the Communist banner.

"Not as you might say joined," said Harry, "but my pals are there mostly. I told young Mac I'd come and give him a hand."

"He's here, I suppose?"

"Yes. He got arrested last week. But they only give him three days and a telling-off by the magistrate as if he was a kid."

"I didn't know. What for?"

"Saying what he thought of Coke-Brown."

"Which Coke-Brown?"

"The *Sallington News*. Him. He was saying what he thought of our lot in his dirty paper, and he gets paid for it, and then when young Mac gives him a bit of what-for back, they goes and arrests him!"

"How rotten. It is a disgusting paper. Tom was talking about it this morning."

"Ah! Talk!" said Harry.

Dione thought he didn't seem as friendly as he had been at the election. Or perhaps it wasn't that. He spoke and looked friendlily enough to her, but he had a good deal of hope still then, and he had very little now. Or, at least, not in the Labour Party. She shook hands with him again and went on through the crowd to where she saw Donald MacLean. She wasn't going to mind if they did glare at her ribbon from hard, serious faces, different from most of the cheerful Labour ones.

"Good-morning," she said, "I'm so sorry to hear you've been arrested. I do hope they didn't give you a bad time."

" I was more fortunate than most," said Donald MacLean; " the magistrate talked to me as though I were a fool, but he gave me a light sentence indeed. I was fearing I would be missing May Day."

" Who was the magistrate ? "

" Och, old Bridie."

" Another Scot ! "

" That was not in consideration ! " said Donald MacLean angrily. Then he smiled a little : " Still on the nationalism, Mistress Galton ! "

" But you weren't hurt ? " Dione said.

Donald MacLean regarded her : " You will never have been arrested, I'm thinking ? Nor arrested as a Communist agitator. Well, I'll be after showing you." He pulled his sleeve up—the coat sleeve was loose on his arm and there was no button on his shirt-cuff. Both his arms were bruised purple in patches between wrist and elbow.

" Oh, Donald ! " Dione said, and took his right hand quickly in both of hers ; she felt all jolted by this on May Day, but knew she ought to be jolted. " Was that the police ? " she asked.

" Mhm. But that is nothing at all in the Party. Soon they will be doing far worse to us."

" How do you mean—soon ? "

" When the proletariat of England and Scotland find out the truth about your Party, as they must and will with the growth of class-consciousness. Then they will turn to us. Then the time will come for us to take action. Then it will be for us here the way it is for our comrades in America. Prison and shooting and beating-up. Machine-guns in the streets of Sallington."

" I wonder," Dione said. " Well, I must be getting back to my own Party ! In the meantime, if we can ever do anything to help you—bail you out, for instance—do let us know."

"I doubt your Party would not like that, Mistress Galton," said Donald MacLean, "a Labour candidate's wife bailing out a common Communist!" But he was friendly enough as he said it.

"Nonsense!" Dione said, "Tom and I don't let *that* Elephant bully us!"

"Ach, you and your beasties! You'll be seeing kelpies next."

"But he *is* a kind of kelpy," Dione answered, half seriously, and then: "Anyway, I'm glad we'll both be in the same procession to-day."

Donald MacLean put an arm round her shoulder and smacked her gently on the back: "You get running along now or they'll be after you! Maybe I'll see you again in the park."

She disengaged herself from the Communist group and went back to her own. It had surprised her rather, Donald MacLean touching her that way. Of course, in the Labour Movement she was always being touched, her hand squeezed between eager hands, or arms round her shoulders like this; it meant—brotherhood. Did Donald MacLean feel that, too? It was nice if he did.

"Why, you weren't ever talking to those Communists, were you?" said Mrs. East. "I shouldn't if I were you, Mrs. Galton; you stick with us."

"Oh, it's all right, Mrs. East," Dione said, "not a serious Left deviation, but an old friend. You've got a new hat, haven't you?"

"There!" said Mrs. East, "if you aren't the first that's noticed it! It's my last summer's made over by my sister. D'you like the buckle, Mrs. Galton?"

The Marshbrook Bridge contingent were lined up, four

deep, and by and bye, and jerkily, the May-Day procession started. From the Market Square they turned south and then east, making a circuit of some of the poorest parts, the Smedbrook division, where a Labour man had sat during the last parliament, and through a corner of Sallmouth. These were grimmish streets, narrow and dirty-looking, with small shops and sometimes tram-lines. Between blocks, up narrow, paved passages, Dione caught sight of a nasty tangle of back-to-backs, indefinitely pressed in behind the comparative respectability of the real streets. They crossed under the railway bridge that carried the main London line, and heard somewhere near hootings and shuntings and busyness. At each side of them, as they walked, there was a small crowd, standing along the edge of the pavement three or four deep, mostly sympathetic or faintly mocking, men without collars and women with black shawls who put sparse pennies into the collection boxes. Others leaned out of the windows; at corners there were a few more; they would walk with the procession for a few minutes, attracted by some speaker or some decorated lorry, and then fall back. Hardly one of the children was up to the physical standard of a North Oxford child; almost all the adults had bad teeth, a practically inevitable result of pregnancy for the women; their skins were dirt-filmed like the Sall water; the damp weather brought out the sour, choking crowd smell. They called out to friends in the procession and laughed a lot whenever there was anything to laugh at. The procession sang spasmodically and in bits; each division had its favourite songs, but the "Red Flag," "England Arise" and "Jerusalem" re-occurred regularly. Dione remembered suddenly Muriel telling her how "Jerusalem" had first been set to music for the women in old suffrage days. Now it had passed on.

One bit of the procession never knew what was happening behind or in front of it; sometimes it straggled, but then, when it was held up at a crossing, the ranks would close again. Dione had no idea where the Communist group was. She told Tom, who was walking bareheaded beside her, about Donald MacLean's arrest.

"Well," said Tom, "so long as you don't go and join the I.L.P.——!" And then: "About Donald MacLean, he'll probably get into serious trouble some time. The police are on the look-out now. Naturally, I'll do what I can, but he won't say thank you to either of us!"

From Sallmouth the procession turned west up the main road again, keeping to the southern river bank between wharfs and warehouses; it was tiring to walk on the cobbles. For a time she carried one pole of Edna Boffin's banner; rain was coming now, gustily, her hands slipped on the banner pole; Tom's hair was curly with the wet. Here there were fewer people watching them. Then they came to the tram fork and the main bridge over the Sall, and turned across it. This was fine, marching above the sticky river and the barges trailing slackly on the current. Here one was aware of the sea; the Sall was faintly tidal, so that sometimes the floating cabbage leaves and sticks turned up-stream instead of down.

Their feet echoed on the bridge, out of step; at the far side they went past some larger shops; here there was some hostility among the onlookers, people deliberately turning away with a disgusted look; once or twice it even sounded as though there was being a disturbance of some kind in some other part of the procession. At one corner they passed a large modern concrete building, refreshingly simple after most of the Sallington edifices. "What is it?" Dione asked over her shoulder of Mrs. East, who was walking just behind her.

" That's the new skating rink," said Mrs. East, and Dione was a little startled ; she connected skating so much with the other life, so little with Sallington. Then they turned up, through three or four sloping residential streets, where women looked out at them from between lace curtains and beyond privet hedges ; a few larger houses showed nobody at all. So they came to the gate of the Upper Park and marched in, all singing the " Red Flag " and trying to forget it was raining. The procession wobbled about rather confusedly, before each contingent could manage to find its pitch. Tom had been told to report at platform 8, a Co-op. lorry backed by banners, and here, in increasingly heavy rain, he told a patient-looking crowd of umbrellas and macintoshes about what May Day might mean to them yet. It occurred to Dione, as she tried to hold still a flapping, dripping banner, that any political party which could guarantee sunshine in England for even eight months in the year would deserve to get everyone's votes !

Gradually people drifted away from the park ; there was no climax. The patient Co-op. horses were reharnessed and moved off with the lorries. Tom and Dione began to walk back towards the gate ; there was a good view at one point, down across Sallington and over Sallmouth way. Just now it all looked incredibly colourless and lifeless and unattractive. Why go on bothering about it ?

Near the gate they met the Communist demonstration, still going on. *They* hadn't got to bother about it, thought Tom, because they were part of it ; they had no choice. At least it was simpler for them. Donald MacLean was speaking when they came up ; they stayed and listened to him. A few of the audience were obviously put off by his accent, though it seemed clear and pleasant to Tom and Dione ; he spoke with the fluency and pattern of a Highlander, using very few words that were in any way strange, though sometimes the turn of a phrase was as annoying for most of the audience as it was pleasing for Dione. Occasionally he would use definitely Biblical phraseology; it fitted in rather well. He was talking fairly simple correct revolutionary propaganda, with little (though what there was contemptuous) reference to the Labour Party, and that rather obscured by his always calling them the social democrats. The rain was against him, but he made a fine peroration. Tom clapped him; it seemed a simple matter of courtesy; they had been in the same procession. Then he and Dione moved off, back to their own side of the river and a change of shoes and stockings, and tea at the Taylors'.

The Communist meeting, too, gradually broke up from formal or semi-formal speech-making into talk. They also discussed Daniel Coke-Brown. The *Sallington News* had commented pretty unpleasantly about Donald's arrest, omitting all their evidence and putting the police evidence in full with cross-headings; deliberately, it seemed, trying to provoke them. It was not the first time.

"We cannot do anything yet," said Agnes Green, competently folding up a strip of red bunting, "the Party could not possibly countenance it."

"Do you suggest we act as individuals, Comrade Green," Donald said, "or—that we do not act at all?"

"There have been definite instructions to the contrary," she said, "you know that as well as I do."

"I tell you they have no idea of the local situation!"

"The time is not ripe," Agnes Green said. She thought he looked terribly tired; probably he hadn't had enough to eat for days; she knew that look; she was beginning to see it on the faces of some of her school classes now. She went on: "I must leave it to your sense of what is best from the standpoint of the world revolution, but we could not possibly recognise your action in any way. I do not in any case see how you could do anything useful, Comrade MacLean. We have to think first of the Party."

"If the Party were less averse from action——"

"What do you think the Party is, young Mac—a bloody dog-race?" said another voice. "You Clydesiders want something going on the whole bloody time—round and round and round, chasing a . . . rabbit into the . . . hole every time!"

"Aye," said Donald MacLean, "but you . . .s down here have lost all touch with action!"

"Now, comrades," said Agnes Green, "there's nothing to be gained by swearing. Not that *I* mind. But it's all of a piece with criticism of Headquarters. We don't know what they've got to put up with. I've been a schoolmistress long enough to know that! We all sympathise with how Comrade MacLean feels about the Coke-Brown paper, but we cannot support his suggestions about the action which he thinks should be taken. No, Comrade Pritchard, let me take the banner; I can dry it in my room so that it doesn't run."

Idris Pritchard, the curly-haired, brown-eyed Welshman, tied a piece of string round the banner and gave it to her. He had a jaunty way of moving, and when his hand met hers over the red wet cotton bundle, Agnes Green felt a little uncomfortable; she didn't quite know why. Donald was talking to the ex-Service man; he shook his head impatiently, arrogantly, hardly able to let the other man finish his sentences. Agnes Green turned to them quickly and asked them both back to tea; she was determined not to ask Idris Pritchard, though she half wanted to. Donald and his friend accepted; they liked talking to her; they liked her cosy room with the books and bulb bowls and photographs of other women. They walked back, all three discussing Communist Party matters, and relationships with the U.S.S.R.

"Who was that Labour Party woman you were talking to?" Agnes Green asked.

"That was Mrs. Galton," said Donald, smiling a little.

"What—the Marshbrook Bridge bloke's wife?" said his friend. "What does she want to come sucking up to us for?"

Donald shrugged his shoulders, and Agnes Green said abruptly: "If she comes again, I should like to talk to her. Perhaps if one put the facts before her——"

"What the hell good is that?" said the other man, "she's not our class."

While they argued about it, and then about other matters, Donald moved on ahead of them impatiently. Every hour now it was being borne in upon him that he would be compelled to act as an individual if the Comintern could not see that these newspapers must be dealt with. These newspapers that Daniel Coke-Brown and his like sold on their betting and football news! He shivered suddenly, remembering yesterday afternoon, just through with the cold quiet of prison, and he trying to sell *Daily Workers* to the football crowd beyond at Greenapple. They'd looked at him—ach, a set of dirty English toughs! He'd been near being beaten up again, sharpened nerve-tight to stand it. He'd known a couple of lads been handled that way up in Newcastle; he'd seen them stripped afterwards. Ach!

That was the thing Daniel Coke-Brown did with his newspapers, and yet that had within it the seeds of its own downfall—aye, it was proved right by the dialectic! —by its own weapons of violence. Weapons. And he thought again of that thing in his friend, Adam Walker's room, and would the chemical stuff in it have kept right these fourteen years? . . . And then there would be the trial and him speaking . . . and then, then there'd be an end of Sallington and the dirt and the cold and the ugliness and the English voices, and passing by the warm lighted bars and movie-houses, evenings, and hating the women who stood there, ready to sell theirselves and be sossed about by any man for a bit silver. Aye, there'd be an end of all this scheming to live, waiting for the revolution, ever held back from taking action.

But then, what would come to the Sallington Party? Agnes Green, Pritchard, wee Ginger, Doris from London, Hart, the lads from the docks, the mill girls, all the comrades. Known to the police. But he would say at the trial that it was his own individual protest! One man would die for the Party, as it had always been. It was not the Party would suffer. Surely, surely he would make that clear in his grand speech at the trial . . . and then . . . aye, there would be action taken in Sallington once and for all!

SUMMER term continued. Again it was magic for a generation of undergraduates. Again the drifting May blossom on Cher water provoked romance. Tom found himself called upon to stand between the college authorities and two of his pupils. Silly young fools, he thought, if once they start being martyred, that'll fix them for life. He lectured them on the fact that there are other things in the world besides the fulfilment of the individual impulse, however essential it may seem. They listened dutifully, but they were in the individualistic stage. They determined not to be caught next time.

Young Hawkes fell suddenly for a Cowley Road girl, and, failing other means—he was in many ways a very innocent young man, having come from a good house at Winchester—proposed marrying her. "Father won't like it," he said gallantly, "but I must. This'll get me out of my class boundaries, Mr. Galton!"

"Nonsense," said Tom, who knew the girl of old, "Beattie Newall's not class-conscious; she wouldn't help you a bit, and she'd be quite determined to get into your class."

Hawkes then went on to talk Lawrence, not noticing that his tutor was getting more and more restive.

At last, at a pause, Tom said: "I'm sorry, but I'm fed to the teeth with Lawrence. He was impressive enough when one first got hold of him, and his books are all right still, but so many idiots have made him an excuse for doing anything in the sex line that they want to do, preferably so as to hurt other people, that I'm sick and tired of it! Lawrence was all for people marrying, but are you and Beattie Newall going to be the right sort of couple? You've read your 'Fantasia of the Unconscious,' I take it? All nonsense and about three-quarters true. Well, now, is Beattie going to look up to you as the working male—the man she's going to respect and follow for ever?" Tom suddenly noticed that his pupil was wincing at the unrespectful way he was referring, out of old habit, to the lady in question, and decided at once to be formal; he went on: "Lawrence says himself that's only possible when the man knows exactly what his job with life is. You don't. You've just told me that what you want Miss Newall for is to get you out of your class—for her to be the leader. Is that Lawrence doctrine?"

"Yes, but the whole relationship between man and woman——"

"Look here, I take it you know that Miss Newall has had plenty of relationships, as you call them, with men?"

"Yes," said Hawkes nervously, "I—I understood so. But that doesn't affect my opinion of her!"

"If you mean that you don't regard her with moral disapproval—well, I should hope not. But, don't you think it may affect her opinion of you? I take it you've lived a pretty virtuous life?"

"Well—yes."

"I'm all in favour of that in reason. But it warps one's judgment on matters of sex. Couldn't you manage to sleep with Miss Newall once or twice before bringing up the question of marriage again? My dear chap, don't take offence, there's nothing wrong with the suggestion."

"Well—well, did *you* sleep with your wife before you married her?"

"No, but of course I ought to have. As a matter of

fact she wanted me to—women usually have more sense about these things than men, that's to say if they have any sense at all—but I was too damned romantic. Anyway, there was the war on and little enough opportunity. Even in the last year one could get leave for an official marriage, but not for an unofficial one. Anyhow, think over what you mean to do about Miss Newall. Shall I lend you a volume of Havelock Ellis ? "

Everyone in Oxford had a party during summer term, to kill off friends, acquaintances, colleagues and pupils ; garden parties were cheap and, if it was fine, satisfactory. There was something very English about the men of all ages in light suits and elegant flannels, the women in art cretonnes and washing silks or even more sophisticated materials, and the children wolfing ices. The Bickerdens received the Galtons' invitation for their garden party.

" How odd to have it just before they start for Russia ! " said May, " but that's just like dear Dione ; she *is* a little odd. You know she hasn't been to the Bach choir at all since Tom took up that constituency of his. I expect he works her too hard. Don't you think so, Phil ? "

Phil looked up from the *Proceedings of the London Mathematical Society* which he was reading a little inattentively, with a view rather to disagreement than to acquiring knowledge. " No, I don't," he said ; " she likes politics for some reason. I suppose she's bored with the Bach choir. Sensible woman to chuck it if she is."

" One ought to persevere with music, I always think."

" Probably. Are you going to their party ? "

" Well, just as you like. It's the same day as the All Souls evening At Home to meet Professor Einstein——"

" Old tease," said Phil, sitting up suddenly. " I should think you might as well go to their party and I might look in. See how work goes."

"How is it going, dear?"

"Oh, so-so." He dived into his *Proceedings* again.

May thought rapidly. Could Phœbe Bathurst be going to be there? Surely dear Dione wouldn't have——? Or would she? People who go to Russia might—— In any case, she had nothing to be afraid of. Even if Phil met and talked to Phœbe Bathurst. Indeed, why not? May prided herself upon being a modern woman. She really had nothing against Mrs. Bathurst—nothing—only was it quite fair on poor Mr. Bathurst, who had never quite recovered from the Great War? People said that Phœbe Bathurst went and stayed in London with other painters—men painters. That was all very well in London and in artistic circles; besides, there might really be nothing wrong, only—no, the woman hadn't been good for Phil! He hadn't been happy; she remembered how she'd first met him when the affair was still going on, and he was all nervy, not eating as much as a man should and working much too hard. At any rate she, May, had made him happy, she'd always known she could make someone happy; and she'd stopped him working so hard—taking him for little runs in the car—Baby's playtime—and she was sure he'd get the Professorship in another ten years. Yes, it would be quite safe, in any case, to go to the Galtons' party.

The children were looking forward to the party; it was fun for them having Aunt Phœbe and Aunt Muriel and Uncle Alex all staying in the house. Uncle Alex had a camp-bed in the barn; Morag brought him guinea-pigs to look at while he was shaving. He and mother had all their things packed for Russia, and after they were gone Aunt Muriel would come and stay on and off—anyhow, week-ends—till the end of term, when they would go up to Auchanarnish. They looked forward to Auchanarnish, too; George and Elizabeth weren't coming this time.

Rosalind had written to Tom about it, explaining that as things were she preferred not to let the children go to Scotland this year. Tom had rung her up one week-end when he had been staying at Marshbrook Bridge, and they had met for tea at the large Fuller's in the Square. Rosalind had asked him if he couldn't take another constituency, and he had said he was damned if he would, and went on to ask her whether she had taken up the complete Coke-Brown position.

"I'm not *interested* in politics," Rosalind insisted; "I'm interested in all kinds of things you don't understand, Tom."

"Deep-breathing exercises," said Tom unkindly; it had been Yoga last time.

"I've got beyond you," said Rosalind, "that's how I know they're so unimportant, all the things that happen on this plane. You don't ever get off the earth, Tom; if you did, you'd understand how trivial it all seems from—the Other Place."

"Well," said Tom, "I wish you'd induce Reginald and his relatives to be a bit more other-planey. But so long as they insist on profits-on-earth, you can't expect the rest of us to do the goodwill-in-heaven stunt."

"I'm sure Reginald will see *in time*," Rosalind said, trying not to be angry, for that is so bad for one's aura. "He reads some of my little white books in the evenings. But he is so oppressed by these heavy, earthy difficulties; he can't escape; he can't attain aeryness."

"No," said Tom thoughtfully, thinking of his brother-in-law in his business suit.

"And so many of his difficulties are due to you and your ideas. Can't you see, Tom?"

"That's what they're meant for, Rosalind, to stop people like Reginald from feeling they're God Almighty, to pull him down out of heaven, to stop him having special privileges and powers and thinking he's deserved them! Can't *you* see?"

"It makes it so awkward for me and the children," Rosalind said, crumbling the edge of a macaroon in nervous fingers. "We were having tea with Daniel and Gwendolen last week, and——"

"Look here, Rosalind, don't have tea with men like Daniel Coke-Brown! He's foul; he really is. He's ignorant and greedy and has no regard for anything fine or beautiful!"

"Tom! He's in the service of the Empire—our beautiful Empire that our fathers loved and worked for and died for. The man you're called after, I remember mother telling me, Thomas Galton who was out in India with John Company——"

"Oh, cut it out, Rosalind! Those men worked and died all right, but they made a lot of other people work and die harder and faster and a damn sight more painfully than they did. The British Empire is red with murder and rape, and we pretend to children that they ought to love it and honour it and go down on their knees to Mr. Bennett at Ottawa and swallow whatever lies Daniel Coke-Brown dishes out to them in his newspapers!"

They were both on their feet now, a plate of éclairs and cream buns lying calmly between them; people turned to look. Rosalind recovered herself first and glanced at her little diamond watch on the moiré ribbon. "I must be going," she said, "but you see why I can't send the children to Scotland. I'm sorry they won't see any more of their little cousins. Can I give you a lift, Tom? No? Well, good-bye."

She offered him a cheek; it was an old gesture, something from childhood, but it had ceased to mean anything now. He touched the skin with his lips, noticing that it was smoother than Dione's, though Rosalind was ten years the older of the two, and that his sister was using some very elaborate scent. He wondered if she bought it or if it had been given her by Reginald Coke-Brown. He thought suddenly of his sister's trousseau, the year before the war, all lacey and frilly. His sister sleeping for nearly nineteen years with that man! Could she have? Yes, God, she'd been paid to! If she'd ever had a lover she wouldn't be so hellishly thick in it now. He crumpled his bill savagely, then smoothed it out, thanked the waitress politely, paid for the tea, and bought a small ark of chocolate animals for Lilias, whose birthday it was going to be in less than a month. It occurred to him in the train that she was rather young for so many chocolate animals; he might keep them in his study desk and give them to her one or two at a time during the ten first days when Dione was away in Russia and he was still being kept over his examining; two at a time wouldn't hurt her, and anyhow she was too young to tell Nurse!

On the morning of the party Dione, pleasantly aware of packed suit-cases, typhoid inoculation over, passports visa'd and all arrangements in the competent hands of the Intourist Office, who undertook all Russian travel, did quite a lot of furniture moving. It was a lovely day, so she moved tables and chairs out under the shade of the walnuts and the orchard trees. The odd-job man and Alex had marked the tennis courts freshly; the gate to the river path was opened, so that couples could go down there if they liked, and even take out a canoe. Morag had got up early and washed Bran before school. After lunch the food and drinks were taken out. Miss Williamson, now white-haired but still perfectly accomplished at her job, who had waited, it was supposed, at all Oxford parties since Jowett's time, came and supervised. Tom got back from college ; he had just had a friendly letter from his publishers, telling him to expect the galley proofs of his book in time to take them to Russia with him. Everyone changed. Lilias looked like the best sort of party cake herself, in pink and blue sprigged muslin. Phœbe was wearing an Austrian dress that she had bought from a bankrupt painter friend ; it had the strangest kinds of flowers all over it and a hard bright edge of a curious blue-green ; definitely rather an alarming dress.

" You will be decent to poor May ? " Dione said, a little nervously.

" I shan't smack poor May's face, if that's what you mean ! " said Phœbe.

" No, I don't, but I only asked them because I believe you've become slightly more adult about that affair."

" If you mean I've given up hoping ever to sleep with Phil again, that's right. Adult. Yes, how nice, I expect I am ! " She looked at herself in the mirror in Dione's room. " At any rate, if I may permit myself one childish remark, I think this dress is about right for May ! "

Then the first people began to come, shy first-year undergraduates and undergraduettes on bicycles : they were sent to play tennis and talk to one another in the orchard. Then the great mass of Oxford, North Oxford, Headington and Boar's Hill. There were more women than men ; Zita Baker had not persuaded John to abandon the biology labs., and the wives of Heads of Colleges delegated as ably as ever for their husbands. The Ruskin girl turned up ; she was an energetic tennis player—Tom wondered what chance she'd get of that later on in her industrial town. He was standing by his sister for the moment, lighting her cigarette.

" She came to see me last vac," said Muriel, between puffs, " such a nice girl. And going to spend the rest of her life doing the work of a four- or five-roomed house in a street of four- and five-roomed houses, and forget all she's had such a struggle to learn! Yes, and it's a waste of our struggle—*my* struggle for women's education. Why can't you tell your pupils to live in sin, Tom?"

"I do sometimes," he said, "but the ones that ought to don't like it, and the ones that oughtn't to do without being told."

Dione was smiling, shaking hands with people, forming and reforming groups, watching to see who was out of it, struggling to remember names for introductions, sure that she had made at least an occasional floater. Morag and Kenneth came rushing back from school; Nurse caught them and made them wash and change, then they burst out and began ragging with their father's pupils. Ian had suddenly become rather shy, but Lilias was going round showing off and disputing the juvenile honours with Bran, the puppy. There was a noise of tennis balls and chatter; people had begun to eat and drink; there were strawberries and cream and raspberries and cream; the roses were at their best; the plain clove-scented pinks were thick and deep, the Alwoodiis delightful; most of the keen gardeners spent some time over Dione's iris bed; at the edge of the orchard there were Penzance briars, and species roses growing unpruned, a glorious Moysii starred with single deep-red blossoms. The Oxford clay was doing its best.

The parlourmaid came out of the house and whispered to Dione that there was a man who wanted to see her.

"Oh, bother, I can't see anyone now! What sort of a man, Alice?"

"A working-man, I think—I did tell him to come back to-morrow, but he seemed very urgent, ma'am, so I thought——"

"All right," Dione said quickly, "I'll come." It might

be someone from Marshbrook Bridge—or a fraud. She walked across the lawn, smiling right and left, in through the big sitting-room, where a few people were having tea, and across the hall to the front doorstep, and Donald MacLean. He was rather white, and he stared at her and said nothing. " Oh, that's all right, Alice," she said, " you go and help Miss Williamson, you were quite right to call me."

Alice went back to the garden; Donald said in a low voice: " I would wish to speak with you privately."

" Right," Dione said, " in here," and took him into Tom's study and pushed him gently into the big chair. Still he didn't speak. " What is it ? " she said, and then: " Donald, what have you done ? "

He answered: " I have killed Daniel Coke-Brown."

Dione's fingers went on, stupidly, instinctively, tracing round the edge of Tom's writing-table. Dione heard her voice say: " Oh ! Are you quite sure you have ? "

He nodded: " You will see it in the evening papers."

" And—you killed him on purpose ? What with ? "

" A hand-grenade. I took the pin out and counted and threw. He was alone in his car. The driver was posting a letter. No one else was hurt."

" Donald. Do they know it was you ? "

" How can I tell ? But they'll have their suspicions. Aye, they'll trace it. I doubt they'll get me. Shall I go ? I will not be blaming you if you tell me to go."

" Of course not. My dear—wait a minute." She ran out of the room and came back with a plate of strawberries and cream and cake. " Now, eat that, and tell me several things. First, how have you got here ? "

" But I must tell you first, it was not Party instructions ! I was acting as an individual. A protest had to be made ! In general I disapprove of assassination, but I have thought

—aye, it was borne in upon me that Bakunin's arguments relate to England now! And I have always held there is a strong case for assassinating newspaper proprietors. I did not mean to escape. I thought I would be caught and maybe lynched or maybe stand my trial and my hanging. I was needing to say it was not the Party, but only me! But when I saw the confusion there was, I dodged and ran and I sprang into a lorry and hid between cases and—and so I was on the main southern road. And I found another lorry and the driver was Red, so I told him and he took me along. When I saw it was Oxford we were getting to, I thought, well, maybe—and by chance a young girl on a bicycle told me your house." He was gasping now, and had spilled some of the cream on to the carpet.

"So that was all right, but I hope to God your lorry driver was to be trusted!" Dione said.

"He was a Red."

"All the same, we can't risk it. I'll need to hide you at once. Finish your strawberries like a good child and come along." Donald MacLean did not move, but tears ran down his cheeks into the strawberries; he scrubbed his face across with his coat sleeve. "There, there," Dione said, patting him, "it must have been beastly. I hate bangs myself."

Donald MacLean giggled weakly through his tears: "Aye, it was an awful big bang! I'm—I'm coming. I've no' let myself cry in front of a woman in all my born days before."

"How silly of you, Donald," Dione said, "why shouldn't you? Now, I'll just peep into the hall and see no one's about, and then we'll go up quietly." As she opened the study door the party noise came buzzing and clicking at her, jarring with voices and tea-cups and laughter. But Alice was helping in the garden and Nurse was out of sight; she said softly over her shoulder : " Come on," and led the way upstairs. The Talking Crow was level ahead of her; the rough back of the gules lion, awake for a moment, arched itself under her hand. At the top of the house there was a boxroom under the slope of the roof, lighted by one small window, and with the cold-water cistern in the middle. " Get in behind there," Dione said, shoving him past a bundle of spades and pails. There were suit-cases to sit on and the remains of a tent. " That's all right for the moment," she said, " but we've got to decide what next." She tiptoed out of the boxroom and looked over the landing banisters; Morag was passing across the hall, carrying a jug of lemonade. Dione whistled and beckoned to Morag, who put down the jug and ran up. As she watched, Dione was thinking hard. The image of the crow gave place to the image of the tractors. The place where she was going. She whispered to Morag: " Fetch Father. And fetch Uncle Alex. Do it carefully, so that no one else sees."

"What is it, Mother?" asked Morag, flushing. "Is it—is it politics?"

" Yes," said Dione; " be as quick as you can."

She knelt behind the banisters, saw Morag run out towards the garden, saw the bowl of roses in the middle of the table suddenly shed three yellow petals, saw them blow lazily across the polished oak and run along the floor into a corner, saw a young couple—Teddy and one of his many girl friends—cross quickly, both laughing, the girl swinging her hat like a tennis racket. Then she saw Alice go to the door, and in a moment show Phil and May Bickerden across the hall; an echo of May's voice came floating up; the Phœbe problem reasserted itself for a moment; she was worried at not being there. She heard Tom saying how-do-you-do to the Bickerdens, just out of sight under the landing. A moment later he was coming up the stairs, two at a time. Then Morag and Alex together. She hadn't meant Morag to know at all, or not for years and years, but now she couldn't think how to get rid of her quickly, and it was urgent to tell the whole thing at once. "Morag," she said, "this is secret," and caught the Flora Macdonald look, and was satisfied. She pulled them all into the boxroom and told the whole story.

By the end Donald had come out from behind the cistern; he wanted to interrupt, but Dione wouldn't let him yet. Morag looked at him, the murderer, not with horror but with romance. The drip of the cistern was the moss dark spring in the cavern under the corrie; the plaid was on his shoulders; the eyes and mouth were right.

Tom said very little; it struck him immediately as being all extremely silly, though he was pleased that Daniel Coke-Brown was dead. "Obviously," he remarked, "we can't trust your lorry driver. He may develop a conscience any moment, or a desire for publicity, especially when he sees it all in the papers. You weren't such a fool as to tell him you were coming here?"

Donald shook his head: "I said I'd get off at Oxford. It just came into my head."

"Well, we've got to get you away within the next twenty-four hours at latest."

Donald said abruptly: "Maybe I should give myself up. I did this as an individual, not as a Party member, and maybe I should testify that this was so. Headquarters would not approve; it has never been their policy. I should submit myself to the Party discipline. Maybe they'll not have me——" There was a horrid pain in his voice.

"Oh, let the C.P. look after itself!" said Tom; "has anyone a plan?"

"I am putting you to inconvenience——" began Donald.

Morag stepped over and stood beside him, shy of touching him still, but wanting to give reassurance; he looked down at her, not understanding.

Dione said: "I've a kind of plan. Alex, have a look at him. Isn't he very like you?"

Alex stood a minute, looking closely at Donald in the pale light of the boxroom. At last he said: "Yes. And still more like my passport photograph. Go ahead, old girl."

"That's it," said Tom, "if we can pull it off. God, Alex, you'll have hell with the Foreign Office if anything ever comes out! Look, I've got to keep out of it if I possibly can because of my party position; anyhow, with luck, no one'll ever know. You've got your passport?"

"Oh yes. Rotten, missing the trip with you, old girl. Mm, I'll need to disappear somewhere for the time I should have been there or there'll be the devil to pay. You must send postcards from me to Mother!"

"There'll be a frantic amount of details!" Dione said, half despairing, "but I think it's the only thing to do." She turned to Donald MacLean now. "Donald," she said, "you're coming with me to the U.S.S.R. on my brother's passport, and when you get there you must fend for yourself."

Donald held on to the corner of the cistern. "There," he said. "There. Where I have longed to be." He turned to Alex: "I am taking your chance?"

"Och, that's nothing," said Alex, embarrassed by his tone, "between Scots."

And Morag quoted to herself in a low voice and very seriously, from a piece of real modern romance: "O.K. by me, pard."

"Now," Dione said, "we're going by car to-morrow morning at ten; the boat sails at two from London.

Nobody should know you've been in the house except us and Muriel and Phœbe, whom we must tell; we must put you into the car during the night, under the rug, and Tom and Alex must put the luggage in—*not Alice.* Morag, you must clear up in the boxroom afterwards if it looks funny. You must change into Alex's suit, Donald—the one he was photographed in."

"He can have my suit-case," said Alex; "I've just put in oldish clothes, some drugs, a few books. Mm, I'll just need to take out my papers and photos."

Tom was suddenly anxious. "Do you think you can really pull it off? Dione, if anything happened and you got into trouble out there——"

"But it won't," Dione said. "Donald, you can play up, can't you? You can pretend to be my brother in front of the other people? We can talk about Auchanarnish!"

He nodded. "I will do anything," he said; "I—I thank you all."

Dione said: "I must run or the garden party will miss me, and it'll begin to look odd. You stay, Alex, and tell him the main facts of our common childhood! Tell him what a bully I was!" She turned and went downstairs, composing herself for the party.

Morag pulled her arm: "Mother! May I take him something to eat?"

"Yes, but don't let anyone spot you. Not Kenneth."

"Oh, Mother, I do wish Brian were old enough to guard him!"

Dione went through the sitting-room and out on to the lawn between the two great lilac splashes of aubrietia under the standard roses. In a moment the garden party had closed round her again, without having missed her.

Phœbe, talking amusingly and Londonishly at the edge of the orchard to Dick Crossman and two other young dons, had spotted Phil out of the corner of her eye, but had not hesitated in a sentence. When the Bickerdens came near, unsuspecting, drifted on the tide of the party, she turned round, her face prepared. "Hullo, May!" she said, "*so* glad to see you again—and what an amusing hat! Hullo, Phil—you look years older than when I saw you last."

May Bickerden said how-do-you-do, wondering rather flusteredly what could be amusing about her hat, which she had bought at Peter Robinson's sale, and whether or not to take it as a compliment. Phil shook hands, and suddenly smiled and looked right through Phœbe's prepared face. His smile turned into laughter: "Well, *you* aren't any older, Phœbe! Nor, I should think, perceptibly wiser!"

May wasn't used to her husband laughing like that! Nor, for that matter, were the young dons, who had looked upon Bickerden as completely grown-up and pre-war. May knew she must act, but didn't know how—and then her host came up and took her by the arm, and before she knew where she was she was being given tea over at the table and Phil was not beside her!

Phœbe had said: "Oh, I'm much wiser. I've done some goodish stuff lately—not that anyone's buying. I've just finished the blocks for a Golden Cockerel Hans Andersen; you know, I terribly wanted to ask you about one of them—it was full of higher mathematics—I had to get it all out of a book and wasted quite half a day doing it!"

"Why didn't you ask me?" Phil said.

Phœbe shrugged her shoulders: "I managed. Well, how are the old electrons?"

"You know I finished up the rare earths—thalium, urbium, disprosium. You remember, I was on them when you—when I——"

"Married May. Yes, I read your paper."

"You did. Good. Understand it?"

"More or less. It was rather dull—by itself. And then?"

"Ah, then I got on to Spin. You remember Spin, don't you?"

"The thing you were having a song and dance with Goudsmit about? You were thinking you'd get on to iodine atoms, but they were being a bit of a nuisance."

"Yes, I couldn't get my methods right. Phœbe, I spent nights and nights thinking about them, and then they wouldn't work out in practice. That bloody Stark effect blurred over everything. Whatever I tried, there was always a mess. I couldn't get my results precise."

"Yes, I know the kind of thing. Technique's the devil when it gets between oneself and what one wants to do.... Phil—does May help a lot over that?"

"Of course not. She's had no laboratory experience. Why should she help? Well then, I tried the other business of watching the band spectra in the molecules. The ratio of intensities. But then I came up against the photometric problem."

"Remind me how the spectra are affected by nuclear spin, Phil. I've forgotten it rather."

"Well, take helium, where there's no nuclear spin. If you start looking for hyperfine structure . . ."

The three young dons who were historians or economists had faded away, quite unable to make out how Phœbe Bathurst could conceivably be interested in this stuff. But interested she obviously was; there was nothing put on about that. For the moment at least, she understood; it had made a contact. The hoopoe was gobbling his facts again, the feathers were lifted and glinting. She and Phil were walking through the orchard now, he still talking hard, looking her full in the eyes as he brought out point after point what work he had been doing.

"So it hasn't gone as fast as you hoped?" said Phœbe. She had stopped beside the Moysii rose and raised her hand up one of the main stems, as she often did to feel at its great shapely thorns.

"No," he said, "I suppose not," and looked at her again. "You are pretty, Phœbe," he said suddenly; "no, stay standing like that. Oh, what an ass I've been to forget how pretty you are!"

Phœbe stood by the rose tree and her strange-flowered dress moved about her body, swaying out or clinging. The rose tree in the witch's garden and Kay again. She stood silent and looked at Kay, at Phil. She looked past Phil to steady herself, steady the beating of her heart; and beyond Phil was the garden and the party and the teacups, and suddenly people crying out and running; and exactly in front of the house the Elephant, come for her again. And she sprang away from the rose bush and Phil Bickerden; she saw the bread-knife on the table; she was going to get the Elephant this time or be killed herself!

Dione was round the corner of the house, showing the iris bed to the Warden's wife, who was seriously adjuring her not to be misled in Russia, nor to suppose that what she was shown would represent the real state of the country. Dione promised not to be bamboozled by any Russian, and pointed out the beautiful bronze-and-winey Ambassador irises standing high and strong in front of the snowy syringa bush. She wondered if Donald was daring to look out of the little attic window and watch them, but she did not look up. Then she heard a half scream, raised voices, a disturbance, and thought what can it be? And knew with dreadful certainty that it must be the police already, and hurried the Warden's wife round the corner of the house, and saw in a state of dazed stupidity that the police had disguised themselves, appropriately enough, as an Elephant.

" It's an Elephant, an Elephant ! " shouted Kenneth, and he and Morag and Ian and two or three other children rushed at the Elephant, and the Elephant, rather frightened, backed clumsily towards the house, treading on a plate.

Morag said : " Oh, we must be nice to the Elephant ! " and ran over to the table and seized a sugary cake in each hand. Keeping her brothers and the other children back, she advanced towards the Elephant, cooing at it, and the Elephant timidly put out its trunk and took one of the cakes.

" It's a *real* Elephant," said Ian contentedly, and he too got a cake and brought it to the Elephant.

" And a little child shall lead it," said Phœbe, standing behind, and her voice shook a good deal. She had dropped the bread-knife. Dione had hold of her arm. " You thought it was *that*, did you," she said. Behind them Phil Bickerden was protecting his wife with a half-opened parasol. The Ruskin girl had picked up Lilias. Zita Baker, in fits of laughter, had sensibly collared the puppy.

And then Tom came hurrying out of the house with two keepers. " Escaped from Mr. Gray's Zoo, has he ? Well, look at the mess he's made of the border ! The least you can do now is to give the children rides." Oh, it was a most successful garden party !

Dione said to her sister : " So you see, he wasn't after all. Perhaps he never is. Perhaps if we were all as sensible as Morag he'd come and feed out of our hands too."

A personal trunk call for Mr. Galton ; he hurried into his study, leaving the keepers to deal with a tranquil Elephant. " Hullo, who's that ? "

" Sallington wants you. Hold on."

" Hullo."

" Oh, hullo, Mr. Galton. I'm Margaret Coke-Brown speaking. Oh, you know ! I came and drove for you last election. Dione came to our wedding. Got there? Listen, Daniel Coke-Brown's been murdered. I thought you'd like to know."

An alibi, thought Tom, if I'm ever suspected! "My God," he said, "you don't mean it!"

"I say, I thought you'd be pleased!" the girl's voice said; "he was an awful old man. He gave us the most rotten set of fish-knives for a wedding present!"

"How was he murdered?"

"Someone chucked a bomb at him. Jolly sensible. Don't you think so, really? Mr. Galton, we've been rung up by horrified relations, and I thought, well I must ring you up, you won't be horrified. You aren't, are you?"

"Well, not so very, perhaps. But it's a serious thing. Did they get the murderer?"

"No, thank goodness, he's got off. Of course the police say they know who it is."

"*Do* they know?"

"Well, I heard someone say it was a Communist agitator. The *Sallington News* is always jumping on the Communists. I think they're quite right."

"It's not part of their official programme. One can't just go murdering people one doesn't like."

"I suppose you've got to say that in the Labour Party, but if you go on saying it I shall jolly well join the Communists! This sort of thing is going to brighten Sallington no end, and oh, gosh, it *does* need brightening! You've never lived in Barstone, Mr. Galton!"

"What does your husband think?"

"Oh, *he's* all right. We can sell the fish-knives now. Oh, it's going to be so funny at all the tea parties! I say, tell Dione I'm starting a baby. Quick work, isn't it? Yes, I'm feeling fine. You are *really* pleased, aren't you?"

"Well, yes, I suppose I am, but for God's sake don't tell

anyone in Sallington, especially not my sister, or I shall get into a row. Yes, thanks most awfully for ringing up! Time's up—right-o, good-bye, all the best to your husband."

The Galtons' garden party began to disperse ; those who were teaching and those who were taught must both be punctual. Children's bedtime loomed in North Oxford. Nurse collected Ian and Lilias. The other two were going to stay for supper of delicious remains with the grown-ups. Muriel and Phœbe were both told ; there was nothing much for them to say—it was a *fait accompli* by now. Muriel was going to see them off and drive the car back from London ; Tom wasn't able to go—there was a lecture he couldn't cut. " Just as well," said Muriel, " you'd look all goo-ey and jumpy about your Dione and give the show away." They decided Alex should drive up with them and see them off; he obviously had to *start* from Oxford, and when they were at the boat they would say he was another brother or a cousin—it might be as well to have him in case there was trouble, too. But none of them knew quite what trouble there might be. That was the worst of it. " I'm glad you decided all this on your own," Muriel said to Dione; " you're getting better, you know ! "

" I couldn't get hold of Tom at once, so I had to decide. Besides, I couldn't possibly have done anything else."

" No, *you* couldn't," said Muriel. " Well, I hope he'll be nice to you. He's a decent sort of chap, isn't he, apart from being a murderer and all that ? "

" Oh yes. He must be a sort of a dim cousin after all. I expect he'll propagand me a lot. Look, Muriel, it's just on supper time ; I must wash."

While Dione was washing Morag came up to her and whispered : " I took him some more strawberries and cream, Mother ; isn't it awful ? he said he'd had no strawberries this year ! "

"I hope they won't make him sick," Dione said. "But you see, strawberries are a luxury just now; they oughtn't to be, but they are. And it's a real luxury to have strawberry beds of our own, like we have. They ought to be everybody's strawberries."

"I felt an awful pig when he said it," Morag said. "I've eaten tons this year. And then he said, 'I've killed a man and you give me strawberries and cream.' What do you think it feels like having killed somebody?"

"Well, Father killed people during the war. Ask him. You know, Morag, if they caught Donald now they'd hang him. They'd kill him back. So remember, lamb, try not even to look as if you had a secret to-night."

Dione went up and said good-night to the littles; she felt very sentimental about Lilias, feeling that she'd have grown up a whole month before next time. Supper was a rather awkward meal, because of Kenneth. After supper they made what arrangements they could, and then Alex and Dione had a long talk; both were rather gloomy, because somehow they had put a good deal on to going to Russia together, and being uninterruptedly brother and sister again. Alex wrote two sham letters which were to be put in with Dione's to their mother. It was difficult to think of anywhere to go without a passport; and he had spent all his spare cash on the Russian trip, which was all paid for in advance. "I might go up to one of the bad areas in this country," he said—"South Wales or Durham or Newcastle, or even Glasgow."

Later in the evening, when all was clear, Donald changed into Alex's suit, and his own was burnt in the incinerator, just in case it might turn up as awkward evidence. He had very few papers; a few newspaper clippings, a letter from a comrade at Greenock, which he burnt, a slogan badge, his trade union card, and his Party card, which for the moment Dione took charge of. Then they took him to the garage and gave him cushions and a rug to sleep on, and told him to get into the car early next morning and cover himself up, just in case the odd-job man looked in.

Tom and Dione both slept badly that night; it seemed as if there was a lot to be said, but neither words nor time to say it in. Both were taking chances and trusting to the future; any answer to any question had to be provisional.

Then it was morning. The papers were all full of the Coke-Brown murder; Communist propaganda was blamed—it was obviously political. The *Herald* was full of the blamelessness of the Labour Party. The *Manchester Guardian* had rather cattily put it on to a back page, but had also given it a leader. *The Times* obituary had obviously been re-written in parts, and there was grave comment about this new danger to English liberty of thought and speech. They sent out for other papers. The *Express* definitely said it was a Communist Party assassination, and prepared to lead a crusade. The *Mail* was about the same. They didn't let Donald see either of these, because they were afraid he might determine to give himself up and explain that he wasn't a Party agent. And then it was time to be off. Muriel and Dione got into the front of the car, Alex behind with the suit-cases, and Donald under the macintoshes and the bunch of roses which Morag had put in.

When they were through Oxford and out on the Henley road they let Donald sit up a little, but decided that he had better not be seen going through towns or even when they passed other cars, just in case there might be a police description out. Dione was driving. At first she drove at her ordinary pace, which, in a full Morris-Oxford, was not anything startling. Then, as she got nearer and nearer to safety—and also perhaps to danger—she began to press on the accelerator and cut corners. She passed a good many cars on the Benson by-pass, and took the long slope through the chalk cutting on top, dodging round a lorry that she would ordinarily have followed. They swung up and down the hilly country before Nettlebed, and after the corner went all out through Nettlebed Woods. At fifty the car began to jar on the driver's hands ; Dione swore at it, but kept her foot hard jammed on the accelerator ; let the little brute shake itself to bits ! " Let me take on, Dione ! " Muriel said, " you're not safe."

" Yes, I am ! " Dione said, and plunged downhill towards Henley, going blind at the corners ; " I've just had the brakes tested," she said over her shoulder. Fortunately they met nothing. Then down the straight between the elms into Henley. Donald didn't realise how fast they were going, and wasn't nervous, but both the others were.

" Slow down through Henley, you idiot ! " Muriel said, " or you'll be caught for dangerous driving."

This pulled her up a little, and she wound her way through the main street very respectably, over the bridge, and then accelerated hard for Henley Hill. Once she glanced over her shoulder. There was nothing behind her, not so much as an Elephant. There might be. The tractors were miles ahead. Normally she took twenty minutes between Henley and the centre of Maidenhead ; she gained seven on this. From Maidenhead she counted three-quarters of an hour to the outskirts of London, the other end of the Great West Road. There was no speeding now ; the road was too full of traffic, except on the Colnbrook by-pass. Bear left ahead, it said, bear, bear, Russian bear, white teeth, steel claws, we're coming, we're coming, we'll be safe with you. Beyond the by-pass they were widening the road, and twice she had to slow down for single-line traffic. She was sweating now, but felt very calm, in very good control of the car.

" Let me take her through London," Muriel said; " I know it better than you." This was only sense. They swopped over on the Great West Road; she was five minutes better than time. They had decided now that Donald had better sit up; it would look much too odd for him to bob out of the bottom of the car at Hay's Wharf. Muriel drove carefully past Hammersmith and Olympia; at the crossing beyond Olympia they were held up, and Alex felt Donald next him quivering with nervousness. Past South Kensington, all so calm and nice, Barker's Summer Sale coming on, crowds on the pavement, nurses and prams, everyone going their own way, seeking their own ends, crossing one another's purposes, wasting hope and energy. London under capitalism. They turned through the Park, one murderer and three accomplices driving past the Row. They swung in the one-way circus at Hyde Park Corner and into St. James's Park. Alex pointed out Buckingham Palace to Donald, who had never been in London. So down to the Embankment and quickly along under great hotels and past the Temple, another stronghold of property. Down Queen Victoria Street and into the City. Muriel stopped to ask her way to Hay's Wharf.

They crossed the Thames, and below them, to the left, was the little Soviet ship, the Red Flag with the hammer and sickle neat in yellow on the corner. Alex felt suddenly desperately cross that he wasn't going. He couldn't answer Donald's murmur of excitement. Muriel drew up at the wharf. They got out, collecting their suit-cases and coats. There was a policeman about, but he was not interested in them. Some loading was going on and several men were just standing and watching. They wondered what to do. There was a gangway down.

" Come on," said Muriel, " this is a sensible ship; we're allowed just to go on board."

They crossed the gangway and hesitated. There was no one about. Donald stumbled over a loose rope and a Russian sailor who was passing, bare-foot and bare-headed, laughed. Then a competent-looking girl came up. "I am Intourist," she said, "you are on the B party, no?"

"Yes," said Dione, "my brother and myself: Mr. Fraser and Mrs. Galton." And she pointed at Donald.

"All right," said the girl, "you are early. I will show you your cabins." She spoke rather contemptuously, thought Dione, as if she were a not very kind nurse and they were a lot of extra-silly children. "And these?" she asked suddenly.

"Just seeing us off."

"Oh." Dione and Donald were taken off to their very comfortable shared cabins, one at the men's side of the ship, one at the women's. The people they were to share with had not yet arrived. They came on deck again. "And your passports," said the girl; "Intourist keeps them while you are on the ship." Dione and Donald handed them over; the girl looked at them. "All right," she said, "you will have cards to fill in. Ah, the rest of your party begin to come." She trotted off to collect the rest of the group as it arrived.

"That seems to be that," said Muriel.

"I never thought——" Dione said, and shook her head impatiently; she was half crying. For a time they stood by the rail and watched the ship being loaded; Muriel and Alex and Dione talked to one another a little, but Donald said nothing. Dione knew one or two of the others in the group, and when they came on board introduced Donald as her brother and Alex as her cousin. It was all rather funny, but a very tucked-away, inside sort of fun niness. They all ate sandwiches and strawberries together. It was then about half-past two and, as the ship was due to sail at two o'clock, Alex and Muriel thought they had better be going. The ship showed no great haste, and for some little time there was a line of friends and relatives waiting at the quayside, having said everything there was to say. Those on board were impatient, shivery, mostly rather afraid and very much excited. At last, with very little extra fuss, they were off. Dione waved to Muriel and Alex for rather a long time.

A little tug had charge and pulled them along past strings of barges through the dirty, powerful Thames water, like a child pulling along an out-of-breath mother. The arms of Tower Bridge opened ahead of them and let them out. Dione put an arm on Donald's shoulder: "You're safe now, Donald," she said.

He had been staring at the Tower of London, but now he turned and looked at her, and beyond her on the mast-head, high up, the tiny Red Flag. "Yes," he said, "we're safe—Dione."

# PART III

## THE HOUSE OF THE INTERPRETER TO THE HOUSE BEAUTIFUL

"Surely now any doubts you ever had are over
You, when you reflect the world, and you too
When your nerves and muscles all are awake, then
Receptivity can begin and the news comes roaring in."

CHARLES MADGE.

For two hours Donald and Dione stood side by side watching, as the Soviet ship was towed down loop after loop of the Thames, nearer and nearer to open sea. It was a Saturday afternoon, so little was going on. The wharves were shut, the shipping was quiet. But somehow it looked worse, quieter, than even a week-end warranted ; it looked as if those cranes hadn't been worked for weeks, those dock gates permanently locked and bolted. Here was a row of sailing barges laid up next one another, there a glimpse of big cargo boats docked in one or another of the creeks.

" Did you see the shipping laid up in the Gare Loch, Donald ? " she said.

" Aye," he said, " I worked there."

Dione had never known how far London stretched, had never guessed at this other London, somehow right out of the Oxford-Cambridge-London triangle that she knew. At first, looking back, they could see known landmarks—St. Paul's, the Tower, or some fine new office blocks, their Portland stone not yet smoke-greyed but shining and prosperous-seeming. These would swing about from side to side behind them as the ship looped south or north down the bends on the widening Thames tide ; then they dropped out of sight and out of mind. They passed Greenwich Hospital, wide and dignified, grey stone and trees, the last of stately England, but London still went on. Then far ahead and to the left was the delicate high pylon of the Barking Creek crossing, and then the Barking Power Station, squared and modern, catching at both their hearts for its likeness to the Power Station on the Sall; beyond it were the red-painted unfinished pylons of the Thames crossing above the strengthening rippled water. She turned to him and said in a low voice: "Do you think you will ever see England again, Donald?"

"Maybe," he said, "I will come back to a different England. One of the World Union of Soviet Republics."

"But would one feel the same," she said, hesitating, "about England if she were—that?"

"The same—no!" he said, "but proud: instead of ashamed."

"Yes," she said, "I see." But she winced away from the thought behind the words. She was—yes, she *was*, and she was right to be!—proud of England as it was now, of England and Scotland, of Magdalen Tower and Folly Bridge, New College cloisters, Trinity Great Court, the Backs; of Auchanarnish and the sea lochs, and the great squares of Edinburgh; of Hampton Court and Kew and the Stratford Theatre and the new Underground building; of Cotswolds and Quantocks and South Downs and the road from Helm to the Undercliff. She was proud of Dunbar and Shakespeare and Donne; she was proud of Virginia Woolf and Lawrence and Shaw and Wyndham Lewis and Aldous Huxley! She was proud of Sickert and Gill and Phœbe Bathurst. She was proud of her own children and their allies, brave, kind, sensible children; and she was proud of the Labour Movement at Marshbrook Bridge, of all the men and women she had worked with and made friends with. She wanted to say all this to Donald.

And then she thought, what does it all mean to him? No one has ever given him Oxford or Cambridge to live in; London to him would be mean streets and dockyards; Edinburgh would be dark, weary-staired closes, one privy to each tenement, no water above the basement. Auchanarnish—yes, but he had turned his back on the sea lochs. Cotswolds or Quantocks would only be steeper walking for a workless man going from town to town. Shakespeare and Dunbar—perhaps. But the moderns were all from the enemy class, bourgeois, traitors, even Shaw a Fabian. The painters were bourgeois painters. Her children had taken the bread from the mouths of his friends' children. The Labour Movement—no good either!

Just then a woman came up and spoke to her: "Wasn't that Muriel Galton I saw saying good-bye to you? Are you a relation of hers by any chance?"

"Yes," said Dione, "I'm her sister-in-law, Dione Galton. And this is my brother."

"What fun!" said the woman. She was tall and well dressed, with silk stockings and good shoes, but bareheaded; Dione could see a few strands of white in her hair, but the face was unwrinkled and very much alive. "I'm Nan Ellis," the woman said, and shook hands with them both. Dione, watching carefully, saw that she noticed nothing odd about Donald.

"I've heard Muriel speak a lot about you," Dione said. "Birth control, married women teachers, equal pay for equal work—oh yes, I remember her showing me a newspaper photograph of you being arrested in a Suffragette demonstration before the war."

"Yes, and I was a minor—rather a kid minor too—so they wouldn't do anything to me. It was a shame! But that started me off as a publicist."

"Are you going to Russia to write about it?"

"I sincerely trust I'm not. Just a spot of high-class journalism perhaps, but definitely not a great book. I'm going to learn. You look as if you wanted to, Mrs. Galton. What do you expect it to be like?"

"I suppose I expect to see equality really happening.

And I expect freedom—some kinds of freedom. I shall be awfully disappointed to find conventions there."

"And what do you expect?" The tall woman turned to Donald; he didn't seem to know what to say.

Dione answered for him: "Donald expects the Kingdom of Heaven!"

"On earth," Donald corrected firmly.

"Communist? Yes, it must be all lovely going out feeling like that. And you're on B party? That's good, so am I. I want specially to see things to do with women's work, birth control and abortion clinics and so on. Do you, Mrs. Galton?"

"Yes, I do. I want to see everything, I'm afraid! Goodness, what an excited ship-load we must be. Do you think everyone is expecting as hard as we are?"

"Not them! Or at least—differently. I suppose by 1932 everyone who reads the papers has made up their minds what they think Russia is like, and if it isn't, it's jolly well got to be. We shall all see what we mean to see."

"Shall we? I mean to be so open-minded. I can't help thinking I am, too."

"Of course you're not! I'm not myself, though I don't belong to any of your nasty political parties, none of which are any good to me. Is your husband coming out?—that's Tom, isn't it?"

"Ten days later. And—Muriel never said!—are you married?"

"Oh yes! But I kept my own name. He's a farmer. I can't bear living in towns, nor can he. He can't come away just now, but he probably will later. I've got my daughter with me. Over there. Yes, the pretty one. I made her ridiculous school let her go a month early. One must bully these institutions. Have you daughters?"

" Two."

" Good. I have three. Two younger than Jane. Well, see you later."

She nodded to them and walked off; she seemed to know several people on board and intended to know any of the others she liked the looks of.

" Who was that ? " Donald asked.

" Lady Nancy Ellis. A feminist. A very good speaker, I believe."

" One of the English aristocracy," said Donald, with an intonation of scorn.

" Donald," said Dione.

" Mm . . . well ? "

" You'll have all the rest of your life to be a good Communist in. Don't be more political than you can help now. It's so—tiring. I know you've got to be a bit, we all must, living in the world as it is. But don't bully me more than you need."

" I did not know I was," said Donald uncomfortably.

" Well, just think a little. You see, I miss Alex rather a lot. We'd looked forward to this. Try and be like a brother, won't you ?—a nice brother. You don't really want to make me uncomfortable the whole time, do you ? Or do you ? "

" I'm sorry," he said, " Dione. I was not meaning to hurt you. I do not think of you yourself as an enemy."

" That's all right, then. Oh, there's a bell; it must be tea ! Come along."

There was tea in glasses with slices of lemon in it: Dione was delighted, but Donald thought the tea tasteless and the lemon a nasty idea. After tea they decided to go and unpack. Dione found that her cabin companion was a girl of about twenty-six, secretary to a Conservative M.P. " So you've come for a change ? " Dione said.

" Well, I'm really going to collect some material for him," she said. " It would be rather awkward for him, coming himself. I've got some introductions," she went on, carefully taking out a couple of dresses, " and I shall keep my eyes open and not be taken in by everything I'm shown."

" How very interesting," Dione said noncommittally. She took out " The Fountain " which Phœbe had given her at the last moment and which was squashing her dresses, and also the yellow Russian grammar, which she took up on deck with her. Now the Thames estuary had widened out, London had at last dropped behind. They had finished with piloting; they were off on their own under the Red Flag.

For a few minutes she talked to a man she had met in London once or twice, a Jewish writer and journalist, who pointed out to her a fairly eminent Labour politician, standing romantically by himself on the upper deck with his hands clasped behind him. " He thinks he's Lenin," said her companion, and winked. " But they'll show him ! "

" Have you spotted anyone yet for our Lenin ? " Dione asked.

" Not yet; but England has a large Jewish population. So you've got the little yellow book, Mrs. Galton ? What lesson are you at ? "

" Only lesson seven. But I've mastered the alphabet."

" Ah, I'm at lesson twenty-five ! "

Then Donald came up and was introduced; he had unpacked Alex's grammar. " It's not just that easy," he said. They wandered about the ship a little and talked to one of the engineers. Dione was thrilled to see the women sailors, jolly, stocky girls in overalls. Donald was less enthusiastic.

" I believe you're shocked," Dione said.

Donald shook his head. "I'm not just used to it," he said.

"Who's in your cabin?"

He lowered his voice: "Dione, it's some man called Medingley. He seems a friendly-like man, but he says he is a Liberal."

"Well, for goodness' sake don't try to convert him, Donald, or you'll give the show away! Please—do remember. You'll suddenly find yourself saying something awkward."

"I cannot deny my faith."

"Oh yes, you can; there aren't any cocks on board! Besides, I'm not asking you to deny anything. Just be sensible."

At dinner they shared a table with Lady Nancy Ellis and her daughter Jane. Donald was a little awkward and embarrassed at being waited on, but was very polite. He looks a dear when he smiles, Dione thought, watching his effect on Jane. After dinner some of the passengers and some of the ship's officers began to play chess and Donald accepted a game. Nancy Ellis whispered to Dione: "Tell me about that brother of yours. He's younger than you?"

"Yes," said Dione, thinking, this is the first time, how often——? She went on with their agreed story: "He's a Communist, and has been working as a dock labourer in Scotland. He may be going to settle in Russia."

"He's charming. You must be an adventurous family. Any sisters?"

"One: Phœbe Bathurst, the artist. Do you know her work?"

"Don't know one end of a picture from the other. I suppose she paints these modern pictures, all bars and squares and corners—rabbit-hutch pictures, I call them. Well, I'll look out for her name. Does she sell?"

" Pretty well. But the market's bad just now. No one seems to have any money."

" Plenty of money about. But everyone's afraid to be caught spending it."

Dione watched Donald play. He wasn't such a good player as Alex and was beaten fairly quickly.

" I'll teach you some good openings, shall I ? " she said.

" Do you play ? " he asked.

She frowned at him—it was an unbrotherly remark. " Of course," she said, " don't you remember playing in the schoolroom at Auchanarnish ? "

" At Auchanarnish," he said. " Aye, I remember fine."

Some of the passengers sat up latish, experimenting on vodka and having political discussions, but most were tired with excitement and sea air and went off to bed. Donald was finding the details of his disguise rather difficult. He watched Medingley, the young barrister, trying to see how much it was usual to wash. He was shy of undressing in front of him. Medingley was friendly and tried to talk, but found Donald difficult ; still, he supposed him to be of his own class. Donald kept on wanting to contradict, to say what he thought of Medingley's ideas and way of life. The knowledge that he mustn't drove him dumb. He had nightmares all that night. He had never slept on a ship before, and, although it was very smooth, the slight movement and jarring bothered him, the softness of the mattress, the smoothness of the sheets. He would have preferred violence or discomfort now. He did not at first fall asleep enough to forget he was on the ship, but the police seemed to be on it too ; they were creeping down the passage, converging on him. Now—oh, he was no longer prepared for death ! They seized him, they were going to beat him up, he saw their faces, he stiffened against the coming pain and woke with a jump and his heart thudding. Two or three times he had variations on that dream; sometimes Dione came into it. Or else he was still preparing for what he had to do, still handling the Mills bomb, wondering whether the stuff had kept. He became terrified of talking in his sleep and being overheard. He was worried, too, by Alex's pyjamas; the legs bothered him and the string round the waist. He had left Auchanarnish to go as a student with a good set of night-shirts, and had only taken to pyjamas when he gave up the ministry. But when they wore out he hadn't had the money to buy any more and had slept in his shirt like the rest of his mates. He turned and twisted about and listened to the noise of the engines and wondered if Dione Galton was asleep. She was the only point he was certain of on this ship, and he was not very certain of her.

Towards morning he fell more heavily asleep and dreamt he was going to do a job of work on a boiler. He had his tools with him and he had to go through one boiler to another; rust crunched under his feet; he had to go through a narrower boiler, he couldn't see, there were narrowing corners ahead, he was terribly afraid of getting stuck. He woke uneasily again. This time they were scrubbing the decks outside; he got up and began to dress. He wondered how often he ought to shave and decided that as he hadn't yesterday it might be on the safe side to do it this morning. This safety razor was just fine to shave with, no pulling and tugging, he wouldn't mind how often he did it with this! As he was finishing Medingley woke up. "Did you get any hot water?" he said. "I couldn't get that tap to work."

"No," said Donald.

"Clever fellow, shaving in cold. Wonder what time we get breakfast."

Donald grinned to himself. He had never been accustomed to shaving in hot water, and lately had not had it for months. He went up on deck. There was no land to be seen. He tried to talk to the sailors, but they didn't want to talk to him. He wished he had his Party card, but Dione was still keeping it; perhaps it was better not to show it yet. He went up into the bows and met a man who looked like the sort of man he was used to. "'Morning, comrade," he said. The man glared at him, not liking the look of his clothes, and Donald suddenly realised that this was another way he might betray himself—safer than the other, but still—— He must try and do what Dione wanted. He became embarrassed and didn't get the conversation he was hoping for.

Other people came out on deck, and then it was breakfast; it was queer, getting so much to eat. Dione was in a pretty striped cotton frock. After breakfast most people went up on deck; they brought their grammars with them and offered to hear one another's verbs. Others had books of statistics, or diaries they were writing up. The sun was brilliant, the sea lovely. Most of the men had changed into shorts. By eleven o'clock a few were already in bathing-dresses. Dione took him aside and said: "I'm sure Alex brought some shorts with him—why don't you put them on—and take your tie off?"

"I'll take my tie off," said Donald, "but——" He couldn't explain to a woman how uncomfortable the idea of wearing shorts made him.

"Go along," said Dione firmly, "or would you rather get a bathing-dress? I'm sure he brought one, too."

"Ach, no!" he said. He wasn't going to do that, anyway. He compromised on the shorts and open-necked shirt. He felt a fool, like he would have now, wearing the kilt; he wasn't a wee boy! But no one laughed at him, and by and bye he got used to it. Dione came out in a green bathing-dress ; he could scarcely look at her at first ; it was like those capitalist papers with the photographs of actresses and that. Her legs were bare all up. He could see the shape of her ; he was compelled to think of her as a woman ; he didn't want to have those kinds of thoughts. He dug into the Russian grammar with his teeth set, trying not to look up for any of these women passing him.

At dinner—she called it lunch—Dione had a coat on over her bathing-dress, but he knew now what she was like underneath. The young girl, Jane Ellis, sitting next him, was wearing a bathing-dress and a wrap too ; he edged away from her arm brushing his, or worse, her bare knee might brush against his in these clothes he was being made to wear. He could scarcely eat. And then the two older women began talking—in front of the young girl—about abortion and whether it should be allowed by law. He was horribly interested, he had known of things happening so often, friends of his who'd got a girl that way and there was no remedy, for the chemists' shops were no good, and maybe they had to get married and get working for a crying angry-voiced woman and a dirty baby with its things all lying about the room, instead of coming to meetings and working for the cause. Or there were old women who did things ; he didn't know what, but it was dangerous, it was horrible. A man should keep out of these things. And now these two were talking of it, using words he didn't know. Hastily he began to talk to Jane Ellis about the difficulties of the Russian tongue.

He was tired in the afternoon and went to sleep, curled angularly in a sunny corner of a bench—he'd slept on benches often enough before !—and when he woke Dione was sitting beside him. Thank God, she was dressed. The shadow had come round, and there was a coat over him ; he looked at it.

" I thought you might get cold," she explained.

He was surprised ; it made him feel soft ; why should she fuss over him ?

" Didn't you sleep well last night ? " she said. " I expect you didn't."

He said : " I had some awful nasty dreams." Suddenly he wanted very much to tell them to someone. He looked round to see that no one was listening, and in a low voice told the police dream. " And one time I thought you'd given me away and were helping them," he said. She smiled and patted his bare knee. He told her about the boiler dream after that. " I've often worked in boilers," he said, " but they were that narrow. I was afraid for them."

She said : " That's a universal dream in some shape or other. It's nothing to worry about. Do you know the interpretation ? "

" Ach ! " he said, surprised and rather disgusted that she believed in such things, " I don't hold with the interpreting of dreams !—dream books and all, it's just a pack of superstition."

" But I didn't mean that sort of interpretation ! " she said, laughing. " This is the scientific kind. Freud and Jung. Donald, don't tell me you've never heard of psycho-analytic interpretation ! "

" I've heard of psycho-analysis," he said cautiously, " but I always thought it was—och, just havers."

" Some of it is," Dione said, " but the part about dreams and repressions is all right. I don't expect you're bothered by repressions, though."

" Repressions ? "

" Well, when you really want a thing but won't admit it. And as far as psycho-analysis goes, it usually means a sexual repression."

"But—I thought that was all—dirty talk. Is it—scientific?"

"Goodness, yes. It's proved, it's used for curing people. But you've probably lived a normal sort of life, so it hasn't come your way. It's only we wretched bourgeois who get into tangles and can't satisfy our good healthy instincts. That's what's wrong with an awful lot of art and literature. Tom says——" She broke off short and looked at him; he was trembling a little. "Are you cold, Donald? Or—don't you understand what I'm talking about? Or—Donald, am I shocking you?"

He shook his head; he couldn't say anything; he wanted her to go on; it was like something breaking.

"Donald," she said, "I suppose you've—had girls?"

"No," he said, very low.

"Not—not at all? Listen, think I'm really your sister and tell me. Why not?"

"I was frightened for them," he said, still very low, facing away from her. "The ones I could have had—och, they were not nice girls at all! And the other ones—I needed to keep free for the Party, not to get having kids!"

"But you needn't have; nobody need nowadays. I thought—oh, Donald, I thought a riveter would surely have his girl to match him, a strong jolly girl who wouldn't fuss and be intellectual and talk about it the way we do! I thought of men like Lawrence's miners. Didn't you want girls?"

"Aye," he said, "in the nights. I was needing to rise up and walk the room. Or read. I have read most of Engels that way."

"Poor old Engels," said Dione. "Donald—did you ever go to movies and look at—oh, postcards and all that?"

"Once or twice," he said, "when I was working. But they are no' fit for a Party member."

"And in the Party—there weren't any girls you were fond of?"

"It is not in our ideology," said Donald firmly. Then he said: "There is Agnes Green I am fond of, but no' that way. And the young girls—well, they maybe liked Pritchard. I was not looking at them. I was not looking at women at all."

"Donald," Dione said, "you were a bit bothered about seeing us in bathing-dresses, weren't you?" He nodded. "I thought so. Now, what's to be done about that Elephant?"

Donald jumped up and shook himself. "Ach," he said, "we'll just not be thinking of it."

The tea bell rang again. They went down. After tea Donald, wandering about the ship, came into the middle of the ship's committee in full swing. He and two or three of the other passengers sat on benches at the back, and a friendly Russian-speaking Jew, a hairdresser, interpreted for them. He was fascinated and forgot everything else for the moment.

But Dione was thinking hard. She was working something out. There is a Labour Party Elephant, she thought, and there is obviously also a Communist Party Elephant. But there can't be a Socialist Elephant. It couldn't exist. If I can only be sensible like Morag, I can deal with the Elephants. If I can only be sensible and see things steadily. If I can see what I ought to do as a Socialist woman.

## UNDER THE RED FLAG 2

DONALD didn't want to talk about that any more. So in the evening he got arguing with some men. There was a Russian woman, a Party member, who had been on a mission in America, and she came in on his side. But he wished there had been no women in it at all. That night he went to bed still excited by his argument, and could not sleep at all, so he began thinking of those women and girls in bathing-dresses. He thought, supposing maybe he had touched one of them, how would it have felt running a hand up her leg. And he fidgeted and turned over and thought about what Dione Galton had said. Then, if it *was* scientific, if it was to be believed—had he been a fool? Could he have had girls without getting tangled up in it? There was that girl Jessie he had kissed in the pub. at Girvan, a bonny girl, aye, a nice one. She'd had some understanding of his political ideas. If he had gone on then—— Ach, he began fidgeting again, was that Medingley asleep? Did he have these thoughts? Did other men—thinking about girls. He kicked off the bottom part of the pyjamas; they were worrying him. If he had gone home with Jessie that night after the meeting, as he'd half thought she'd like him to—well, would he not have been sitting in Girvan now, a family man, with no time after work to read more than the football news, slopping about in-ben by the fireside in stocking feet instead of coming out to speak and think and do propaganda—or maybe out of work, maybe breaking his heart seeing his kids on the Means Test and so afraid every Saturday night it would mean another—aye, he'd heard talk enough!—that he'd be better without a woman at all? Would it not have been that? Instead of—— Ach, there he was on it again! There, there, back in Sallington, in that room, handling that queer-like sectioned iron thing, letting it tempt him to action, boiling up over marked copies of the *Sallington News*. And could he be sure now that it was not just over his own arrest he had been angry, the things that man had said about him—which mattered little—which did not matter at all? Had he not acted on base, individualistic motives, had he betrayed the Party, was the Party maybe now hurt by what he had done? He had meant to explain that, to put it all right at the trial in a grand speech, and now—oh, now Dione Galton had snatched him away and there was nohow he could get turning the ship round to take him back to England and undo the mischief he might have done to his Cause! Exhausted, he dropped into an almost dreamless sleep.

He heard a group after breakfast the next day discussing the Coke-Brown murder, but he could not join in—he took his grammar back on deck and went at it. It was sunny again, and again there were bathing-dresses. Dione would come up in one, would sit down near him, within touching distance. Maybe she wouldn't mind if he did, seeing she'd said she was his sister? No, no, that would make it worse. He fled off to those that were more like his own folks, and spent all morning with the third class, who rolled up their shirt sleeves but at least wore trousers. The worst was, there were some English-speaking Russian women, going home after a holiday, and they wanted to teach him Russian, only they'd taken off their dresses and underneath they were in kind of petticoat things, awful short and showing at the neck, just nothing but a wee flimsy bit of ribbon over their shoulders, and no stockings, only the garter marks reddish on their legs by the knee.

The third class passengers on the Soviet ship were mostly workers, with a few of the poorer or more logical *intelligentsia* among them. They slept more to a cabin and had rather less good food, but all classes shared the sitting-rooms, and there were none of the usual notices that most passenger ships have: First class only—Second class only. Most of the third class had very definite political and class convictions; some were delegates, others were hoping to get work when they got there. Donald felt himself at ease among them, and yet felt that they weren't at ease with him. However, as time went on, there was a good deal of fraternising. Jane Ellis made friends with a boy in the third, a young American I.W.W. member, and through him with some of the others. The Jewish writer found compatriots and talked Yiddish with them. And Dione made friends with an Australian workers' delegate, a long, fierce, difficult man; the job of making friends with him took her mind off some of the other things which were occupying it, and she could watch Donald without bothering him.

At lunch Jane Ellis said: "Mother, it is true, isn't it, English policemen don't have revolvers and things? I told that Levin boy so and he said all capitalist police were armed by their Governments."

"No," said her mother, "ordinary police only have batons, but they can be very rough all the same, when they arrest one. Of course I wriggled a lot—and it was a long time ago. But they haven't improved. I've watched them arresting prostitutes: and taken notes. Have you ever been arrested?" she said brightly to Dione.

Dione shook her head: "Not yet. I wonder if one will be. I know I shall hate it."

" And you ? " she turned to Donald.

He nodded. " Aye. Two—three times. It is remarkable what they are able to do, even without weapons."

" Perhaps they thought you had bombs on you," she said.

Donald froze and looked past her. " They will be giving us the fruit now," he said.

" Mother," said the girl, " you know that Aussie. Well, he called me comrade ! "

" Did you like that ? "

" Ooh yes, it was lovely ! "

" Members of the Communist Party," said Donald, " are commonly called that by one another."

" Do you think he can have thought I was ? " the girl asked.

" I doubt he'll not have thought quite that," Donald said, between friendliness and irony, " but maybe he thought you had a promising look."

" I wish I knew more about Communism," said Jane, with something like a glad eye at Donald. " You've no idea—the *rot* they teach one at schools and call it modern history ! "

" I would be glad," said Donald, " to give you an outline of the materialist conception of history." They went out on deck together. " I wish I had my books," Donald said.

" I've had too many books," said Jane firmly.

Donald began at the beginning. He had his authors and his material at his fingers' ends, but he had a habit of dropping into the platform manner. When he did that Jane fidgeted. He wished she would wear a more decent dress ; he could have taught her more easily so.

Dione, with half an eye on it going on, as she leant on the rail, watching the low horizon which must, they thought, be North Germany, asked Nancy Ellis whether she would mind if Jane swallowed it all whole and wanted to join the Communist Party.

"One of my daughters, at least, is certain to go in for politics," said Nancy Ellis, "and if they must join a party I should sooner they joined a serious one."

"You don't count mine as serious?"

"No," said Nancy Ellis, "at present, at any rate, I am afraid I don't."

"But——" said Dione, and then realised, heavily, the kind of reason why intelligent women like Nancy Ellis didn't take the Labour Party seriously. They had seen it in office and watched it dither to its inglorious end. They had read the declarations of its leaders and the resolutions of the trade union conferences. They had noticed the advertisements in the *Herald!* What had she to put against that? Her idea of Socialism, Tom's idea—she couldn't separate them—and oh, she was bad at explaining ideas! And beyond that and far solider, the really serious thing, the Labour people of Marshbrook Bridge, the strong, the loving body whose little head waggled so fecklessly in London. Medingley, too—she had talked to him a little and realised how an uncompromising, a liberal Liberal, could politely despise her Party's compromises. And she thought, if only we didn't compromise, we could probably rope in him and people like him. The educated English admire courage. And then she thought, but is he wanted? Medingley, and Tom, and I. Are we wanted or ought we to be scrapped? And Jane Ellis? She began to wonder if Jane Ellis could solve her other problem for her, and then thought, no, it wasn't fair on Jane; he'd probably be very difficult now, she was too young, she would be frightened. But if only she could, all the same!

At dinner she asked Jane if anyone else had called her comrade.

" No, only him," said Jane, over her shoulder at Donald.

" You know," Dione said, " I'm rather looking forward myself to the first time someone calls me tovarish."

" But that's only the Russian for comrade, isn't it ? " said Jane.

" Yes," Dione said, " but at my age it seems much more romantic in Russian ! "

" You are a pair ! " Nancy Ellis observed, " probably everyone in Russia is too civilised now to say that to foreigners. Jack Lambert—that's the newspaper man, look, over there, the bald one with the eye-brows, I know him of old—told me he was going to wear his best suit and a stiff collar. They liked the Trade Delegation much better when they did that."

" Oh lor'," Dione said, " I can't believe that ! " For if there is an Elephant there, she thought, a big red Elephant, well I may as well give it all up and go back to North Oxford.

After dinner there were games with the crew ; the wireless operator, a big blonde girl, organised things. Most of the third class passengers were there, and some of the others. There were three or four young things about Jane's age, though mostly without her gumption. The Labour politician played for a short time, but he was not naturally a playful man. Dione played because she enjoyed it. They had fox-and-geese and twos-and-threes and an amusing and rather brutal game that consisted in beating people round a ring with a knotted towel. " This is the sort of game Attila played with the chief Huns," said Medingley, breathless and a little bruised, retiring from the ring. But Dione thought, how nice the sailors really are ; they might so easily amuse themselves by smacking us really hard, we bourgeois who've come to look on at them like the Zoo, but I know that man in the blue shirt didn't hit me nearly as hard as I hit him, and what fun Jane's having, and how good the wireless girl is at running it all!

After the games they began singing, and Dione sat on one of the hatches among the Russian girl sailors; they grinned at her, and one suddenly patted her hand. They sang a couple of funny folk-songs, the choruses going quicker and quicker, and ending in a shout. Then someone sang "Stenka Razin." Dione disliked that, because she associated it with studio parties. She looked round; the sunset was blazing with colour behind and at each side of them, and flat, marshy-looking land was closing in. It was the beginning of the Kiel Canal. There were several fishing-boats quite near them. What did the North German fishermen think of this new sea bird?

Then there was dancing; the crew produced their gramophone. Dione danced first with Medingley, then with the Australian delegate, who waltzed stiffly but well. Jane was whirling round with her American boy, and anyone else who could get hold of her. Dione's cabin companion was dancing nicely in an elegant little black velvet coat over a semi-evening dress. Dione, talking priggishly about education to the Australian, who rose like a fish at every correctly modern platitude she made—well aware that they came out of books, not out of her own experience! —suddenly noticed that Donald was not dancing. She went over to him: "Won't you dance, Donald? Ask Jane—I'm sure she will." He shook his head. "Dance with me, then."

"I cannot dance these London dances," he said, scowling a little.

"Come and walk round the ship, then," she said; "it's a lovely evening."

"I'll be glad to," he said, "I have never liked looking

on at the dancing." They went up to the top deck and watched while the ship waited at the entrance to the canal, and a man came on board selling cigarettes and small illegal bottles of spirit. This shocked Donald very much, but Dione was amused.

Then the ship moved on again, up the canal; the sunset stayed long and beautifully, like a Highland sunset. The lengthening ripples stretched back from their prow to the flat banks on either side, from which the smell of hay came drifting up, enclosing them. The dance was still going on. They went up into the bows and leaned over, watching and smelling. Donald said: " This is sweeter than anything since home."

She saw there were tears in his eyes. What does a Socialist woman do? " Are you at peace, Donald?" she said softly.

" Aye," he said, and put an arm round her shoulders. Her heart jumped and thudded. What does a Socialist woman do? She turned a little in his arm, getting closer to him. He was looking far out along the canal to where they were going.

After a time he too turned slowly towards her, looking at her questioningly. What does a Socialist woman do? She said the magic word: " Tovarish," and held his eyes with hers, and slowly his grip tightened on her and his other arm began to come round her. For a time he held her half-way from himself, trembling. Now they were pushed off, in the current, there was no need for her to do more than be very kind and very certain. If she could be. A Socialist woman must be. He was squashing her rather against the edge of the boat, some metal thing; it hurt her arm; she took no notice. She was suddenly glad it wasn't Jane. He might have hurt Jane. Jane, hurt, might have broken the moment for him. He couldn't hurt her. It was not part of what she now was to be hurt by a mere bit of metal.

"Dione," he said, "are you mad?"

"No," she whispered, "I was never saner. And so will you be soon."

"It must be I who is the mad one," he said. He kissed her then, putting his hands behind her neck and squashing her face against his.

For a moment she half dodged it, the strange flesh against hers set up fierce burning in her cheeks. Her lips met his; his lips squeezed hers, biting, not knowing what to do. He let her go, and took a deep breath of the hay-scented air. Blindly, violently, the image of Tom took possession of her; she felt herself inwardly crying out to Tom, to the kisses she knew and wanted. Deliberately she lifted her arm and began to stroke Donald's head. He had soft, springy hair, very different from Tom's. She kept on wondering when someone would come along and bump into them. It was dark now, but they were used enough to the night to see one another.

He said: "I have never kissed a woman that way. I did not kiss Jessie that way. I never thought it would be that way at all. Ach, Dione, tha mo ghaol ort!"

"What are you saying to me?" she asked, very gently.

After a time he answered: "I was saying, I love you." He picked up one of her hands and began to kiss it very contentedly; it was a little cold from the land dew that had begun to fall.

She said: "You mustn't say I love you, you mustn't get tangled with me. I am here to untangle you. You mustn't tangle me either. We are both of us Socialists, we love all mankind, and so we love one another. Isn't that right, Donald?"

"Yes," he said, but he had not listened much.

She said: "It is all going to come right for you. Only you mustn't ever love me too much. I don't belong to you."

He looked up then and said, startled: "I had not thought—what will *he* say, Dione?"

"Tom is a Socialist too," Dione said firmly; "he will lose nothing on this."

"But," said Donald, puzzling, letting her hand go, "have you done this before?"

"No," she said, "never; there was no need."

He took her in his arms again and kissed her, harder, less tentatively already. The bones of his face hurt her, pressing against hers, so hungry, so starved. "But what will we do? What will we do?" he said.

"What do you want to do, tovarish?" she said levelly. A Socialist man must answer.

"I do not know," he said stumblingly. "You have given me so much. You have given me this evening. I will not be asking too much of you."

She felt terribly moved. It was like when he came first after the murder. She wanted him to be a baby to be picked up and kissed well again. "I wouldn't be that sort of woman," she said, "I wouldn't promise you and then not give." There were voices near them in the dark; it was difficult to tell how far they could be seen. She sat down under the shadow of the bulwarks; the deck was damp and cold.

"When we get there," she said, "will that do, Donald?"

"Aye," he said softly, lingeringly, and she felt his hands over her hair, feeling it. They slid down on to her face; he nearly put his finger into her eye. "Why are you doing this for me, Dione?" he said.

She thought, I must give him the truth, and said low: "Mustn't Socialist people be kind to one another? Mustn't we share everything? It's wrong, isn't it, Donald, to be one thing in politics and another in living? I'm trying now to live the same way that I think. How could I leave you all oppressed and bound as you were?"

"I think I am understanding," he said.

They crouched together under the dark shade of that prow moving steadily north-east towards the Baltic. Her weight was all on one knee; she was stiff, cold away from him, burning where he touched her. His hands stroked down over her arms. "I think I am being a good Communist to you, comrade," she said, and rubbed her cheek lightly over his.

Night and day the Soviet ship went on through the still, calm, blue Baltic. The ship-load was mostly very happy. If they had not been, they would not have been able to talk to one another so easily. For some it was the promised land they were coming to; the Australian saw it as that. There were Russians returning from exile in far places. Those who wished ill to the land they were approaching were few; the feeling of the boat was against them. There were many on board with a non-Communist set of principles, good Liberals like Medingley, despisers of parties like Lady Nancy Ellis or the Jewish writer; but the friendliness of the ship had drawn them into the common hope and excitement. One evening there was a cinema; the next there was dancing again. That was the last evening of all. They had seen islands to the north, illusive, uncommunicative. But islands under the Red Flag. Towards midnight the water horizon shouldered up for a short time over the sun. But there was no darkness; instead a green light like some unknown fruit, like the light in the fairy hills, glowed between sea and sky. Jane Ellis danced with the sailors; they taught her their own dances. Dione and Donald wandered about the ship; they were further north than the Shetlands now, but it was warm enough in the white nights. For him it was the promised land. It had always been that, but now there was the other promise. He did not know how it would be, he could not imagine, but the sight of her in the short bathing-dress had not distressed him during these last two days, for now he need not snatch his eyes away from her ; he could picture what he liked.

He was not really worried about Tom. Dione's husband was not very real to him ; he was a public figure, not someone warm and within touch. But Dione herself was more anxious about Tom than she cared to admit to herself. If only she could explain to him beforehand ! Then it would be all right, then he couldn't mind. But she would have to explain when it was all over. And supposing he hated it—supposing it spoiled Russia for him—but he oughtn't to hate it, she kept on saying to herself. But if he did ?

What would have happened by the time she told him ? Would Donald still be there ? If so, wouldn't it all be very awkward ? Her imagination shifted uneasily over practical details. No, it would have to be all over, all tidied up. She would have to explain that to Donald.

When Tom saw her again, what would she be ? She would be a Socialist woman : as she had always been. She would be an adulteress. She would be changed. She would be one of the sort of women she had always supposed she would never be. Would she look at herself in the mirror and see herself different ? Nonsense, half her friends had done it ! Well, not half, but several. And without her reasons. If one did it for this kind of reason perhaps one wasn't an adulteress. Nobody had thought of that. If one did it for someone else, not because one wanted to oneself.

It must be very different if one wanted it. A different kind of waiting. No fear. None of this awful backwards feeling, this shrinking of the flesh. Perhaps it had been like this being a virgin; she couldn't remember now. Dear Donald, she was so terribly frightened of him, and she must not show it. A Socialist woman must not be frightened, would not be. Out of the strange waters by the ship as she passed Cronstadt, seals rose through the waves and mocked Dione. Not undressing, she slept for a little; and most on that ship slept uneasily, their luggage ready beside them. And then the water horizon shouldered down again, the green and orange cleared from the sky, and in a blue and brilliant morning the Soviet ship sailed into port, and a dozen or so of the few idle people in Leningrad came down to the quay to look at the foreigners out of the strange outside capitalistic world.

For some time they waited at the quay for anything to happen, staring at everything there was to see, a cart passing or bridges and buildings which might be historical. Everyone was sleepy and anxious and excited; they pointed and whispered or fell suddenly asleep on top of their luggage. After a time officials came on board, some from Intourist; they were friendly but rather superior. Passports were given back to their owners. Now for the first time since the beginning Dione and Donald began to be very nervous. Dione was acutely conscious of having Donald's Party card at the bottom of her pocket, under her handkerchief; obviously she was not going to be searched, but that made no difference to her feeling of guilty embarrassment. Nobody among the passengers knew quite what formalities there might be, and most felt a little like new boys coming to a very large school. Donald stared out of the ship on to what looked like another real world, no longer now the small, magic, conditional world that Dione had brought him into, the world where no one seemed to be considering the important things—the difference between one shilling and two—where there was infinite leisure for discussion and no one was hungry or cold. Well, that was over. Reality would begin again.

Dione came up to him. " All right ? " she asked. He nodded. " Well, we've just got to wait. I wish——"

" What ? "

" Oh, I don't know. I wish Tom was here."

Then suddenlv they were all leaving the ship, the little

magic world between worlds, they were walking down a gangway, they were in a building full of benches ; they sat close, waiting. There were pictures on the walls. Donald nudged Dione : " Look : Lenin." She took his hand and squeezed it. But Lenin for her was a history-book name, someone remote like Napoleon, someone not connected with life. Only she could see the name made something different happen inside Donald ; she did not yet know what, but she tried to share it.

Two or three names were called out, loudly but rather unintelligibly, into an immediate silence. The Labour politician went through, and two others. A door opened and shut behind them ; for another moment there was silence, as though people were listening for screams. The mere tension shook Dione into a fit of laughter she could not explain to Donald. Then other names were called out ; soon it was B party. They went through into a room beyond where the luggage was examined. Everyone was now on edge, especially those who had slept little the night before ; giggles rippled about the room as one by one the opened suit-cases of the English exposed rolls or packets of toilet paper and every time it was explained to the customs officers by one of the interpreters. For most of the tourists the examination was not very thorough, but Dione watched the real immigrants having their baggage mercilessly ransacked ; at first she was indignant about it and sorry for them, and then she began to wonder whether after all it didn't give them a fine sense of importance. If one was in no hurry it did no harm. By this time she was recovering her sense of normality. Nobody had asked her whether she was carrying the Party card of a murderer ; nobody had looked suspiciously at Donald's passport.

All at once it was over, and the Intourist guide was shooing them all rapidly into a 'bus, and it started, and after a minute or two almost all of its occupants began to tell whoever was next them their Impressions of Soviet Russia. Dione felt herself taking rapid mental notes, even though she was already aware that she would be bound to alter them very soon; she observed the cheap, shapeless dresses and red head-handkerchiefs on the women, the embroidered shirts and eastern-looking coloured caps on the men; she observed the crowded pavements, the worse-than-crowded trams. They were in a great main street now, lined with shops. She peered hard at the shop windows, trying to see what was for sale, but they were like the sheep's shop in "Alice Through the Looking-glass"—she never could quite make out what was in any of them. Subconsciously she was waiting for what one expects from any capital city—the luxury quarter, the fine dresses, the cafés, the advertisements, the temptations to spending, the flower of civilisation as we have known it. She waited for Regent Street and the Avenue de l'Opéra; they never came. And her astonished subconsciousness registered the fact that it *was* true after all, that there really weren't any class distinctions, that these people in the shabby frocks and shoddy shoes and patched trousers really were the owners of this one of the world's Capitals.

While she was still taking this in, the 'bus drew up and they poured out again and stood on the pavement, saying, "Oh, look!"—till the Intourist guides managed to remarshal them and get them into an hotel. The guides ran about with lists and ticked their names off; they were put firmly into rooms. The rooms were very comfortable, but were always shared by two or three people. Dione found herself put into a room with the girl who had shared her cabin and another woman whom she had only just got to know on board. When she met Donald again she found he was sharing a room, too. At the moment there was nothing to be said or done about it—the party were all talking at once, not attending to the guides, who were trying to give them breakfast. But Dione felt a dreadful sense of relief. Not yet, she thought, not to-night.

Again their conscientious sheep-dogs mustered them; it was already becoming apparent which members of B party were going to be restive and which to be good. Now they were being taken for a drive round Leningrad; Dione sat between Donald and Jane; it was very hot and the roads were very bumpy, and it was difficult to remember which was the Winter Palace and which was the Admiralty and which was the Hermitage. Every now and then they stopped at the side of some square or another and were lectured to; during these lectures a small crowd always collected; after a time the guide would appeal to the crowd to move aside and let the foreigners see their country. Dione could hear at last the magic word said in schoolmistressish tones by competent guides: tovarishi. And reluctantly the crowds would move away a little. B party would dutifully look in the required direction. Excitement and sleeplessness were telling on B party. They began suddenly to fall asleep on one another's shoulders, regardless of the distress they were causing to the guides. They were shown more and more buildings; those who had looked Leningrad up most conscientiously began to be lost. And still another building! Dione thought through a haze of sleepiness, and got out on to still another hot pavement. "Smolny," she thought, "what's Smolny?" and remembered vaguely out of her history books as though it had been Anne Hathaway's house or Kenilworth Castle.

They went in. What did these corridors remind her of? She remembered: Mädchen in Uniform. She looked round; Donald was staring and troubled: "I have had this long in my mind," he said, "but it was not—not such a grey, empty-like place." The guide led them along the corridor to the great hall, with the benches and the flags and the daïs with the picture above it. This was rather magnificent, Dione thought, beginning to wake up more thoroughly, this light, this white and scarlet and unpainted wood, and the great low-brow picture of Lenin! This place is what it ought to be like. From there they went back along a corridor and came into another room; there was a little furniture, cheap and ugly, there was a window without a view, and there was a sense of something enormously big, something pushing out intruders. Dione found herself pressed against Donald, and he was whispering: "He was here, Lenin was here; oh, Dione, we were not here helping him!"

But again Dione was setting other values against this. What is it like? What is it like? It is like the first London show of Van Gogh pictures, the chair, the cornfields, the lauriers-rose—those pictures that oppressed one like this does, like this hurling one back out of the room, by some force in them, some dæmon. Yes, there was a dæmon here, she thought, the Talking Crow, going where it will, without a ticket or passport, going to what nation or what epoch it will, to whatever man can bear it, the Crow's weight heavy on his hand, the voice that will not let him rest, that he cannot escape from, driving him—driving him, on to Cloud Cuckoo Borough, without a ticket or passport. . . . Lenin. He was undoubtedly the greatest single figure in modern history. The greatest events of modern history happened here and hereabouts. What was I thinking of all that time? For I certainly didn't realise what was happening. Very few of us did. The newspapers. Yes, but one can't blame the newspapers for everything. Some people saw. Donald, who was only a boy, saw. But I? I was thinking of Tom being safe back from the war and

Morag a darling baby. Oh yes, and Ireland. I was all in a fuss about the Black-and-Tans. When all this was going on. Odd how one misses the 'bus.

Again they were outside. Lambert, the old journalist, said to Lady Nancy Ellis: "Well, now we've seen Bethlehem."

"You think it's that, do you?"

"Yes, with a touch of Calvary."

"It must have made things a lot simpler," Dione said, a little enviously, "to know that the further one went in one's chosen direction the more right one was. None of this bother about compromise and seeing the other side."

"But that was not always so," Donald said; "here, at Smolny, maybe, but not afterwards. Remember, Dione, how he needed to go carefully with the peasants, how for the sake of the future he allowed the New Economic Policy—and in face of many in his own party. Aye, he could see realities. He was no theorist."

"And when one thinks of the mess we made of the General Strike——." Dione said.

"*We?*" said Donald. "If it had been in *our* hands —— But it was in yours."

"The difficulty was," Dione said, "it wasn't in anybody's hands. It had—fallen out and was lying on the floor in bits before anyone knew. Oh dear," she went on suddenly, half to herself, "I wish it had all happened then and we'd got it over!" And then she began to wonder, as they drove on again, whether if it had happened she would have been able to have Ian the next year all the same.

That evening, after the guides had left them, she and Donald walked about Leningrad together, watching people. It was strange seeing so many happy, confident faces, mostly rather ugly, but in some way attractive. It was odd seeing that amount of gaiety after Sallington. "Look at those girls," Dione said, "tossing their heads up and kicking their toes out as though they owned the place!"

"But," said Donald, "they *do* own it."

"Yes," she said, "yes. So they do. If only they were dressed a little better. I don't mean elaborate stuff or trimmings, and I like the short skirts, but if only they'd put the waist line at the waist instead of round their hips and have a little more fullness in the skirt—it's just a matter of cut. Oh dear, what fun it would be to redress Leningrad!"

Donald laughed and took her arm in his; he did it very clumsily, hauling her along, with big strides she found it difficult to keep up with. "This is fine!" he said, "I will like fine living in this country!"

They decided to do nothing about looking for a job for him till they were in Moscow. Both felt that Leningrad was a little too near. Donald was quite confident that he could get work in Moscow; they were obviously short of metal-workers. Dione was a good deal worried about how it was to be done, about what would happen over the passport. She did not tell him quite how much worried she was, but she felt he had better avoid all Government departments. She did not propose to use any of Tom's introductions unless it was absolutely necessary. Government departments, she felt, are dreadfully alike all over the world. Even here they might—no, she thought, they *can't* send him back!

They were walking along the Fontanka now; there were other couples, arm in arm or hand in hand. She saw two young people saying good-bye to one another—the girl was bare-legged, in one of those shapeless cotton frocks, with a cheap beret that didn't match, and a string of beads, the boy wore an embroidered shirt and grey cotton trousers; both were fair-haired and northern-looking. They kissed in the middle of the pavement and parted casually, he along the canal, she with a wave of her hand, across a small bridge. "I suppose this is all right for them," Dione said; "they needn't cling to one another and be miserable, wondering when they can afford it, and thinking they've got to be careful."

"No," said Donald, "there's none of that here."

She extracted her arm gently from under his and took his hand instead; it seemed friendlier and was much more comfortable. "Whichever of those two has a room, it does to take the other to. And when they have a baby they know it'll be wanted as another citizen, the State will be pleased with them, they'll have done something worth while." Donald said nothing, only his bony fingers tightened, squeezing hers together, the hard palm of his hand, scarred in one place by a burn. She knew his hands now. "Donald," she said, "I'm sorry about to-night."

He turned suddenly and looked down at her; he was nearly a head taller than she was, a little taller than Tom. "I'm wondering if you *are* sorry, Dione," he said.

"My dear," she said, "my dear, I—I want to make everything right for you."

"But you do not want it at all yourself, Dione," he asked, "not at all?"

She wondered, confused, having to answer at once, what does a Socialist woman do? Does she lie? Can she cheat? "Donald," she said, "you know there's no question of my being in love with you. And you wouldn't want that, either. You know I like you, Donald, I respect you. I—I think you're a good sort of person. I think you have power and that you'll use it well. That's what matters, isn't it, not one's silly personal desires?"

"You have not answered my question, Dione," he said, "or—maybe you have. Well, I'm going to kiss you,

Dione, whether it's your personal desire or not, for it's surely mine ! "

For a moment the impulse against being kissed in the public streets made Dione dodge and shove him away. " You are being a bourgeois, Dione," he said, laughing and holding her hands, and kissed her accurately on the mouth.

" Sorry ! " she said, when she'd got her breath again. " I know I was. Don't hold me, Donald. So long as none of B party see us ! "

" Well, aren't I your brother ? " he said, and kissed her again more thoroughly.

" Brothers don't kiss like that," she said. " You're improving, Donald."

" I'm needing to make the most of my time," he said, in a queer, hard kind of way.

As he held her tight in his arms, half leaning against the parapet, she heard some laughing comment in Russian from a girl passing by. She felt horribly uncomfortable. She felt like a housemaid with her young man. With her out-of-work riveter. She was sacrificing herself to her ideas. And then suddenly she thought, that isn't how a Socialist woman behaves ! Sacrifice—what a dirty, novelette-reading, hole-and-corner mind I've got. Sacrifice ! She put her arms up quickly round his neck, and held him down to her fiercely, kissing him back. Did she like it or didn't she ? Very probably she did. Anyway, who cares. If someone was kissing her she would bloody well see that he had a good time of it !

" Aye, that was better," he said, half letting her go, looking down at her face again, " but you would rather not have had it at all. Wouldn't you, Dione ? "

" Oh, don't," she said, " don't ! Don't be always asking questions, pulling things up by their roots ! "

"You have set me such a question yourself, Dione," he said.

"Oh no!" she cried, "not a question. An answer." And then, taking a quick breath: "Donald, you'd better have your Party card now."

She opened her bag; she had put his card into the fold of her own Oxford Labour Party card; he saw that. "Yes," he said, "maybe it's true you do like me a little, Dione."

They stayed in Leningrad three days. They saw the Hermitage, and Dione showed Donald the technique of Greek vase painting, and told him the story of Peisthetairos and the Crow and the founding of Cloud Cuckoo Borough, and made him laugh over that early and so successful piece of anti-religious propaganda. The Jewish writer spent a good deal of time over the pictures, but they did not seem to say much to Donald; he always wanted to know what they were about, and was worried by the constantly recurring Christian theme. They saw the Peter and Paul fortress. They saw hundreds and hundreds of Soviet propaganda posters and leaflets. They were taken out to Tsarkoe Selo and picnicked on smoked-fish sandwiches. Nancy Ellis made the guides very nervous because she would sit on the grass. "Nonsense," she said, "it does no harm to sit on the grass. Everyone sits on the grass in England."

"But the notices——"

"Sheer bureaucracy. I shall certainly sit on the grass."

Some were taken over a factory, others over a crèche. Some were already beginning to react against the propaganda, others didn't mind it. Dione's cabin companion wrote copious notes every day; she particularly emphasised the bread queues and the general messiness, she was delighted to find housing conditions still bad, and kept a sharp lookout for beggars, of whom there were a certain amount, almost always old women—left-overs for whom nothing could be done, who would have been miserable in institutions.

And in the evenings Dione and Donald walked about the streets. Leningrad was always crowded. There were always people in the parks and by the Grave of the Revolutionaries. In these white nights no one seemed to go to bed. After work the citizens wandered along the river and canal banks, talking and singing; sometimes they took boats and rowed; sometimes they sat on benches reading text-books on economics and engineering, or newspapers.

Dione said: "I shouldn't be afraid to go anywhere in this town alone."

"Are you afraid in other towns?" Donald asked, interested.

"In most foreign towns, anyway," she said, "I hate being stared at. I shouldn't much like walking through Piræus or the dockside quarters in Marseilles. For that matter I always get a bit frightened in the East End of London or Leith."

"What for are you frightened?" Donald asked, "you are surely not frightened they would hurt you in the open streets? Or is it robbery you are frightened for?"

"I'm not sure," she said. "I'm a bit frightened of men looking at me, I expect. Yes, I suppose at bottom I'm frightened of rape or at least—of people coming up behind and—kissing me or something. But I'm frightened of women sometimes, their eyes and hands: women who've been hurt, probably, and who want to hurt back when they see me wearing nicer clothes than theirs. I'm frightened of the places one feels one's a stranger in—an intruder, an alien—the sort of person they're bound to hate, to want to do down in some way!"

"That seems to me like class-consciousness," Donald said.

"Very likely. And education. The way girls were educated. To hold themselves apart, a kind of—precious thing. But I don't feel it anywhere in Marshbrook Bridge, and I don't here. I would just—oh, say I was a Socialist. And it would be all right."

"But can you not see," Donald said very earnestly, "it would be the same in the other places?"

"I'm not sure," she said.

"Dione," he said, "I'm thinking you have as much to be cured of as I have." He put his arms round her. "They're folks like me," he whispered, "they've been out of work and hungry and they're seeing you've never truly had to care for the difference between having a shilling and not having it. They've had the police after them, and they're seeing you're the kind that the police would always be respectful to. But if you are not frightened for me, you will learn not to be frightened for them."

"I see," she whispered back, admitting it.

"But you are frightened for me still!" he said. "What will I do, Dione, how can I do more with you when you are that frightened?"

They came in late from these walks. The last day, Nancy Ellis said, "I suppose after this, if your brother stays in Russia, you'll not see him again for years?" Dione nodded. "You're very fond of him, aren't you?"

"Yes," Dione said, "and we've a lot to talk about."

"Why don't you ask these Intourist people to let you share a room with him in Moscow? I'm sure they'd do it for a brother and sister."

"Oh," said Dione, "I wonder if one could. They—they seem always to have arranged everything beforehand."

"You mustn't let yourself be bullied," Nancy Ellis said firmly, "of course you can ask them. My dear child, don't look so alarmed, I'll do it myself." And so she did, and the Intourist guide made a note of it to send on to Moscow.

B party were put on to the night train for Moscow. They leant out of the windows, watching the country in the evening light. Now they were all brimming with experience, wanting to communicate it. Their minds were in a turmoil of things seen, comparisons with hopes or fears. They thought of people and buildings; they thought of what had happened ten and twelve years back. The sense of history gripped them. They remembered Smolny:

"In that room, on the two iron bedsteads,
He slept, and Krupskaia.
They had no fun.
There are two red stuffy armchairs, there is one sofa,
There is one cheap wardrobe.
There are no flowers.
Pictures are not Lenin,
Stalin is not Lenin,
Nobody else is Lenin,
Lenin is dead.
He has no fun, no heaven,
Only remembrance, only authenticity.
The people in the streets remember Lenin,
They have their fun now,
The fun of being brothers, of certainty,
Knowing they're right, although
There are still no flowers.
Walking their streets in the light evenings, talking, whispering, hand in hand,
The people remember Lenin.
But the room at Smolny
Is quiet, empty the bedsteads, the sofa unlain on, the table
Not covered with papers, nor in the wardrobe even
One greatcoat for winter.
Empty the room, empty the walls, the window, empty the air he breathed.
Lenin is dead, is dead.
He had no fun, no flowers.
The people shall have them."

The train took them steadily east across Russia. They came to Moscow and their hotel. Again the rooms were given out.

"You and your brother in room 317," said the guide, handing Dione a key. It was on the fourth floor, looking on to a courtyard, with the usual shower and plugless wash-basin. They looked at one another.

"Well, then, this is all right," Dione said, as casually as possible.

"When ?" said Donald.

"To-night, my dear," she said.

"Not now ?"

"I—I've got to get ready," she said, "and there's not time. They'll have things arranged for us." She bent over her suit-cases, unlocking them, taking out her dresses.

Donald watched her : "Frightened ?"

"A little," she said. "I can't help it. Don't bother about it, Donald."

"Ach," he said, "if only you could be wanting me a little, Dione—only a little !"

Ought she to say she did ? Ought she still to be truthful ? Oh dear, she'd got into the habit of being truthful with Tom. "I like you, Donald," she said, "I like being with you. I like seeing all this with you. I think I like you kissing me."

"I'll try to be gentle, Dione," he said, low and not very happily.

Nancy Ellis knocked at their door ; Dione was rather relieved—they wouldn't have had time. "The party's splitting up to-day," she said ; "there's a visit arranged for a factory, but I've been told I can go and see an abortion and birth-control clinic, so one or two of us are going off there. Will you come, Dione ?"

"Yes," she said.

Donald said: " And I'll go to the factory."

Nancy Ellis nodded. " Come along down, then. We shall start at once after breakfast."

Dione and Nancy Ellis and three others went off to their clinic, Donald and Jane and the others to the factory. " And I thought Leningrad was crowded," Dione said to herself, " but this—this is unbelievable! And the dust, and the sun, and the people hanging like flies on to the trams, and the walls of the Kremlin like something Moorish, almost. God, what a place! "

Their clinic was large and competent. They were shown into the room of a doctor, whom they questioned through an interpreter. The answers were long and appeared to be medical, but the interpretation was always given a correctly Marxist twist. " And v'y is der reason for dis? " said the guide, with the accurate American accent which is generally taught—and, after all, the population of the United States is considerably larger and more important than the population of England, and seems likely to be going to have a revolution sooner—and then out would come the economic interpretation of contraception or whatever it was. Nancy Ellis shook her head impatiently: " I can get all that out of a book! " she said, but it had no effect.

Abruptly the interview came to an end and the guide passed them on to another doctor, a woman surgeon in a white overall. " I am not come with you," said the guide. " I—I am sensible." And how right she is not to come, thought Dione, also a person of sensibility. I don't want to see this a bit! However, they were all five put into white overalls and taken into an antiseptic-smelling room with a special operating-table in the middle, and a pretty, youngish woman on it, who turned and looked at them; her knees were over supports, she was all ready for the abortion to be performed.

" But she *can't* like us looking on ! " Dione said.

" I don't suppose she's been asked, my dear," said Nancy Ellis, " but, as I understand no anæsthetics are used, she will probably be too acutely occupied with her own sensations to mind whether the whole world's looking on."

The woman surgeon put on her rubber gloves and called them all to attention. It was all done with extreme competence and rapidity. At first it did not seem to hurt much ; then blood began to flow and the woman on the table shut her eyes and went white. Now blood and tissue poured out of her ; the surgeon took another instrument and for a minute or so there was the peculiarly unpleasant sound of metal scraping against human flesh. Once the woman on the table gave a little gasping cry ; no one heeded her. The surgeon swabbed round with cotton-wool, turned and smiled at the onlookers ; it was all satisfactorily over. She went out to get ready for the next case. Dione looked at her watch ; it had taken less than five minutes. The woman on the table opened her eyes and moved her head from side to side ; she was still very white ; her upper lip was drawn back from her teeth. " Ought we to do anything ? " Dione asked, but none of them knew. A porter came in with a trolley, a short, thick-set man, rather stupid-looking ; he put one arm under the woman and shifted her over, helping her to cover herself ; he seemed to do everything far more gently and tenderly than any English hospital nurse.

So that's what it comes to, Dione thought, the smell of blood in her nostrils, the look of the woman, so terribly uncovered, branded into her imagination. That's what all the fuss is about, that's reality. They went on to the birth-control clinic : the alternative, when it worked. Nancy Ellis tried to get hold of their figures of failure and success, but it was difficult to be sure of them. The place was full of the usual propaganda posters ; Dione suddenly felt she was sick to death of them. There was no freedom here, either. What was the good of putting so much pain and effort into exchanging one bondage for another ?

After that they saw another clinic, and then came back, hungry and tired, about 4.30, for dinner. The factory party had come back and had theirs already. " Where's Donald ? " Dione asked, and Jane said he had gone out alone after dinner ; no, he didn't say where.

Dione went up to her room ; she was tired and hot. She finished unpacking and made everything tidy, then had a shower bath ; she was dusty under her socks, down her neck, everywhere. She dressed again and brushed her hair. She was ready now. She was waiting. It was seven o'clock. She had brought these contraceptive things for herself and Tom ; it seemed somehow indecent to use them for herself and Donald. She was cross with herself for thinking that, but the thought remained. And if they failed ? Supposing—with someone new—she didn't know what effect that was likely to have. Well, she thought, if they fail I shall have an abortion. Like the one I saw. Because that's how it ends logically. That's a real end. Blood and pain and ugliness. After that you stop fussing about fine points. She wondered if Donald would make a frightful muddle of it. Probably, the first time. That was why she hadn't wanted it to be Jane. She mustn't let him know if he did. She must make it seem right for him. Then he'd be better the next time. In a year she would be laughing at herself for this fuss.

She lay down and began reading " The Fountain." She couldn't keep her thoughts on it. Tom, she thought, oh Tom, oh Tom, if only you would come and tell me I was doing the right thing, tell me to go on ! Oh Tom, it's such fun with you, so warm, so friendly, so kind, so happy-making. It's all right with you. And the end isn't blood and pain—yes it is, but it's not shameful, it's clean blood, it's Morag and Kenneth and Ian and Lilias ; it's lovely and sweet and new. Oh Tom, she said, half aloud, oh Tom, and began crying into her pillow, and wondered why Donald didn't come.

Someone knocked. But it was Jane Ellis. " Mother said, would you come and have supper with us ? Got your supper card ? I say, have you got a headache or anything ? "

Dione shook her head : " No, I'm just tired. I wonder where Donald is."

" Oh, he's sure to be all right," Jane said ; " he'll probably turn up when we're in the middle of supper."

They went down and had supper, but Donald didn't come, though lots of other people came into the restaurant who might have been him, but weren't. " We're going to the cinema," Nancy Ellis said, " won't you come ? "

Dione shook her head : " No, I'll wait for Donald."

" He may have gone off to the cinema on his own," Jane suggested, " do come ! You'll make the guide frightfully cross if you don't—she's got the tickets and she says it'll be good for us ! " But Dione wouldn't.

She went up to their room. She couldn't read. She began looking through his things and decided she'd better wash his socks. She found a dirty shirt and smelt it tentatively ; yes, this was how he smelt. What did she think of it ? Nice, not nice ? She didn't know, she couldn't make up her mind even about something as easy as that, she couldn't this evening be sure of anything in the world. She washed his dirty things and her own, boiling some water on her spirit-lamp and cutting a piece of cork to fit the plugless basin. She put them out to dry over chair backs, noting one sock that wanted darning. It was getting late. Could anything have happened to him? Wouldn't someone let Intourist know if it had? What was he thinking of? How could he treat her like that? Anger and anxiety tossed her about. It was past eleven o'clock. Nobody came.

## UNDER THE RED FLAG 4

When the other bit of the party did not come back in time to have dinner with them, Donald went out of the hotel. If he had stayed someone would have talked to him, and he didn't want that. He wanted to walk and not think too much. To-morrow he would get on to seeing about work. That would be real. To-morrow. It was difficult to look as far ahead as to-morrow. What could he do to-night if she was that frightened, still not wanting him at all? Maybe he'd hurt her. He could not bear to hurt her. But why had she been so brave at first? For it was surely she that had begun it. Maybe it was that he'd done something wrong since. Maybe it was all wrong; it came of letting himself look at those women in their bathing-dresses—he had known he should not have looked—and then the hay smell along the Kiel Canal and the green light on the Baltic, the bonny great sea loch, and walking with her those evenings in Leningrad. Maybe it was naught but a snare and a delusion to take him from his work, and from seeing Communism in action. Aye, and from seeing her as she was, as a bourgeoise. An enemy. If she were an enemy, he should be glad to hurt her this way! But it was not in him to hurt her. Not now.

He walked along the tram-lines; after a time he came to a bridge over a branch of the Moscow River. Here he turned and walked along the waterside; there was a parapet wall on his left, and on his right some oldish, broken-looking houses. He heard music ahead of him. He didn't want music; the evening was charged enough with feelings.

The music came down the water from the direction in which he was walking. By and bye he came to three girls sitting on the parapet above the water; one was playing some stringed instrument and they were all singing. They wore cotton dresses; two had red head-handkerchiefs, but the player was bare-headed. Their legs and arms were bare and very brown. They turned and looked at him, staring with their bold eyes. The one who was playing stopped and said: "American comrade?" She had a bit of an American accent herself.

He hesitated. "No, Scottish comrade," he answered.

"Scottish?" said the girl.

Donald wanted to go on walking; at the same time he had to explain; he knelt down, picked up a stick and drew in the dust a map of England and Scotland. The three girls came tumbling off the wall to watch. Their bare legs stood solidly all round his map. Light hairs on brown skin. He began to put in the towns. London; they knew that. "Here, Scotland." He patted the hot dust with his hand. "Glasgow."

That seemed to mean something, too; two of the girls were talking hard in Russian, and he heard the name repeated. At last the American-speaking girl tapped him on the shoulder: "You—Glasgow, Scotland—working?" He nodded. "You—working in zavod, in factory—Glasgow, Scotland?"

"Metal-worker," said Donald, and on an impulse turned the palms of his hands towards them.

They seized hold of his hands. "Ah," said the girl who did the speaking—she had laid her instrument down on the parapet—"You—work with hands. Me too. She too. She too." Laughing, they all held their hands palms up beside his; they were working hands all right. "Me," said the girl, and she screwed up her face, thinking of the word, " me—engineer. She engineer: electric zavod. She: learning."

" What do you do ? " said Donald, interested and a little bothered at these women engineers.

The girl laughed and made the appropriate movements with her arms and hands, like a clever child.

" You're on a lathe ? " said Donald.

" Yes, yes! The words—I forget. You say them. English—I not speak well. I understand. You say. I Marfa." She pointed to herself. " She Nina. She Maria. You——? "

" Donald," he said.

They laughed. " Don-ald! Don-ald! "

He didn't much like being laughed at. " Here! " he said, and took his Party card out of his pocket.

Marfa knew it at once, snatched it away from him, and explained it to her friends, reading it aloud in English and translating it. She found his name: " Don-ald Mac-Lean." Oh, he had got so tired of being called Mr. Fraser by the passengers on the ship! Suddenly she burst into a torrent of Russian, checked herself, frowned, stamped, and said: " MacLean. I know that name. MacLean, he was one great leader—in Glasgow—you come from—in the Party. He was—Bolshevik."

" He is dead," said Donald, " aye, he was a grand man. I have heard him speak."

" And you," said the girl, " you are—active member—propaganda, yes ? "

She had taken him by the hand, she was looking into his eyes, she was all alive and oh—not frightened. He took a half-step towards her: " Listen, comrade! " he said, " I killed a man. I killed a capitalist, a newspaper owner. I threw a bomb at him. I escaped. I came here, I want to live here, in the U.S.S.R." He waited while Marfa translated it excitedly to the others ; all three had their hands on his arms now, all three asked questions. " Yes, yes," he answered, disentangling Marfa's questions and exclamations. " You read about it—that was the one ! Yes, Coke-Brown. Yes, I am he. Some friends helped me to escape. Now I need to get work and live in the U.S.S.R."

They all talked at once. Marfa turned and clapped her hands down over Maria's mouth, and shook her fist at Nina till she was quiet for a moment, too. " Now," she said, " I have a friend. Yes. We—call him up. He is English Party comrade—Comintern. He will—make the investigate. Then—maybe we find you something. Some work. Come. We go—post office."

" In the Comintern ? " said Donald, and for a moment he held on to the parapet wall.

" Sure," said Marfa, and then : " Why—why frightened, comrade ? " She laid her hand on his gripping hand, looking at him with such warm and positive friendliness that he had to try and explain.

" They'll know in the Comintern, the way things were. The way I got letting my own individual pride and anger persuade me—against the Party. And they'll not know I had been meaning to put it right—at the trial. But it will be best I get it over. Aye. Will we go to the post office now ? "

He stood straight, his lips narrowed, his eyes steadied again. The girl was looking at him still. Had she understood at all ? " He is nice man, the Comintern comrade," she said reassuringly, " he—help you live here. I got a thought too, maybe, how you live." She put a hand on his shoulder, watching him closer. " Comrade," she said, " it is—all right. Not—not sad, comrade." And suddenly she put both arms round his neck and kissed him.

On the way to the post office she explained the others to

him. He was glad to have that to think of. All three of them were sharing a room. Maria, the eldest of the three, was a peasant's wife ; she had worked so well, organising a kolkhoz, learning to read and write and teaching others, that as a reward she had been sent to Moscow to work half-time in a factory and continue her education. She was a Party member. She had two children whom she had left in the village with her husband. Nina, the youngest, who had black eyes and comparatively elegant shoes, worked at a glass furnace in an electrical spare-parts factory. Nina was also still being educated ; she was a comsomol. And she herself, Marfa, she was a Party member, and on the works committee at her factory. She had been married to a locomotive driver who had been five years in America ; that was how she had learnt English. Now they were divorced.

Donald looked at her curiously. He had never to his knowledge seen a divorced person before. " Why ? " he asked.

" Oh," she said, " Dmitri, he was—one great mutt, one bone-head. He love me too much. He want me not work. We—fight. I have—different ideology. I say, I work in factory, I not love you too much. So I get one divorce."

" He loved you too much, did he," said Donald. He seemed to have heard that before. " And now—do you see him ever ? "

" Oh, sometimes," said the girl, " but—he make too much drama. He is nice man, but—we not true comrades. You understand ? "

They got to the post office and telephoned. He stood back, watching them, trying to listen, hearing his own name repeated. For a time, for a week, he had been lulled by this other thing, as the man in the song had been on his way to battle, when the fairy maiden had put her word on him. Dione had done that, for a week she had made him not think of the wrong he had done against the Party, getting him away when he should have stayed, stopping him thinking when he should have thought most. He could tell her that, hurt her with the knowledge of the harm she had done. Dione in room 317.

Marfa turned from the telephone, beaming. " English Comintern comrade, he come," she said, " good—yes ? " She tucked one arm through his ; the stringed instrument was under the other.

" What do you call that ? " he asked.

" Balalaika," she said, " after, maybe, we will play music. Now—come."

They went along together. He wanted to find out something about this Englishman, but it was difficult. The girls kept asking him questions, about his work, how much he used to make, his hours, what he had to eat. Then about unemployment in Scotland, then about Party work ; again he tried to explain that the assassination was not Party instructions but an individual protest ; it was queer how here he was already forgetting the sharpness and bitterness of his temptation to do it. The girls did not seem to worry much ; they laughed ; there was one capitalist the less. They came to a block of flats and went through a passage into a small courtyard ; in one corner a boy was cleaning a fish—he turned and shouted to them. They went up stone steps to the third floor, and Maria unlocked the door. It was a square, lime-washed room with a big table, a bed with an embroidered linen cover, very clean, and two sofas, each with a tidily rolled pile of bedding on it, two cupboards, a lot of plants in pots, and behind a screen in one corner a wicker cot. Marfa pulled the screen away and a small, curly-headed child sat up in the cot. " That my kid," said Marfa, and hugged it and put it back. Nina and Maria took off their head-handkerchiefs ; Nina combed her short dark hair and then handed the comb on to Marfa, but Maria undid a great long plait that came down nearly to her knees, and began brushing it slowly. Nina went over to one of the pot plants in the window and broke off a flower and gave it to Donald ; it was a big, very sweet jasmin.

Then there was a knock, and the man from the Comintern came in. He was an ordinary-looking man in rather shabby clothes, but not flauntingly untidy like so many of the Russians. He shook hands with them all and said, " 'Evening, comrade," to Donald ; he had a Staffordshire voice. He saw Donald's hungry eyeing of the *Daily Worker* that was sticking out of his pocket, and handed it over, grinning a bit, while Donald silently passed across his Party card. Then he talked to the girls in laborious Russian, still with the Staffordshire accent ; they all laughed ; he was making the kind of jokes people in the Potteries make, and they didn't translate very well. Still, the intention counted.

Donald looked up, and he was rather white ; he put the paper down on the table, smoothing it blindly from side to side with the tense pressure of his fingers. " So that is what they are saying of the man that killed Daniel Coke-Brown," he observed in a hard kind of voice.

" Well," said the Comintern man, " you didn't expect them to go saying you was a hero, did you ? Not after you were as near as makes nothing to breaking up the Party. Haven't you seen the *Moscow Daily News ?* "

" No—I——" How could he say how little he had been thinking of the papers even ? Or had she—could Dione have been hiding it from him ? Anger against her jerked through him, mixed with a bitter knowledge of what he had to do. " I—I am thinking—I had best get back to England—and—put that right."

" And how did you think you could do that ? "

" By saying—before they hanged me—that the thing was

done — as my — individual — protest. Against — Instructions."

"If you could put it right that way," said the man, putting the *Daily Worker* back again into his pocket, "we'd send you off all right. Don't you worry! But you wouldn't. You'd only stir it all up again. Why, lad, it'll be half-forgotten already. And it didn't break the Party. Takes more than that! Now then, you cheer up, we've got your record. That's all right. I knew Comrade Green a bit: was in that little affair at Preston with her. The best thing you can do now is stay here and keep quiet." He handed back the Party card and began explaining to the girls.

Donald took the card. He walked towards the window and looked out across the courtyard of the flats through the green jasmin leaves. As the view blurred he put his hands up over his eyes and face. He felt the girls come closer to him; they patted his shoulders. "Tovarish," they said, "tovarish." He minded their touching him less than his shrinking away meant. He almost liked it. Marfa was standing beside him; he could smell her hair, not like Dione's, a stronger smell. She had her arm round his neck, she pulled his hands away from his face, and brushed the palm of her own hand across his wet cheeks. She was laughing a little, but not to hurt. "Listen!" she said, and shook him. "I have one comrade. She is—manager—in a metal zavod—at Kharkov. You are skilled metal-worker, Don-ald, yes?"

Donald said slowly: "I was a skilled riveter, but I can turn my hand to any kind of metal work."

Marfa said: "I send her—one long telegram—you go to her factory, yes, no?"

"Will you?" said Donald, staring, "oh, will you truly? Now? Oh, comrade——"

Marfa had hold of the Comintern man and was explaining

to him in Russian; he nodded, asked a question, agreed. Maria, the peasant woman, came over and stood by Donald; she took his hand and stroked it, held it close to her own cheek. She said something to him, but he shook his head, not understanding; Maria laughed and patted his hand before she let it go. He didn't know what to say or do; only he knew he liked this room and these women and the flowers and the Staffordshire man, who had produced out of his pocket a grubby half-sheet of paper and a pencil. They began to write out the telegram; it was long, and Marfa and Nina chattered and laughed like children over it. When it was finished the Staffordshire man winked at Donald and pocketed it. Donald offered to pay.

The man shook his head. "That's all right, lad. You stick to what you've got. You'll need it as likely as not, where you're going. So long, comrade." He went out, with a kiss on the way to Nina. Below in the courtyard the boy who had been cleaning the fish was singing bits of a song, but sometimes he forgot the words. Marfa turned to Donald and said: "Now you stay, have supper with us."

Supper? His mind swung back, but the last hour still stood between him and where he was before. Supper already? He said: "I should be going back. They will be waiting on me coming maybe."

"Why?" said Marfa, "you stay with us, sure."

"There is someone waiting," he said. Dione in room 317.

"Who? One comrade? We will call up—telephone—yes. He come too."

Donald hesitated. He couldn't see himself fetching Dione to supper with the girls. Was she a comrade? She had said she was. But she had kept the *Moscow Daily News* from him! What did she mean by it anyway? Not the same that these girls meant. Not what it meant really, only some fancy idea of hers, some kind of a mad-like story she had made out of a thing that was as real and solid as steel plates. She had made him wait. Well, now she might wait for him. "It doesn't matter," he said, "nichevo. I will stay with you."

"Good!" said Marfa, and went off to the communal kitchen of the flat in which they had a room, and made tea; the other two rummaged in the cupboard, found a clean cloth, glasses and spoons, sugar in big shapeless lumps that they told Donald to break for them, biscuits, cucumbers, and a plate of potato salad. Donald helped them to lay the table and pull the two sofas up to it; Maria showed him proudly her pile of books, an algebra book with the page doubled at the beginning of quadratic equations, one on elementary physics, several copy-books half-full of what might have been essays, and three text-books of economics or Marxist history. Then Marfa came back with the tea and hot water and they had supper, all talking hard; the curly-headed child sat on Marfa's knee and ate biscuits. Nina and Maria kept on asking Donald the names of things in English, and telling him their Russian names; he hardly had time to think of anything else. They cleared the supper-things away; again he said he must go. Again they told him: "Stay. Stay! We have music now."

He wanted to stay; these girls were real; they'd been talking about real things, work and wages and food. He was comfortable with them. He resented Dione being at the hotel, waiting for him, the fine stuff of her dress, her soft skin and hair, her mind full of things he didn't understand and didn't hold with. "Well," he said, "I'll stay maybe half an hour."

Marfa picked up the balalaika: "I play—what?"

He said: "Do you know any revolutionary songs, now? I'd like fine to hear some."

She nodded and struck up, playing and singing; the other two sang with her. In a little Donald had hold of the tune and some of the words: "Zavodi vstavaite, sherengi smikaite. Na bitvu shagaite, shagaite!" . . . They went on from that to others. This was what he liked, what he wanted; they stirred the blood like pipe tunes!

"Now you sing," suggested Marfa. "Sing—music from Scotland."

At random he began singing the "Hundred Pipers." That set Maria off on to peasant songs, sketching the movements of a dance with her hands and feet. Nina peeped round the screen and gestured back that the child was asleep. Again Marfa sang, this time something softer; the plucked strings of the balalaika vibrated long and sweetly. It was beginning to get dark. What would he be saying to Dione?

"That was—what you call love song," Marfa said. "Now—you."

"Maxwelton braes are bonny," he sang. He must go. He must go soon. In a moment he must go. Her promise true. His promise. He had promised nothing. His only promise was to the People. The Party.

"Sad," said Marfa, "sad! You have a girl, yes, no?" Had he a girl? Was Dione his girl? She had said she was not his, she would not belong to him. She wasn't a girl anyway, she was—a lady. A frightened lady. He shook his head. Marfa said: "You stay, you sleep with me, Don-ald, Scottish comrade. Please." She said something very quickly to the other two; they seemed to agree. She said: "They go out now—little while. They walk. When they come back you sleeping—so." She made the gesture of laying her brown cheek flat on her arm and shutting her eyes. Still Donald said nothing; he didn't know what to say, it was as though his body did not belong to him any more. He looked at her newly. She was brown and strong and thick-set. She took his hand, snatched it up and laid it over her left breast. He could feel she must have nothing on under the cotton dress. His fingers of themselves closed a little, feeling through the dress; a sudden briskness began to come over him; he lifted his head. "You not understand?" Marfa said impatiently, "I want you," she pointed to the bed, "there. You." She laid a hand on him where no woman's hand had ever lain before. "Me." She drew his hand down over her body to where no hand of his had ever lain on a woman. The briskness in his body began to take shape and meaning, but still he was too unsure of himself to speak. "You have a sickness there, maybe—Don-ald?" she said.

That shook him up. "No," he said, "no! But I—I have never done this. I have never gone with a woman."

"Not true?"

He nodded.

She threw back her head and laughed: "I teach you. Then—you teach Nina." She translated to the others, who laughed too. "Nina, she say, she comsomol, she like sleep first time with Scottish Party comrade. But—I show you first. Comintern comrade, he say, you good man. But you sad—a little. Not sad with Marfa. So, that is all right, O.K. yes?"

The other two went out; he heard the door shut, their steps going away. Marfa began to undress him, to pull his coat off; he was sweating now; he could feel his shirt clinging to his arm-pits and chest. She was sweating, too, a little under the arms; her dress was cut straight across like a child's dress, a pinafore; he couldn't help but look. Her hands on his buttons—he couldn't let a woman do that! "I do this, comrade," she said.

She took off her dress; she had thick breasts, a warm

brown, something wild-like and strong and—useful, he thought, not the same as the white chickenny breasts he'd seen on postcards. She was wearing dark cotton bathing-drawers, like a man's; he put out his hand uncertainly. Suddenly she said: "You got—rubber goods—comrade?"

"No," he said, checking and drawing back from her.

She smiled and shook her head. "That no matter. Nichevo. Maybe I have another kid. Maybe not. I don't care. I like kids. Only—not like other husbands." She took his hands in hers and laid them over the cotton stuff stretched across her hips. "You take—them pants—off me, Scottish comrade," she said.

He was trembling a good deal now. "We'll—be quick?"

She laughed: "Quick, quick!" she said, and gave a leap and a bound out of his hands on to the bed and with one throw-out of her arm tossed off the embroidered cover and was round on to her back. He plunged down, feeling desperately, clumsily, for what he needed; her hands helped him. He gave a choking cry of violence and release. This was it, then. This was—it. He fell and fell and always her soft breasts and belly and legs were there to stay him in the dizziness of his falling. Always a comrade. He fell and fell into a lovely softness, a drowsiness, a darkness, kind voices, freedom, night.

## UNDER THE RED FLAG 5

DIONE woke. It was 8.30. For a moment she didn't know where she was. Then she did. She looked across at the other bed to make sure; it was flat and empty. She dressed and pinned up her hair in less than four minutes and ran downstairs. She tapped on the desk; there was no one about who spoke English. She tried German: "Mein Bruder—wo kann er sein? Ja, mein Bruder! Er ist nicht hier!"

One of the clerks arrived. He was not very helpful. "Your brother?" he said, and shrugged his shoulders, "perhaps he has found friends. You have friends in Moscow, yes?"

Then a competent Intourist guide turned up. "Reassure yourself, Mrs. Galton," she said, "if anything happens to our tourists, we know. The police tell us. It is all right, yes. You are, I think, in a highly nervous condition?"

"But," said Dione, nearly in tears, "something *must* have happened to him. Oh, don't stand about! Can't you *do* something?"

"Your brother is all right, yes," said the guide, firmly, "I will see if there is a telephone message at the office." She turned towards the door of the hotel. "That is your brother, I think, yes?" she remarked, with the air of one who has scored again.

"Oh, Donald!" Dione said, her voice all quivery. "Where *have* you been?"

"Come up," said Donald and took her by the elbow and led her upstairs to room 317. She sat down on the bed and mopped her eyes ; he came and sat beside her and put an arm round her. " What for are you crying ? " he said.

She leant her head back against his nice, solid shoulder. " I didn't know what had happened," she said. " I was afraid you'd been run over or something, Donald." Suddenly she turned and seized him by the shoulders and began to sob violently, her face burrowed hard into his chest.

He stroked her hair ; he felt he could be infinitely gentle to her now ; he understood women now. After a time he said : " Listen, lassie." She lifted her face, red and wet with crying ; he kissed her forehead. He went on : " Dione, you were frightened and I could not be frightening you more. You did not want me at all. So I found a Russian girl, a working girl like I am a working man, and she did want me, and I slept with her last night. And now I have had a woman and I am free of that. And now I will not be bothering you nor frightening you, Dione, for I have done what I needed to do ! "

Dione found it a little difficult to think consecutively or sensibly. She sat back on the bed, rather away from him, yet not so as to appear unfriendly. She looked down at her own hands ; they conveyed nothing to her. So that was why he had not come. Simple. She might have thought of it. A working girl. She took a deep breath and looked up and smiled : " So it's all lovely, Donald. My dear, I'm glad you've got what you wanted. Was it—was it as good as you thought ? "

" Aye," he said, " it was better far. I had never guessed —afterwards, the sweetness, the peace of it. Passing all understanding."

" What was her name ? " Dione asked. " Keep on talking."

" Marfa," he said. " She is a Party member."

" How did you find her ? "

" By the river side. When you were late coming back I

went walking. I found three of them there, her and two others. And, oh, Dione"—he suddenly remembered —" she has sent a telegram to a metal works at Kharkov to ask if they'll take me on, and I am going back this afternoon to get the answer. And—and—maybe I'll be going off there at once!"

"My dear . . . that would be fine. She must be a good sort of person."

"Aye, that she is."

"Donald?"

"Mmha?"

"When you go for the telegram, will you take me to see her?"

"I might," he said doubtfully. He was puzzled. Marfa had said to bring a comrade. Did Dione count?

"I wish you would," she said; "I—I haven't made any friends yet, Donald."

"They'll no' be the sort you would be wanting to be friends with, Dione," he said.

Her voice had gone rather choky: "But I thought you said—she was a working girl—like you were a working man."

"Don't get crying, Dione," he said, "I only meant—ach——! And I thinking you'd be that glad of it all!"

"I *am* glad," Dione said; "I *wanted* you to be happy, I *wanted* you to get what you needed, and I'm sure it's better this way. I'm sure she did it better than I would have. Only, I do hate feeling I'm right away from you again."

"And she so near. Well, there it is. But you were never of my class, you never wanted me."

"You know that's nothing to do with class. It's because —because I'm really in love with my husband. That oughtn't to interfere, of course. Perhaps—perhaps another time I shouldn't do it so badly." She looked away into the corner of the room blurred through tears; she couldn't remember ever having felt so worthless before, such a worm. She hoped he would take her to see the girl, but, now that she came to consider it, she couldn't see why he should. They were the people of the future; she wasn't. She'd failed in what she had intended to do. Failed through cowardice, a lack of nerve. She hadn't even got the aristocratic virtues apparently, the things a Highlander should have, the qualities she should have inherited as Fraser or MacLean. She looked round at him; he was frowning, worried; at least she would have the courage not to spoil the memory of his first night for him! She jumped up: "Come along, Donald! You must be starving. Let's have breakfast; then we're going off sight-seeing."

She washed her face and came back into the room; he was standing looking at his half-dry shirt: "Did you wash that, Dione?"

She nodded: "Of course. I've never known a man yet who could wash a shirt!"

"I've washed my own mostly," he said, then: "I do like you, Dione." They kissed one another solemnly and went down to breakfast.

"So you turned up after all," Nancy Ellis said. "Your sister was so worried about you!"

They all went off to see the Kremlin; Dione remembered very little of it afterwards; it seemed rather flimsy compared with the scene she couldn't help trying to reconstruct in her imagination. Donald liked it; he would have liked most things that morning. In the Red Square there was the usual long queue waiting to go in to the Red Tomb, workers, soldiers and peasants, men, women and children, waiting and moving slowly towards it. Their guide put them in at the head of the queue. Several of them protested. " It is all right," the guide said ; " they know you are foreigners, have little time." That seemed only sensible, yet some of them would rather have gone with the crowd. The U.S.S.R. was beginning to affect them that way.

Among a shuffling of feet they went down past walls of very beautiful polished granite, reddish with a blue fleck in it like butterflies' wings. They turned corners, lost their sense of direction ; they had shuffled into a double file. Nobody spoke. They came into the central chamber. Under a blanket, in a glass box, Lenin is lying. He is so tired that he must sleep for ever. His mouth is gentle, his face is sweet, because he has loved mankind. Because he was so good and loved so much, he worked so hard that he died. He is not sleeping, he is dead. It is all as simple as that, so simple that a child or a peasant can understand it. A child or a peasant can become better by thinking of Lenin. You or I can become better by thinking of Lenin. If that is a religion, then a religion it is. If that is sense, then it is just sensible.

They came out of the tomb. Jane Ellis was crying.

" What is it, Jane ? " Donald whispered to her.

" Oh, it's all right," said Jane, and swallowed hard ; " only—only I don't *want* him to be dead ! "

" We can go on with doing his work, Jane," said Donald, " he is not just a person now, he is an idea. That way he can't ever be dead. That thing in there is not really him, but only a shape that the idea took for a time."

They went back to the Intourist office. There were questions of future arrangements. Donald looked at the clock. " Come on, Dione," he said, " it's time we were off."

Her heart leapt delightedly as she followed him out of the office. On the pavement she said : " Donald, are you going to take her anything ? "

" How did you mean, Dione ? "

"Some kind of present. Wouldn't it, perhaps, be graceful?"

"What like of thing could I take her?"

"I don't suppose you can buy anything, but why not take her something to wear? I've got a pair of new silk stockings, or there's that red and green scarf of mine that you liked. I could put it in tissue paper—it doesn't look worn a bit."

Donald debated in himself. At last he said: "No, I think I'll not, Dione. She's a Party member, and she'd maybe not like yon kind of thing. Let alone she did it without thought of that. It would be a queer-like thing, a pair of silk stockings coming from a hunted murderer!" He added: "If it had been you, would you have been expecting presents from me, Dione?"

"No, of course not," she said, "that would have been different. You could have given me a curl of your hair if you'd liked."

"You can have that anyway," he said, "only maybe I'll wash my head under the shower first—I'll have got it dirty in the train."

They took a tram, working their way through like worms from the back where one got in to the front where one got out. Then they walked, and Donald told her more about the girls. "They are all on morning shifts," he said, "so they'll just be home by now." They went through the courtyard and up the stairs; for a moment Dione wished she hadn't come. Then she told herself not to be an even worse coward than she'd been already. Donald knocked and a girl's voice called out something, and they both walked into the room. Donald shook hands with the girls, who had all been busy. Marfa was sewing something, Nina attending to the plants, and Maria doing algebra. "This is my sister," Donald said.

Dione shook hands. As she was shaking hands, last, with Maria, her hand was seized and turned palm upwards. The three laughed and Maria said something to the others. Dione didn't understand, but Donald blushed, half understanding. Marfa pulled him aside: "She say—that girl not working girl—that girl not sister. She say, if that girl sister—she been—kept by one man."

Donald said angrily: "She is a married woman, she has four children."

"She not wash floor," said Marfa, and laughed. She added: "One long telegram come. My friend, she say all right—wel-come to Scottish comrade—she meet train Kharkov to-morrow morning—she speak little English."

"Then I'm going," he said, "I'm going to-night!" and turned to Dione: "It's all fixed! I've got my job and I'm away off!" And he gave a queer sudden bound and a kind of war shout. The gules lion awoke.

The three Russians all laughed and talked at once; Nina, the youngest, held on to his arm, saying something, and Marfa interpreted: "She say, when she finish here, she go Kharkov, live with Scottish comrade. You take her—yes?"

Donald grabbed hold of Nina and gave her a hug, and then did the same by Marfa. The peasant woman, standing by the table, one finger still stuck in her algebra book, nudged Dione and said something in a low voice. Dione told herself that Donald wouldn't have been able to kiss two girls that way before; she was glad of his gaiety; she had never seen him gay before, never seen him doing anything he liked and wanted; there had always been the background of Sallington and rain and cold street corners and oppression. Now all that was wiped out. She kept her eyes away from the bed with its tidy embroidered cover. Maria smiled at her and motioned her to take off her hat;

when she did, Maria put down her algebra book and patted Dione's hair. Then she pointed at Dione and said: "Communista?"

Dione shook her head. For a moment she had been tempted to assent, to say "da-da-da—!" to be included in the group. But instead she said: "Nye, tovarish—Socialista." Maria said something she couldn't understand, a question. Dione shook her head again. Maria repeated it. "Nye ponimayu," Dione said, bothered, hating not to understand. If only that other woman would interpret! But she had both arms round Donald's neck—Donald was sitting on the sofa and she was behind it, and Nina was sitting on Donald's knees, putting jasmine flowers into his hair. It was, she thought, an extremely pretty scene, a pastoral: shepherd and nymphs. People ought to be able to behave like that always. How happy he looks. Then she said: "Donald, I'd better go and arrange about your ticket for to-night and see if I can square Intourist. I'll expect you when I see you."

"Hi, lassie, get off me!" said Donald, jumping up. "Will you so, Dione? That would be fine. I'll no' be long."

"Dosvedanye, tovarishi," said Dione politely, out of her conversation book. They all shook hands, but they did not call her tovarish back.

She found the right tram. She got out of it at the right place. She talked like an aunt to the Intourist office—she hadn't known she had it in her to be so firm with anyone. They produced a hundred excellent reasons why Donald couldn't go to Kharkov that night, and when told he had got a job, said they must talk to the police and the appropriate Government department. Dione said that could be done best at Kharkov—she thought that once Donald was settled in a factory and proving himself a valuable worker, as he surely would, there'd be considerable difficulty in turning him out. While she argued with them, Nancy Ellis came in and joined forces with her. After an hour, Intourist suddenly decided that the ticket could be bought, but intimated that she and Donald were very naughty children and giving a lot of trouble to their kind governess. Deflated, Dione went back to the hotel; it was amazing how much energy one could expend in this kind of way.

"You've never dealt with a Government department, have you?" Nancy Ellis said; "they're just the same. One's got to be as pig-headed as they are themselves to get anything done."

It was dinner time at the hotel, and when they were in the middle of dinner Donald turned up, hungry and cheerful. Then they went up to room 317 to pack. The washing was all dry; Dione found the sock with the hole and took out her darning-needle and wool. "You'd better take some stuff for mending, Donald," she said, "I believe it's hard to come by here, and you'll probably find someone to do it for you." She was thinking of Nina.

"I'll do it myself, Dione," he said, "if you can spare it." She also gave him the chocolate and raisins she had brought with her, and her little spirit lamp; it was only sensible. He said, rather embarrassed: "I have never had so many —personal possessions—in my whole life before. You are making a capitalist of me, Dione!"

"Well, you can give them away if you want to," said Dione, "and even I know enough Marxism to realise they aren't capital! Yes, and you'd best take an extra bit of soap."

"I'll take a shower now," he said, "it'll maybe be a thought difficult at Kharkov." She heard him turn on the water and begin splashing about; she suddenly wondered what he was like naked, and had half a mind to go and see. Then she thought, no, that would still bother him, and she went on with the sock. He came back, damp and cool-looking, and went on packing. After a time he looked up and said: " Dione, will you not take that bit of my hair? It's clean now."

" All right," Dione said, and added: " Your mother would like it."

He handed her the scissors and knelt on one knee beside her for it to be cut. A romantic pose. Suddenly he said: " Dione, if you're cutting a bit hair for my mother, will you not take it yourself too? I would like fine for you to have it yourself. I—I've nice hair."

" All right," she said again.

He laid a hand on her knee: " Dione, are you angry at me? "

" No," she said, " why should I be? "

" What is it, then? " he asked, " can I not help? "

She said, looking aside: " Well, I was thinking of you saying that when I'd learnt not to be frightened of you, I should stop being frightened of other people, stop being shy and class-conscious and stupid. But now I shall go on being frightened."

" Would you have stopped with me? " he asked.

" I don't know," she said, " there's the difficulty, you see! But I was frightened of those girls to-day."

" The silly besoms! " he said. " Dione, was what I did wrong after all? "

" No," she said, " no! It was plumb right for you, and very likely it was best for me. Very likely I'm best left to myself and my own—class. One is what one's been made. I'm too old to change now."

He kissed one of her hands that still held his darned sock. " I love you, Dione," he said; " that's a queer thing, isn't it. I thought it was only just—the other thing. But now I'll go on and it'll not matter that I'm far away and not seeing you. Will I write to you, Dione ? "

" Please—comrade," she said, and bent over and kissed his soft hair, still damp and smelling a little of soap.

He looked up and said : " Maybe, if that's how you need to be stopped getting frightened, you'll get it from some other man."

" Maybe so," she said, and then : " Oh, Donald, I meant to ask you, is there no one at Sallington I should try and get news of you to ? "

He thought for a moment. " If you could get word with Agnes Green, she's safe. She'd like you, Dione, if you'd let her."

" I never stop people liking me ! " Dione said, rather indignantly.

" Ach, but you do ! You're for ever making barriers." He got to his feet and found pencil and paper and wrote the address. Everything was packed now. " When I have an address I'll send it you," he said, " and—you will be writing, Dione ? "

" Surely," she said.

He walked about the room a minute or two ; then he said : " Dione, I would like fine to have a piece of your hair."

She unpinned a plait and shook it out : " Look, cut from behind my ear : here." He did. A long lock lay in his hand. " I'll tie it up," she said, and then : " Last time I did this was for Tom, in 1917, when we got engaged. I sent it out to him in France. It was fairer then. I'd just started putting it up." She tied the hair with a piece of ribbon. Then she said : " Wait ! " and hunted through her handkerchiefs and found a dry sprig of white heather. " Put them together," she said, " it comes from Auchanarnish. My mother sent it me and said young John MacLean of Lerguligan—he's your cousin, isn't he ?—had found it and brought it in." She put the hair and the sprig together into an envelope and saw him put the envelope into the breast pocket of his coat next his Party card. She took another envelope and put his hair into it ; on an impulse she said : " You might put your name on it."

" That way you'll not get mixing it up with any other body's ! " said Donald, and signed it with a big " Donald MacLean."

An Intourist guide came and knocked, and said it was time to go. She saw him off at the station in an immensely crowded train. She stood on the platform waving a handkerchief. For a moment it became the leave-train at Victoria Station, that one train of all trains that women of about Dione's age, or rather older, find it very hard to forget.

She went back. He had apparently forgotten nothing. There was no trace of him, and the hotel had moved her into a smaller room, as they needed the extra bed in room 317. She stuck down the envelope that held the lock of hair and put it into the bottom of her suit-case. It was all satisfactorily over, like an abortion. An Elephant had been killed, even if she herself had not been in at the death.

The next morning she had another complicated hour, dealing with the Intourist office, waiting while people telephoned or didn't telephone, or said : " Just one minute " and vanished for ever. In the middle of it Medingley turned up and asked if he could help. She explained the situation and said she thought it was smoothing itself out. Donald could deal with the other end. Medingley didn't answer for a moment, then he looked at her and said : " By the way, Mrs. Galton, he wasn't really your brother, I take it ? "

She gasped and said nothing.

He went on : " You see, sharing a cabin, one's bound to notice little things. I take it he was—a fugitive."

Dione said : " Well, as a matter of fact——"

" Quite," said Medingley, " now—one more guess : after all the law's my trade !—was he by any chance the Sallington murderer ? "

" Yes," said Dione, very low.

" So I supposed. Well, naturally, this is entirely between ourselves. Trying fellows, these newspaper proprietors. I think you acted with great sense, Mrs. Galton."

The next day, after dinner, Dione thought she might as well present one of her introductions. It was from Phil Bickerden to a colleague, a mathematician. They had met at a conference, and when Phil came out to Moscow for another scientific conference in 1928 he had stayed with them for a week. He had explained that there was the father, Peter Nikolaevsky, his wife who was a doctor and who had been a very keen Ukrainian patriot, and about three half-grown-up children. Since 1928 he and Phil had corresponded rarely, writing to one another about twice a year, entirely on technical subjects. Dione took her letter and walked off to find the address, armed with a plan of Moscow. It was extremely hard to find the address, as it was a newish block of flats built behind some others; she found her way there at last down an unfinished pathway half-blocked with heaps of gravel, and climbed three flights of stone steps, none too clean and rather like those that went up to the three girls' room. She knocked at the door; it was opened by a girl of about sixteen with bare legs and a pinafore dress. Dione handed her the envelope and was proceeding to deliver a prepared Russian sentence when the girl interrupted, speaking very clearly and with only a slight American accent: "You are English, I think—yes? Please come in. This is for my father. I am Neonila Petrovna. How do you do? I am quite well, thank you."

Dione shook hands and walked into a rather dark hall and through into a long narrow room with a good many books, some very battered-looking—a stove, a sofa, some pot plants, a few chairs and a table at which four people were sitting, drinking tea and eating black bread with an egg-and-cucumber salad. The girl said : " This English lady has a letter for our father," and handed it to a rather worried-looking man with a short beard, who put down his glass of tea and began reading it.

The woman beside him, whom Dione identified as his wife, got up ; she was a rather beautiful grey-haired woman in a yellow-and-white embroidered linen dress, the nicest Dione had seen yet in Russia. " Welcome ! " she said, speaking slowly : " you sit down, please, Mrs.—— ? "

" Galton," said Dione.

" Mrs. Gal-ton," repeated the hostess, " voyons, c'est là notre fille aînée, Oksana—ah, pardon, je me trompe !—this is there our eldest daughter Oksana."

The other girl, who had been sitting beyond her father, got up and shook hands ; she had obviously been reading a book during supper, for it slipped off her lap ; she picked it up and put it on the table—it had a picture of a three-propellered aeroplane engine on the cover. It struck Dione at once that Oksana was very beautiful, like her mother, but quite young with very brown skin, lighter brown hair and brilliantly blue eyes. She wore a cotton dress, much the same as her sister's, but better-fitting.

" And this my son Leon."

The boy shook hands, saying nervously, " Thank you very much." He seemed to be half-way between his sisters in age and darker.

Mrs. Nikolaevsky made room beside her on the sofa for Dione, and then her husband finished reading the letter and looked at Dione suddenly from over the top of it. " Good that you come," he said, " we are glad seeing strangers from Ausland. And how is my dear colleague, Bickerden ? "

Dione gave the news of Oxford. All the family listened

to her hard. She felt she had to be very accurate! The hostess poured her out a glass of tea, regretting that she had no lemon.

"And you yourself, what do you do?" said the girl Oksana in very good English. Both the girls spoke English much better than their brother or their parents.

Dione answered: "I have four children. And I do all kinds of things! But I'm afraid I've no regular paid job. Quite few women in England have."

"Ah," said Oksana to her sister, "this is typic of the life of the petty bourgeoisie."

"Vraiment, 'Ksana, tu es incroyable!" said their mother crossly.

"And what do *you* do?" said Dione. It seemed the only thing to say.

"I am radio specialist," said Oksana, "and now I am taking interest in aeroplanes. My father, he is mathematician: you know. My mother, doctor. My brother is cinema technician. My sister, she studies languages; she thinks to become for a time Intourist guide, perhaps."

With a charming smile, Neonila said: "I had thought to go on the stage, for I have temperament—but alas, no technique. So now I think to be a Guide, as that is near the Stage, and my temperament shall have outlet. Besides, I am interested to observe tourists. Tell me about the stage in England."

Hastily Dione laid before them all her knowledge of the English stage. They had read a good deal of Shaw, the whole of Shakespeare, and some Galsworthy. They had heard of Noel Coward and wished to understand his ideology. Dione did what she could, added something about the cinema for the benefit of the boy and something about the B.B.C. for Oksana, whom she very much wanted to make friends with. They filled up her tea glass.

"And now," said Oksana firmly, "tell us about the unemployment problem in England."

Dione made a little gesture of despair: "If you really want to know, you must ask my husband when he comes! He's a politician and can give you the figures."

"A politician," said the father, frowning, "how? My colleague Bickerden says an economist."

"He would," Dione said, "but Tom is also a—Socialist candidate."

"Socialist?" said Oksana.

"Labour Party," said Dione firmly.

"But," said Oksana, "do you not know, Mrs. Galton, the English Labour Party is only a Social-Democratic Party —it is not truly Socialist——"

Dione interrupted: "I know that's true in a way, but it'll take hours if we start on it now! Won't you wait till Tom comes himself and discuss it with him?"

"Good," said Oksana, "I will explain and I will argue. He is nice, your husband?"

"Yes, very," said Dione, "look, there's a photo." She took one out of her bag, and another showing the children. They were handed round and thought well of.

"He is a nice man," said Oksana firmly. "I would like to have children by such a man. You have four; that is good. Will you have many more? If you have no profession, you can."

"It's very expensive bringing up children in England," Dione said; "I'd like to have more, but—there's clothes, food, education. Besides, if we do have any kind of revolution in England, it makes it much harder to act if one has young children."

"That I understand," Oksana said. She came and stood beside Dione, looking down at her, "and a revolution, you want?"

" We want *something*," said Dione.

" But you do not understand yet what. Listen, you will be friends with me, comrades, yes ? How long do you stay in Moscow ? "

" I'm going to Nijni for three days with some of the party," Dione said, feeling pleased and warm, " and then coming back here to meet Tom, who will have come from England. Then we shall be here together a week. Then I go back to England and Tom stays another ten days. He may be going to do the Volga trip."

Oksana nodded : " Well then, for a week we see one another, many times, yes ? Do you like sport—swimming?"

" I love swimming."

" We will swim together. In ten days I have my holiday."

" And my colleague Bickerden," said the father suddenly, " when he was here in 1928 I remember he was in love. He told me—very much. And of his beloved—she also, very much. He is married, yes ? "

" He is married," said Dione, " but not to the one he was in love with then."

" But how not ? He was much passionate. And she, I think."

" She was married already to someone else."

" But why could she not divorce, and marry my colleague Bickerden, who was so much passionate ? "

" It's very difficult getting divorced in England," Dione said, " especially if one wants to be. If she had been divorced because of Bickerden she would have had to give up her children whom she loves, and he would probably have lost his fellowship at Oxford."

" That is typic of petty bourgeois morality," said Oksana, " and stupid. You agree, yes ? "

" Oh yes, I agree. But also she is very fond of her husband."

“ If they are good comrades, then she should stay married to him, but our father’s colleague, Bickerden, should be her lover, yes ? ”

“ Very likely,” said Dione, “ but it didn’t happen. She’s my sister, by the way. She’s a painter and she works very hard. She earns about three-hundred pounds a year.”

“ That is good,” said Oksana, “ and has she children ? ”

“ Three.”

“ But they are by her husband, not by our father’s colleague, Bickerden ? ”

“ By her husband only. Look, I have a photo of her, too.” Dione took out a snapshot of Phœbe at work, frowning over her tools, her tense hand holding the graver rather out of focus but very beautiful.

The mother said : “ She is ill perhaps, poor one ? She has the air—I would say—allergic.”

“ No,” said Dione, “ she’s only thinking about her work.”

“ Ah, but no ! ” Oksana cried, “ the work should make one feel happy—gay. It is not the work. Ah, I should like to give her to our father’s colleague, Bickerden, to be made happy ! ” Dione, astonished, saw that Oksana’s eyes were full of tears. And suddenly Oksana threw her arms round Dione’s neck and sobbed : “ Oh, I am so sorry for you all, living in the capitalist countries ! Books say to me it is your own faults, but oh, I am so sorry ! I wish you could have revolutions, quick, quick, and be happy like us ! ”

“ Oksana ! ” said her mother, and poured out a torrent of protest in Russian, and Neonila said : “ Ah, ’Ksana too has the temperament.”

The next day Dione went off to Nijni Novgorod with most of the party. It seemed as good a place as anywhere else, but some of the first magic had gone. She would be glad to see Tom. He would be in the Soviet ship now, in the little world between the two great worlds, steaming across the blue Baltic. He was going to cut short his time in Leningrad, perhaps taking it on his way back, so as to join Dione earlier. She had got one letter from him, enclosing a letter from Morag, asking her mother to give her love to Prince Charlie. But Prince Charlie was in Kharkov and hadn't sent his address yet. Bonny Charlie's noo awa safely o'er the friendly main, Mony a heart will brak in twa. . . . What was that woman Marfa thinking about him now? Tom's letter had said that no arrest had yet been made in the Sallington murder case, but the police were supposed to have clues. There had been a letter from Alex, too, writing from North Shields of all places, a puzzled kind of letter. She wondered what was happening to him; she had already enclosed one of his sham letters in her letter to their mother.

It was curious how she was now finding herself assailed by all kinds of Liberalism; she was hating the propaganda, the cocksureness. It did not seem to her particularly good or clever that a child of four could say why Capitalism is wrong and Communism right; it was on a par with the shorter catechism, and only showed that children were tractable little animals when trained young. She had been shown the wall newspapers of factories and schools; she hated this business of people telling on one another—nasty priggish little boys, scribbling up that other little boys had spilled the ink! Where was the place for the rebel, the boy or girl who wouldn't fit nicely into any orthodox scheme? Sometimes it seemed to her that the whole place was like one vast school, all becoming more and more imbued with that public-school spirit which all sensible women are up against: here was the house spirit, government by public opinion and if necessary public chastisement, the dear old O.T.C. very much to the fore, and Stalin something between head-boy and head-master!

She went to Nijni feeling very prickly and was not appeased by the inefficiency that was apparent there. She had rather a sore throat from the dust; several of the party by now had sore throats or eyes, or some form of digestive trouble. A pair of shoes belonging to the Jewish writer had been stolen. A large orchestra, left over from old times, had played grand opera very loud indeed during all meals.

Nancy Ellis was not quite sure that the position of women was really as good as she had hoped at first. She did not object to the fact that every second woman she saw in the street was in an advanced stage of pregnancy, though she felt they would have to get out of the habit within the next twenty years or so, or it would make considerable difficulties; and she approved of women going on working while pregnant—obviously the women themselves were perfectly pleased; very few of them looked strained or haggard in the way that a pregnant woman in Walworth or Stepney is. But afterwards? It was all very well for the woman who was working at a well-organised factory, for instance; only so many seemed to be doing factory or office work and also looking after a home and children, much as in other countries—and where, as a matter of fact, were the women in high positions, about whom she had heard? The same two or three names occurred over and over again, obviously exceptions. She and Dione discussed all this at length. Or again, the State prisons, where people were cured instead of punished, were wonderful; but what about the G.P.U.? What about the militarism? What about the peasants? One way and another all kinds of serpents erected their heads in Paradise.

Tom and Dione fell into one another's arms in the middle of the hotel lounge. Each found the other extraordinarily fresh and interesting and delightful, both talked at once.

Dione took Tom up to wash. He asked at once where Donald was. Dione said he had got a job at Kharkov. "Has he!" said Tom, "he's got some guts, that chap. How did you like him, Dione?"

"Rather a lot," Dione said. "Tom, would you like to know all about him and me?"

"Him and you. Why, did you—you got to like him as much as all that? He was a nice chap, I thought, and nice-looking. Yes, tell me, Dione."

She told him the whole story: "Would you have minded, Tom, if I had?"

"I hope I shouldn't. I feel as if I shouldn't. It's difficult to tell now. Sweetheart, I almost wish you had."

"Why?"

"Well, you'd have got it over and I should be quite sure, about not being jealous and beastly; at least I hope so. But now you've got all ready and it hasn't happened.

'And she that will not when she may,
When she will she shall have nay.'

Aren't you feeling a bit like that?"

"Yes. How clever of you, Tom. I didn't even know I was."

Tom was doing a terrific wash; he hated sleeping in trains and getting dirty, and he had soap all over his neck and ears. "Dione," he said through the soaping, "I wonder if you wouldn't like to go to Kharkov now and—see what you feel like."

"No, I've got you now. Besides, I don't know his address."

"Well, that *is* a reason. But I think he must be a good fellow, your Donald. If all the C.P. were like him—instead of just hindering. By the way, have you fired off any of those introductions?"

"Oh yes," said Dione; "oh, Tom, how nice you look! I found the Nikolaevskys."

"What's he like?"

"Like a mathematician. But the elder girl is awfully nice—she's called Oksana—that's Ukrainian, I think—and she's one of the most beautiful people I've ever seen."

"I never think your taste in women is very good," Tom said with decision.

"But she's—special. She really is. She's like I hope Morag's going to be. Tom, she's coming round this evening to take us to one of these Parks of Rest and Culture, and you'll see. And she's going to take us swimming."

Tom was finding it all very exciting. During the five days' voyage he had recovered from term and done his proofs; now he was all ready. After their day's sightseeing he took Dione off walking through Moscow; the only thing that was wrong with it as a town was the absence of cafés. Tom refused to admit that there is anything unideological about cafés, properly used, as in French provincial towns, as social centres for argument, chess, the writing of books and love letters, a reasonable amount of thirst-quenching, and other intelligent occupations. Dione agreed; it was extremely hot; café glacé would have been about right. They wandered about very happily; it was ridiculously nice just to be together again in a foreign town. Tom was not yet bored or distrustful. "This is all right, Dione," he said, "these people are all right; they aren't being oppressed. I should like living here. They're a cheery lot, but they're serious-minded, too. It's like Scotland without John Knox."

"They've got the same passion for learning that we had in Scotland two generations ago."

"There's more to it than that. Of course you're a miserable Highland aristocrat who's never done a hand's turn but driving cattle, but I'm an honest lowlander and my people were used to hard work: they've been doctors and engineers and architects, in University and Government Services—yes, and Ministers most likely too!—and on my English side we're Northumberland, which is all the same; we were ploughing our own fields not so far back. And I could damn well turn to and do any kind of job of work that was worth while—and pretty well anything would be worth while in this kind of state."

"You'd like doing something with your hands for a change, wouldn't you, Tom?"

"Yes. Like in the war. Till one saw it was no good and it all got nothing but a bloody bore—as most work is to most people in most countries now. It's *praxis* I need. I'm right away from *praxis* at Oxford—up in the clouds, the sort of man Aristophanes, who knew a thing or two about *praxis*, had the courage and sense to laugh at! But they're right down to it here."

"I'm not so far from *praxis* as you are, Tom, after having had four children; modern medicine hasn't got far enough to prevent child-birth being devilishly alike for all women. That's where I'm at ease with the women at Marshbrook Bridge, just as men are at ease together over drinks. Even Highlanders don't escape that! Have you noticed, Tom, how many new babies there are going to be in Moscow within the next month or two?"

"Yes. Jealous?"

"Oh well. I should think it was pretty uncomfortable: I take it they're put on one end of a conveyor belt with the babies inside and come out at the other with the babies outside—and standardised."

"You think it's all going to be one great lovely, Fordised new United States, don't you? But there's a lot to be said for the material comforts, even if they are all the same shape and size. I don't suppose either of us realises quite how much. And my god, when one thinks of the hand-made, picturesque, peasant-and-prince, filthy muddle this place was in before, one doesn't wonder they enjoy a bit of standardisation." He threw out his arms in a wide gesture, a kind of embrace; Oxford was falling off him.

"I'm glad it's such fun, Tom! But don't walk *quite* so fast—I'm melting."

"Oh, sorry. But—it may be disgusting presumption, but I'm inclined to think I should survive a revolution!"

"Yes. You'd enjoy putting up barricades across Banbury Road, Tom! Or at Sallington. I wonder if I should; I hate bangs. Tom, shall I survive the revolution, too?"

"You bloody well will!" said Tom, and put an arm round her. How much better he was at that than Donald! Or was it only years of practice? She couldn't remember now what he used to be like; perhaps she was more pliable in the old days. Now everything they did together seemed to fit; for fourteen years they had grown up like two trees, twining their branches in amity towards the sun.

In the evening Oksana turned up to go with them to the Park of Culture; she was pleasantly dressed in a cotton pinafore dress with a short-sleeved white muslin blouse under it, and she wore a little white beret. She seemed rather depressed, and after a time explained that there had been a row with the other occupants of the flat; they had three rooms—her mother and father slept in one, she and Neonila in another, and her brother on the sofa in the living-room—and in the other two there was a proletarian family. "I like them," said Oksana, "but then, I am not at home much. Mother regrets that they are not—sanitary; she has taught them much, but not all. She has a high standard of sanitariness because she is a doctor. Also they have little children, and it happens sometimes as it does to-day, that they are crying when my father, he wants to work, and then there is a—how do you say ?—a hell of a row. Neonila, she became temperamental, too ; she was learning English poetry by heart : the poet Wordsworth. He was a bourgeois. But still he had a good vocabulary. So mother and I, we had to make the peace. And mother, she had many forms to fill in for her hospital."

" Have you a maid ? " Dione asked, " or do you do the housework yourselves ? "

" No, there is a peasant girl who comes. She lives with friends : some have their maid sleeping with them—we not. Neonila tries always to teach her economics, but she is not intelligent. She goes to church even ; it is sometimes so with the peasants."

At the Park Tom enjoyed himself very much ; he began playing games with a group of men, first rather childish games of balancing and pushing one another off a pole, then semi-serious football. Oksana and Dione left them to it and wandered off down the river, talking. " To-morrow is my sixth day," Oksana said, " I will take you to swim : not here, but beyond."

" What do you usually do on your free day ? "

" I play games, swim, tennis, ball, high jump. I hear much music ; there is always music in the parks. I dance. Mostly I am with the comrades. Sometimes I stay home, read, make radio apparat, help mother, do a great cooking with her perhaps, or filling in hospital case sheets. She is a nice woman, my mother, she finds it hard perhaps sometimes, the new life, but she believe it is good because of what is coming. Some of my friends, their mothers grumble, grumble, make things not nice for them at home. But my mother is—what do you say in English ? "

" A darling," suggested Dione. " You know, people in

England say there is no family life over here—you've destroyed the sanctity of the home and all that."

"But," said Oksana, "while we crowd so much, before all the new flats are built, there *must* be family life. Too much sometimes! Of course there is now no force. A man cannot now beat his wife and his daughters. That is good, I think. But when we are comrades, when we all work for one thing and hope so much over one thing, it is good to live together."

"It's very—Hellenic." Oksana looked puzzled. "Like old Greece. It's obviously like Plato's Republic. And these parks—they're like Sparta—it would be lovely if everyone went quite naked, not only their arms and legs! I expect the Spartiates were a good deal more like your people here and less like English public-school boys than we make out, and your State is all Spartiates and no helots. But it's not only that. I believe that in the fifth century people in the city-states were as boring about democracy as the Communist propagandists are here. Sorry, Oksana, going off on to ancient history! I was brought up on it."

"No," said Oksana, "I like to hear about history. I like most of all learning. But ancient Greece was a system founded on slave labour."

"I'm not sure how much you can press that," Dione answered, frowning. "Early on it was feudal—or something like it—and slave labour began to tell by the time the silver mines at Laureion got going, and of course in the fourth century. But what about the middle fifth? There seems to have been a time when people there got some new ideas that could set the human mind flaming as your new ideas do now. They seem to have done things for non-economic motives. What about the Eunomia in Sparta? When they stopped being a prosperous, productive, happy kind of State, and started being uncomfortable on principle? I can't believe that was entirely a military necessity."

"But afterwards," said Oksana, "Greece — went. Because it was founded on an unsound economic basis."

"Or because the ideas wore out," Dione answered, "in the way ideas do. What do you think will happen to Communism in five hundred years?"

"The Communist State is not here yet," Oksana said eagerly. "We are only transitional. Look now at the peasants! Most of them do not understand. We need another generation of education. In the meantime—oh, to guard the thing we have, the little young lovely Socialism, to keep it safe from the people with power who want to tear it away from us and kill it!" Again there were tears in her eyes, and her brown strong hands grasped on to Dione's.

And Dione wondered, in a detached grown-up way, if there had ever been anything she cared about like that, except personally—her own baby children—Tom in the last year of the war. . . . And she wished she were young like Oksana—and as hopeful. She would have liked to give Oksana something—the whole world and a new pair of skates, as the Ice Queen promised to Kay. And suddenly she wondered whether Phœbe's Hans Andersen was printed yet, and she wished Phœbe would write to her.

They wandered back and found Tom sitting on the ground in the middle of a dozen men and boys; a mixture of German, English and Russian was going on; they were discussing world economic conditions and the general slump in prices. "Pupils?" Dione asked in a pause.

"No," said Tom, "too damned intelligent. They ask the wrong questions. A committee meeting!"

They stayed in the Park till dark; there was singing, and some good funny side-shows, and they came back late and pleasantly tired. It was fun for Tom and Dione going to bed together again. She'd been moved into still another room! "How do you like my Oksana?" she asked.

"Oh, she's alive all right. They are here. God, if one could get Marshbrook Bridge feeling this way!"

"But don't you think she's beautiful, Tom?"

"Yes, probably. I didn't notice much. I expect I was looking at you, Dione! She was wearing a funny sort of dress."

"She liked you. She said so."

"They're all amazingly friendly here, considering the way we come and stare at them. God, I like this place. Socialism in action—I'm so sick of theory. It makes me feel that what I've been after all these years isn't just dead and academic as it sometimes seems to be—specially at the end of term—but something alive that's quite likely to be really going to happen soon."

OKSANA came early the next day and snatched them away from Intourist, clamouring to take them to see sights. A good many of the party were doing things on their own or with VOKS introductions ; it seemed improbable that they should all be hoodwinked by wily propagandists the whole time. Those used to Western European accuracy and punctuality tended to get very impatient; one of the sillier people had been arrested, but had been let go after an hour or two.

They took a tram and then a little river boat. Twice Oksana waved and shouted to friends as they passed. The river boat was rather fun; there were so many people carrying those mysterious bundles that look so neolithic to the descendants of bronze and iron wielders. The sky was cloudless ; Tom was beginning to sunburn a rather hearty red on his neck and forearms. They got out and walked through rough pasture along a kind of towpath; after a time they came to a group of poplars and alders. " Here," said Oksana, suddenly interrupting a political argument she was having with Tom, " we swim."

They undressed; Tom, with English discretion, behind another tree. When she took her dress off Oksana was wearing a solid cotton brassière and knickers, but she had obviously sunbathed a good deal, as she was equally brown all over when she took them off. She kicked her shoes off and stood for a moment with her strong legs apart and arms stretched over her head. Her body was a most lovely golden-brown colour, as though some metal suppler and more varied than bronze had taken a fruity bloom; her breasts were high and firm; the light coming down through the poplars dappled gold flecks into the long bob of her hair. She had not the fashionable boyish figure, for her hips were broad and her belly more rounded than the Paris or London mode allowed. The calves of her legs were thick with muscle, and when she reached up on tiptoe, her toes spread and gripped the ground like a savage's. Dione, who did not usually admire women naked, gasped with admiration, and hoped Tom was looking. "You are lovely, 'Ksana," she said; "doesn't everyone fall in love with you?"

"Sometimes," said Oksana, "but I have not much time for that. Nor interest. Besides, they say always, marry with me and have children. I say, not yet. When I am a great technician, then I marry—perhaps. I must have children; we double our population in thirty years."

"What fun it must be," Dione said, "to feel that everything you do is quite certainly worth while—work and children and even play: all for a purpose."

"Yes," said Oksana, "we do not play for—holiday—but to make ourselves stronger, better workers. You swim now? We need not wear anything here."

"Oh, good," said Dione, "then Tom can see you." She shouted to him to come as he was. The three of them swam and dived; Oksana said the water was cold, but it seemed delicious to the two Scots. They came out and lay on the bank in the sun. Dione and Tom were dreadfully pale and undressed-looking compared with Oksana, who looked exactly right against the grass, but Tom was a good shape, square and not fat anywhere. After a little Dione collected a towel and put it over her back; she didn't want to blister. Oksana was still drying her hair; she had no bathing-cap—there wasn't yet enough rubber in Russia for that. Tom had been shy of looking at her at first, but now they were arguing again, and while he talked he stared at her, half to make the points of the argument and half in admiration; he was going into the early history of the English Labour Party, explaining how it had developed, and she was putting difficult questions; she knew a good deal about it.

Dione was extremely sleepy from the sun and the swimming; she put on her frock, but not her shoes and socks, and went to sleep under a poplar. When she woke up, the other two had put out the picnic things. Oksana was dressed except for her shoes, but Tom had still not put on his shirt. He looked extraordinarily young and happy. They ate the sandwiches, laughing a good deal. Tom and Oksana had a tussle over one, and Oksana jumped up and pushed Tom over; he seemed rather pleased; it was as though he'd known her for a long time. The running argument had for the time died down. When they had finished, all lighted cigarettes, which kept the flies off. Tom made a tiny bonfire of sandwich paper and chips and lit it with one match, taking a lot of trouble over it; Dione knew that he only made tiny bonfires when he was really happy. Oksana went down to the river and sat there dabbling her feet and humming the marching song: "Zavodi vstavaite . . ."

Dione still felt lazy; it was the first Russian day that she hadn't been violently doing something the whole time. "Why don't you go and talk to her, Tom?" she said.

"I have been talking to her," Tom said, and blew away the ashes of his tiny bonfire.

"Haven't you been kissing her, too?" Dione asked; she didn't quite know why, only it seemed such an obvious thing to do.

"Yes, I have," he said.

It was, when he said it, a slight shock, very slight, only just perceptible; it passed. "How sensible of you, Tom," she said. "Wasn't I right about her?"

"She's an astonishing person," Tom said; he added: "If she's at all typical of the country—and I think she is—it'll be all right."

"They're either like her and wildly keen about everything or else they're Easterns and muddle things. Was it nice, Tom?"

"Yes," he said, "very." He went on: "I don't know if it's her or the whole thing. I feel——" He couldn't express it at all; he shook his head. "I feel as if anything could happen."

"How lovely," Dione said, "and did she like it?"

"Apparently. We were in the middle of an argument. Dione—you know that you and I have both had flirts of one kind and another. We've both kissed people occasionally. But this is rather more serious. Tell me, Dione, shall I chuck it? After all, I've got lots to do and see here, and I can just forget all about to-day."

"No, no!" she said. "It's all part of the same thing, isn't it?—all this coming alive. Don't let's refuse it, Tom."

He took her hand in his: "Listen," he said. "I think I'm rather falling in love with her. It's ridiculous in a way, because she must be nearly twenty years younger than I am——"

"Oh, not quite," Dione interrupted, but he paid no attention.

"And I shall be seeing her another half-dozen times, perhaps. But during those half-dozen times, either I let whatever's happening go on, or I don't."

"What would be your reason against going on?" Dione asked, as impersonally as she could, looking at his broad, clean hand holding hers.

" Not to hurt you."

" I thought so, Tom. But that's all right. You wouldn't hurt me."

" I love you so, Dione," he said suddenly, and raised her hand quickly to his mouth.

" I know. That makes it all right. But you mustn't hurt her. Isn't she more—vulnerable—than I am ? "

" I don't know. She seems so tremendously certain and assured. I feel as though it would be in her hands. Just because she's part of this enormous thing. It's like trusting oneself to a very high-powered engine."

" A tractor," Dione said thoughtfully.

" She'd think it was silly of us, sitting here talking about it like—adolescents. She's finished with that."

" You know a lot about her already, Tom," Dione said, " but it *is* silly. Look, she's coming back."

" All right, Dione," Tom said, and kissed her lightly and got up and went towards Oksana. Dione wondered if they would mind her looking on at their meeting. But either they didn't mind or they didn't notice. On the way back Oksana walked between them and kissed them both, and they her. It interested Dione very much to notice what Tom kissing someone hard looked like from another angle ; she had never been able to see properly before.

Oksana went home and found Neonila reading Marx in German for practice, and her mother nailing a new piece of stuff on the sofa, where Leon was beginning to wear through it. " You go and sit down, Mother," she said ; " I can do this much better than you."

" Very likely," said her mother, " for I am very bad indeed. What is making you so happy, 'Ksana ? "

" Because the Englishman, Tom Galton, has been kissing me. It makes little funny pains run through my body—

here. It makes me feel glad and light and it makes me feel I am living for ever."

"That is because hormones are set loose in your bloodstream—speaking inexactly—and are having a strong effect on your sympathetic nervous system. The same thing will be happening to the Englishman, Tom Galton, but with a man it has a more localised effect——"

"I know that," said Oksana, and laughed. "He had no clothes on. We had been swimming. Besides, I know about men."

"It is very bad for a woman," said her mother, watching the skill and quickness with which she hammered in one nail after another, "to have an abortion for her first pregnancy. Besides, it hurts very much, and I don't want you to be hurt that way."

"Well," said Oksana, "I am not sure about all that. You see, Mother, the English are very shy, and he is married. His wife is a nice woman, I think—don't you? She is bourgeois, of course, but she tries to think in right ways. I like her."

"Even if she thinks right and you like her, you could hurt her, 'Ksana. It is a pity to hurt people; they are sure to be hurt enough one way and another during their lives."

"Well, I do not really know about her. I wish Leon were old enough to make love to her. Look, Mother, how well I have mended the sofa!"

"You are a clever girl. Tell me, 'Ksana: do you feel as if you wanted to be with this Englishman always?"

"Oh no! Why, Mother, he doesn't agree with me over some of the most important things. Remember, he is in the English Labour Party!"

"I cannot remember all these foreign parties. Is that social democrat?"

" Yes. But I am arguing with him. I am changing him a little already."

" Perhaps you might hurt his wife more that way than by sleeping with him."

" But it is *good* to change his opinions. The other would be—only him and me."

" Perhaps. What does he think of you ? "

" He thinks I am beautiful. As some of the comrades have thought ! I expect I must be beautiful."

" You are certainly beautiful, 'Ksana. It is very awkward for you, I know. But I meant what does he think of you ideologically—and about everything ? "

" I tell you, Mother, I am changing him. But he is, I think, at least—Socialist. It is like making something ! "

" A new five-valve set ! It is good when one finds one can make something, but dangerous. Both for you and him."

" It is like a set that gives me something new—some station I have never heard——"

" I thought you said he told you nothing the comrades haven't told you ? "

" He is a—different wave-length. I want to know what happens next."

" It is probably very simple what happens next. It is always the same thing."

" Mother, don't laugh at me ! Do you find it of no consequence how your eldest daughter loses her virginity ? "

" Nothing you did would surprise me, 'Ksana. And you would always find a good reason for it, too. I am only surprised that you have kept your virginity so long, as things are."

" I am surprised, too, when I think of the games I have played with the comrades ! But perhaps it was because we were comrades. There was nothing new about them.

I did not want to—explore. They might be good to marry with and have children, as I shall do later. But not this."

The next day Tom and Dione went with B party to see a kolkhoz. It was not entirely reassuring, but at least it was producing a fair amount of small crops. In the evening Oksana came round again and had supper with them. Tom had got a bottle of wine at Torgsin. Nancy Ellis fell for her and said all sorts of pretty things about the U.S.S.R., which she had certainly not intended to say. Tom said he would see her home; it seemed a very English thing to do. Dione went up to bed and decided to go to sleep and not wait for Tom. It was not so easy as she had thought, going to sleep, but still she managed to in time. When she woke the next morning, Tom was very sound asleep; she lay propped on her elbow watching his face. She was not going to—lose him. There would be no nonsense of that kind. But he might go a long way off, as he was now, sleeping so deeply. He might go far and far into Oksana's country—which was good country, but fairyland, oh, fairyland for anyone from England or Scotland, from Oxford and Marshbrook Bridge. And if he ate fairy fruit there—— No, it wasn't fairyland; it was the Debatable Land that lies between here and fairyland, it was where Jean MacLean went, and though one comes back from there, though there is no question of staying there seven years or being sent as teind to hell, yet one comes back changed. Yes, changed. Why not? Isn't life made of changing? Isn't that good biology? Am not I, too, she thought, giving my mind to the plow tractors to furrow as they will? There is nothing wrong, there are no kelpies here, no Campbell Women; if there is anything wrong it is my mind, which is full of black wriggling seals like the tide race beyond Jura.

The next evening they went over to the Nikolaevskys',

who were all very nice to them both ; even the boy did his best with conversation. Dione caught Mrs. Nikolaevsky looking at her curiously, but kindly ; Oksana, though, seemed intensely at ease. They talked politics of course ; it seemed impossible not to. Once during the evening Tom and Oksana quarrelled violently for about five minutes. Both of them were on their feet, flushed and gesticulating. It seemed to Dione that she had heard a good deal of what Oksana was saying from Donald—and wasn't it better not to argue about it ?—one did no good, it was so much a matter of what point of view one looked at a given set of facts from. She tried to mediate, but Mrs. Nikolaevsky said : " Do not distress yourself for this, Mrs. Galton ! They are—children. It is for the moment only."

What does she know ? Dione thought, or doesn't she ? For she is right. It is for the moment. It is because they are not being honest with one another, perhaps. They are in a state of strain. Tom is being like this because he is changing ; he is hot iron being beaten upon. And she—she too——

Neonila said : " I have always read that the English are so calm, have so much control. It is interesting to see for oneself that this is not so."

Oksana suddenly laughed and said : " I have not lost my temper so since two years. I am known to the comrades as—sensible. What is this Tom doing to me ? " And she kissed his ear, and then went and sat on the sofa beside Dione and was charming to her.

Dione began to recognise quotations from Oksana in Tom's conversations, with her or with others. She wondered why this annoyed her so much ; she was angry with herself, suppressed it. Why should she mind if Tom was influenced by someone ? Surely she didn't suppose he was such a super-man that he oughtn't ever to be influenced !

But—by Oksana? Well, why on earth not? Why should she, Dione Galton, a rational woman, be annoyed because Oksana was a woman, too? Hadn't she herself admired Oksana, both for her body and her mind, long before Tom had? Dione was firm with herself. The difficulty was that Tom himself was fidgety and jumpy and no great help; he did not realise that he was being anything but normal, but Nancy Ellis noticed and suggested pills. Well, at least it was only for three more days. Then she herself was going home, and Tom was going down the Volga with Lambert and the Jewish writer.

She had just had another rather disturbing letter from Alex; he said first of all that he had written to Christina Campbell proposing marriage, and she had turned him down. In a way it was a relief. He had wanted to take a definite step of some kind, only he hadn't exactly wanted to marry her. The letter went on: "Do you remember my dealing with a case for Simpson and Bone, the paint manufacturers? Well, I've got them to let me have some casks of paint at wholesale prices delivered here, and I am giving it out cheap (or free, but they usually like to pay something) to the unemployed men hereabouts to paint their houses and furniture—red, or any other colour they like. It gives them an interest in life, and if they haven't got that they will certainly die off like flies the next time there is a 'flu epidemic, and that would be a pity, as they are a very decent, intelligent set of men whom it's a pleasure to be with." Alex, she thought, with barrels of paint——? What was at the bottom of it all? Sensible of Christina Campbell, but one could trust that girl.

By the same post Tom had a rather gloomy letter from Mason at Marshbrook Bridge. Things were going badly; everyone was dispirited, meetings were badly attended; people were dropping out. Reuben Goldberg was showing signs of going to the I.L.P. Edna Boffin had been difficult. Lots of the members were out of work, including Taylor, who could usually count on getting work as a bricklayer in summer. If you were out of work, you didn't get enough to eat and your strength went. He, Mason, had been having his rheumatism worse than ever. And he hoped Mr. and Mrs. Galton were enjoying Russia.

Tom chucked it over to Dione to read, but before she had finished it he began fidgeting. At last he said : " About Oksana."

" Yes ? " said Dione. It usually was !

" I can't leave it like this. Having got so far. We seem to have made contact in some extraordinary way. You know, Dione. You told me first."

" But what can you do, Tom ? " She put the letter down.

" I've been talking about it to her. Listen, it's such a chance. She gets her holiday now—it starts the day you go back."

" And you're going with her. How lovely."

" You don't mind, Dione ? You're sure you don't ? "

" That's all right, my dear. But what about her ? You—you haven't yet——"

" No, but she wants me to."

" I'm sure it's much better than going on as you are now, fidgeting one another. Only, aren't you likely to get rather permanently entangled ? "

" We've got to take the risk now. You told us to go on, Dione."

" Tom, I'm not really responsible for everything. You—you aren't going to stay in Russia and never come back ? " She discovered herself to be horribly near tears. She went over to the window and stood with her back to him ; some way off and below there was a view of one corner of the Kremlin ; she fixed on that.

For a moment he didn't answer, then came over and stood beside her. " Sweetheart," he said, " I couldn't do that if I would. And I don't want to, believe me. My life's not here but in England. I take it Oksana and I will always think very closely of one another—love one another perhaps—whatever that means. We've got into one another's blood rather a lot. We shall write to one another, I suppose, but—we shan't even count on ever seeing one another again. She'll certainly marry, though perhaps not yet. In the meantime she says I'm good for her work. She's certainly good for me. And I—well, it makes no difference to how I think and feel about you, Dione. Yes, it does; it makes me respect you more than I did. You aren't crying, are you ? "

She shook her head, tightening up the muscles of her face and neck : " No—Theotormon."

He laughed, picking it up : " All right, Oöthoon! You've found me a virgin of furious gold, my dear."

" Is she——?"

" A virgin—yes. Why not ? She's got to stop being some time—she's older than you were. I shall be careful of her, you needn't worry. I think I know the—main points."

" But——"

" What ? "

" Well, you obviously don't want to let her start a baby, and—it's always I who take the precautions."

" I'm going to take them now," said Tom.

" Have you been able to get—things—here ? "

" Oksana's mother produced them. She's a doctor, you know ; she—gave me a bit of a lecture on them." Dione burst into a splutter of laughter. Tom said, a little hurt : " It was damned nice and sensible of her."

" Of course it was," Dione said, " but—oh, dear, what would they think in Marshbrook Bridge ? "

" In fifty years—no, in twenty perhaps—they'll see and approve. In the meantime they don't know."

Dione turned away from the window into the room again, and began twisting up a corner of Mason's letter; " How long do you think you can stay ? "

" An extra three weeks."

" Like Elinor Glyn."

" Shut up, Dione ! "

" Sorry, I was only——"

" Yes, I know. I didn't mean to bite you. Look, will you be all right about Scotland ? "

" Yes. Will you be all right about money ? "

He nodded. " It's bound to cost a bit, as I'm a foreigner. But——"

" My dear, it's obviously worth it. It'll be—good for you. Put it down as election expenses. By the way, is Oksana going to pull you right out of the Labour Party ? "

" I think not," he said, " though I—admit the force of her arguments. Probably we shall each see the other's point of view better when we're not in a state of strain."

" But you will be," Dione said, " you'll both be thinking, it's such a short time. She'll feel she's only got so many days to convert you in."

" She won't. She'll know that's the wrong way to set about it. Don't you worry."

" Tom," said Dione, " I want to ask you something. You think of her, and treat her, as completely an equal, don't you ? Well, have you ever done that with a woman before ? "

" What a horrid idea ! " said Tom, startled, " don't I treat women as equals ? "

" Of course you don't. Think again ! They're always something above or below, to be looked up to or looked down on, in varying proportions according to your mood.

Perhaps I'm putting it too fiercely, but it's about right. And you aren't treating Oksana now or thinking of her as men in England think of and treat the women they're in love with. Yes, Tom, I believe this will be a very good thing."

During the next three days they saw more things and more people; several of the introductions had proved interesting. But Dione hadn't made up her mind about Russia yet. She swung between one point of view and another, sometimes she thought she'd got it clear, and then some new sight or event would come and alter her idea. Before she went she left Tom two or three books, including "The Fountain," "The Orators" and "The Waves." People in Russia were still starved of English books and wanted them. She couldn't quite imagine she was going back.

Most of the party were leaving with her, but some were going by Kiev. Tom and Oksana both came to see her off. She walked along the platform with Oksana; it was difficult to know what to say; if she had liked Oksana less it might have been easier. "You'll take care of Tom?" she said. Oksana nodded and hugged her. There was something extraordinarily nice about Oksana's skin; it was cool and smooth in this hot weather like the skin of fruit. It was there for use, not for attraction, yet it was lovely to touch. The feel of it stayed on Dione's lips for miles and miles of train travelling, underneath and closer than the feel of Tom's.

## UNDER THE RED FLAG 8

THEY had walked up from the little house on the edge of the new town called Sea Grass, and all the way they had picked flowers, and now their hands were full of them. Tom told her the English names of the flowers which were the same as English flowers: pinks, larkspur, love-in-the-mist—but it was a grey foamy colour, never the nigella of garden borders—mullein, lemon thyme, sea lavender, mignonette—but it doesn't smell—marigolds, chicory, everlastings. But this and this and this, that starry one, this spiky one, the blue that matches your eyes? She told him their names, but she did not always know them herself, for they were different from the northern flowers or the Ukrainian steppe flowers that she had known as a child.

Both of them took off their shoes and socks, and Tom took off his shirt; he had bought Russian linen shirts at Torgsin—they were cooler to wear than his English ones with buttoned sleeves. She wore a thin cotton dress with shoulder straps; she leant back against Tom and he slipped a hand down it, fondling her strong little breasts, till she turned her face up to be kissed. They were flooded with the heat of the sun and the heat of their own bodies. Here, on the top of the kurgan, they were quite alone. They could see for miles, north and west the queer hillocks of the kurgans, the Scythian grave mounds, rising out of the dry, flowery, unfenced Crimean steppe, and south the Black Sea, as beautiful as the Ægean. South-east was their town, Sea Grass, the low lines of the huts, and the big semicircle of the new buildings, and between it and the kurgan a flock of spotted goats belonging to the kolkhoz.

Tom had not much liked the idea of spending their honeymoon in a hut at the edge of a newly developing industrial town, but Oksana had decided it. She said she wanted to see the new town; she was interested in it. So Tom dutifully went with her, and fairly soon he began to see what she meant.

After a long train journey they had spent their first twenty-four hours at Dnieperstroy, on their way south; this again was Oksana's choice. Tom had seen this holiday in terms of gardens, tall trees at evening and fountains, or calm light rooms where they would be alone to see one another and think of one another. But instead they had gone out that morning of all mornings, and Oksana had said: "I want to walk over the dam—at once." So there they had gone, and Oksana bounded along the new shadeless streets like a wild creature, and when the sentry with the bayonet wouldn't let them by, she had thrown her arms round his neck and talked to him hard, but whether it was an account of her political convictions or her biological state, Tom couldn't quite make out: from the words he understood, he thought probably both. At any rate the sentry had let them pass, and they had walked across, she leading, jumping alarmingly over gaps in the planking of the half-finished roadway above the heavy green thunder of the falling water, piling down to the foam and fury of its rapids. The dam was finished, though not all the works connected with it. Above it was the lake, spreading now over acres where once there had been wooden huts and a few ragged crops and little hope or joy, only a vague trust in the magic of the household ikons. Below the lake and the dam was the power station, the force of the Dnieper waters hurled down dark spirals against the steel blades of the turbines, and then the revolving of enormous shafts, the busy picking-up of the current, then transformers and condensers, an elaborate and ordered web of pylons and wires and the shining fairy fruit of the insulators.

Two men were riveting a pylon: one held the red-hot rivets in place with long metal tongs; the other went at them with rapid, swinging, accurate strokes of a great hammer. They were half naked, with brown, leaping muscles like men in a propaganda film. Tom suddenly wondered whether Donald was doing this kind of work, and thought of him for a moment with vivid sympathy.

Oksana said: " That is idiotic. They should do it with a machine." Which was, of course, true. For a few minutes they stood watching the riveters; Tom thought she was comparing their muscles with his and hoped that he was standing the comparison; he thought he'd—done well by her. She said: " Now I will tell you what I did dream last night—after. I was making a radio apparat and it seemed to me I was needing to make some necessary correction in every part. I had to do again all the blue prints. I know them so well, the blue prints, and at every place I did need to make that so essential correction. I did that in my sleep for long, and when I waked again I was still seeing those same blue prints. That was when I waked you, Tom, when you were so sound asleep. I wanted so much to make myself sure it was still you."

" That wasn't really a nasty dream, was it?" Tom said.

" No," she said, " only—interesting. Did you dream, Tom?"

" Yes," he said slowly, then: " Well, I'll tell you. It was when you woke me, then. I'd been dreaming in a rather muddled way, about the war, nothing really bad though, and when you began to wake me, moving against me, I thought you were Dione—in 1918—and before I was quite awake I called you by her name."

" But you said Isobel."

" Yes, that's her other name. I used to call her that then. Especially—at nights."

" That is good, then. I wondered a little who was Isobel."

" And didn't tell me ! "

" No ; it was your affair. But it was nice you thought I was Dione. Because I like her so much."

They had sat for a time in the new park, looking down over the lake and the works ; it was all blazing and sweet with cannas, lobelias, African marigolds, blinding red geraniums, godetias, nemesias and snapdragon, with the hammer and sickle bedded out in lavender bushes. Someone passed on a bicycle and Oksana said : " Oh, I would like to have a bicycle and go so fast always ! "

" But you must have one ! " said Tom. " I'll get one sent out somehow——"

" Don't be stupid ! " said Oksana, and blushed violently. " I do not want a bicycle—like that. Besides, you could not import one. When all in the Union of Soviet Republics have bicycles, then I will have a bicycle, too. And it will not be long to wait ! " she ended provocatively.

" Sorry," said Tom and kissed her hand. He had been made to feel humble that way once already, when he had wanted to change luggage with her. He had a newish rucksack and a solid English fibre suit-case with good leather corners and handle and excellent locks ; she had a rather battered cardboard case, secured with string, and an ancient rucksack of her father's, which he had bought as a student in Germany some time during the 'nineties. He had so wanted to swap suit-cases ! But she had laughed at him : " Are you ashamed of me, then ? " she asked.

" No," he said, " but I'm rather ashamed of myself."

" Then you shall stay ashamed," she said, and swung her toes at him in the railway carriage.

But since then she had taken one of his rough silk ties, that he had got from Hall's in the High at Oxford, to use as a belt. And he hoped he'd persuade her to take as many as she would of his handkerchiefs ; or his hat ; or anything at all ! She liked dressing up in his clothes, stalking about the hut or outside in the starlight in one of his shirts and nothing else ; she liked wearing his pyjamas. That was all the use they were ; but it was, anyway, too hot to sleep with anything on.

From Dnieperstroy they had come south to the Crimea and the little house. A new deposit of ore had been found, and a factory town and harbour were being made. Now there was a single-line railway, rows of wooden huts for the workers, and a canteen where Oksana and Tom usually ate one meal a day. Oksana knew one of the engineers who had found them the hut ; it had two rooms, one with a tiny stove and a basin to wash at, and a good verandah with a vine growing over it. Oksana and the engineer had made all the arrangements, and Oksana had paid. Oksana had paid for most things except the railway fares ; she said very sensibly that everything was very expensive in English money, and when Tom suggested that he could get a better illegal exchange than the official one—as Lambert, who knew the ropes, had done already—she was really shocked and forbade him to do anything of the kind. She was getting quite good pay as a student and technician ; it would do for two. At first Tom found it extraordinarily embarrassing.

" But *why?* " asked Oksana. " We are comrades—it is reasonable that I pay for you. Here you are not earning wages—I am."

So Tom had to resign himself to being a gigolo, and after a few days he ceased to mind. When he asked himself why, he discovered, rather to his horror, that it was because nobody seemed to be shocked or inclined to laugh at him. He had, then, in his previous relations with women, acted entirely in deference to public opinion. When he said that to Oksana, she said: "But the public opinion comes, I think, because in your country the women are in a bad economic position." He agreed that this was so, and Oksana stood him meals at the workers' canteen, and he felt very happy and curiously humble. He had laid down at the feet of Oksana and her State some burden of pride and assurance and responsibility. It had been partly economic, he thought, his class position; and partly national—though the position of England was economic too, due to the industrial revolution and nineteenth-century imperialism; and partly because he was a teacher—would he ever be able to go back to Oxford and assume un-self-conscious superiority over his pupils?—or to Marshbrook Bridge and assume superiority there as their candidate? If only he could be happy and innocent like this always, stripped and new-born.

It made him sensitive to other people as he had never been before; he was a far better lover to Oksana this way, for he followed and understood her moods of body and mind, without trying to impress his patterns; he could tell when she wanted gentleness and when she needed violence. Yet there was nothing subservient about it—everything came naturally. But he felt that now he would never be able to deal with anyone without thinking of them first and immediately, not as some category of person, classifiable according to his old prejudices, but each as someone new and individual and to be learned from, yet touching him so intimately that he could not feel separate from them. He tried to write all this home to Dione, and wondered how it would carry, for a ten days' post out of the U.S.S.R.

He had after all very much enjoyed being in and about the

new town. They had gone all over it, Oksana asking questions and translating the answers to him—though he was beginning to understand some Russian. They had not started on the ore yet, beyond the assays, but they were busy on the harbour and the great blocks of workers' flats, which had been planned on a fine scale with a view out over the sea. The factories were not going to be built till all was ready for the workers. There would be shops too, and already they were busy on roads and gardens ; a little park with cinder paths was flowering gaily, with coloured tobacco plants which smelt sweet in the evenings, and little trees planted. In the meantime the workers lived very roughly in the huts with wooden walls and earthern floors, three or four to a room, nothing in each but camp-beds and a rough table and most likely a picture of Lenin with a bunch of wild everlastings stuck up over one corner.

Men and women workers were in separate rooms, except for a few married couples, Oksana's friend the engineer, and two doctors, and the teachers who had charge of the adult school for the Tartar workers. It was like a wild-west town, Tom thought, and then had to modify the idea, for there was no alcohol—no bar for heroes and villains and low-down or golden-hearted prostitutes to meet in—no gambling, and no six-shooters. And, above all, there was no one out for himself or herself, no one trying to make money out of it ; Sea Grass was the workers' town and every worker not only knew it intellectually, but felt it while he worked. They were all interested, all felt it was worth while living uncomfortably and working hard—they might have been, Tom thought suddenly, rich young folk out roughing it in some wilds, determined to get value out of every experience !

By winter the flats would be finished, and no one living in the hutments. In the meantime they didn't need baths any more than Tom and Oksana did, for they went down and bathed in the Black Sea most days. After bathing, and especially on their sixth day, they would play the concertina and sing and dance. Everyone joined in, the school teachers and architects and doctors, the farm workers from the kolkhoz that gave them milk and eggs and vegetables, the lorry drivers and railwaymen, and Tom and Oksana. There were more men than women, but not so very many, as a good many of the navvies were women, and there were a few children, including the school teachers' little girl; they were deep in the affairs of the town, like little Athenians watching the Parthenon go up.

Oksana was paying for their meals by dealing with the radio sets for the whole of the hutments and advising on the installations for the new flats. It only took her an hour or two every day, but Tom was very envious of her—almost at once he began to want to work for Sea Grass himself!—and at last he found something he could do. They had started keeping rabbits; he went and saw them with Oksana, who was deliciously and femininely enthusiastic over them; she had never had a rabbit to stroke before! Tom, however, thought they were not well, and conversed with their guardian, who was worried, for they were semi-sacred animals, a State experiment for helping the U.S.S.R. over its food difficulties. Tom said tea-leaves. He wished Morag had been there; she was the family expert. But he knew a certain amount about them himself. He and the guardian in consultation altered the prescribed diet of the State rabbits. And in two or three days the rabbits picked up and throve. And Tom felt like the spinster lady who has embroidered a pair of slippers for the curate!

And now they were lying here, up in the sun on the kurgan, with the wild flowers all round them. Below them, sixty feet down, were the bones of some Scythian chief, his wives and slaves and horses. Perhaps there was gold with them, like the golden beasts in Leningrad, or perhaps that had been stolen by Tartars hundreds of years ago. Once, slaves had come day after day bringing loads of earth and pebbles to lay over the stone burial chamber of the chief; they had made the hill, and all the other hills, sweating and bleeding under the loads of earth. And now flowers had grown on the kurgans, and sweet herbs and the sparse green that goats crop, and people's minds had turned at last from the chiefs who fought and wore golden beasts on their coats and golden crowns on their heads, to the slaves who had been hurt and oppressed and killed on the same earth, in the same sunshine.

Tom had put his shirt under Oksana's head and shoulders to keep her from little stones and prickles. In return now she had his cheek resting on her upper arm, his eyes looking into hers. This must all be very good exercise, she thought, for afterwards I feel as if I had played a game of football—or perhaps as if I had come up to the surface after a long swim under water, in sea caves, in deep shining caves, and now I am resting, rocking on waves, I am so light—and yet so heavy—so softened—so tired—so utterly rested—so happy and delicious. It was as simple as this to be happy, and she hadn't found it out till now. But must it be one only man or would any man do? It was after all very unlikely that Tom should be the only man who could do this for her. Any good sort of man, she thought, anybody worth while, whom one would want to explore, to help to make—whom one could let touch one, so closely, one's body and mind. If I make him, he makes me, she thought, and wished fleetingly that she could let him make her a baby—if it weren't such a bother afterwards—if she could have a baby by him and then give it away to the new town, like the radio set she had made for the canteen. But probably I should be silly and like it too much to give away, she decided, and then it would be a responsibility and hinder my work. When the time comes I shall have babies, three or four perhaps, by someone not Tom, but like Tom, who will be strong and kind with me like Tom is and for whom I shall feel like this. There will be such another man later. But after I have worked for several years and played games and thought and come to decisions, and have forgotten about this except as something very sweet, something nice that happened to me when I grew up and became a woman—and it shall happen to my daughters like this—and I shall have forgotten Tom except as my comrade, for we shall stay friends always and always, and perhaps there will have been a revolution in England by then, and Tom will be Bolshevik, partly because of what I have done to him. But in the meantime there is us, and all the little things about him which I like so much. His smile. He is looking very grave now, but I will make him smile, I will look at him the way it pleases him so much that I should look, softly—his eyes—there, he is smiling, oh Tom, I have pleased you—his hands—his voice. " Oh Tom, please : say me something in English."

Tom began to say, in a low voice, not lifting his cheek from her brown live arm, and keeping his eyes still on hers :

" Oh, death's old bony fingers
  Shall never find us there
In that high, hollow townland
  Where love's to give and to spare.
Boughs have their fruit and blossom
  At all times of the year ;
Rivers are running over
  With red beer and brown beer.
An old man plays the bagpipes
  In a gold and silver wood ;
Queens, their eyes blue like the ice,
  Are dancing in a crowd.

" The little fox he murmured :
' O, what of the world's bane ? '
The sun was laughing sweetly——"

" Oh, stop, stop ! " said Oksana. " Explain to me—everything. What is a townland ? "

" That is a kolkhoz in Irish. Queens with eyes blue like the ice, are you and your friends. It is a poem by the Irishman Yeats—I told you some of his political poems."

" That is the man who advised illiteracy, yes ? "

" No, no, that's Auden. And he didn't advise illiteracy exactly—only not always to be thinking and reading books and having no *praxis*."

" But one must have theory, too."

" Yes, schoolmistress ! But you liked him really ; you know you did. ' The two worlds in each other's arms '—you remember that ? "

" Yes," she said, " I remember that. You reading it to me and holding me. It was nice of Dione to leave the book. Was she perhaps thinking of that line ? "

" Perhaps," he said. He shifted his head enough to kiss her arm ; the skin was a little salt from much swimming in the Black Sea.

" Sing me something," she said, " something of your revolution."

" Casey Jones ? " he asked. She liked the tune of that, and approved the words, which she considered really proletarian. He thought it a childish taste, but still—it was hers.

" No," she said, " not American. Something of your own in England."

He began very softly singing to her :

" Bring me my Bow of burning gold :
Bring me my Arrows of desire :
Bring me my Spear : O clouds, unfold !
Bring me my Chariot of fire.

" I will not cease from Mental Fight,
Nor shall my Sword Sleep in my hand,
Till we have built Jerusalem
In England's green and pleasant Land."

" Do you like that ? " he said.

She looked at him innocently : " That—but that is, perhaps, Zionist ? "

He sat up suddenly. " Oksana," he said, " you know perfectly well it isn't. You ought to be smacked ! "

Yes, she had known all along from the way he sang it. But she had wanted to tease him—it was, oh, so romantic, not realist, not proletarian !—only perhaps it meant very much to him, perhaps her teasing had hurt him. Teasing people helps to make them, but hurting doesn't. " Yes, Tom," she said, " I did know. Perhaps you should smack me, yes ? " She flattened herself away from him looking down at her, frowning, and she had a small delightful moment of physical fear, a kind of shiver like before a high dive.

He pulled her up roughly by the wrists and half across his knees ; she was a slack delicious weight of she-flesh, she-nerves. He pulled her frock up ; she felt the sudden heat of the sun on her bare legs.

She murmured, with her eyes half-open looking at the flowers and tiny shining pebbles : " I would like to be smacked a little, Tom."

" Sorry," said Tom, " I can't. I respect you too much. Even upside-down. If you really want to be a masochist—"

" What is a masochist, Tom ? I want to be smacked."

" Someone who wants to be smacked. You had better go off and marry a peasant. I expect some of them still keep up the good old practices. He'd probably do it every Saturday night before bedtime. On a tumbler of vodka."

" Ach ! " she said and suddenly rolled over, off his knee.

" That is not nice of you, Tom! That is—serious. For it does happen still—a little—and it is terrible! I—we—we are so lately free that we shudder still to look on our chains."

Her voice quivered; he took her in his arms. " Soon—soon," he said, " that will be over everywhere. It will be over, my 'Ksana, as it is over for you and me. Men and women will not be enemies any longer; they will not hate one another. They won't want to grab at one another and cheat and lie and hurt one another. That's only because we are still mostly each out for his own—as your peasants are."

" But," said Oksana, with her arms round his neck, " even here, the comrades have wanted me to be theirs, to belong to them, to marry and be always there for them to have. It is so with many of my girl comrades who have married; at first they have perhaps liked it: afterwards, not."

" That is because it is easier to be a political Socialist than a Socialist in living. Perhaps in Russia you have thought too much about politics and economics and too little about living."

" It was necessary."

" Very likely. But the other has lagged behind; it will probably be still another generation before we can any of us be real Socialists in our lives."

" When the economic basis is right," decided Oksana, " then the other thing will come." And her arms on his shoulders shifted and caressed him, and her lips on his neck.

" In England we can perhaps work for both," Tom said. " May I go as far from the economic basis as that, Oksana?"

" I think yes," she said, hanging from his neck and looking up at him. " Oh, Tom," she said, sighing deeply and happily.

But his eyes clouded; the look which answered hers was

different, was out of another place and time. He began to sing again :

> " Had we never loved sae kindly,
> Had we never loved sae blindly,
> Never met—or never parted,
> We had ne'er been broken-hearted.
> Ae fond kiss.. . . "

For a moment he dodged her kissing mouth, then gave in to it.

" No ! " she said. " No ! that is one of your national songs and it is all wrong ! That is not—being a good Socialist, Tom. We shall not regret anything. We shall not let this—personal thing—disturb us afterwards. We will be working together for the same thing, I in my country, you in yours. We will always be together that way. And this—will have been good, and enough. Now, we have ten days more—so long, so long ! There is no hurry, there is nothing to be sad for, Tom."

" Oh, my love, my love," he said, and fell to kissing her again, up in the sun on the kurgan, above the unremembered bones and gold of the Scythian chief.

# PART IV

## THE VALLEY OF HUMILIATION, BY VANITY FAIR, TO DOUBTING CASTLE

"What shall we put in the daily paper?
What shall we put in the daily paper?
What shall we put in the daily paper?
Early in the morning?
Workers on the dole who guzzle,
Communists who need a muzzle,
All the winners and a cross-word puzzle,
Early in the morning!"

G. D. H. Cole.

## LONDON I

THAT evening on board the Soviet ship going back to London everyone was deciding on their impressions of Russia. Most were glad to be getting back, for one reason or another, often perhaps small reasons, but they piled up: baths and W.C.'s that worked; posts that arrived; trains, trams and 'buses that were not intolerably crowded—yes, and taxis—or one's own car; freedom from hotels and especially being herded by guides; English cookery suitable for English digestions, with plenty of fruit and vegetables—ah, Dione said, but I shall still find some strawberries up in Scotland!—the possibility of buying soap, razor blades, safety-pins, the thousand and one little things that stick life together; newspapers with one's own kind of news—at any rate an exterior calm and dignity and sense of safety first. "One can't deny," Medingley said, "that their standard of life is intolerably low."

"Yes!" said the M.P.'s secretary, "I saw the most dreadful slums when I was poking about by myself."

"One has to consider where they started from," Dione said, "the incredible state of chaos they were in at the end of the war."

"They've had fourteen years to get right in," said Medingley; "there's my difficulty about that."

"How can they ever get right," said Nancy Ellis, "when they're such a race of incompetent, unpunctual bunglers? What amazes me is that they keep going at all."

"There's the minority," Dione said, "who are so keen to pull it through that they make up for the others." She thought vividly of Oksana.

" Ah yes," said Medingley, " I grant you the Communist Party. Though no doubt there are some compensations for their hard work. But here's the test, Mrs. Galton, would you go and live there ? "

After a moment Dione said : " Honestly, no. Not as I am. But I would if I were a Russian, whatever I were to lose materially."

" I wonder if you would, Mrs. Galton," said the secretary girl ; " just think of the conditions. Think of the overcrowding and the dirt and the dreadful food—you couldn't bring up children there."

" Well, I'm not sure," Dione said, " I'd take a child over ten." Morag and Kenneth, she thought.

" It's not entirely a matter of food and housing," Nancy Ellis said, " but those schools—the lack of equipment bothered me a good deal."

" And too much parrot-fashion teaching about the glorious doctrines," said an American school-teacher who had joined the group.

" What do *you* think, Jane ? " Dione asked.

Jane answered shyly : " I believe one would learn a lot more there because one would be wanting to learn. One wouldn't have to waste time on school chapel and ragging the mistresses and being serious about hockey every winter afternoon ! "

" If you went to school in Russia, Jane," said her mother, " they wouldn't let you off a month to go and visit England."

" Oh, I don't know," said Jane ; " I bet you'd bully the Commissar for Education till he let me go—anyway you'd probably be him yourself."

All exchanged names and addresses, and Dione mentioned that she was going to stay a night with her sister-in-law. " I'll come and see you," Nancy Ellis said ; " too sad your leaving your brother behind."

"Yes," said Dione, not daring to look in Medingley's direction.

They got in early one morning and Dione went straight off to Muriel's and they had a very gay breakfast together with grape fruit—two for Dione!—and beautifully fresh English eggs, toast, country butter and marmalade. There were letters from Auchanarnish; Kenneth had been up the burn with MacCallum and had caught his first burn trout. Tom had told Dione she could tell his sister where he was and why, but she wasn't inclined to yet. Suddenly the telephone bell rang. "I'll answer," Dione said, "and pretend to be your highly trained parlourmaid! Hullo?"

"Hullo, is Mrs. Galton there—Dione Galton?"

"Speaking." Who on earth knew where she was!

"Thank god, you're the third Galton I've tried! Medingley this end. Mrs. Galton, have you seen the morning paper yet?"

"I've just glanced at it. Why?"

"Got it there? Good. What is it—*Manchester Guardian?* Same here. Look at page nine, third column."

She looked, and her voice came sharply over the telephone: "But I don't understand! How *can* they have arrested someone for the Sallington murder?"

"It was up to the police to catch the murderer, and—as they couldn't get *him*—they've got someone else."

"But then it must be someone innocent!"

"Of course. But—look, Mrs. Galton, I'm coming round. We can't discuss this over the 'phone. Yes, at once."

Muriel had picked up the paper and read the paragraph. "Now, steady, my dear. Drink your coffee. There. We're going to get this man off."

"Then I shall have to tell!"

"If you do that you'll be liable to all kinds of penalties

for aiding and abetting a murderer. And they'll enforce them. It'll smash Tom politically, and at Oxford too."

"But I can't let them hang an innocent man!"

"No, and you'll probably have to lie like hell. You're a bad liar, Dione."

"I know. And I've not got to involve Tom."

"If you involve yourself you involve Tom; it would be the same at his constituency. If you involve Alex you involve yourself. No, we've got to keep off the truth."

"But if we can't get him off without the truth——"

"Then you may have to choose between this man's life and Tom's constituency."

"But it isn't only the constituency! It isn't only me and Tom—and the children. It's the whole Labour Movement that'll get involved! Yes, I know, I *did* think of it, only I had to act as I did, I still don't see that I could have acted otherwise—but oh, my goodness, the headlines!"

"It's just not got ever to get to headlines."

"If only I could ask Tom——"

"This is only the preliminary business. The man won't be on trial for a long time. Apart from his mental anxiety there's no hurry—we could leave it ten days till Tom got back. I don't suppose it would be safe to write to him."

"But he won't be back for three weeks. Oh, Muriel, I hadn't told you, but he fell in love with an awfully beautiful girl over there, and he's staying with her. And he'll have a frantic amount to do when he gets back, so I must settle this if I possibly can."

"My dear Dione. This is—this is new, isn't it?"

"Yes, quite. But—Muriel, I really don't mind. Or hardly at all. Nothing to count later. Naturally, we—we can't grab one another."

"Well, I hope you'll find yourself someone fairly soon."

" I don't think I really want to. But don't be angry with Tom, Muriel. We both saw what was happening. We decided it was the right thing to do."

" No, I'm not angry. I merely remark that men are exceedingly selfish."

" Very likely. But not Tom. Now, let's think. I wish I could remember just who this man Adam Walker is. I know Donald told me his name. Wait a minute. I don't think he's actually a Party member." She dug her head into the corner of the sofa, her fists at her ears, thinking. " Got it. He's the man Donald got the bomb from; the bomb was a war souvenir. I suppose they traced it to him through neighbours and then found it missing. The question is, has he told the truth."

" He might try to shield Donald."

" He's much more likely just to have been frightened and said a lot of things that were half true and half lies and look very suspicious. In any case—Muriel, the best thing we can do is to forge a confession from Donald."

" I don't think they're likely to take that."

" But Donald was a suspect. No, I think pretty badly of British justice, but I don't think they'd hang a man with that in front of them. They'd be more likely to hang him if he really was a Communist, but he's only in the N.U.W.M. and he's an ex-Service man. The British Legion might help, though they're none too keen on the Left in any shape. Still—— Let's draft some confessions."

" What about the signature ? "

" I've got one on—oh, an envelope. I can forge it."

" How ? "

" The usual way. Oh—probably you don't know. Phœbe taught me. Oh, lord, if only I can pull it off ! "

For a time they made drafts, laboriously trying to think out something absolutely clear and yet in Donald's phraseology. As they discarded a draft, Muriel burnt it. Then there was a ring. Dione slipped the nearly finished one under the blotting-paper, in case it wasn't Medingley; but it was. She showed him the draft.

"This is all right as a confession," he said, after a minute; "that's to say, it reads genuine. But have you got to put in all that about the Communist Party's views on assassination?"

"Yes," said Dione firmly. "I'm sure Donald would want me to. He was desperately anxious not to involve his Party."

"Would you mind particularly if the C.P. were involved, Mrs. Galton? They're a nasty, prickly lot. Always going for *your* party! You don't think there's conceivably something to be said for their being discredited? After all, Donald MacLean got his main ideas from them and their propaganda. They *are* to blame."

Dione shook her head: "Nothing doing. That stands. What about the rest of it?"

"We want some corroborative evidence—something that the police can test to try if it's genuine. Somebody who saw him escaping, or with the bomb, for instance. Rather difficult without local accomplices. Yes, I take it you're right about the C.P. Mustn't descend to Continental methods, must we?"

"This evidence is going to be a job. I don't know the C.P. people in Sallington. And—I can't tell about Marshbrook Bridge. I really don't know who I'd trust on this. They might get all fussed up about telling lies. That means one of us. But none of us were there! And—oh, hell, the lorry driver who took him to Oxford may squeal!—when he hears this man's involved. And then they'll suspect us!"

"I very much doubt it. Umm. You might conceivably

say he came to you asking for help and you gave him money ?"

"Or else that I saw him on May Day—I did, you know—and he said he was going to commit this murder. And I tried to dissuade him. Which would be best ?"

"Certainly not *both*. What he said to you isn't evidence. Put in that he came to you afterwards, and give your Oxford address. Then you can think up a conversation. But that's really not good enough by itself. We need someone on the spot."

"Hold on! I remember something. He told me—yes, this is it! He told me that the night he had the bomb with him in his room the chap he shared with asked him what the parcel was—seemed suspicious. If we could get him!"

"That's good. What was his name ?"

"Some odd name. Something to do with plants. Gardener ? No. Oh, blast, Sutton . . . Carter . . . Barr! Zacharias Barr. Eden Grove, they lived. It sounded utterly filthy. The room was under the street level, and there were bugs. We'll put him in—pencil, please. How's that ?"

"Better. It's worth trying. I take it these Scotticisms are right ?"

"Give it me," said Muriel, sitting down to the typewriter, "I'd better make a few slips. They'll recognise the make of course, but there must be thousands of Remington portables in London."

"What paper are you using ?" Medingley asked, picking up a sheet to look at the water-mark. Dione was kneeling beside her suit-case, which she hadn't unpacked yet, rummaging in the bottom for the envelope.

"You'd get that make anywhere," Muriel answered. "Nothing that can be traced." She wrote it out. Once Dione altered the phrasing of a sentence, remembering hard back to the way Donald talked. Muriel slipped it out over the platen and handed it across.

Dione had the signed envelope on the table in front of her. She had chosen the right thickness of nib. The first letters were all right, but she wobbled on the capital M. "Damn! That won't do. Wait a minute. Give me some sheets. I'll sign them in the right place and then you can type above the best." She began again. Medingley watched her with a professional fascination. At last she produced one that passed completely. Muriel typed above it and then typed a small manilla envelope to the Sallington police. Medingley took it, saying he would post it in the City.

"You should expect to hear from the police, if they want your evidence, within the next few days. They may even go the length of a trunk call. Will you be here? Oh well, if you're in Oxford they'll get at you even quicker. If you come up to town again we might do a show?"

"I'd like to, but I hope I shall have been sent for—— Oh dear. And if I'm not. . . . . ."

"We've done what we could. If this doesn't work: yes, well, we shall have to think it over. At any rate, they can't conceivably trace it."

"But you *do* think they'll take it seriously?"

"I haven't enough criminal experience to be certain, Mrs. Galton. I think it will depend on what other evidence they have. Obviously it won't do the trick by itself—they must be used to sham confessions. But supposing this Adam Walker has some kind of alibi, as he well may have, a document like this might be the turning point. Well, good-bye, Mrs. Galton. You'll burn those other signatures, won't you? Good-bye, Miss Galton. Curious the effect Russia has on one. I still don't feel that any of us have been behaving at all oddly."

Muriel let him out of the flat and came back to the sunny room with the breakfast things. Dione was still unpacking, slowly taking her things out of the suit-case and laying them on the pretty bed in Muriel's spare room. She came on a snapshot: "There's Tom's girl friend. Pretty good, don't you think, Muriel?"

Muriel looked at it and from it to her sister-in-law: "I wonder if Tom is going to be as changed by that place as you are."

"*Am* I changed?"

"Certainly."

"But I didn't accept it—whole."

"I should hope not, indeed! Don't you still believe in a certain modicum of liberty?"

"But I don't think liberty and *laisser-faire* are really compatible. At any rate till people begin to have an automatic sense of decency—loving one's neighbour as oneself—Communism, I suppose. When we're all Communists we can all be free."

"You mean when men begin to be brought up in the feminine tradition of self-sacrifice?"

"But even women aren't supposed to be self-sacrificing all round. Only for their aged parents and their children—so long as they're helpless. And their husbands—so long as they're faithful."

"Yet they've done rather well over being self-sacrificing for a Cause, Dione. Did Nan Ellis talk to you at all about old suffrage days? But—I wonder if Tom will come back from Russia all romantic about Communism. You seem to be. You haven't had much to do with the Communist Party of Great Britain in Sallington, have you?—apart from Donald MacLean. No, I thought not. I've had something to do with them on committees and things. A maddening lot. Can't see anything except from their own wretched point of view and quite willing to play hell with everyone else's work just to get some fiddling little thing of their own through. You Labour people are usually helpful and comparatively broad-minded."

"Yes," said Dione uncomfortably. "I know the Communist Party are an awkward lot. I expect the early Christians were, too. Wouldn't see other people's point of view. The Labour Party will be just the same when it starts being persecuted."

"Nonsense, it never will be. How can you be so silly, Dione!"

"Our people are victimised quite a bit already. It doesn't do in a good many works to say you're a Socialist."

"Everyone sensible is a Socialist—more or less. It's only a matter of time."

"But when manufacturers and people say they're Socialists—more or less!—all they mean is that they want to be taken over by the State and made nice and secure and respectable. Muriel, I don't see how we're going to avoid something horrid happening in this country, too. People being really killed and suffering dreadfully."

"Then how *can* you work for it, Dione?"

"Because the alternative isn't just going on happily and securely and traditionally. If it was—well, I should be tempted. I expect I should fall to temptation. I do so hate violence, and I know I don't love my neighbour as myself. But the alternative's pretty clearly war. In a few years, just when Kenneth's old enough. And a great many more people get killed in wars than in revolutions. That's putting it on the most selfish grounds. Oh, Muriel, don't you see, I'd simply love to go and live gently under a palm tree in the South Seas, but I *can't* run away. Can I?"

"I suppose not. Though it would be good for us all

to have a little peace. You can't be said to have had much of a holiday in Russia, my dear ! "

Dione glanced down at her browned arms. " I have in a way. But—yes, I do feel a bit chawed up, what with all I saw, and Tom and Oksana, and now this. I'd like to start everything fresh. Only how can I ? I wonder if people felt like this in Eleusis after Initiation. There must have been a good deal of chawing up on that. You had to die and then be reborn. It all seems silly and unreal to us now, what one knows of the ceremonial ; yet perhaps it was rather like a month under the Soviets."

" Well, I'm glad you realise that all this Communism is a religion exactly the same as all its forerunners."

" But it isn't, Muriel ! At any rate it annoys them frightfully if you say so, and all ordinary religions are proud of it."

" Quite. This is a new kind—on that point."

" But Communism is scientific. Far more scientific than most of the University science we're used to."

" Scientific. Naturally. It has to be : the *Zeitgeist*."

" No, but—anyway, damn it all, I'm not a Communist ! I don't see why I've got to defend their position ! "

" No," said Muriel, " nor do I." And she laughed and slapped Dione on the back in the hearty way she often did with other women.

After some hesitation Dione decided that she had better go back to Oxford the next day, so as to be there in case the police wanted her. She had, anyhow, to spend a day or two at home, paying bills, answering letters, and making various household decisions. It would be good for her to have a lot of jobs to do. As it was, she hadn't got so much as a sock to knit at Muriel's, and Muriel disapproved of needlework for women to such an extent that she didn't even darn her own stockings if she could possibly help it.

There was nothing to be done but smoke cigarettes, as if she'd just been a man, and telephone to people, most of whom were out of London. She caught Joyce Ward, in town for a day or two between visits, and found herself suddenly asking Joyce all the kind of questions she had been too shy to ask before. Joyce, giggling rather at the other end of the telephone, decided that Russia had bucked up Dione no end, but disclaimed all entanglement with Pussy. However, she asked affectionately after Alex. Dione, with practically no hesitation, told all about her brother in Russia, but then dried up and became non-communicative and ordinary again.

That night Dione was quite unable to sleep. This was the first time in her life that had happened to her, and she was both astonished and annoyed. She realised that it was quite useless to worry about what might be going to happen; it could only result in making her a less efficient instrument for perjury or whatever might be necessary. It was no use considering at this stage her alternatives if the Sallington police did not take the confession. If Adam Walker came up for trial. If she had to tell the truth. If.

She got up and took a couple of aspirins. It was not quite three in the morning; the time people came back from dances. She lay down, consciously relaxing her muscles but still unable to defeat the tension in her nerves, on Muriel's comfortable spare-room bed, hearing the sparse noises of London's earliest morning traffic. She missed the faint cradling of the boat. Wanting sleep desperately, she turned to cushiony thoughts. That Sunday last term up the river with Tom. The warm hay-field miles from anywhere. The sweet hay round and under them, the hour of sunshine taken clean out of the stream of work and worry and public events. Tom. Tom. Awkward keeping her mind on Tom alone. No, Oksana, you can't come in now. No.

Deliberately she shut her eyes, calling her body to quiet softness of physical memory. But behind her dark, pulsing eyelids came no Tom but another naked man, Cranach's Adam, Adam Walker, stalking naked and afraid through Eden full of newly created kelpies. Muriel's soft bed stiffened under her. She shifted heavily, her aspirined imagination beginning to blur, unable to fix any longer on too remote Tom. She supposed her eyes were open, still seeing the dim outline of Muriel's wardrobe. Adam Walker, naked, walked into the room and disappeared into the wardrobe. A policeman, clothed, walked into the room and disappeared into the wardrobe. A small seal's voice behind her said Bolsheviki tempo. And what would the Marshbrook Bridge Elephant say if it knew that the Labour Candidate's wife had two men in her wardrobe probably murdering one another? Of whom one was a Communist put there by Tom. No, he wasn't a Communist, was he?—or was he? The Elephant would say he was. Shut your eyes, Dione, stop looking at that wardrobe, go to sleep, rest, rest your body, unstiffen, stop feeling the rumpled hot bed against your back. Go to sleep from the middle outwards. Blood trickled out of the shut wardrobe, the policeman performing an abortion on Adam Walker. Sterilised. Who comes smelling blood? I, said the fish, with my little dish. The Campbell Women whispering: can't quite catch—keep quiet, Dione, quiet and you'll hear. Trickling and whispering. His heart's blood dyed its every fold. Tom!

Muriel came running in: "My dear—what is it? You yelled!" She switched the light on and caught Dione glaring at the wardrobe. She pulled it open: "Look, baby, there's nothing there!"

Dione sat up, rubbing her eyes and sweating. Only just past three. "Too idiotic of me," she said; "it must be the change of food. I expect I ate too much fruit."

"I expect you're worrying about that brother of mine. But it'll be all right. Marshbrook Bridge is never going to know! If this doesn't work we shall manage something else. Obviously it's going to be all right."

Dione felt curiously calmed. Muriel's voice was like Tom's. She had it on the tip of her tongue to say: "And the revolution?" If she could be reassured about that, too. No, keep it to herself. She got up and pulled the sheet straight. "That's all right, Muriel; I'll go to sleep now. No, don't stay. You've got to work to-morrow."

"I've things in the afternoon, but I'm more or less free all morning. We'll leave your luggage at Paddington; then we can lunch somewhere and you can catch the 1.45. We'll lunch at Gunter's. I'll stand you a strawberry ice! Will that be nice, Dione?"

"Yes, lovely. I haven't been there for hundreds of years. There were those beautiful plane trees in the Square." Beautiful plane trees. After Muriel went out she was thinking of beautiful plane trees. Beautiful plane trees along water-courses in Samos and Naxos, plane trees with cool dark springs, mavro mati, bubbling up under their roots. Plane trees hung with garlands for their greenery and comeliness. And, so thinking, it became light behind Dione's curtains. Morning quietly asserting itself through the summer-green, far-reaching plane trees in empty Berkeley Square, morning occurring in other more crowded and less dignified parts of London, not known to Dione, but known on the whole to Muriel Galton and her committees, known to the Labour Party and the Communist Party and the police. London not emptied in August, but tending to appear even more overcrowded than usual because the children, out of school, played all day and half the night in the street, having nowhere else to play in, and now at dawn slept heavily, five or six to a room, or stirred and cried, nails scratching at new, red bug-bites or pinched perhaps by summer diarrhœa, another thing which Muriel Galton, in collaboration with the Medical Officers, tried to deal with, on the whole with only fair success, as was inevitable, considering the housing, and that, in turn—— But Dione had got to sleep at last, and was still asleep at nine o'clock when Muriel brought her in a tray with coffee and toast and scrambled eggs.

Muriel spent the earlier part of what she had optimistically called a free morning in dealing intelligently with several things which had to be dealt with : the housing of some girl-student delegates, the tackling of the Ministry of Health by a small committee of sensible but rather easily circumvented doctors, the collection of some combined housing and mortality statistics, and finding somebody who could translate Chinese into readable English. A practical engineer's job really, making connections, seeing that gears functioned, greasing up all round. Dione thought she could help with the students, mentioned names, offered to write a couple of letters to Oxford people. Then they went off to Paddington, left the suit-case, and walked back across the corner of Hyde Park to Berkeley Square. Even at this unpropitious time there were one or two orators still in the space by Marble Arch ; poor dears, only the rather mad, whose mythical audience was always with them, could face an ordinary English week-day blank.

Turning inward from the Park to Mayfair, they began to pass the discreet and rather impressive luxury shops, those which only advertise in journals which cost a shilling and over, specialists in some particular thing, appealing mostly to women's ideas of themselves as consumers and to some extent as happy-makers, at any rate as objects of man's pride and competition. Dione suddenly remembered seeing just that little delicately labelled perfume bottle on Joyce's dressing-table at Auchanarnish. Her pace quickened a little. She found it all both shocking and in a horrid way disquieting—there hadn't been any looking into shop windows in Moscow. Up rose a nest of horrid little individualisms, unashamed little lusts crying I want, I want—I want those silk stockings, I want that dress, I want that star sapphire pendant, I want those silky-soft undies—or, rather more subtly, I want to go to bed with Tom in that nightgown, it would make everything feel different, he'd see me, touch me, fresh in that—back vision of Oksana's solid cotton knickers and brassière. If one does live in a capitalist society, let it damn well give one its best!

She shook herself, talked to Muriel about Moscow, and turned her eyes resolutely away from the shops towards the traffic—and across it. Oh that flower shop! And a shop of men's clothes. Tom would look ripping in that sweater. People's relationships oughtn't to depend at all upon clothes. But they do. The Marshbrook Bridge trousseaux. The men in purplish best suits, and stiff collars in homage to the Elephant, and shiny ties. The underclothes: the pink or peach locknits with machine-lace insertions, the disastrously splitting art-silk stockings in all the shades that look wrong on a human leg. Though probably you couldn't get anything really nice anywhere in Sallington. The younger Coke-Browns came to London for their elegancies. And, oh dear, here was a window full of the most adorable children's clothes! She trailed a little. Muriel laughed and stopped. "Much better look if you want to," she said; "they're never so fetching as when you get half a glimpse!"

"It was the organdi," Dione confessed; "yes, the one with the posies—*I couldn't help seeing Lilias in it!*"

" She's quite pretty enough as it is—yes, and quite vain enough. She'll never look nicer than she does in that smock you made her. Though I confess I find it quite maddening to watch you smocking ! "

" And the embroidered linen for Morag——"

" I bet it hasn't got any pockets—and what would my poor Morag do with her knife and her string and her diary and her precious fountain-pen and her baby guinea-pig and her collection of fossils ! Let Morag alone and don't make her frill-conscious yet. She's going to be attractive enough without that. Come along, Dione ; this is mere æsthetic masturbation."

" I know. Too silly of me. Come along yourself ! " Shocking. She was shocked at herself. What would Donald have said—or Oksana—or—or the Sallington police. And then in another window there was a single dress thrown carelessly over a stool, a white evening dress—no, just off white—with a belt of softly twisted colour, and the line, the thing which really matters—How good one would feel in that dress, how well able to make people happy and confident, to get things done, to work magic !

" Next Christmas," said Muriel, grinning at her, " I shall give you a dress."

" Nonsense. I don't want one."

" Liar. No, Dione, why shouldn't I ? My brother does from time to time, I gather, and I hope you don't count it as For Services Rendered."

" Muriel, I swear I shan't want one when I'm out of this ! These shops really ought to be censored, they're bad for me." She thought hard of girls in Moscow. Ahead were the plane trees of Berkeley Square. Still further ahead, Sallington, the man Adam Walker in danger of hanging. How, with that in the immediate future, had she been able to think in terms of personal vanity ?

Muriel agreed that these shops were, in effect, evil. "They make it harder for women to be different, to get free. Very few women can afford to shop hereabouts unless they're kept, either as wives, mistresses or daughters. I shouldn't mind the shops much but for that. You, I take it, would object anyhow on Socialist grounds."

"Women couldn't get into that position in a Socialist State, even if they wanted to. And when a thing's impossible you cease to want it, especially if there's an alternative —as there would be."

"I wish I knew how many average women would be attracted by your alternative—as I visualise it from your descriptions of Russia. Certainly not all. And yet there is something very attractive about it. Only of course I can't believe you, my dear. You and Tom, you've been got at, not really by wily Russians, but by your own minds wanting to be got at. I shall be interested to hear what Nan Ellis has to say about it."

They lunched, Muriel paying, on *foie gras* sandwiches and large strawberry ices; with the ices they had sponge cakes with crumbled nuts on the top and chocolate leaves. They drank large dripping glasses of water with the ices, as one must; it was soothing and definite in the mouth between the bland liveliness of the sweet cold spoonfuls, the silver clinging with a tiny frozen bite to August-warm she lips. Water is a good drink, especially plain English water, either the hard water of London and Oxford or the faintly root-tasting spring water of the Highlands, water uncorrupted by nasty little pieces of ice, the unpleasant fruits of the tree of prohibition. Russian boiled water is not so good, and one tires of *Narzan.* English fresh bread, impeccably and eternally wheaten, such as is cut with clean knives for Gunter's sandwiches, is good too, as good as any food in the world. Some prefer sponge cakes in the plain golden,

Victorian tradition ; Dione, faintly heretical, preferred the added crispness of nuts. Chocolate leaves, too, are largely a matter of texture, for nibbling front teeth and healthy molars, though the tongue has its fun, distinguishing between the cold, slick sweetness of the chocolate and the fire-warmed nutty sweetness of the biscuit. Would one be so aware of these things unless oneself and they were on an edge of danger and uncertainty—Russia behind—Sallington ahead ? Yet how quiet, how secure stays Gunter's, tucked in the corner of plane-green Berkeley Square, wafting out with special blessing wedding cakes and christening cakes for the aristocracy of England. Page-boys of an earlier date no doubt have flattened their noses vainly against the plate-glass, while sweet aromas tickled up their gastric juices towards an action which their economic position restrained them from taking. Who ever heard of the rape of Gunter's ? In London on the whole the lower classes have had bread : no need for them to eat cake. It is possible—what with hired agitators, not to say the pernicious influence of the movies—that things are different now.

That evening Muriel, sitting over coffee with Nan Ellis, was rung up from Oxford. Dione had been called upon most politely by the Oxford police and asked if she could make it convenient to have a word with the Sallington police. It was best to say as little as possible over the telephone. No, Dione was quite all right. No need for Muriel to come up with her. Yes, everyone had been very friendly and nice. Yes, Muriel might let Medingley know. Yes, quite all right. So long, Muriel.

" What's up ? " said Nancy Ellis.

" Oh, she's only got to go and give evidence somewhere. Nothing important. More coffee, Nan ? "

" That brother of hers was a nice young fellow. Wonder how he'll like living out there. Suppose those years working as a labourer will have made him used to roughing it. Wonder how he could stick it; must have been to a public school and all that. Funny, we never talked about that in the boat or in Russia. Matches, please, Muriel. Somehow there was a whole lot one never had in mind all that time."

"What do you feel about Russia now, Nan?"

"It's no place for middle-aged Liberals. But—you should go, my dear."

"*Are* we middle-aged Liberals?"

"Not in one sense. Not Simonites or Lloyd Georgeites or anything parliamentary. But we're the Liberal tradition. By the way, Muriel, these schoolmasters are working up for a drive against us: the idiots are going through all their little hoops about not serving under women—keep the top jobs for men, in fact. We shall have to look out."

"There's none of that in Russia, I gather."

"No. Not that. If only one could trust the Russians to behave sensibly and consistently! Like Western Europeans."

"We aren't always sensible and consistent."

"You are. I am, on the whole. But men——! Well, well, no doubt one's prejudiced. Now, what about getting down to business. I got the Ministry on the telephone this morning. My dear, that man who deals with figures is a perfect fool! But I think I've made him see our point."

## AUCHANARNISH 5

Curious going back to Scotland. When she woke in the third-class sleeper Dione had a moment's muddled feeling of being in Russia, then she looked out of the window and everything steadied and cleared. After all that very nearly unbearable anxiety, it had been so simple. She hadn't even seen Adam Walker. The Sallington police had been very polite; they had recognised her as a lady! The man who had examined her was a fellow-Scot; he came from Peebles. Each, detecting the voice of the other, had felt a slight sympathy, a stirring of racial trust. It had made Dione able to put much more conviction into her story of how Donald had come to the house. She had spent a couple of hours writing out that imaginary interview and what exactly each had said, trying to fix it all into her imagination till it was as plain as memory. The Peebles man had scolded her a little for not having been more sensible, not having realised at the time that Donald was the murderer. She had accepted the scolding meekly, like a nice woman.

She had been shown the confession, and had read it with the greatest interest. She had asked intelligent questions. Now it was all right. Her evidence and Barr's, and his rather muddled alibi, among them had cleared Adam Walker. She suspected that it was just as well for him that he was not a member of the Communist Party—if he had been he might have needed something stronger. Of course we all know how splendid British justice is; no one would have put him through the third degree like those nasty

Americans, or invented evidence against him like those nasty continentals. But still— however, Adam Walker, though a member of the N.U.W.M., definitely denied being a Communist, and was undoubtedly one of the heroes of the Great War. Not that this would necessarily have helped him twelve years later supposing he had gone Red—traitor to all he'd fought for. Well, Adam Walker was free, although this might not be much help to him over getting a job. At least he had been decently fed in His Majesty's prison.

Dione dressed and breakfasted. No need to worry. No need to think of something fresh. Going home for the holidays. Home to Auchanarnish. It was a lovely morning in the Highlands, but yet just that much cooler than in England.

Jimsie from the garage met her on Oban platform and took her suit-case. He drove the car when her mother was alone. He seemed pleased to see her, really pleased, as though she were a friend, not an employer, not belonging to an alien class; she wanted to ask him all sorts of questions—why he liked her, what he thought of her having so much more money than he had, whether he really supposed she was a good driver or only said so out of flattery or politeness—much the same thing in the Highlands! But she was too shy.

The station master came up and shook hands with her, and so did her old friend, the porter, another MacLean, who hoped she had not found Russia too bad: "But you're looking well all the same, Mistress Galton."

"There's nothing wrong with Russia," Dione said; "I enjoyed every moment of it!"

"Ach, don't you be telling me, Mistress Galton," said MacLean, the porter; "we'll have none of your Reds here!"

Jimsie explained that he had brought in young John

from Lerguligan, who had to see the dentist; would she mind their fetching him back? "Of course not!" Dione said, delighted at the prospect of seeing young John—she wanted to talk to him about Russia. They found him waiting for them at the dentist's; he shook hands, but instead of getting into the back of the car with Dione he got into the front with Jimsie. She talked to them a bit, leaning over, and wondered whether if she'd been driving the two men would both have got in at the back. But the bad road made leaning over rather difficult, and by and bye she sat back; young John and Jimsie began to talk of the prices of stock. She was cross with them; she wanted something different to happen. She had a wild impulse to tell John about his cousin Donald; that would make him sit up! She wanted to pull his nice brown hair—very different from Donald's, though. It was no use. What she'd said about Russia hadn't really interested them either; it was too far off.

At the corner of the fuchsia hedge Morag and Kenneth met them and jumped on to the running-board. That was all right anyhow, and when they came crunching round on the gravel drive to the front of the house there were Ian and Lilias—such a big girl!—and her mother. Huggings and greetings. "Oh, you *haven't* cut down the beech, Mother!"

"But it interfered with the view, dearest; you know how I like a view."

"Oh, Lilias, what have you got, Lambie—oh, a *lovely* stone." The smell of the house, pot-pourri, dogs, old furniture and hearth-rugs, and roses, and scones being baked. The same old smell. Her own room, rather full of children. "Look, Lilias, a lovely dollie from Russia. A picture-book for Ian—like Russian children have. Just little oddments for you two—I hadn't room. Morag darling, it was so nice getting your letters. Oh, stop Bran eating my slippers! I say, where's Phœbe and the others?"

"Oh," said Kenneth, "that ass Brian went and caught something or other—at this time of year—he *would;* so they won't be up for another week. I say, Mother, we've made a ripping house at the edge of the loch. Come and look at it—now." So there she was again.

But was she? During the next few days she began to wonder. Part of herself was there, another part wasn't. It was—where? She wanted to talk to people in a kind of way she usedn't to want, but they retreated. The first two days she had talked Russia hard, but she noticed after this that both her mother and the children tended to dodge the subject. And the things they seemed to want to talk about didn't interest her. Morag asked about Donald as soon as they were alone, but when told he had got a job and was safely settled in Kharkov seemed to think that ended it, and began to talk about school. The only person who wanted to talk Russia was Robert Finney at Carse of Easland, but he was apt to get rather cross if something Dione said didn't agree with what he had already made up his mind must be so.

As she had agreed with Donald, she told his father and mother that he had gone over to Russia and found work there, and that she had met him accidentally. Mrs. MacLean wept about it, quietly and with dignity. It was as though her son were dead. More than dead. Not even with much prayer and reading of the Good Book could she come near him now. His father said little, but was extra-cross with the children when he found them among the raspberries.

Dione felt curiously out of it—as though she had been to a magic place and come back into the ordinary world, but it had lost its value. She re-read some of the witch trials, trying to make out whether they had felt like this. She couldn't tell; there were too many real centuries between her and Green Jean. She didn't know what or whom to fix her thoughts upon. She shied away from Tom and Oksana; it was all right, but she didn't want to imagine the details. Donald hadn't written. Phœbe hadn't written. Her tractors were plowing other fields.

On Saturday she went into Oban to fetch Alex. Half-way she saw a man walking with a bundle in his hand, and slowed down; she could very seldom find people to take lifts on this road; usually they shook their heads and grunted. This man accepted rather doubtfully, but got in. Dione asked him questions; he talked a form of Scots which she found very hard, Highland heavily overlaid with Ayrshire. He talked reluctantly, but Dione discovered that he was out of work, that he had been with his people in Campbelltown, but they couldn't go on keeping him, and now he was after a job again. If there was nothing in Oban, he could work his way south-east from there. He added that he was a riveter.

"Oh!" said Dione, "I had a friend was a riveter on Clydeside. Maybe you knew him? He was called Donald MacLean."

The man said there was a wheen MacLeans on Clydeside, and looked at her suspiciously. "There was the one MacLean," he said slowly.

"Ah yes," Dione said, "you've heard him speak?" The man nodded. Dione said: "Are you a Communist?"

The man answered: "Ah dinna hold wi' they parties. Ah'm a Red. Ah wud hae followed MacLean. Ah wud follow ony man that wud lead us."

"But they all let you down," Dione said; "is that it?" The man didn't answer. Dione said hesitatingly: "I'm Red, too."

The man looked round at her and the car, circling his thumb at it: " Wi' thon?"

Dione said: " It's my mother's. No, that's not fair. We've got one, too. But I'll be very willing to chuck all that when the time comes. Do believe me!"

" Aye, Ah'm believing ye," the man said, and then he began to talk, about difficult times on the Clydeside, keeping up with his union, meetings he went to where nothing new was said, and unemployment, first sporadic, then continuous, and the gradual lowering of the standard of life. Every now and then Dione failed to understand him, yet the general thing was clear enough; for the first time for days she felt in touch again; this man too had been to the forbidden ground. Dione put him down at the cross-roads; " Good-bye, comrade," she said, " and good luck."

The man took her hand. " Ah'm thanking ye," he said, and seemed as if he would say more, but it never came out.

Alex got off the train; his likeness to Donald startled Dione rather—and she thought it was more pronounced. " Well, old girl," he said, " here we are again. Are we going to be able to pull it off with Mother?"

" What—about being in Russia together? Of course we are. Now, Alex, tell me all about the paint barrels."

" Well," he said, " my main idea was this, and it's not a political idea, Dione, so I warn you. It doesn't fit into any of your damned parties. Shall I drive? All right. Well, I went up to Shields—I thought I'd maybe get a bit of a Russian feeling there! And it struck me pretty soon that here were all these men out of work and ashamed of being out of work. It was the shame that was destroying them. And it seemed likely they'd be out of work for maybe ears. So I thought to myself, what's all this about work? Why do we all take it so damned seriously? When the thing has destroyed our happiness. Other people don'—happier people—dagoes, Arabs, you know, Dione."

"Yes," she said, "the Greeks didn't hold with it, either. But it was the aftermath of the Puritan revolution here; they hadn't got anything but work left to enjoy. Besides, the manufacturers last century educated it into their factory hands."

"Whatever it was historically," Alex said, "it's here now, and when people aren't working they feel wicked—and then they go and commit crimes as often as not, to justify themselves, poor dears. So, I thought, why not teach them to be properly leisured and jolly and all the things we're taught in public schools? Teach them to play games and lie about and discuss poetry. But I found games weren't much use; it made them too hungry. Besides they'd seen through games—they suspected them of not being work. Then I did this stunt with the paints. I gave Bone and Simpson my real name—I had to—but I had a fake name to the others."

"What did you call yourself?"

"MacLean. Thought I might as well do a complete swop."

"How damned funny," Dione said. "You know you look more like him, too."

"That no doubt comes of living on bread and margarine and strong tea for a month. It's interesting to be—not oneself. I found my—they—my advisers trusted me better so."

"Who were they, Alex?"

"Two chaps. And a girl."

"A girl?"

"Yes. I knew I'd have to tell you sooner or later. May as well get it over. She's—just a girl."

"Have you married her?"

He shook his head : " No, no, it's nothing—respectable. I doubt if you'll approve, Dione. She's—a bad girl. I take it you know about all that kind of thing. But I don't want to upset you."

" I expect I know a good deal, in theory, anyway. Tell me some more. Is she a—prostitute ? Sorry, they're hateful words ! "

Alex said : " She's a working girl, but there wasn't enough to live on decently. She . . . supplements. She's not exactly a professional."

" How did you pick her up ? "

Alex looked at her : " Well, Dione, if you won't be shocked—I was so sick at not going to Russia—God, how lovely these hills are !—and then at Christina turning me down, that I just picked up a girl on a street corner. Think of it, Dione, a girl in a black costume—a bit shiny at the elbows if you looked hard—with Woolworth art-silk stockings going at the heel and worn shoes and a little red beret and paint on her face. I took her to the pictures and squeezed her up, thinking of you away in Russia and my not even being able to go home, and then we went to an hotel. I thought of all the good little books tell one, and I was damned if I cared what I caught off her. I didn't, though. And then we began talking, and—I take it I gave her about three times what she usually got, my poor Nelly. We arranged to meet again. We went on talking. And then she took me to her home ; I made friends with her brothers—they're good chaps. It seems a funny business, talking about it like this. It was all right there."

" Of course it was all right. Are you going back ? "

" Seems like it. When I can get away. It makes Edinburgh and the office look pretty damned silly."

" Yes. I say—Alex. Well, look here—do you think

it's necessary to—actually to sleep with people—before one can get on to real terms with them? People, I mean, that one finds it difficult to be on intellectual terms with at once."

"Meaning the working classes and all that? Thank the Lord we can talk about all this! It's been all bottled up inside me in the office. None of them would have understood. No, I don't think it's necessary, but it's a short-cut at any rate for people of about our age. It makes things easier. If it comes off. Though God knows it's easy enough for a man to have a working-class girl without altering his point of view one bit. It's happening the whole time."

"There's nothing to be done with some people but—abolish them. Don't you think so?"

"Maybe so. Abolishing's not my line. Oh, look, there's Ardfeochan! And the loch colour. I never had any paints to match it."

It was not so difficult as they'd thought to manage conversation about their joint holiday, because Mrs. Fraser definitely didn't want to talk about Russia. It was as though the U.S.S.R. was something not quite nice. Alex had arranged to stay till Monday night; he and his sister wandered about, discussing things, and were late for meals. On the Monday Dione got letters from Russia, one from Tom and one from Donald. Tom wrote from the Crimea, a fairly long letter, but not, somehow, telling much except about Dnieperstroy and the new town; about the rest of his life he said little, except that he was happy, and at the end there was a postscript from Oksana sending her love. Dione read most of it aloud to the family, but as far as she was concerned she had got almost nothing out of it.

Donald's letter said: "Dear Comrade, I should have written you before, but I have been that busy I have had no time for getting stamps. I am busy on the riveting again. We are finishing off the calorifier tanks for the new thermal power station they have made for this city. I have got over seeing it—they let us see over works just whatever way we care to, the like of churches. It is heating the whole of Kharkov as well as making power, but you will not understand, so I will not get explaining it all now.

" But, Dione, I will try to say something of what it feels like. It has me astonished the pace everything goes, most of all when I remember how most of the comrades who are working with me on the job are unskilled. There is half of them come straight from the country with no knowledge of tools. But I get teaching them and they are very willing to learn. Some of them are just fools, and I have to keep remembering they have not had the benefits of a decent education, yet with all that it is fair amazing what gets done. They call this the Bolshevik tempo ; there is many bosses in England or Scotland who would be glad to see this much speeding-up ! There are even blind men at work, turning out small screws.

" I had expected much of this from what I had read ; you will remember what I was telling you on the boat and at first you were not listening to me. Yet it is queer seeing it in practice and knowing for certain, the way we all know, that we are out of the old ways for ever. It is very heartening to be sure our factory is working under the Triangle, that is the management, the factory committee and the factory branch of the Communist Party. I will tell you another thing that is queer, too, Dione, and that is that one is just taken for granted as a Communist. There is no need to be always thinking of it, nor always angry. At first I had considerable difficulties ; they were even wanting to send me back. But the woman who is manager was a good comrade to me and went with me and argued with them. I was needing to play up to her, making out I could not understand them. There is a boy on the committee speaks a bit English and another woman. But I am getting on fine with the Russian; I can understand most that is said to me now. I think I am here for keeps or anyway until things are different in England.

"I hope you are well. I am well. I would be glad of books or newspapers. I get the *Moscow Daily News*, which is fine, but I would like fine if you could send me some *Daily Workers* or maybe something that deals with literature. There is little of that here.

"Kharkov is about the size of Edinburgh, but it is growing so fast it is hard to say what size it is one day to the next. The new buildings are mostly in concrete; they are unhomely, but maybe I will get to like them. I am living now in a room with three other comrades. There was one that was not clean, but he is better now. We have fine posters up on all the walls and we can get baths at the factory. I am putting in for a room to myself and think I'll get it before winter. This will not sound very grand to you, but it is away better than I was used to my last year at Sallington and the food is fine now I am getting used to it, though I could wish their porridge was made with oats and not with maize, the same we give hens in Scotland. Well, I must close now. Your loving comrade, Donald."

That was very satisfactory in most ways, but again it left out a whole category of things; again it did not help Dione to any feeling of stability or value. She made up her mind to write back to him and ask for more, and also to ask him to send a letter to his parents. That evening she drove Alex in to Oban, then did some shopping for her mother, waiting some time for the little dressmaker who was doing over Mrs. Fraser's tea-gowns. By the time she had finished it was fairly late, but she thought she would be back for an unpunctual dinner, and certainly before dark. Then she had a puncture. The wheel jammed and by the time she had got it off and the new one on she was trembling with effort and annoyance. Then, as she lowered the jack, the new tyre squashed down gently into the road. She discovered it was only a loose valve, which she could tighten, but it meant a longish turn at the foot pump, and by that time it was nearly dusk. She hoped she would meet someone on the road who would take a lift, but there was no one.

She hated driving alone in the dark! She knew how silly it was and had told herself time and time again not to be a coward, but it was no use. She was terrified of the dark emptiness of the back seat, inalterably behind her, and the fact that the noise of the engine covered any noise that Someone or Something rustling there might make. Every now and then she would glance round, just to make sure; one couldn't tell from the driving-mirror. There was nothing, only so far an emptiness which seemed to be waiting to be filled, shadows which seemed quite likely to take the form of a kelpie. One would know a kelpie by the feeling of dampness and then a damp touch. Oh, shut up! She began singing the "Red Flag." Or a Campbell Woman might lean over, just not touching so far, and say very politely through thin lips: "Now let us have a little talk, Dione." Oh, shut up! With heads uncovered swear we all—— "Of course," the Campbell Women would say, "we can offer you terms. Special terms because of our old relationship with the family. You must give up this nonsense and come back to us. After all, *we* know you don't believe in it," they would say, "it's not *your* song."

Yes, it is, it's a stupid song in a lot of ways, it's low-brow if you like, but it's mine and Tom's.

"Tom is several thousand miles away. He wouldn't even hear of what had happened for a week or so. Not until after the interment. He'd never see you again. I wonder what he will say to Oksana about it."

The People's flag—the People's flag—make an effort, think about something—do something—invent something! The People's flag is deepest blue, but then of course it wouldn't do. And kelpies of course join seaweedy fingers round one's throat to drag one back into the shadows. Another six miles yet; the People's flag is deepest yellow, it sheltered once some other fellow. Think of Lenin.

"He couldn't come between you and our fingers touching you; he couldn't stop the touch from shivering and shivering you till the shiver gets to the place in your brain where shivers really begin to hurt. He is an abstraction now. Once he was alive, as you are alive but are going to be dead. I wonder if he met us or the kelpies while he was dying? Something funny happened to his brain, you know. Perhaps that's what it's like at the end, even for Lenin, or for any of them. Perhaps we always get them in the end. Eli, Eli, lama sabachthani."

Shut up! The People's flag is deepest black, because they gave us all the sack, and e'er our limbs grew stiff and cold—— Another five miles. The People's flag is deepest green, but then I wished it hadn't been.

"How interested you all were in Ireland ten years ago, to be sure, and now that's over, Ireland is a bore. Naturally. And in ten years Socialism will be a bore too. But you'll be old, Dione, too old to make up for lost time or do any of the things you might have done. And we shall not be able to keep our terms open indefinitely. No. It seems a pity, doesn't it, not to accept? You see, Jean MacLean didn't accept, and we got her; it was very unpleasant for her in the end, quite as unpleasant as the rack and the boot and the pincers. The things that happened to the other witches. Oh, such nasty things happened to other women, Dione, not so very long ago. Only two hundred years since the last witch was burnt hereabouts. Just outside the door, Dione. People could get back to that quite easily. But we can make special terms for you."

Four miles. The loch edge pretty close here. Lapping dark. So that they could slide out. Skidding on kelpies' long arms, over and over into the loch, in among them. Drive carefully, you fool! There, you're past the worst bit. Though naturally they'd follow. And it wouldn't help you to go fast. A question of relativity. They would be geared to one's own speed. Tractors, tractors, where are you? But I didn't see any at the kolkhoz. Perhaps at Tom's new town. Nine fifteen. What time would it be there—further east—bedtime? The People's flag is deepest white, because they gave us such a fright. Three miles.

"You thought you'd got rid of us, Dione, but you haven't. And you won't till you have something as strong as we are. I wonder if you ever will have. It doesn't seem very likely, does it? No, the tractors aren't here. And the crow has gone. No, Saint Finnigal is no use; we have frozen her. A painful business being frozen: Green Jean found it so. And her baby too, no doubt. Quite. Oh yes, naturally the children suffer. They burnt them at any age. Yes, we have our eye on them. Particularly Morag. She has the capacity for suffering."

Shut up! I shall see the garage light in a minute. I shall call Jimsie.

"You don't really know Jimsie, do you? He might be on our side."

Jimsie likes me!

"But supposing it really came to something. Supposing

the people on the other side of the door got through, the witch burners. Think of the Southern States, Dione, think of Scottsboro. Oh yes, we were there. Are you sure Jimsie wouldn't be on the side of the witch burners? He'd rather enjoy it, wouldn't he? He'd throw a can of petrol. Whuff, up it would go, a stinking flame in your face, Dione, burning your hair off. Or Morag's hair."

Shut up! Here is the garage. No one about. Anyway, nothing can possibly happen in two miles!

"Oh, can't it, Dione, *can't it*, CAN'T IT——"

The brakes screamed like snared rabbits as she pulled up, the car rocked and slid on the road. Dione got out her torch and looked hard at the whole of the inside of the car.

"Have you lost something, Mrs. Galton?" It was Dione's nurse, Mrs. Finney, and the shepherd's wife, all out for a walk, in thick coats and shoes.

"No," said Dione, "I only—I only—would you like a lift back or are you going on?"

"I'll come back with you," Nurse said, in her comfortable Perthshire voice, and climbed in. Naturally, the Campbell Women were not on the back seat. Nurse said: "I was wanting to speak to you about Morag, Mrs. Galton. She's been having bad dreams. I think she is frightened of something."

"She hasn't said anything to me, Nurse," Dione said, "and she usually does."

"Perhaps," said Nurse, "she was thinking you were frightened too, and she has a very good heart. She would not be wishing to give you trouble. You *are* frightened of something, are you not, Mrs. Galton? You were frightened just now."

"Yes, Nurse, I suppose I am," Dione said, "and I thought I wouldn't be after Russia!"

" You put too much on that, if you don't mind my saying so," Nurse said; " it was like—the way Kenneth looks forward to Christmas."

" Wouldn't you like to go there yourself ? " Dione said. They were past the fuchsia hedge now.

" Indeed, I should," Nurse answered. " It would be a very interesting experience. I was thinking, perhaps you could be telling me something about it one day when you are not too busy." The kelpies had all gone right down to the bottom of the loch now ! The gules lion yawning in his sleep could chase them away.

Phœbe and Robin and the children all came up the next week. Brian was looking rather pale, but nothing really out of the ordinary. Robin was being at his best. It was so much a matter of health, and his leg hadn't given a lot of trouble lately. He invented good games to play with the children. Bran, the puppy, began to follow him about till Morag got quite miserable ! And he was charming to Phœbe. It was a pity he didn't shoot, but he fished a little. Phœbe seemed very cheerful, and was nice to everybody, even the neighbours. She had brought some small canvases up with her and was doing a certain amount of painting ; she said she had started on another big canvas at home —it had got to a stage now where she could leave it. " After all, paint's really my medium," she said ; " I know about all there is to be known about wood-engraving now."

" Why didn't you write to me ? " Dione asked. They were walking along by the loch ; the hay, only just cut up here, was smelling soft and sweet from the meadow beside them ; sweet as the Kiel Canal perhaps. Close to the loch there were bog myrtle bushes—every now and then she stooped and nipped off a leaf or two. It was the Campbell badge, but that didn't matter ; the scent of its leaves, mixed with the hay, making something peculiarly Highland and heart-searching.

Phœbe said: "Well, it was like this." She stopped and laughed and then went on: "I thought that old Elephant had spoiled everything; but it hadn't. Phil rang up the day you left—from the lab. He was rather a dear. So we went up the river together."

"And then?"

"Well, you see, I'd imagined it all pretty often, and I was terribly thrilled. I wore the most unsuitable dress, just to be not like May. And then in about half an hour I discovered that I wasn't in love with him any longer. I may have stopped being ever so long ago, only I hadn't known."

"But didn't you enjoy it?"

"Oh yes, I enjoyed it all right. I very much like hearing about physics. It's the kind of thing that seems to me worth while having a conversation about. And Phil, you see, had made up his mind to be awfully good and loyal, so he sat in one end of the canoe and I in the other, and I found I didn't even want to kiss him—but he wanted to kiss me!"

"And did he?"

"Oh yes, and I enjoyed that, too. But—I just enjoyed it. It wasn't life and death any longer, and I noticed that he was getting the tiniest bit bald. But he was all over the place. And he is still."

"But you're not?"

"Not a bit. And I've started this big picture. I'd got all held up till now, messing about without colour, just because it hurt me to use it. Now I'm off again."

"But isn't it going to be frightfully bad for Phil's work?"

"No, I don't think so," said Phœbe thoughtfully, half watching a heron which was flying across the loch, "though it may be bad for his professorship! You see, we talk about it, and he finds it quite consistent with being a good husband to write about it, and I can see the new ideas bubbling up in him like hydrogen."

" Sooner or later you're going to give him hell."

" My dear North Oxford silly, do you think I'm going to be a pig about anything he wants? I don't want to hurt him like he hurt me; it would be ridiculous. But—I should be rather sisterly!"

" Then it's his handwriting I've seen on letters to you? I thought I knew it."

" Twice a week, lassie! And Robin's been sweet about my picking up with him again. He was always nice about Phil."

" What about Pussy? Has he evaporated? I should have thought this particular path might have brought back a few tender memories!"

" Pussy? Oh, Pussy won't paint a picture like mine if he lives to be a hundred. Pussy and his wriggly nudes!"

" You're on a peak, aren't you, Phœbe? It's terribly exciting for me when you are. Your valleys are so long. Do stay like this for a bit; it's good for us all."

" Yes, you've done a bit of a slide, Dione, haven't you? What exactly happened in Russia?"

" Oh, I don't know. Nothing depressing really." She didn't want to talk about that. " I'll race you to the hay rig, Phœbe—coming?"

August went by. The last of the raspberries and gooseberries were over. When Alex came for the week-end he and Dione went off shooting at Ardfeochan. After considerable meditation on the roe-deer, Dione had decided that there was no reason why she shouldn't do it after all. Phœbe painted. Robin seemed to be enjoying himself. The children rushed about; Nurse said Morag's nightmares were getting better. Brian hadn't been sick. At last Dione got a wire from Tom saying he had arrived and was coming north in three days. The next day she had a letter from him ; it said :

" Dearest Dione, I am writing this in the boat and shall post it at Harwich ; you will have my telegram before you get it. I must go to Oxford and Sallington on my way north.

" Well, I came back by Kiev. You can imagine I felt pretty lonely and gloomy there, and I can't tell you how glad I was to find your letter. You are a dear. I stayed there a day. In the evening I went with several Americans to a concert ; it was good enough, but they seemed very strange. I couldn't talk to them, but I talked to the Intourist guide a bit. She said she supposed I was glad to be going back to England ; I said what came into my head, that I hated the idea of going back to the capitalist countries after the U.S.S.R. She was curiously pleased—people can't have said that to her much. Yet I can't see how anyone intelligent can avoid feeling it. But you know, don't you, that as far as you are concerned I *do* like coming back ? You do, don't you ?

" I read ' The Fountain ' at Kiev while I was waiting about. I wanted not to have to think too much—you see, don't you ? It's obviously extremely good by all the standards by which in the past one has judged non-technical books, the style all one can ask, and the story moving and new. While I was reading it I was inside it—and it must have been good to get at me like that just then ; it touched on a lot one had thought and felt about since the war. Yet when I looked up it all dropped off me ; it was as though it were about some other century, almost some other world : a place full of curious sanctions and customs and taboos which are as unnatural as nose-ringing and totemism are from the Banbury Road ! You see, even in this short time I'd accepted the practical implications of Socialism. It makes me hopeful that one will be able to get used to the future very quickly after all.

" From Kiev I went to Warsaw, after the usual fuss at the frontier, not that anything of mine made difficulties, but some people have a passion for smuggling as such. It was odd getting out at Warsaw station and seeing the whole place so fine and prosperous-looking. One immediately questioned oneself: what splendid and successful Plan had this country had to look like this? Then I walked out and through the town—munching hot rolls made of *white* flour, feeling as greedy as at school!—and I saw beggars, and soldiers all dressed up in pretty uniforms, and large private cars, and women who obviously didn't work, and I realised it was the same old business again, civilisation standing on its head, a pyramid precariously balanced upside-down and pretending that's the only rational way! The old mortal sickness of rich and poor in the same city. It seemed like going back to barbarism, something as silly and wasteful and wrong as serfs and barons, witch burnings and human sacrifices.

" I got the only French paper I could see, the *Ami du Peuple*!—which was full of denunciations of pacifists and pro-Germans, and a rather ancient *Morning Post* which was all beautifully calm and August-ish, all about the bags on various grouse moors, and some row about a church somewhere. How can I write down the *silliness* of it, Dione—or did you feel it too? I expect it doesn't strike one so suddenly, coming by boat.

" Then I got to Berlin. I only had three hours there; I should like to have stopped longer, but I have to get back for this meeting at Marshbrook Bridge. I said to the porter, taking a chance: ' I have never been in Berlin before. I am a Socialist—tell me what to see.' He looked at me rather grimly and said: 'Go and walk down the Sieges Allee.' Well, I did that. It's an odd place, Dione, with ridiculous marble groups of kings, arc lights and patches of shade, and rather fine trees behind. But I saw what he meant. There were benches all along and on the benches men and boys sitting with these faces of despair and misery that I'd forgotten in the U.S.S.R. Faces I've seen often enough in Marshbrook Bridge and taken for granted. After the U.S.S.R. one doesn't take them for granted any longer. Plenty of people look worried or cross there, but that's an utterly different thing from the eyes of men and women who can't see any future.

"I suppose I was looking at their faces very hard, for a boy on one bench looked up and murmured something—I didn't catch what. I spoke to him, in my rather rusty German, and almost immediately realised that he was trying to get off with me. I told him I was only in Berlin for three hours, and asked him to come to supper with me. He accepted and we went on together; he seemed to think, poor chap, that he ought to give some kind of return for his food, but I told him I wasn't that sort. We talked about general conditions instead. He was a nice boy, not, by his build, a real homosexual; but of course it's a regular trade in Berlin. Not that it isn't in London, but it's more specialised perhaps and less in the open. He seemed to have no hope in any political party; when I said I'd just come from Russia he shrugged his shoulders and laughed—if one can call it laughing. 'I have friends among the Communists,' he said, 'but they will be done down in the end like the rest of us.' He walked back to the station with me and pointed out some others in the same profession. And of course there were women, too. I'd forgotten in the U.S.S.R. the way that women look at one in other countries, showing themselves off, pricking one with their eyes and calculating how much one's good for. I wonder if you found the same about men looking at you? I gave the boy five marks. But if I were a German I should certainly belong to the Communist Party; it's the only practical one there.

"Then it was Holland. The guard of the train was very much interested and we talked Russia on and off whenever he came to look at tickets. And then it was the crossing, and appropriately enough there's a thick fog to arrive at England in! I still feel dazed.

"Well, my dear, I shall be with you as soon as I'm through with the Marshbrook Bridge stuff; I must bring up a hell of a lot of papers. Have you got your typewriter? Love to the brats. It will be good to see you again. Will you be glad to see me this time? I wonder. I hope so. I love you. Tom."

Oh, but she would be glad to see him! There wasn't any question. She made no reservations. Why should she not be glad? They would have long walks and go fishing together; she looked over his flies and casts. They would sleep together again. Was he going to like that? Would he keep on comparing her with Oksana? Well—what if he did?

The day after a letter came from Donald. It said:

"Dear Comrade, You ask me to write about everything. I know well what it is you are wanting to know. Well, I am thinking of getting married. It is not to Nina, as she has not come, and anyway maybe she was not just my sort. She is a girl in the same shop as me; she is called Anna, but I call her Annie. She is a bonny girl with yellow hair like a Lowland girl, and a fine worker; she is on the committee, and I am being put on it next month. We are thinking of getting registered then. I have got my room and I am trying to get it nice for her, but it is hard to come by stuff and any furniture that is decently made. That will be better next year.

" I told Annie about you and what you did for me, Dione, and she says when we have a girl we will call her after you. Will that please you ? I would like it. I would like to try to tell you what this is for me. A year ago I had not thought it was anyways possible I could ever get married, still less have children ; for in England or Scotland a decent man who has any regard for a woman cannot go doing that unless he has a steady job, and few indeed have that. I thought, too, that if I got married it would knock me out of my Party work. Yet I wanted a child of my own awful bad, and God knows, Dione, I seem to want a woman now there is nothing against it. So now I am getting what I want, and what every decent man wants, and I am grateful to this country which is giving it to me and which is my country now, and you will believe I am grateful to you. When Annie and I get having this baby, I will send you a photo, and I will send one to my mother, too. I have written her.

" It is queer what you say about Adam Walker. I am wondering how he was got off. And I am thinking it was you did it again. Will you tell me one day ? And will you tell me what happens to you ?—everything, as you said I was to tell. Will you tell me when you stop being frightened.

" What do you think of it now you are back at Auchanarnish ? Are you angry at me for writing to you this way, me who is son to your mother's gardener ? Tell me that, too. Or maybe you'll not write me more at all now you are back and forgetting Moscow. Or am I wronging you ? Would you ask me into the grand drawing-room and have me sit on the fine silken sofa ? Would you kiss me again ? I have your hair, Dione, the long lock. Annie says it is softer than her hair, and I am thinking it is. Have you mine yet ?

"Thank you for the *Daily Workers*. How did you get them? I can see you: Labour Candidate's Wife caught buying Communist daily! Is he back yet? What did he make of it all? Or it of him? Thank you, too, for the books. And will you send me news of the Sallington folks if you go there? And do you love me at all, Dione? There now, I have written you a letter the like I have never written before. Annie said to me to write what was in my heart. I wonder, was she right? Your loving comrade, Donald."

That was a nice letter to get. It would be lovely to have the baby named after her. She wrote him back a long letter. About Auchanarnish she wrote: "I wonder whether you'd like sitting on the big sofa to talk to me—with my mother looking on! I'd like that better at Oxford—you never saw my drawing-room there, and if you came back I wouldn't have to hide you behind the cistern. But up here I'd sooner walk along the loch with you or up by Saint Finnigal's well among the ferns. I'd sooner pull gowans with you than sit in drawing-rooms. And I have your hair, Donald, and perhaps if we saw one another again I'd kiss you better than I've done before. There, you can tell Annie that is what is in my heart, Donald! And give her my love and say I think she's a lucky woman."

She went in to Oban to meet Tom. She arrived twenty minutes too soon, and walked up and down the platform, too excited to talk to anyone. The train was signalled and puffed in cheerfully. Tom got out; he looked supremely well, burnt a splendid red-brown, which made his hair look light and young and his eyes very blue. He came to Dione. "Well?" he said, but after he had looked at her for a moment he didn't seem to need any answer. And it was all quite respectable for a husband and wife to kiss on the public platform of Oban station.

## SALLINGTON 7

Yet, all the same, there was something. What was it? The first few days Tom was extraordinarily happy and gay and nice to everyone. Then he began to cloud over. It was partly just being very busy; his extra three weeks had piled up work. There were page proofs to go through—and now he wanted to rewrite the whole book! There was a certain amount of routine University work as well as his next term's lectures to get ready. He had promised to write some articles for the *New Clarion*—he dictated these to Dione, who typed them. Then there were the affairs of S.S.I.P. and the Socialist League, which bothered him a good deal. And then there was the Leicester Conference at the beginning of October; he had to make up his mind how he stood with regard to the Party before that. He hadn't much time, with all this, to go for long walks or have family tea with the children; he let the first spate in the burn go by without touching his rod. He worked late in the old schoolroom at Auchanarnish and went to bed tired, and after a fortnight or so Dione began to see him getting sudden moods of depression for no obvious reason.

She found that at these times it was no good petting him; he didn't respond. One evening, when he was changing for dinner—her mother liked that—she went into his dressing-room; she had meant to brush her hair there—it was usually a good time for talk—and found him sitting in shirt and socks, with his head in his hands, miserable and faintly ridiculous. "What is it, my dearest?" she said, all sore for him as though he had been one of the children. "Can't I do anything?" He shook his head. "Tell me at least what's worrying you."

"I'm just realising slowly and carefully," said Tom in a grim and level voice, "that I'm not going to sleep with Oksana again, or kiss her again, or look at her again or speak with her again, ever any more."

Dione was horrified at his way of saying it. She answered, hesitating, "But Tom, you always might go to Russia again——"

"That's no use, my girl," said Tom; "it was part of the bargain that it was to be—temporary. And she should marry someone else. And I shouldn't get entangled!"

His voice was frightening. Dione didn't know whether to touch him or not; when she did, uncertainly, he shrugged his shoulder away—and then apologised. She was terribly sorry for him; she saw how it was hurting, now the first bravery and glory of it was over. She wondered whether Oksana was feeling the same thing, poor darling, and then wondered if Tom was wondering about Oksana too. She wanted to write to Oksana to tell her about Tom, but wasn't sure if Tom would like her to—but if she asked Tom it would be like doing it on his initiative, not her own! Oh, it was all so silly, when all three of them felt so warmly about one another. Perhaps these things would have an easier convention in a hundred years. Little comfort now! She worried, too, about Tom sleeping with her. She so much didn't want him to feel that he ought to show her any signs of affection—let alone the whole thing—that she herself became shy and cold to him. And then he became shy of her, and felt hurt—oh, so silly, so silly, and nobody's fault!

The holidays came to an end; the Bathursts went back to Helm. Lady Ann had bought one of Phœbe's pictures and had been rather embarrassed when Phœbe told her it was an excellent investment—she had looked upon it as a neighbourly act towards dear Mrs. Fraser's eccentric daughter. It wouldn't mix with the Raeburns, Phœbe thought, and wondered aloud during lunch whether it would finally end in the servant's water-closet. Mrs. Fraser found Phœbe harder to shut up than Dione, when she really got going—and the dear child had been so full of spirits all the holidays; it must have been because dear Robin was so much better.

They were going to try the experiment of sending Brian to school for a term with Morag and Kenneth. He was rather thrilled with the idea, especially that he was going to get through part, at least, of the winter in a house with electric light—that he could turn on himself and frighten all the cornery things away. So Dione took him back with the others. After this, Morag would have only one more term; the awful problem was, where next? She couldn't face the idea of an ordinary girls' school, especially after what Jane Ellis had told her.

The first week or two of Oxford was always pretty strenuous, especially in autumn after being away for so long. There was infinite work to do in the garden, and all the preparations for term, letters to answer, people to see and so on. The worst of it was that it took up a lot of time, but somehow there didn't seem to be anything real or worth while to show at the end of it.

In the meantime Tom was at Leicester, writing rather gloomy letters about the Conference. Socialisation of the banks had gone through, Trevelyan had made a good speech, Cripps was coming to the fore, people were talking about Cole's ideas. It was the best Party Conference he'd been at, but, all the same, it was a bit uninspiring after the U.S.S.R.! Sixty-four pages of resolutions to be got through in a week: well, it was obvious what happened. The old hands knew the ropes and could deal with the conference machinery. The young ones got done down. Half the trade union leaders smoking cigars in the hotels like so many caricatures of themselves! And as to the new men who were coming on, some of them couldn't be trusted, one or two put everyone's back up, they were as jealous of one another as chorus girls. Yet it did seem worth it when, just occasionally, a wave of enthusiasm would come over the delegates—just once or twice they *had* looked like Socialism. That must mean something, mustn't it? Or was he only kidding himself that it did? Was he only in the Labour Party because of his social and economic position that kept him compromising, that kept him where he wasn't directly attacking his own world? Did Dione think he was justified in staying in it? "I don't feel that I'm a Communist," he wrote, "except in so far as I'm a Socialist and also accept most of the Marxian interpretation of history and society—but not all. I don't at any rate feel like joining the C.P., who wouldn't presumably have me. They'll never do the trick in England. But how much of my refusal to accept complete Communism is due to my job and the fact that I'm a success at it, and also to the knowledge that I've taken on the responsibility of you and the children?"

Dione wrote back to say that he mustn't let considerations for her and the children influence him against his conscience. Yet she knew it wasn't as simple as that. This was not a thing anyone could decide completely by himself—as though he were alone in the world.

Another letter of his crossed hers. No one had dealt adequately with unemployment and the Means Test. They'd shied off it. The *Daily Worker* was quite right about that—and they'd let down the Lancashire strikers. So Tom had taken to the *Daily Worker* now, had he! Well, if he went on, she could send his old copies to Donald. Some of the Marshbrook Bridge people were there. Mason, of course, he was good at dealing with the Standing Orders Committee. Edna Boffin had come as a visitor, besides Reuben Goldberg for a couple of days. But John Collis and the Wool Workers were taking up the old-fashioned trade union point of view. Tom was fed up with them! These conferences were the devil; one was much more in touch with the great body of the movement at Marshbrook Bridge than here.

One of Dione's autumn jobs was putting away summer holiday clothes. She had brought down Tom's country things from Auchanarnish and began to put them tidily in their drawers. Tom had spent a hurried day in Oxford, repacking, on his way back from Russia, and all his things were still unsorted and in heaps in his room. Some had come back from the wash—she liked these embroidered shirts—but there were papers in drawers and on the table and everywhere—Russian grammar and phrase book, photographs, pamphlets, the usual accumulation. When she opened the tie and handkerchief drawer, Dione found a bundle wrapped in a Russian newspaper, and, when she looked inside, found they were dry flowers, pink and mauve everlastings and a few poppy heads. She left the parcel and went on tidying. She very much wondered if there were letters or photos of Oksana among the papers, but scrupulously didn't look.

It began to occur to her that it might be better for Tom not to have too much domesticity this term; a few nights in college wouldn't hurt him. And when Alex wrote and told her that his Shields people had formed a discussion and drama club and wanted her to come and talk Russia, she accepted at once. Then she became very nervous;

she hated speaking and this might be extra difficult. Alex had warned her that she mustn't talk down to his people; she wasn't the candidate's wife or anyone special here, just someone who'd had the luck to get to Russia.

She went there for the week-end, taking all the Russian photographs she had, and talked to the club on Saturday night. It was much easier than she had thought; there weren't too many of them and they picked up her points at once, laughed encouragingly at her jokes, and asked questions afterwards; she particularly liked these North-country girls, doing their best for themselves with bright-coloured jumpers and rather badly painted lips. These were Tom's people on his non-Scottish side. Perhaps that was one reason she liked them. Alex, having introduced her, went and sat among the audience; Dione supposed the girl he was sitting next was his Nelly, and at the end she was introduced. They all accepted her and were jolly to her. On Sunday they went for a walk down Tyneside; she liked Nelly; she liked these men, who reminded her a little of Tom. She was so encouraged that she wrote to Mason, asking if he would like her to come and talk Russia in the constituency.

Mason wrote back that he would gladly arrange meetings and that it would be a good thing if she stayed with the Taylors; things were going badly with them now and they'd be glad of a little extra from her. So Dione, having assured herself that everything was all right and Brian very happy at school, went off to Sallington. Tom had settled down to term and was working furiously. He had got another book in his head—or perhaps the same one as he now wanted to write it!—but there it must stay till the vac.; he could do no more than make notes. He approved of her going to Sallington; he was bound to go down there himself once or twice before the Municipals. Whether he realised her other reason for going, she didn't know. The flowers weren't in his handkerchief drawer any longer; perhaps he had taken them to college.

The first evening she was there Dione found out all about Taylor; he had been out of work for a couple of months—all the time she'd been in Russia—and of course Mrs. Taylor hadn't been able to give him the food he was accustomed to and his strength went down. Then he got a job of bricklaying on the new Sallington hotel, and the second day he was there he fell thirty feet off the scaffolding and broke his leg. He was taken to hospital and his leg had mended, but now he was home—the hospital, Mrs. Taylor said, had discharged him the first possible day, they were that full; there'd been going to be a new wing opened, but since these economy times there'd been no more heard of it. He was walking and the doctor'd be sure to pass him next time. The thing was—Mrs. Taylor told all this to Dione while they were in the kitchen peeling potatoes—that now he was having awful nightmares almost every night about falling off that scaffolding, and if he went up on it again he'd be sure to fall off, but the firm had promised to take him back, which was very decent of them, and he didn't dare miss the chance of a job, what with winter coming on and work getting scarcer and the Means Test. But if he did go back—Mrs. Taylor began crying over the potatoes. "And I've always done my best!" she said, "and I give Emmie oranges, like it said about vitamins in the papers, and plenty of bottled milk, but now I've had to cut down her milk, which is all wrong for a growing child, as you know as well as I do, Mrs. Galton!"

"Yes, yes," Dione said, thinking rather guiltily how she'd always insisted on Grade A milk for hers—and yet she'd been right to!

"And I'm always mending and doing over, and there's a bit from the garden—we're luckier than most—and yet I can't do it on the money—and what we'd do if we had to go on the Means Test!—like the Thompsons next door, and they've got four children. But it'll be a great help having you, Mrs. Galton, only you must say if anything's not as you like, and you won't go staying on when you don't want, because of us, will you?—because I can manage!"

"Things must change soon," Dione said. "It's impossible to go on like this." And she patted Mrs. Taylor's shoulder.

"There, my dear," said Mrs. Taylor, putting the margarine to frizzle in the pan, "I've no right coming putting all this on you. You've got troubles of your own, I'll be bound."

"Not this sort," Dione said, "and I want to know. I don't really know how most people live, Mrs. Taylor—only out of books."

"Well, we can show you that," Mrs. Taylor said, "though dear knows, Mrs. Galton, a year ago we'd have said we were a bit above it. We'd got this nice council house, and making up our minds only to have Emmie, though I did want a little boy, and taking a library subscription—we thought we was, oh, regular highbrows! But Taylor he says we're real proletarians now. Not that I can feel the same as them down in Carisbrook Road, Mrs. Galton, with a dozen children and never knowing what it is to be clean."

"We're all pretty near one another," Dione said, "it's only a question of something ceasing to function. Suppose all the colleges at Oxford stopped getting any interest from their endowments, it would be the same for Tom and me, and I'm sure I shouldn't manage as well as you; I'd be one of the Carisbrook Road muddlers!" But all the same, she suddenly thought, we'd have about £400 a year between us, more than a pound a day, and Auchanarnish—unless that all came to an end, too.

Mrs. Taylor laughed and said: "I always say it's nicer cooking when there's two to it. I always like a bit of a talk and mostly I don't get it. I used to go to my evening classes more for the discussion than what I learnt. But I haven't been since Mr. Taylor's accident; he likes company in the evenings, even if it's only me sitting by him while he reads his paper."

"Still it's a pity to drop your classes. What did you like best?"

"We take what we can get. But I liked a bit of history or literature or pretty well anything. There now, if you'll just take in the plates——"

Mr. Taylor sat by the fire with a pencil and paper. "Still doing cross-words, Mr. Taylor?" Dione said.

"Yes," he said. "You see, it takes my mind off."

"I wonder if you'll ever win one."

"I knew a man once," Mr. Taylor said, "that knew a man that won a cross-word." He sighed and put down the *Herald* and came over to the table.

Dione talked about Russia to three or four groups, mostly women. At each meeting someone came up afterwards and asked in a hushed voice if it was TRUE that . . . and Dione reassured them. Gladys Wills turned up at one of these meetings. Dione was pleased to see her again. She had got a good job as typist with a big firm of Sallington solicitors and was living outside the division. If there was another general election or a crisis of any kind, she would come back and work for the Party, but in the meantime she was rather bored with it. It was easier in some ways to make friends at Marshbrook Bridge without Tom;

she was less official. Now that there was no immediate crisis, except the municipal elections in which only a gallant few felt any interest so far, she had not got to be in any way special. She was just a woman—in a large political movement where women had only lately begun to be taken at all seriously.

Mason was, as usual, rather worried, once you got under his ironic surface cheerfulness. He asked Dione what Tom was up to. " He was all over the shop at the Conference," Mason said, " asking questions—well, I mean, Mrs. Galton, the sort of questions we haven't got an answer to yet! One can't run a Movement that way."

" But it won't keep alive unless people ask questions, will it? " Dione said, " and they've got to be new questions. The old ones answer themselves. Russia makes one ask questions, you know."

" And I thought at first he wouldn't be one of those ones! " Mason said and laughed. " I didn't think he'd go off on his own. Perhaps he'll do better this way for some of our young folks. But the older members, they like things to go on the way they're accustomed to. And they don't want too much talk about Russia."

" The people I've talked to have been keen enough."

" Yes, but they've mostly been young ones—haven't they? The young women in the Movement, when they're any use at all, they'll stand anything as far as I can see. But some of the old ones, they came because they wanted to be shocked. And I bet you shocked them! Oh, I know them, the old cats," Mason said, " they'll go home and pick it all to pieces. Never mind, Mrs. Galton, you do more good than harm, both of you. But I do hope your husband will be careful about his meetings here. If Morrow Hill thinks he wants a revolution——! "

" But we *do* want a revolution, don't we ? Or something very like one."

" Bless you, yes," said Mason, " but it doesn't do to say so all the time. It may have done in Russia, but not here, not in Sallington. I know what I want all right. I've worked with my hands and under a foreman, long enough to know ! You folk who come into the Movement from outside—not that we don't count you as one of us now : we do—you always want to go talking revolution. Yet I'll bet I'm more of a revolutionary than you ! "

" I'm very glad to hear it," Dione said, " and I expect you are. I'm really very frightened of it. I do terribly want equality, but I hate hurting people and I hate being hurt."

" That's just what we don't need to have in England," Mason answered.

" But can we avoid it ? When the Coke-Browns and people hit back ? We've got to be prepared for that, haven't we ?—not just wait till our heads are cut off and then look surprised ! That's what the Taylors, for instance, don't seem to see. Pacifism won't be any good then."

" But there's all the difference between pacifism and going round with bombs in one's pockets—sooner or later one goes off, and what good does it do ? Look at the *Sallington News* now—it's no different."

" Yes, but its circulation's gone down a lot," Dione said. " I found that out. It hasn't got the same personal touch. So *that* bomb was some use ! "

" Well, for goodness' sake," said Mason, with a face of comic concern, " don't you go saying that at a meeting ! "

" No," said Dione, " I promise I won't."

The more Dione saw of people the more she realised Mason's difficulties. There was Miss Waterhouse, who saw the Labour Party entirely in terms of immediate local problems—though they needed dealing with badly enough; there was Sam Hall, who had wanted to stand as councillor at Barton's End, but they had a local man they liked better, and now Sam Hall wouldn't work in his own ward; there was Edna Boffin, who wanted to stand next year, but Mason told her there wasn't a "woman's seat" in the division. Dione rashly sympathised with her over this, and was told off by Mason, who said it wasn't so much her being a woman as her having two or three pet causes that she would run at the same time, and which annoyed half the voters. The number of causes there seemed to be!—good, bad and indifferent. Esperanto and folk dancing, the League of Nations—for or against it according to how you looked at it—the F.S.U., anti-vivisection, Christian Science, secularism—that was Jo. Burrage—the protection of animals, children and aborigines—and poor Mason had to deal with them all, as well as legal questions, affiliation orders, and the constant collision between individuals and local or Government authorities! No wonder he wanted her and Tom to give as little trouble as possible.

Every now and then she would come up sharply against something very trying, most often among the women—a kind of idea that the new millennium would mean more and better co-ops., everyone with a five-roomed house and vegetable garden of their own and earning £5 a week. Everyone a cut above the poor streets, which somehow seemed to be left in the picture, but full of Tories! She went round one evening and talked to Reuben Goldberg about it. He was gloomy: "There's not ten per cent. of the Labour Party here who're class-conscious," he said, "and here am I saying it, a skilled engineer in a sure job, earning three times what most of them do! I don't mind telling you, Mrs. Galton, I had a look at the I.L.P., but half of them are no better. It's heart-breaking, Mrs. Galton, it is indeed. When one thinks of the hopes one's had!"

"How long have you been in the Movement?"

"Twelve years. Ever since I was a young man."

"Yes, that's longer than I."

"Mrs. Galton, I should like to ask you something. You usedn't to be so keen, used you? Not when you were here first. No, in a way you were keen enough, but you didn't seem somehow to be part of the Movement."

"I didn't feel part of it at first. But now I'm beginning to think this is more my real place than Oxford or even Scotland, and you're more my real friends. Did you always live here?"

"No, we've been about a bit. I'd two years in Birmingham, and then I had a year at Barking, at the power statior there. Ever see it, Mrs. Galton? A sweet station it is."

"Yes, I saw it, going down the Thames in the Soviet ship. Do you like this better?"

"I like most of the people in the Movement here. For that matter I liked the I.L.P. chaps. But there, three-quarters of them don't know what they're after. They're not educated. They've time for books, a lot of them, but what do they read? Not Marx or Engels, but these rotten newspapers that are written and sold to take their minds off the struggle! Spotting winners! As though horses had been created to make more money for rich men and women instead of being ridden in green fields for the strength and pleasure of the workers!"

"Have you ridden at all?"

"When I was a boy I used to ride my father's pony. He was a butcher—a kosher butcher. Not that I believe in all that now."

"Horses are nice, though. It ought to be like that on May Day, oughtn't it?"

"There, Mrs. Galton, that's what I've always thought!"

In the meantime she had written to the address Donald had given her: Agnes Green, 27b Saffron Street, Greenapple, Sallington. What a romantic address, she thought, but Mason, when she asked where it was, said: "There's no apple trees there now, Mrs. Galton! It's up between Smedbrook and Sallmouth. Oliver of the A.S.E.'s in there—though his majority came down badly last time. But it's a real working district, no Morrow Hill there. No, I don't know Saffron Street, but you go to the Town Hall and get an Upmill tram—73, it is."

So when she got a formal note from Agnes Green asking her to come any evening after 6.30, that was what Dione did. She found the number in Saffron Street, and rang. It was bitterly cold, waiting for the bell to be answered—as cold as this time last year, canvassing. The little slatternly sixteen-year-old who answered stared at her, then took her upstairs. Agnes Green came out on to the landing and shook hands. "Come in," she said. Dione saw that she was the woman in the coat and skirt whom she had noticed last May Day. There was nothing very marked about her; it was as though she could have slipped unnoticed in and out of any crowd. Her room was small; there were books on two sides, a folding-table, a small divan with linen-covered cushions, one obviously embroidered by a child, a large leather chair and two smaller ones, and a good many exercise books and papers covered with children's writing. "I'm just making tea, if you'll sit down for a moment," Agnes Green said.

"Don't bother, please——"

"I am making it for myself in any case," Agnes Green said, and Dione felt squashed and sat down. She wondered when this calm woman would speak of what she had come about; it was up to the hostess! At last Agnes Green, having poured the boiling water into the tea-pot, said: "And now, Mrs. Galton, you tell me you can give me news of Comrade MacLean?"

Dione sat back in her chair. "I suppose you know, Miss Green, that it was he who murdered Daniel Coke-Brown?"

Agnes Green, busy over the tea things, said in an even voice: "I supposed so."

"He came to me," Dione said, "rather by accident, and I happened to be able to help him to escape." She told the whole story, watching the other woman carefully, and astonished to see how little anyone's face could show. "His anxiety all the time," she ended, "was that the Communist Party should not get the blame for what was his individual protest."

"He was certainly right to be anxious about that," Agnes Green said, "we all were. It did us no good. However, the action was probably sound in itself. Daniel Coke-Brown was the kind of man who has to be got rid of. I take it you are in agreement, Mrs. Galton?"

"Unofficially," Dione said, "oh yes!"

For the first time Agnes Green smiled in a human way as she handed Dione the cup of tea. "Nothing you say here will go beyond the Party, Mrs. Galton."

"Would you like to see his letter?" Dione said, and gave her the first one, adding: "He has written since this, but it was mainly personal, saying that he was getting married to a Russian girl." She thought she saw her hostess start a little then, but she was not sure.

After reading the letter Agnes Green handed it back; she was definitely more friendly now. "I gather from this," she said, "that you were—on very good terms—with Donald MacLean before the end?"

"We were on kissing terms," Dione observed.

Agnes Green suddenly blushed and looked for the first

time really like a schoolmistress : " And—your husband ? "

" Tom is a good Socialist," Dione said firmly, having at last scored a point.

" Yes," Agnes Green answered noncommittally, " but isn't this—rather a special application ? "

" I don't think so," Dione said; " remember, he aided and abetted." And suddenly she caught Agnes Green by the hands and said : " Try to think of it our way for a moment ! Can't you see, Miss Green, we're not enemies ! We're both after the same thing, your Party and mine. I see it as two wings, one that won't compromise and keeps the flag flying and the ideals strict and bright—that's you. And one that does compromise so as to get things done, that keeps in touch with the mass of the workers, the muddled, brave, kindly people who aren't yet any of the things you say they are—one wing that believes in *praxis*. That's us. And my side want to be friends with you, because we can see that we're out for the same thing. Your side isn't allowed to see that, because if it did I suppose it would compromise and cease to be itself. But oh, do try to be brave and see it our way once ! " She stopped speaking, staring at Agnes Green, hoping so much that something had got through, if not from the words, from the touch.

But Agnes Green smiled a discreet and remote smile, saying as she disengaged her hands from Dione's relaxing ones : " I understand what you are trying to say. In some ways I wish it were in any way representative. But it is not, and it is—if you will forgive my saying so—a romantic point of view, which does not correspond with the realities of the situation. Have you studied the beginnings of the Russian movement, Mrs. Galton ? "

" A bit," said Dione, horribly cast down, " the Iskra stuff and so on ? But surely it's different here ? " She wished she had Tom—or even Mason—to argue it for her.

" Not essentially," Agnes Green said, in that cool, assured voice that had dealt with hundreds of unruly children.

" I take it, then, you're up against Oliver here ? " Dione asked. Her voice had gone remote, too.

" Yes," said Agnes Green, " you may take it so."

" It seems a pity," Dione said, " that you should feel called upon to hinder Socialism instead of helping it."

" You consider Oliver a good Socialist, then ? " asked Agnes Green, and, in the same voice, " Another cup of tea ? "

" In general, yes," Dione said; " no more, thank you."

Agnes Green took her cup. " By the way," she said, " we were all somewhat surprised over this affair of Adam Walker. May I ask whether you were in any way instrumental ? "

Dione hesitated : " I had something to do with it," she said, " but again, in confidence."

" That will not go beyond the Party, either."

" You can trust your Party, then—absolutely ? "

" On Party matters," Agnes Green answered her, " yes."

SALLINGTON 8

Early October was fine, but beginning to get chilly at nights. All being well at Oxford, Dione stayed on with the Taylors. She was horribly worried about Taylor; obviously he ought to have gone away for a change after his accident. Normally he was stolid and rather unimaginative, but now he was dreadfully nervous; sometimes he couldn't eat, and then Mrs. Taylor used to cry in the kitchen. He knew he was going to fall off that scaffolding again. The doctor gave him another week before going back to work. When Dione got hold of the doctor and had a talk with him, he said: "But of course, three-quarters of my panel patients ought to be sent to the seaside and given a thorough change and rest and feeding-up. A great deal of what's wrong is under-nutrition; that's what's making this measles epidemic so bad. And they ought to be got away from their homes: no chance of quiet for most of them. But what can I do? I gather they deal with these things better in Russia, Mrs. Galton."

"They do indeed," said Dione, thinking of workers' rest and convalescent homes she'd seen, flowers and gay rooms and good food, enough to make any doctor's mouth water!

"You know," the doctor said, putting the things tidy in his dispatch case, "I don't believe in politics myself, but your people would perhaps at least not interfere with us! The permanent officials at the Ministry are mostly all right, but they're being chivied into economies by these damned politicians—begging your pardon, Mrs. Galton! I thought I'd got my rheumatism clinic fixed up, but——" He shrugged his shoulders.

"The local authorities are worse, aren't they?" Dione asked.

"Oh, they're the utter limit," said the doctor, "though again, it's not usually the M.O.'s—the man at Sallmouth's gone economy-mad, though. But imagine, Mrs. Galton; we'd got rickets pretty well under since the war, especially on the new housing estates, where there's a reasonable amount of sun. Women whose husbands were earning three pounds a week, say, spent every penny they could on food for their children, and quite right too. But now half of them are on the Means Test, not irresponsible people, but women who've brought their children regularly to the welfare centres and done splendidly by them—they're getting two shillings a week for each child. Naturally, we're beginning to get rickets again! A nice look-out for the next forty years. And this is the moment the Sallington City Council chooses to cut down our grants for milk and cod-liver oil!"

"I wish you people could make yourselves felt politically a bit more," Dione said; "you'd be taken seriously."

"We haven't time," the doctor said, "and I must be getting along now. At any rate, while you're staying with the Taylors they can afford more to eat."

Dione went to see Mrs. East at Barton's End and verified all this. The Council estates were well planned and looked prosperous; people prided themselves on keeping up appearances. But inside, behind the white curtains, there was abominable poverty. It was worse in the Carisbrook Road district, or at least it looked much worse. She paid a visit to ex-Councillor Finch's elder daughter Dorothy, who was married and living down there—and on the Means Test. She was a jolly, intelligent girl, with a young baby. When Dione came in she apologised for the smell—Dione had always hoped you didn't notice it if you lived there—

saying it usedn't to be so bad, but they'd had to sell the lino off the floors and now there was nothing but the bare quarries, much worn from earlier tenants. " I scrub and scrub," the girl said, " but I can't seem to get the smell away. The suds go down the cracks between the quarries, Mrs. Galton; they aren't properly mortared in, and there isn't any foundations, like. And there's always a draught under the door, and they're that cold to walk on. And now there's the beetles. If we'd known how it would be, Bill and me wouldn't never have got married, but he thought he'd got a steady job—he'd been four years at the Synthex works—and now there's baby and I don't know how ever I shall manage ! "

She began to cry bitterly, seeing it all as she said it, and Dione sat beside her and petted her, and by and by asked a few leading questions. There was one practical thing to be done : the next day she and Dorothy went over to the Sallington birth-control clinic, which was struggling to keep in existence by collections at drawing-room meetings and amateur theatricals. The worst of it was, it wasn't much good to Marshbrook Bridge, because it was right down on the edge of Sallmouth and a ninepenny tram fare from Carisbrook Road. After the clinic Dione took Dorothy to tea at Fuller's in the Square, and they talked and laughed and enjoyed themselves. Afterwards Dione saw her run across the Square and jump into a tram and wave her hand, and was suddenly reminded of Russian women and was hopeful for a moment, and then remembered Carisbrook Road and the smell and the tiny windows and the cold quarries that Dorothy was going back to, and she was swept with anger for her friend.

It was only five o'clock ; she thought she would go and see Margaret Coke-Brown ; the Barston 'buses stopped just here. Perhaps it would be a good thing to see some different kind of person. " My dear," said Margaret Coke-Brown, " how marvellous of you to come! I've finished the whole of Proust and the whole of Bertrand Russell, and I'm getting so frantically bored, and all my relations in law will bring me things and insist on giving me the most ridiculous advice!"

" When is it due?"

" Another six weeks. Oh, gosh! But it's going to be a super-baby. I shan't let it have a single complex. Come and see my nursery, Dione, looking over the garden, vita-glass windows, and the decoration's really designed—I saw to every scrap myself—not just a higgledy-piggledy scrap-heap like most nurseries."

It was a lovely room; it had everything a baby could possibly need, including light and space. " And here "—she stooped to open a drawer, and what a wonderfully becoming dress, Dione thought, Barri of course—" all presents from the in-laws, but I made them let me choose them myself."

The baby's layette took Dione's breath away; she handled the embroidery and real Valenciennes without saying anything.

" A bit silly," said Margaret Coke-Brown, watching her, " but it's my very own only marvellous baby and I do feel a bit over-emphatic about it! And if the old aunts *want* to give it things, well, why not? I shan't let them interfere with it otherwise!"

Dione found it a little difficult to know what to say. She remembered what a thrill one's first baby always is, and this wasn't *just* luxury. A great deal of it was the kind of thing every baby ought to have, by right. Every baby: that was the point. Not just one Coke-Brown baby. She tried not to say any of this; what was the use, at the moment? But Margaret Coke-Brown saw some implicit criticism in what she did say, and tried to answer it. "Let me know if there's anything I can do for your Labour Party, Dione, won't you?" she said; "I'm—I'm quite serious really, you know."

"I'd like you to make friends with some of the people," Dione said slowly.

"But aren't they—I mean, can one make friends with them? I don't believe there's a soul in Sallington from my in-laws downwards who's got any ideas at all!"

"Then why do you want to work for the Labour Party, Margaret?"

"Oh, I made up my mind about the principle of the thing when I was at Newnham!"

"But that's like—oh, art for art's sake. It's not real. You won't be any good."

"But what can one talk to these people about?"

"Any of the important things."

"But isn't one always making reservations—like with aunts?"

"Well," Dione said, "does one ever say the same thing in the same way to two different people? Often they're slow, but then one must be patient. They know about things that we don't, but they aren't educated to conversation as we've been; after all, a child in an elementary school is usually just disciplined into a few facts—it isn't drawn out as our children are."

"But they have such incredibly bad taste!"

"They have to buy what's sold to them. Sometimes by your in-laws! Come and try, Margaret, when you're up and about again."

"All right," said Margaret Coke-Brown, "I will really try."

Dione felt all fidgeted that evening. Perhaps it was what Margaret Coke-Brown had said about bad taste, but the

Taylors' pictures and furniture, which she had been living with quite placidly, suddenly got on her nerves. It was all very normally ugly and she just hadn't been looking at it, but this evening it seemed to shout at her. She suddenly decided that she would go and skate the next morning a the new Sallington Ice-rink. She had brought her skate with her on chance.

"They say that rink's going broke," Taylor said, in a rather satisfied tone, "starting in such a big way just at that time!"

"Oh, what a pity!" Dione said. "Have you ever been?"

"No, *I've* never been," said Taylor, in a voice as if she'd asked him whether he'd been to the moon—or to somewhere not quite proper. Dione felt cross and rebellious and went off there in her blue fur-bordered skating dress—from Harrods' sale—thinking she was jolly well going to enjoy herself for once in a way!

The rink was rather empty; Taylor was probably right about its going broke. It wasn't as big as the Oxford one, but as there were so few people the ice wasn't badly cut. For a time she just did speed skating, round and round, letting the quickness and rush of air blow all the annoyance out of her body. Then she practised figures in the middle of the ice; she was pleased with her own muscles, pleased with the feel of the changing edges, the balance tilted from side to side. Round her were novices plowing along; two were being helped by uniformed instructors. There were a few other good skaters.

Then dance music began and the ice was cleared for a quarter of an hour's dancing. She wished she had a partner; at Oxford she had several partners, especially one of Tom's pupils, a Canadian Rhodes scholar; she was the equal of any girl ten years her junior on the ice! But here she didn't know anyone. The other good skaters paired off with one another or with the instructors; there were eight of these, three women and five men; the men's black uniforms looked trim against the coloured dresses of their patronesses. One of the girls was probably a Coke-Brown: she was so like Tom's niece Elizabeth. The women instructors were all dancing, their faces in a faint official smile; probably they really enjoy it a lot, Dione thought. All but one of the men were dancing, too. They started with a waltz. It was maddening not to be in it! She felt all her crossness coming back; her skates wriggled sympathetically under her as she stood by the barrier watching. The waltz ended in curves and posturings, and Sonja Henje poses by the women. It was a fourteen-step this time. The partners swung together again. And the other instructor who had not danced last time glided between them to the barrier and said to Dione: "Would you care to dance this, comrade?"

It was like being hit by a snowball: the other world turning up here! And who was he to have the cheek—with his brown bright eyes and confident mouth—in that uniform—and, oh, what fun, she was going to dance after all! "Certainly," she said, and glided out and into his arms and backwards on one foot, and quickening, and the next beat and the next and the next, and the rush of air again, and the swing over, secure of his edges as of her own. The fur border of her dress swirling out, her knees and hips bent and lifted to the music of the fourteen-step, her skates changed over quickly; they were the fastest couple there; oh, he was a splendid partner, as good as the Canadian. He said nothing, but he smiled; he was impersonal in his black uniform; he was her servant and—— The tune ended. They swept round once in a great arc; he held her hand lightly in one gloved hand, encouraging her, too, to posture for a moment. They were at the barrier again.

" Why did you call me comrade ? " Dione said, " and who are you ? "

" You're Mrs. Galton, are you not ? I saw you last May Day."

" In the procession—were you——? "

" I was with Donald MacLean," the man said, with something between a wink and a smile, " and I know all about *that*."

" Are you in the Party ? " Dione asked.

He made a movement which she took for assent. " And now, did you want to dance ? I am not allowed to sit out with a partner." He added : " I'm *3s. 6d.* a time. Sorry. The others are more."

" All right," Dione said, " I'll go a bust and have all I can get."

It was a waltz again, really the best dance, though perhaps the easiest. It swept them from side to side ; he steered marvellously, fearlessly, between the other couples, beautiful deep edges, catching at her breath. Oh, lovely, lovely ! He was about her height and so light, never pressing on her. The dance ended ; she was breathless with speed and pleasure and swinging. " The next will be a tango," he said. " Can you do that too, Mrs. Galton ? "

" Yes ! " she said, and then : " Do tell me some more—what an extraordinary job this is for you to have ! "

" You would not say that if you knew what my life's been," he said, looking round as he did so, as though he were afraid someone might overhear.

" Tell me about it," she said, " after the dancing."

" Can't," he said. " I'm booked up."

The tango music started, calling to their wits and skates and sense of rhythm through the megaphone's mouth.

Sometimes she didn't like this so much, but she did with him. The noise of steel on ice sang under the dance music. Once their skates touched, but he snatched his away in time. She thought of what to say when it stopped—thought of the place. Before the wide half-circle of her finish was done she was impatient to say it. "Come and have supper with me. When do you finish here?"

"At eleven, but this is my evening off. I'll be through at nine." He added: "There's dancing from eight-forty to nine."

She hesitated, then: "I'll be here at half-past eight."

"Right, comrade." His brown eyes snapped at her again. Everyone came swarming on to the ice; there were more here now. He glided in and out and away, and the next thing she saw of him, he was patiently piloting a perfect duffer of a fat woman round and round.

What a thing to do! She didn't even know his name. Should she get out of it? Difficult now. Was she a perfect idiot? What would anyone say? Was she being—doing—was it *safe?* But damn it all, he'd called her comrade. It was like Donald vouching for the man himself.

She told the Taylors she might be late that night, not to worry or sit up for her; she had a key. They usually went to bed about ten. No, she wouldn't want any supper.

They danced again—she'd never skated twice in one day before. Between dances he said nervously: "I've got to change, I shall be ten minutes after the end. You can't wait here, Mrs. Galton. Will you wait for me outside?"

She nodded: "Very well."

"And if you didn't mind waiting along at the corner by the 'Red Lion'—it is all right there, it is very high class, yes, indeed—I don't want them to know I am meeting anyone, least of all a patron."

She laughed ; it was all being rather fun after all—it was like breaking rules at school ! " Right-o ! " she said.

She waited at the corner, watching people ; a man spoke to her, but she froze him. She was excited. By and bye her skating instructor came hurrying along ; he was wearing an overcoat and a felt hat, but his eyes were as bright as ever, bright and a little frightened. And, by the way, what was there odd about his voice ? He touched her hand : " Will you have a sherry ? " he said. She shook her head. " I didn't *think* you would," he said, " but——"

" Now look here," Dione said, " we've got to get everything clear. This is my evening. I pay for everything. See ? "

He hesitated. " Right ! " he said at last and smiled at her. " Well, Mrs. Galton, where are you taking me ? "

She was taking him to a little Italian restaurant she had been to sometimes with Phœbe three years ago ; it would be quiet and pleasant to talk in ; she didn't think it was very popular in Sallington. They took the tram across the river, no chance of conversation there as they had to strap-hang. In the Square she said : " By the way, what's your name ? "

" Idris Pritchard," he said. " I was wondering when you'd ask."

" I remember hearing the name from Donald," she said, " but I can't remember quite what he said." They walked along to the restaurant. " What do you usually do about supper ? "

" I mostly go home and have tea and bread and butter—sometimes I have something at the ' Red Lion.' "

" What do they pay you ? "

He looked at her sideways. " It's not too bad," he said, " All depends on how we get booked for lessons and dances."

"And that depends on your making yourself liked by people?"

"That's the idea, Mrs. Galton."

"It must be very odd. And then you give a percentage to the Communist Party, don't you?"

"That is so."

"That's according to what you get, isn't it? Oh, sorry, I forgot it was all secrets! I won't ask you any more. Here's the place."

She took her coat and hat off and he did the same. How very curly his hair was! "Do you like Italian kind of food?" she asked.

He answered: "You order. It is a long time since I've had anything of the sort."

"Red wine or white?"

"As you like."

She ordered Chianti and a tolerable Italian meal. What was he thinking, sitting silent opposite her? "Do you like your work at the rink, Mr. Pritchard?"

"Sometimes; I liked it to-day."

One couldn't parry a look of that brightness and sharpness, sharp and yet defensive, like some animal that isn't sure one doesn't want to hurt it. She laughed: "But sometimes it must be boring. What do you think of us all?"

"It is just the way one earns one's living. If a good skater comes along we look at them. I looked at you before I saw who you were. And I was wanting to dance with you."

"I take it you usually get what you want!" Having said that, she wished she hadn't—it was obviously rather unkind. Yet his confidence and curly hair invited it; it was the answer she'd have made to a man with an assured income.

" Only when I've got a fair deal," he said, " and that doesn't happen often."

" Why not ? "

" If people of my kind got a fair deal, I would not be in the Communist Party."

" Tell me about that. How long have you been in it ? "

He hesitated, looking across at her. " Would you like to know the whole of my life story, Mrs. Galton ? "

" Yes, I should," she said, " but eat, won't you ? " She poured him out some Chianti. She wanted to know what there was at the back of that smile, which didn't seem somehow to mix completely with Communism.

He said : " Well, I was the youngest son of a farmer in Glamorgan." (So that, she thought, accounts for the accent.) " I was the clever boy of the family, and I won scholarships. So they sent me to college. Well, I was in my second year there when my father found out something."

He stopped and his eyes looked dark, not bright. Already she began to feel soft with sympathy for the boy he had been. " Tell me," she said.

" Well, Mrs. Galton, it was a girl at home, in the dairy. My mother found she was six months gone. She blamed me. And father said I was to come back from college and marry her. He was a very religious man, my father. But I was not coming back from college for her ; I knew she had been with a lot of other men. She did not mind who she had. So I told my father I would not marry her. She was older than I was, too. I was right, surely, Mrs. Galton ? "

" It was rather bad luck on the girl, either way. How old were you ? "

" Nineteen. My father said I was never to come home again and I should get no more money from him to keep me at college. And I have never been home since then. I do not know if my father and mother are alive or dead now. So I tried to stay on at college on my scholarship, but I could not do it! In those days I was apt to spend more money, Mrs. Galton. When I left college that was the first big time I did not get what I wanted."

"I'm sorry," she said; "that was bad luck. Go on." Their risotto had come; she helped him, looking for the nicest bits to give him, as though he'd been one of the children.

"Well, I had a piece of luck after that—it was the college people who wanted to do what they could for me. I had a year as tutor to a Swiss boy; he was sixteen. We lived at Cartigny, near Geneva. Do you know that country, Mrs. Galton?"

"I've only just passed through. It must be nice. Were you happy?"

"It was the happiest time of my life. Especially the winter, yes, indeed! I had skated before, but I learnt to skate well there, and I went ski-ing with Pierre—that was the boy. It is not likely I shall ever do that again."

"Oh, but you will!" Dione said; "you must!" She had caught the slight movement of his shoulders and body, remembering as he spoke of it; it was unbearable that he shouldn't ski again.

He smiled a little. "I got a skating prize that winter—I never knew how useful to me it was going to be!—and in the evenings I often went dancing. Pierre used to beg to come too, and sometimes I took him, but not often. I met a girl there, she was one of the typists at the S.D.N.—sorry, the League of Nations. She was a French girl, but I knew some French then. She gave me Marx to read; I had not thought much about politics before that. And when I got to know her better she told me some funny things about the League. Whenever I see those good little leaflets the League of Nations Union sends round free I think of what Zizi told me."

" What sort of things ? "

" Oh, funny stories. Perhaps you would not care for them, Mrs. Galton. Zizi and me, we were—good friends —at Geneva, but I didn't save. Then that job came to an end. Still, I had read Marx and a big lot of Lenin, in French paper-covered translations, and I knew where I stood as much as one does know at twenty-one. My next job was at a school; it was a preparatory school, low fees, but a fine school crest and a Latin motto and all that. You will not know much about those schools, Mrs. Galton, but there are plenty of them ; they don't pay their masters well. I made less than I make here and worked harder. The food was awful, especially after Switzerland. Still, it was a gentleman's job ! I got some tutoring to do in the holidays, and I was there a year and a half. I didn't have so much time for reading or politics and I had to keep quiet about what I thought, anyway. Well, that was in '27, at the beginning of the slump, and there were real gentlemen looking for work by then, Oxford and Cambridge degrees and the right accent. One of them did me out of my job at the school. Well, I could not wonder ; he was what they wanted. He looked a gentleman—I saw his photo—and I don't, do I, Mrs. Galton ? "

" What *does* that matter ? Don't tell me it bothers *you*, Mr. Pritchard ! "

" And it's against one being Welsh. And my accent—though I'd never been back to Wales all that time—I have a nasty accent, I have indeed, Mrs. Galton."

" I think it's rather nice," Dione said, " but how can you mind about that if you're a Communist ? "

" I don't mind," he said. (But he does, really, she

thought.) "I'm only showing you how I was chucked out of my job on class grounds."

"I'm sorry!" she said. "Oh, will you have coffee, Mr. Pritchard?"

He looked at her. "I was asking myself," he said, "could I dare invite you to come back to my room and have tea with me there? I did not think you'd care to come, though."

She felt the tiniest shiver again: was it *safe?* Would Tom like her to——? Then told herself not to be a fool. "I'd like to," she said, "but isn't it late?"

"You'd have time just to have a cup of tea. I'd like to make it for you. And—you wouldn't call me Idris?"

"Yes, if you like. Then you must call me Dione, as Donald did."

"Dione, Dione," he said gently, "that is a nice name, whatever."

She paid. They took a south-bound tram—a 73, she noticed, the same she had taken going to see Agnes Green. It was almost empty, and as it bumped along he leaned near her and told her the rest of his life: odd jobs, poultry farming with an elder brother, the only one of the family he had kept up with, small parts in films, and two jobs as skating instructor, first at a small south-coast ice-palace, then here. He'd been lucky to get this. They left the tram and walked towards his street; she noticed with pleasure that he didn't try to take her arm or anything silly. Yes, she thought, this is *safe;* I would have been a coward not to come. She asked him questions. Two things kept turning up in his story, one was politics—his growing sense of Marxism, books he'd read, meetings he'd been to—and the other was girls. There was a girl on the films that he spoke about very bitterly. It was horrid to think of one's fellow women being this sort of nuisance in the world, grit in the wheels of life. He was obviously the kind of man who could be hurt and got at by this kind of thing; he was sensitive. How he must hate some of his patronesses at the rink! She wanted so much to be kind to him, to show him that all women are not like that.

They came to the house; he let her in; there was a dim sort of gas light in the hall and a smell of cooking and general mess; she tripped on a hole in the lino going up the stairs. He unlocked a door on the top landing and went before her to light the gas. It was cold, but he lighted the gas fire, too. It was a dingy room, with a tin of cigarettes and some odd bits of china on the mantelpiece—souvenirs—two paper fans, a coloured picture of Lenin, a very Victorian one of Marx with a romantic beard, and a few photographs; she couldn't see them very well, but thought they were girls. There were two chairs, a chest of drawers, an iron bed. On the chest of drawers was an enamel tea-pot, a loaf and butter and one cup. It was horribly lonely and horribly moving; she wanted to cover it all with armfuls of flowers. Perhaps, in the C.P., he didn't mind what his surroundings were like. She sat down and he put the kettle on the gas-ring. He turned round, still kneeling on the floor, and said: "It is not a nice room; no indeed. But the comrades come here. I am that glad you came. Now that we're here, I want to say that I know everything you did for one of the comrades. We at the centre have not forgot. That was why I called you comrade at the rink."

This was lovely! This was what made it worth while doing something. He'd answered as Agnes Green hadn't. She said to him what she'd said to Agnes. For a time, while the kettle boiled, they talked politics, she leaning forward in the chair, he looking up at her. She could make him understand!—he saw what she meant, he would be in brotherhood with her, he was not keeping her out of the thing he was part of! Or—did he evade her a little? She wasn't sure. He poured out the tea. "I have only the condensed," he said; "will you have some?"

"I like it just as it is," she said; "I got used to that in Russia."

"If I had known you were coming this morning," he said, "I would have tidied up."

"But that's all right," she said, "and you oughtn't to try to do anything special for me."

"It is the first time there's ever been a—lady—in this room," he said; "I am not meaning it in a class sense, only you are a different kind, Dione—I can call you Dione?—you are my lady comrade."

She was rather touched and rather embarrassed. "I'm a woman like other women, Idris," she said; "there's no difference."

"Isn't there?" he said. He began to stroke the fur border of her dress. "It is a lovely dress, indeed," he said. "I shall be able to think of it having been here in my room. I do love soft things, and coloured things, and sweet things."

She didn't want him to think about her dress; she began to talk about pictures, sipping her tea. He knew the Sallington Art Gallery pretty well, and the London Galleries. She talked about Vienna and Basel, and modern French pictures at Moscow. Suddenly she saw his eyes get dark again, tears perhaps.

"I could hate you for having seen all that!" he said. "I do hate you as one of your class." He laid a hand on her knee. "But I am not hating you yourself."

She was reminded of Donald. She stroked the hand on her knee. "You shall have them, you shall have them!" she said; "I do so want you all to have them!"

"You do?" he said. "Truly? Dione fach, you want

us workers to have everything you've had, everything of yours?"

"Yes," she said, "yes," wanting so much to dispel the hate and envy in his mind, feeling intensely and painfully his needing all that but having to live in this dreadful, poky room, with nothing to look at but those two pictures of shouting Lenin and silly old Marx. "Yes, Idris," she said.

. . . . .

It was over. He was looking down at her in a curious blank way. She discovered that this jerking which was going on still in her body and mind was herself sobbing. She sat up, hastily, silently. The sobbing stopped. Even her heart was quieting. She still felt sore and bruised, but not in sufficient pain to let it show. She looked at him, staring him down. There was no sound in the room but the purring of the gas fire. "You—you'll want the bathroom." With a fierce effort of muscles she stood up straight and hard and stalked past him towards the door. He jumped in front of her and held it open. "I'll put on the light," he said, and opened the door in front. She heard him feeling about for matches, striking one. The gas-light came on. Again he held the door for her; he looked a fool; she didn't care what she looked like. She shut and locked the door, carefully not banging it.

God, how beastly, god, god. And all quite real. It has happened. Happened to me. Happened—for ever. Whatever else I think and imagine it will never not have happened. All the rest of my life to have my skin feeling, my mind feeling—and I thinking all the time in terms of Donald, thinking of the Communist Party as Donald! What a fool, what a sentimental little North Oxford fool, letting this filthy Welshman get me. And Marx and Lenin looking down at us all the time, and the smell of gas. Those spider words hanging between us in the smell of gas and tea-leaves, nasty hurting little words, bourgeois ideology, class scruples—but if I had really been a bourgeoise I wouldn't have been—decent to him. I'd have ticked him off, I'd have said something so hurting he wouldn't have been able to go on. Oh, if only I had! If only I hadn't been so bloody soft. Being a comrade. But it wasn't being a comrade, it wasn't kindness, he wasn't Donald, he turned into a horrible, blind, hurting animal. Oh, why, why—just because I was afraid of being a prude, afraid of being North Oxford—and then—oh, his cruel hairy legs, his sharp knees digging into me. . . . .

She chucked her head about wildly, wanting to bang it into something, stop it remembering. And then she felt like nothing but vomiting, and sat down on the floor. For a minute or two her head swam, then she lifted it and looked round. It was a dim, pathetic little bathroom and W.C., obviously used by the whole house, cleanish but a bit smelly. Above the bath was a shelf with seven tooth-brushes, all rather discoloured and nasty-looking. The paint on the bath was all off under the hot tap. There was a soft much-used cake of pinkish soap. She looked at it doubtfully, trying to remember what she had read of the disinfectant powers of soap. Anyway, thank God, she needn't be afraid of *that*. He'd been—careful. But oh, the foul, horrifying touch of the thing! She poked the soap with one finger and decided not to have anything to do with it. She washed hard at the cold tap and dried her face and body on her handkerchief; she didn't mind the bathroom towel so much for her hands. Now she had begun to shiver. But at least the feel of her body was beginning to change. It was mostly in her mind now that she felt this sickening shame and anger. She tugged the velvet dress down snugly over her hips. There, that was better. Her hair. She had a comb in her bag, but that was in the other room, and not for anything was she going back to him with her hair messed up. She looked about. There was a comb on the shelf by the tooth-brushes, a black comb, greyish with use. She hesitated, considered she could get her hair washed—yes and waved !—to-morrow, and held the comb under the tap and dried it vigorously on the towel. She combed her hair out flat and did it again. She put the comb back by the tooth-brushes, and suddenly she was overwhelmed by the nastiness, the inadequacy, the pity of this dreadfully private little room where the people in this house were used to strip themselves, see their bodies in the twelve-inch cracked mirror backed by the grimy bath and the tooth-brushes. No wonder Idris Pritchard was like he had shown himself to be. No wonder. Poor Idris. Poor people in this house. In the other houses like it. Oh, poor dears, poor dears, how could one blame them for anything !

She came back into the room ; Idris Pritchard was sitting on the bed ; he hadn't put on either his tie or his shoes. He didn't get up when she came in. " Well ? " he said.

She didn't mind looking at him directly ; at the same time she didn't particularly want to. " Turn on the gas, please," she said ; " I want my bag and coat."

He jumped up. " But you aren't going ! "

" Naturally," she said.

" Oh, Dione fach, not yet, not till you have said you are forgiving me ! You cannot indeed ! "

She wasn't going to be caught by brown hurt eyes any more. " Turn on the light, please," she said.

He stood in front of her ; he caught her hands. " You're angry with me now, are you not, Dione fach, are you not ? You were not wanting it, because you're a lady and I'm only a poor skating instructor that anyone can bully and do down. You hate me, don't you ? "

"Don't be a fool, Idris," she said, "let go my hands." He dropped them. She said: "Turn on the gas and be reasonable, and I'll stay and talk for a bit." He turned it on, looking at her over his shoulder. She found her bag and sat down in the chair where she had been before. "Idris," she said, "you—behaved very badly, but—living as you do, you've got to. I see that. It's society's fault. It's the people who made you live with that bathroom." He looked puzzled. "The people who oppress you, make you a slave. You were being like a slave when you did that to me, Idris—grabbing and hurting. But it's them I blame."

"You forgive me then, Dione fach, you do forgive me? I had to do it—you were so white, so lovely. And now you're so kind—so kind to me—you don't hate poor Idris——"

"Oh, shut up!" Dione said, trying to be patient; "can't you see it's not a personal matter at all? If I were going to be personal about it—but I'm not. I'm looking at it as a Socialist. I'm trying to see you as one of a whole class of people who've had a bloody time and who can't help doing bloody things back." Still he looked puzzled; none of them had ever said anything like this before. "Good god!" she said, suddenly impatient, "isn't that simple enough? Have you got a better Marxist scheme for it? Now, you can just think it over, because I'm going." She picked up her coat and began to put it on.

He watched her; he said: "You will not go, Dione."

"And why not?"

"Because you will be kind and nice and lovely; indeed yes, you will stay with me for to-night."

"I certainly shan't. I've been quite kind enough." She heard her own voice hardening with anger.

"But you will." Suddenly his eyes snapped open at her;

he said savagely : " I have got you now, lady, Labour lady ! I am a proletarian, I am going to show you ! "

For a moment she was astonished and frightened ; then she said : " You aren't a proletarian. You're only an imitation 'Varsity man ! Get out of my way." For he had his back to the door. That hurt him—she saw it did. But now she wanted to hurt. Idris Pritchard calling himself a proletarian—he ! When she'd known, and how well, Donald MacLean's hard, work-scarred hands.

He said sulkily : " You needn't be frightened. I will not hurt you. But you will stay, yes, Dione fach ? I promise, I will be good. Only I cannot let you go from me like this —not so soon."

" I've told you already," Dione said, " I'm going."

" You cannot go," he said, " because all the trams have stopped."

She looked at her watch. It was only too probable. Hell. " Then I shall walk," she said, calculating quickly. Fifteen miles to the Taylors'. No, seven into the Market Square, and there'ld be taxis. She opened the door and was through.

He hadn't counted on that. He caught hold of her to pull her back ; he was a good deal stronger than she was. She caught at the door jamb, slipped and suddenly saw what to do. She kicked with all her force at his stockinged feet, getting him full on the toes with her shoe. He yelped with pain, letting her go, hopping on the other foot. She turned and bolted down the stairs, heard him after her, ran at the front door, praying for luck, turned the right handle, and got out and tore down the street clutching her bag.

Under the lamp at the end she stopped panting. Was he going to follow ? Apparently not. She went down the next street at a half-run, and realised she didn't know at all where she was. The tram-lines ? Perhaps this way ?

There wasn't a soul about to ask, or even a lighted house. Between lamps she looked up at the stars; it was a clear night. That was Cassiopeia; oh, and there was the Plow, over that house, and the Pointers. She'd been going wrong after all. To get to Sallington Market Square follow the Pole Star. This was easier said than done. None of the streets pointed directly north; she looked at their names as she came to them, hoping for a clue; sometimes she ran; but she was getting more and more tired, aching from the middle outwards. Pole Star, North Star, over Scotland, over the dark lochs and the slithering seals, quiet Pole Star over stiff Saint Finnigal. Pole Star, North Star, Polaris. That star drew nigh. Not that star. A different star, another saving star. That star drew nigh to the north-north-west. That would be about over the Power Station from here. The Power Station going on all night. And there it did both stop and stay: right over the place where Lenin lay. Another street. She looked at the name: Saffron Street. The other end of Saffron Street. Again, suddenly, she began to run. She came to the right number, but couldn't see a light. She knocked. She knocked again. She listened; there seemed to be nothing but her own panting, scuffling breath. She heard steps. Someone opened the slit of the letter-box and called: "Who's there?" She recognised the voice—what luck! "It's me—Dione Galton!" She stepped back, so that her face could be seen. There was a fumbling of chain and lock inside, then the door opened and there was Agnes Green in a blue flannel dressing-gown.

"Come in," she said. "What's the matter? Are you ill?" Dione walked in steadily enough and then clutched at the blue flannel shoulder: her knees were giving. "Come up," said Agnes Green, holding her competently under the arm, "can you manage?"

" Yes," whispered Dione, and managed the stairs. Agnes Green opened the door ; there was the same room, the same chair. She sat down in it, shuddering all over, trying to shake off those hands, legs, lips, everything. " Have you any brandy ? " she asked.

" I'm afraid I haven't, but I'll make you some tea."

Dione nodded weakly. " That'll do splendidly." Everything happens over tea in Sallington, she thought.

Agnes Green went out to fill the kettle ; when she came into the room again she found Dione's eyes waiting for her, calling her back. She went over to the chair. " Now, my dear, what is it ? "

" Idris Pritchard."

Agnes Green's hand came down strongly on to her shoulder : " What did he do to you ? Was it—rape ? "

" Something of the sort," Dione said. " But I expect it was partly my fault."

" It always is. Don't bother about faults. Has he hurt you much ? "

" Yes," Dione said ; she was perilously near crying again.

" The dirty little Welsh devil ! " said Agnes Green violently, " now—think carefully. Was he using any precautions ? "

" Yes," said Dione again, lower ; that particular memory was too much for her nerves ; she began to cry hard.

" My dear," said Agnes Green, " my dear," and patted her rather awkwardly. Then she said : " You're luckier than some. There was a girl. She was one of my old pupils. He did the same thing by her, but he wasn't so careful."

" What did she do ? " Dione asked tremulously.

" It's down with her mother in the country. She got her affiliation order all right. But she lost her job."

" Oh, how beastly. How horrible. How could he. A man who does that——"

" He has been very unhappy in his life."

" That's what he told me. Otherwise—I wouldn't have given him the chance. He—he called me comrade. And all that."

" He did, did he. That was a dirty trick. Not even as if you were a comrade."

" Oh—aren't I ? "

" Well, you haven't joined the Party, have you ? But he made you feel—— Oh yes, I know. He's a regular little play-actor. Your tea's ready, Mrs. Galton."

" Thank you. Won't you call me Dione ? "

" If you like."

" You know, Agnes, the last thing he did was to try and make me stop the night with him. So I fought him and ran away. Then I found your street."

" You've had a nasty time, my dear. How are you feeling now ? "

" Pretty rotten. Sort of—all messed about."

" Would you like to stay the night ? You can have that sofa or my bed."

" Oh, could I ? That would be kind of you, Agnes. I'm staying at Marshbrook Bridge and it's such a long way back."

" I've got some extra blankets. My dear child, you're still trembling."

" Oh, he was a beast. One ought to be able to *punish* people——"

" There are several things you could do to punish him if you liked."

" What ? "

" You could tell them at the ice rink that he'd been rude to you—made advances—they'd give him the sack. There are plenty of skating instructors going."

" But I couldn't do that."

"Why not—Dione?"

"It wouldn't be fair. It would be taking advantage of my—economic position. You know that. And it wouldn't be any satisfaction to me either!"

"You could tell his landlady—she'd turn him out. Rooms are difficult to find nowadays."

"That's no good either. I can't be mean to him even if he was to me. I should like just to hit him and hit him and hit him!" Now she was crying again.

"Dione, my dear, my dear, try and outgrow that! Listen, you've done something already. You've complained to the Party officially. That's me, you know. I'll take it up as a Party matter; it's more than a private affair this time."

"He kept on asking if I forgave him, and I kept on saying I knew it wasn't really his fault; it's the way society's treated him. But he didn't understand."

"No, I don't suppose he's often had that said to him before. And you meant that?"

"Yes, honestly. You understand, don't you, Agnes, I—I bear no ill-will against him as part of the people who've been oppressed; they've every right to hit back. I'm ready to be hit back at. It's just as an individual I want to hurt him!"

"I think I see," Agnes Green said; "you don't, in fact, hold it against the Party?"

"Of course not."

Agnes bent suddenly and gave her a funny little cold kiss. "By the way, are you going to tell your husband?"

"I don't know. I hadn't thought. We usually tell one another everything."

"Well, think it over. Some more tea?"

"Agnes, there's one thing that's worrying me. Idris Pritchard will hate me rather after this, I think. After my getting away. And apparently he knows all about Donald. Is he safe ?"

"Absolutely safe. You needn't worry. He's—extraordinarily trustworthy in some ways. And he's intelligent; that's how he knows how to get round people. And he's one we can count on for anything secret or dangerous. You've seen the worst side of him, Dione. He must have been getting at you from the beginning."

"He was such a lovely dancer. And now I shan't ever be able to go there to skate again. Oh dear, I left my skates there, too; I thought I'd be sure to go back."

"Perhaps you will. My dear, how late it is! And I've got a class at nine to-morrow morning. But I'll let you sleep on."

'No, I ought to go back, or the Taylors will worry. Oh, Agnes, Mr. Taylor's ill and he oughtn't to have to go back to work, but he's got to—it's his only chance. Otherwise they'll be getting on to the Means Test."

Agnes smiled. "Well, I won't draw morals to-night," she said. "But you're a nice woman, Dione. I like you."

"You said that just like Donald," Dione said, and yawned.

"Very likely. We've probably both got the same standards. Now come along to my room and I'll find you a nightgown and a hair-brush. You'd better take an aspirin. And be quite sure not to dream about it."

"No, I won't, Agnes," Dione said obediently.

## OXFORD 4

SLOWLY Dione woke up, lifted heavy eyelids, wondering where she was; she saw Agnes Green laying the table for breakfast. Oh, lord, she said to herself, this is next morning; and I've slept like a pig; and I'm feeling all right and this is all there is to it! She sat up, feeling faintly silly in her hostess's wincey nightgown. "I shan't be ten minutes," she said, and went off to wash. The bathroom here was a bit better—the original Victorian *décor* had been painted over—but it wasn't exactly cheerful either. She looked at herself in the glass; she appeared to be much the same as ever. What did it amount to? Certain physical memories, extremely unpleasant, no doubt—so much so that she had better put them away and suppress them hard, at any rate for a few weeks. After that they would probably have lost their force. And beyond that? Well, she'd had something done to her that she'd been afraid of—what she'd told Donald she'd been afraid of in strange, unsocialist towns—and by a friend of his! And now—would she cease to be afraid? Possibly; that remained to be seen. And equally she was still afraid of the revolution, of violence and discomfort and general unpleasantness, and perhaps equally it would break over her like this, but leave her virtually unshaken, and ready for breakfast.

Agnes Green had made tea and toast and was now boiling eggs. "Do you have nine o'clock school every day?" Dione asked. "How on earth do you manage to get anything else done? You do a good deal, don't you?"

"I'm busy at the moment," Agnes said, "over the hunger-marchers. Our contingent is due to start for London in three days."

"Will it do any good?"

"If it does nothing else it will show people what's going on—the thing the newspapers and their own comfortable interests don't let them see. And it will be good for the men to meet in thousands; they'll be able to practise solidarity. Do you like a hard or soft egg?"

"Hard, please. I wonder what Parliament will say to them."

"That doesn't interest me very much, I'm afraid," Agnes said. "We're through with Parliament. I know you believe in it still, Dione, or you think you do. But I wonder if you do really? Can you possibly hope to achieve Socialism by Acts of Parliament?"

"A good deal of it, I think. But of course something else is needed, too."

"Direct action."

"A change of heart."

"That won't come without the other."

"What about education?"

"No time, Dione. Besides, you can educate a few high-brow children, but you don't touch the elementary schools. I spend my working time shoving at the structure of education, hoping to budge it an inch. I try not to let a school hour pass without shoving a little. A good many of us are doing that; we're bound, as a profession, to see things as they are to some extent. But oh, my dear, it's so tiring always to keep on remembering to do it, to keep on thinking of new ways of interesting the children without letting them know what's happening. Sometimes I almost give up; it would be so easy just to do plain State teaching!" She laughed a little, but it was such a tired laugh; Dione realised what it must be like for her to be making this effort the whole time, to be in a constant state of strain.

"Come and stay with us one holiday," Dione said, "and talk to Tom about education; I think you'd agree a lot."

"Should we? Well, perhaps we should. Thank you. I should like to see Oxford some day. You've got children, haven't you? Yes, that must be pleasant in many ways. By the bye, you know that the Lancashire and Birmingham contingent of hunger-marchers will be due to come through Oxford on Saturday or Sunday? Perhaps you'll see something of them."

After breakfast they went as far as the trams together and said good-bye; neither of them had mentioned Idris Pritchard. Dione was back in Marshbrook Bridge a little after ten. When she got to the Taylors' street she realised something was up; there were neighbours at doors and windows and a small group by the Taylors' front gate. Obviously they must be worrying about her—the Taylors must be raising a search-party. Oh, hell, what shall I say? She hurried along to the house, and as she got there Mrs. Taylor rushed out and flung her arms round Dione's neck; and just as Dione, embarrassed and much touched, was going to explain that it was terribly sweet of her but really she needn't have got into such a fuss, Mrs. Taylor sobbed out: "Oh, Mrs. Galton, Mrs. Galton, we've won the cross-word!"

That settled the Taylors' immediate problem. Mr. Taylor, interviewed and photographed by the *Herald*, told about his accident and how now he could go away for a change and rest. Dione was photographed, too; it was rather shaming, but good for the constituency. At any rate, she had contributed two clues! And then, having recovered her skates, she went back to Oxford.

Again a great flood of domesticities overwhelmed her, children and house and garden—the bulbs to get in—and a thousand and one things. But at least Tom seemed more himself; he was able to talk now about his Russian time calmly, and, she thought, happily. It was wonderfully pleasant to have the evenings with him again. She would finish off the household chores and have a bath and change into some silk dress that left her arms and neck bare, and brush her hair carefully; then she would go and say good-night to the children, all warm and cuddly in bed—sometimes Morag had dinner with them, too—and tell stories or sing them songs. Then she would come downstairs; usually Tom would be waiting in the hall, reading a paper, and he would look up and watch her coming down the shallow steps towards him, watch the light on her arms and neck and hair. Then there'd be the table laid in the dining-room with silver and flowers—not chrysanthemums, they were too wintery, but she found crisp late roses, or two or three odd dahlias, or striped African marigolds, or bramble and hip branches from the hedge by the Cherwell. On a fine night she never had the curtains drawn, and they could look out from the candle-lit table to moon or stars over the orchard trees. And—she wasn't really greedy, but she'd had enough strong tea and bread and butter to last her a lifetime!

Here was her Tom again, behind the candles, talking about work, pupils or colleagues or books, the affairs of the world, asking her advice or arguing pleasantly, both leaning forward between the live quivering little lights, each so aware of the person the other one was at the back of the argument! Blowing the candles out and going through into the sitting-room, that wide, happily memoried room, books lying about, chairs one could properly lie back in, good chairs to snuggle up in with Tom, to be kissed or have one's face and hands stroked, and not to have to wash up or think of clues for cross-words. Pleasant —oh, ridiculously pleasant!—to be among decently good furniture and pictures. How nice Phœbe's pictures were, and the Nash water-colour and the reproductions of Degas and Gaugin in her bedroom! Ordinarily she wouldn't notice them for weeks except as patches on the walls, now she looked at them as pictures ought to be looked at. And the wood-fires—that elm she and Tom and the odd-job man had felled last winter!—and the Orrefors mirror and the linen sheets on the bed. It wasn't that she minded cotton sheets, but all the same, oh——! Was it terribly wicked to enjoy it all so much when her friends at Marshbrook Bridge were out of it, when that bright girl Dorothy was still scrubbing between the cold quarries and crying because she couldn't get the smell away?

She didn't tell Tom about Idris Pritchard; that was all finished, she wasn't bothering about it, why bother him? He'd imagine it far worse than it probably was. The first twenty-four hours it was extraordinarily difficult not to tell him; they'd always told one another everything. Yet it would obviously just be selfish to tell this. But she wrote about it to Donald. That was rather a help, because, though mostly she just never wanted to think about it again, yet sometimes the details began to leak past the barrier she had put up and threatened to swamp her unless she got rid of them by telling. Perhaps, though, it was only the first few days that would be so acute.

She did tell Tom about Agnes Green, and he was quite pleased at the prospect of having her to stay. "Thank goodness," he said, "they haven't put anyone up against our people for the Municipals at Marshbrook Bridge."

"They wouldn't have a chance. They've got hardly any membership there."

"Would that stop them? They'd do it for a platform, not to get in. But it would be a bloody nuisance all the same. I believe young David Hawkes is going over to them after all."

"What about his young woman?"

"Oh, Beattie's been adjourned *sine die*. I much prefer the C.P. He may get his heart broken a bit either way, but at least you don't have to wait six months for the decree to be made absolute if you want to get out of a political party. You know the hunger-marchers are coming through to-morrow, don't you? He's going down to the Corn Exchange to help with them; I warned him he might get progged."

"I thought of going too, with Zita; even if the Labour Party won't have anything to do with it officially, it's perhaps just as well to have a few individual members about. And I take it we might make the progs feel a bit awkward!"

Tom laughed: "Yes! I gather from Mason that what's happening at Marshbrook Bridge is that George Grove and Mrs. East have organised a committee on their own, but he doesn't know officially. I'll look if I've got an old pair of shoes for you to take down."

The next day, then, Dione and a few other grown-ups went down to the Corn Exchange and were given jobs by the undergraduate organisers. The men marched in, singing, and flopped on to chairs and floor while speeches were made and supper was got ready. A good many of them were sent off to the first-aid detachment in the gallery; they had been rather badly knocked about by the police at an earlier halt, and there were a lot of cuts and broken heads. When she got back that evening Tom asked her what she'd thought about it. "I'm going back to-morrow morning early to help with breakfasts," she said.

"I'd thought of taking Morag, but I won't. She'd feel all romantic about the chaps with bandaged heads. Some of the undergraduates were feeling pretty romantic about it, too; a good many of them had never seen anything of the kind before, I suppose."

"Yes, they've led sheltered lives, poor dears. Are they—shocked?"

"I think so. Certainly one or two of the girls were. And some of them, I believe, felt that it was really going to be some use, that this was the beginning of the—end. Like in 1914. The war to end war: the revolution to end revolutions. It must be fun to be twenty."

"But what did the hunger-marchers think of them and the whole lovely altruistic soup-kitchen?"

"Half of them didn't think; they were too tired. Some of them were friendly, but I expect a good many thought we were a lot of mutts to betray our own interests like this."

"So we are, so we are," said Tom. "But we can't help ourselves—once we look over the garden wall."

"I take it quite a lot of them are out for what they can get, and a bit of revenge too. And I take it there are a certain percentage who'd chuck it all and go on a lovely blind if one gave them a hundred pounds."

"Lord, yes. People have to be used to money to see it for the rotten thing it is. Equally we don't appreciate how fine the chaps are who don't get corrupted when money still means such a lot to them. I suppose it's a matter of proportion. I wonder whether I'd, say, chuck everything for a hundred thousand pounds? No, it wouldn't be good enough. Nothing under a million would tempt me—and a Pacific Island thrown in."

"They wouldn't ask one to chuck everything; they'd only ask one to be moderate, not to go so quick. That would make it much harder."

"Who's 'they'?"

"I don't know. Representatives of the Campbell Women and the Elephant."

"But one would know them by the cloven hoof, wouldn't one?"

"Yes, if one looked, but one wouldn't look. It's so awkward asking people to take off their boots in the drawing-room, especially if they've started by making an offer. Besides, it wouldn't be straight money for us, Tom; it would be power of some kind: a newspaper: or being Prime Minister. Wouldn't it?"

"Or a title—because one's wife liked it so much. Baroness of Banbury Road. Don't pull my hair! You'd look sweet in a diamond tiara! No, I don't think it's even that, Dione. I think it's the other way on: being frightened of losing what we've got. Of losing all this and going to live for ever and ever in Carisbrook Road. Yes, that gives you the creeps, doesn't it, my girl?"

"But it wouldn't be like that. One would just be overcrowded for a bit."

"Like the Nikolaevskys. But then, you see, they've succeeded in the U.S.S.R. It's all right now. But they didn't know at the beginning that they'd succeed. It was pretty unlikely, really, and it's those people at the beginning who needed the courage. But supposing one didn't succeed —supposing one got involved in an unsuccessful revolution——"

"Then I suppose one would be shot."

"It mightn't even be as easy as that. Some of us might be shot or hanged and the rest imprisoned for life, as some people are imprisoned at the moment in various civilised countries—a thing one might well remember every time one walks in one's garden—and at any rate it would be seen to that one never got another job. Our private incomes would probably have disappeared by then. And if we got safe out of England our children might still be kept and brought up properly by the other side—an interesting form of torture designed by the Fascist Government for some of their refugees. We always talk as if we were bound to succeed, but—oh, it's a jolly prospect."

Dione shivered: "Well, at least we're facing it."

"Not all the time. But still, we have been warned. Well, I somehow hope we shall avoid being gassed, that's all. I'm quite sure the authorities wouldn't mind in the least what they did to us. We'd be vermin. Rats, Dione. Perhaps we'll end up on the dung heap, after all, our faces blue and a little bloody froth——"

"Oh, Tom, chuck it—you'll have bad dreams!" She knew he would if he got back to Nœux-les-Mines; he always did. "What is the use of frightening ourselves, anyway? Tell me something else, Tom. Are you hearing from Oksana?"

"Yes," he said, "you don't mind?"

"Mind——! You great idiot. Is she—fairly cheerful?"

"I think she minded a lot more than she thought she would," Tom said slowly. "But she's taking it out in television and aeroplane engines. Only she doesn't write English as easily as she speaks it, and—letters are always rather unsatisfactory."

"I suppose you could telephone to Moscow?"

"What would be the good? No, we're all right, Dione; don't you worry. It's only every now and then it gets one badly. I wonder if you'd care to write to her some day?"

"Oh, Tom, I wanted to, but I didn't know if you'd like me to! And—I took some snapshots of you, Tom, at Auchanarnish: when you were working. You didn't know. Can I send them?"

"Please, my dear."

So that was a little disentangled. But as to the revolution, as to what may be going to happen, what can one do but act as it seems best at the moment and be aware of danger without being terrified all the time?

On Sunday morning she went down early to the Corn Exchange and helped over the men's breakfast. Most of them had taken advantage of the chance of a bath, and during the morning they wrote letters, mended their clothes and patched up their banners. Dione took a batch of mending and sat down to it. Various men came up and talked to her. Some were convinced and intelligent Communists, some were politically very vague. A few were just cheery popular kind of folk who liked being with pals and playing the mouth-organ. Some were bad at talking and others a little too good. There were all kinds of faces, the narrowed eyes of fanatics, the tough bones and muscles of men who looked like N.C.O.'s and were probably skilled factory hands, the wondering faces of Lancashire lads who'd never been in strange parts before, a few definitely stupid and definitely evil, occasionally a very sympathetic face. Some had fairly solid clothes, but most of them were in an incredibly bad state of repair; shirts could only be cobbled together to hold for a few days longer. A good many boots and shoes and oddments of clothing, as well as money, had been collected in Oxford, and were eagerly taken by those who were worst off. Dione saw several of Tom's pupils, including young Hawkes, but didn't do more than nod to them; she felt she might be either a slight embarrassment or a slight dissipation of romance—like having one's mother looking on!

When she got home she found Tom had hunted out another pair of trousers and some socks. "But I'm not going down this afternoon," she said; "I must let Nurse have a Sunday out—she hasn't all the time I've been away.

And I ought to be at home myself. After all, it's an awful thing for a respectable don's wife to have missed three Sundays in term already! What *did* the callers think?"

"Morag poured out; she loved it. She got off with your Rhodes scholar. But what about my trousers?"

"Look here, I'll ask Nurse if she'd leave them. I know she's going down town." Nurse agreed to take them, and Dione took over the family. It was too wet to garden, so she read to them out of the Golden Cockerel Hans Andersen. "Which do you want?" she asked.

"*I'ld* like the 'Little Mermaiden,'" Morag said. "But it's no good reading it to Ian—he'll only howl. You'd better read 'Kay and Gerda.'"

When they came to the picture of Gerda in the boat, everyone stopped and looked at it. Brian kept on repeating that it was by his mother. Kenneth said he thought it was rather silly. Ian said: "I think it is a sad, sad picture."

"Why?" said Dione.

"Someone is chasing that lady," said Ian.

"I don't think so," Dione said, "she's only trying to find her friend and she's worried in case he's got lost."

"She is being chased," repeated Ian, and added confidentially: "I was thinking of elephants."

"He's been potty about elephants," said Kenneth scornfully, "ever since that elephant that came here. You didn't see it, Brian," he added unnecessarily.

"And it was such a nice elephant," Morag said, "once we'd given it buns. It was only hungry."

"Well, can I go on?" Dione said. "It's really not a sad story, Ian. Kay isn't really lost; she only thinks he is."

"Because she's silly," said Morag.

"Because she's a girl!" said Kenneth.

"Stow it!" Dione said warningly, and went on reading. None of them liked the picture of the ice puzzle, and when

Dione said it was a grown-up picture they clamoured that it had no right to be in a book of fairy tales. The story came to an end. Dione took Lilias up to change her into a pretty frock and told the others to wash. Then she went to her room to put on an Oxford Sunday tea-frock. Morag came to have her hair brushed. "How are the dreams nowadays, Lambie?" Dione asked.

"Oh, they got all right," Morag said, "after you came back. I just didn't know what was going to happen."

"I wonder if I was a pig to let you into it?" Dione said.

"Oh *no*, Mother!"

"But you don't mind still keeping it a secret?"

"Rather not. I've got school secrets that I don't tell you. And I expect," she added, "you've got secrets you don't tell me."

"Yes," Dione said, "I suppose I have. If people haven't started coming to tea, will you sing me something?"

"All right," Morag said, and they went down. "Will you play for me, Mother? I'll choose." She turned over the pages. "This one." Dione began to play. Morag stood with her hands behind her back and sang:

> "Oh can ye sew cushions, and can ye sew sheets,
> And can ye sing balaloo when the bairnie greets?
> And hie and ba burdie . . ."

Her voice rising to it was so sweet that Dione nearly cried. She knew how it would go on, to the woman on the Means Test, the Highland woman, the woman at Marshbrook Bridge, now or a hundred, two hundred years ago—or Morag foreseeing her own life—the voice went on relentlessly to the croon:

> "Hie-oh, ee-oh, what'll I do wi' ye?
> Black's the life that I lead wi' ye,
> Ower mony o' ye, little for to gie ye,
> Hie-oh, ee-oh . . ."

Then the first of the Sunday callers was shown into the room. Morag stopped in the middle of a bar.

It is curious to think of the calling going on at Oxford every Sunday afternoon in term. *O quanta qualia sunt ista Sabbata!* The strict practice has perhaps fallen off since the war, but still dutiful undergraduates and undergraduettes bicycle or 'bus along the Banbury or Woodstock roads, bicycle or 'bus up Boar's Hill and Headington Hill and Hinksey Hill, to call on the wives of their moral and intellectual tutors. And the wives, and sometimes the daughters, of the tutors, have ordered tea and bread and butter and sandwiches, and cakes from Boffin's or even Fuller's, to be made ready, and they are waiting with suitable conversational openings on their lips, and the ritual meal occurs. After that, many of the undergraduates also attend chapel.

Dione cut short the ritual by the necessity for putting Lilias and Ian to bed. Two Somerville girls came and assisted, but it was really rather heretical. Then it was Kenneth and Brian, who only needed supervising and shooing out of their bath the moment they had finished playing admirals with the nail-brushes. Morag always stayed up for Sunday supper, another Oxford ritual meal, at which hospitality can be dispensed without too much expense and often very pleasantly, though naturally it is not always such fun for the hostess who has had to arrange it all, avoiding gaffes, not asking together the protagonists in such University feuds as she knows of, and often having to accept snubs from the ruder and more popular undergraduates. Dione thought that it was on the whole good for Morag to learn the tricks of the hostess, being pleasant to a mixed bag of people, pretending to be interested in one conversation while listening to another, and in general making the wheels go round; Dione considered that all this would be useful to her whatever state of society she grew up into. To-day there were three pairs of young, Teddy the biologist, and the Opies. They discussed sport, literature, science, national and international politics; it was all very intelligent. Intellectually at least they were quite alive, all justifying the title of *homo sapiens*. Several of them were definitely above the average of good looks. There was, Dione thought, carving the cold chickens so that they went round, with enough white left for Lilias to-morrow, a definite case for the Oxford Sunday supper. And how were the men at the Corn Exchange amusing themselves?

Dione asked Nurse if she had left the trousers. "Yes," said Nurse, "and I was fair horrified, Mrs. Galton, at the condition of those poor lads. I and my friend that I was meeting, we stayed an hour mending their clothes. And they say there'll be a contingent from Scotland in the same condition!"

"Yes," Dione said, "it's fully as bad there."

"But then how," said Nurse startlingly, "can you and Mr. Galton rest content with making speeches?"

"But we don't," Dione said. "We're trying to do things as well, and we do get a certain amount done. At any rate, we stop things getting much worse—though some people say we oughtn't to do that. It's all terribly slow compared with what one wants—only look what we're up against."

"Yes," said Nurse, "I understand you have great difficulties, but I had never thought to see shirts the like of those shirts I was mending this afternoon."

The next morning again Dione went down early to help with breakfast and giving the men a good send-off. She found herself marching with them and a bodyguard of police, through the Corn and Carfax and the High, slightly embarrassed, especially as she was immediately under a banner which read: " Our Babies are Starving." She and Zita Baker grinned at one another across a couple of earnest undergraduates. The Proctors were waiting on Magdalen Bridge, but showed no signs of taking action; Dione nodded to the Junior Proctor, whom she knew. They walked up Headington Hill, singing fitfully, and at the top found 'buses waiting to take them another stage of their journey. The 'buses had been subscribed for by friends at Oxford, but the 'bus drivers had given their own time. Part of the police guard got in with them; it was not certain how they would get back.

That, then, was that. The hunger-marchers went off on the rainy Wycombe–Uxbridge road to give their petition to Parliament, and the Oxford Labour Party and Communist folk who had seen them off went back to their various jobs. Dione had lunch with Tom in College—a thing she particularly liked doing; he was always very much the host and his scout was friendly. He showed her his reviews; they were almost exactly what he had supposed they would be, either by bright young reviewers who knew nothing about the subject, or else by other economists or historians; one knew in advance what old So-and-so was bound to say. The *Lit. Sup.* had been dull, the *New Statesman* annoying, the *Economist* intelligent. But he was no longer interested in that book, though Dione, who had typed it all, still was.

Tom had arranged to go down to Marshbrook Bridge to speak for the municipal candidates, on Thursday night this week, and again at the week-end. Dione was coming for the week-end, too, and would stay over the elections. She stoically agreed to speak so long as it wasn't for long. " They don't want you for long," Tom said. " Nobody listens to what either of us says, but it makes the thing look important, and then a few more of them will take the trouble to vote."

The next evening, while Tom was looking over essays, Dione thought she'd better look through the cards which had been left by visitors while she was away. May Bickerden had not called; perhaps that was inevitable. She hoped May wouldn't be a nuisance, and either come and weep or flounce out of other Oxford drawing-rooms when Dione came into them. Still, it didn't much matter.

What did matter? She hadn't, oddly enough, bothered about that so much at Marshbrook Bridge, that question which is at the back of the mind of all Scots—why?—what is the whole end of man? And if God isn't there to be glorified, but, instead and fairly obviously, the devil, the big devil of Sallington, what does one do? One doesn't glorify, but one does act. She had been uncomfortable, worried, angry and indignant there, sometimes almost in despair over what she was seeing and hearing, but she had always found something to do, even if it was a passive thing—being a listener to and sharer of someone else's unhappiness and injustice. She had never had to stop and consider, as she was doing now, sitting in a comfortable chair in a warm room, the visiting-cards in her lap. The water-beetle skates exquisitely on the summer-green Cher water: "But if he ever stopped to think of how he did it, he would sink." How easily one sinks between moments of action whenever one is alone, facing oneself in the mirror of time, trying to peer over one's own shoulder at whatever is behind, the infinite and everlasting background which one blots out with one's own body, or with images of kelpies or tractors. What does one hope to find if one looks hard enough? Pattern. Purpose. Reason. A nice Eddingtonian reason that one will be able to understand the day after to-morrow if one is a good girl and thinks hard enough! Well—is it likely? Why should the universe happen to fit in with the ideas of the upper middle classes of north-west Europe and North America at this particular and non-significant moment of time?

And yet here one is, so complicatedly alive, so capable of taking the most diverse actions, or making what are not perhaps, philosophically speaking, real choices, but which come to the same thing when one isn't fussing about determinism or Pavlov. Here one is, with one's clever hands, so much nicer to have than hoofs or wings, one's legs that run and skate and swim, the little lenses behind one's eyes constantly occupied with colour and line and movement, one's ear-drums vibrating ceaselessly to sound waves, one's tongue ready to taste—oh, all full of such possibilities!—and what does one do with it? One seeks, seeks, asking how to keep it from perishing, behaving all the time as if one were not *it*, but a little separate thing in the middle of it, an engine-driver. One clamours, oh, if only the engine-driver could get out and look round, unobscured by these eye lenses and ear-drums and nerves and brain between one's self (as one calls the engine-driver), and the thing one is experiencing, if only the engine-driver could get a perspective and see what life is all about—look round, take notes, nod to himself and then come back into the body, like Lazarus, and say: now, this is all right, old thing, go ahead. But that doesn't happen. One's thought pushes and pushes deeper into one instead of coming out at the back, as it feels like doing. And if one made it a little hole, a little bullet hole, it wouldn't come out with fuzzy wings or dove-shaped. No, Dione, the mere fact that you have that picture at all shows what a low level of civilisation you're really at—you haven't taken in the thought of the last three centuries at all—you're still obsessed with primitiveness; you're seeing Keres, as the first of the Greeks saw them three thousand years ago. After all, you're not much further on than they were. What's three thousand years? A hundred generations perhaps, no time for mutations, for any real alteration in human structure. Wait another million years, Dione, and then ask your question again, if you still want to.

But in the meantime, mustn't we think at all? Must it be always action? And if so, what then must we do? But to find that out, unless one is prepared always to obey some leader, who must either have taken thought—the thing we had agreed not to do—or else be incapable of deep thought, as perhaps the best leaders are, must we not think? I can follow leaders sometimes, during action; I can follow Tom, for instance, but only because I have made up my mind beforehand that it would be a good thing to do. Good? Good? No, that's a word I can't allow for the moment. Why do other people follow leaders? Lenin, Jesus, Mussolini, Napoleon, Hitler, Alexander, Socrates. The sons of God. No woman, of course. . . . There wouldn't be. Not yet. Wait a million years, Dione. Though, after all, is it a specially good thing to be a leader? (Good again! These dear old moralities.) Is it the leaders only who get to Cloud Cuckoo Borough—the people who've taken action? What about this nasty, unpleasant, tiring business of thinking—thinking with a brain which isn't yet adapted for this kind of thought, which is too near the monkey's still? Does that count for nothing? Oh, Dione, there you are again, with ideas of value going in! Worthwhileness. And one's got to do this kind of thinking alone; one can't share it, not even with Tom. He, being at the moment sufficiently occupied, would tell one, with the surface part of his thought, not to be silly. But is one silly? Hasn't one got to do this kind of spring cleaning sometimes? Isn't it valuable? Value,

value. . . . One can't get rid of these moral concepts, and what do they mean anyhow? They're all in terms of property. Value: that's a trader's idea, a Jew trader. Value: above rubies. And these commercial ideas have crept into all our morality, art and science. Funny. And probably this whole idea of purpose is a commercial idea. We see the universe as a vast transaction, a deal, a merger. And we say, what are we going to get out of it? What is our side of the bargain? Isn't it about time we chucked that idea and got hold of another?

Steady now, Dione, my dear; it seems to me just possible that this is rather a big criticism you've made. You'll have to put it away and take it out again another day and think it over. It's just possible that if you considered it long enough it would be the way out. Out of what? Out of this tangle I'm in. Out of Doubting Castle, where, you remember, people were shut up in separate cells—it was just a mistake putting Christian and Hopeful into the same cell. Yes, having got this far, it's about as far as you'll get to-day. In picking the lock. Images, images! One peers over one's shoulder in the mirror and at the back, instead of kelpies, one sees a great £ sign or a $ sign, or—what was the sign for a shekel? Caught up, caught up in image-making, in the eyes, in the body——

The telephone bell rang. Action! She jumped up, fluttering the cards off her lap: "Hullo?"

"Oh, it's you. Phœbe speaking. I'm in London, at Clare's. Dione, I'm going to the demonstration in Hyde Park on Thursday to draw hunger-marchers, and I want you to come up. Yes, to *draw* them. Because it interests me. Because I'm going to, anyway! And you're to come up, too. Oh, rot; you can easily. You can stay with Muriel. No, that's all right—I rang her up just now and she said she'd love to have you, so there! And listen—there's a studio party in the evening and I told them I was bringing you. Yes, the bloody limit, aren't I. But you've got to come. Tom at Sallington? All the better, you can hop off. Nonsense, the children will be all right. Oh, I'll pay your fare if you're going to be so silly! Yes, I've sold two of the water-colours. Yes, I'll meet you at Paddington. How's old Brian? Good, give him my love. So long, Dione."

"Tom," Dione said. Tom looked up from an essay and grunted. "Phœbe has just asked me to go up to London and see the Unemployed Demonstration at Hyde Park."

"Well, don't go and get arrested."

"Tom. I think I've had rather an exciting idea."

"Good. Tell me about it a bit later—I've got to get this stuff finished now." He sank into essays again. If one ever started term badly or late one never seemed to catch up again. He wouldn't get these essays finished till after midnight. He'd taken nearly an hour writing to Oksana. No, it wasn't writing the letter that had taken the time; it was sitting and wondering afterwards. Sitting alone in his own unhappiness. They were growing apart now, away from that lovely closeness of thought. England, Oxford was getting at him again. And he didn't know a thing about these wretched aeroplane engines of hers. It was two months and six—no, seven days, since he had seen her. The last time. "And miles around they'll say that I am quite myself again." Horrible. She hadn't liked Housman, though. She'd liked—oh, hell, man, get on with those essays!

## LONDON 2

DIONE caught the London train, feeling thrilled and faintly guilty, and settled down in a corner seat while the admirable—the so un-Russian!—Great Western Railway carried her rapidly towards Paddington. The new idea was tucked away somewhere, waiting to be taken out and reconsidered thoroughly on some new occasion. Every now and then she would cast an eye on it, to see that it was still there and not obviously idiotic. It seemed to be lasting. She thought it was a very definitely anti-Semite idea, or rather perhaps anti-Eastern—for she felt it might be welcome to the kind of Jews whom she knew: the Jews who were sick of their traditional pattern. It was an idea opposed to all the bargaining of the East and the Mediterranean basin, opposed to the idea of the scales of justice—taken from corn-growing Egypt into the rest of the world. An idea opposed to the Jealous God of Scotland, the Family Grocer visiting with his wrath those who questioned the price of his sandy sugar or attempted to evade an extortionate bill.

She had tried to explain her idea to Tom, but he was very busy and she was shy at explaining. He had said it was sound Marxist criticism. But wasn't it also opposed to some of the ideas of Communism—at any rate of Communism expressed in action? Idris had said he wouldn't have been a Communist if people like himself got a fair deal. There it was again, the commercial idea. And the dictatorship of the proletariat, wasn't that very much the people who'd had the worst of the bargain so far suddenly weighting the scales their way? Invoking the same old cock-eyed goddess of justice, only she'd got to have the bandage over the other eye!

But Socialism, but the idea of brotherhood? That wasn't really a commercial idea. Brothers and sisters don't bargain, do they? They don't insist on a Reason for the family being as it is, first Morag, then Kenneth, then Ian, then Lilias. Not, that is to say, unless an element of commercialism is introduced, unless the eldest brother gets the inheritance. If that happens, you have Jacob and Esau. Otherwise, you can dispense with a whole lot of moral ideas; that was what Aristotle was after, saying, "When people are friends there is no need for justice between them." That was presumably what Jesus was after, but the East and the Mediterranean were too much for him, and, besides, he hadn't quite got rid of the idea of the Family Grocer; how could he with that racial inheritance and that education—even if he saw through the education very young?

At Paddington Phœbe met her, and they put the luggage into the cloakroom. From there they walked to Hyde Park, talking hard all the time. There was a great crowd at Marble Arch, but none of the marchers had arrived yet, though there were plenty of police, on foot and mounted, who were already beginning to press on the crowd and send it, as far as could be seen unnecessarily, to one side or the other. It was a crowd which seemed very willing to talk, and both sisters got into conversation with people; a good many were wearing badges, Trade Union, Labour Party, F.S.U., League of Nations Union—every kind of organisation; it was as though everyone there wanted in some way to identify themselves; Dione regretted not having her red-and-green rosette. From what they could hear, most people seemed to be in sympathy with the hunger-marchers; at any rate those who were not kept silent. Probably, for instance, thought Dione, those two rather well-dressed women—they might have been shopping at Marshall's, say, and found themselves here quite by accident—they are thinking it's all a disgrace, but they're rather frightened of saying so out loud, even to one another. And that tall man who looks as if he manages or directs something: he doesn't like it at all—dangerous fellows, they ought to have been stopped! And those girls—no, they aren't disapproving, but it's just another occasion for giggles. Phœbe was already leaning against the railings, drawing in her note-book; for once, nobody took any notice or tried to look over her shoulder.

Suddenly Dione spotted someone she knew and dived through the crowd: "Hullo, Mr. Lambert, I haven't seen you since Moscow! At work?"

"More or less, Mrs. Galton, and you? Come to see the fun?"

"What's going to happen? Anything?"

"It depends on what you mean by anything. Not a 1926. Just a London row. It will look best in the foreign Press. You'll have to go to Paris or New York to see it as an occasion. There, they're coming at last."

Now one contingent after another of the hunger-marchers arrived at Marble Arch and were ordered this way or that through still increasing crowds that, on the whole, cheered them and greeted them friendlily. Each contingent had its banners and heads well up, most were singing, some had mouth-organs; often they were accompanied by sympathisers from the London industrial suburbs, and all had police guards marching with them, so that, as this north-eastern corner of Hyde Park began to fill up with marchers, it also filled with police. The Lancashire and Birmingham men came in and Dione squeezed to the edge of the pavement to shout to them—some of them recognised her and waved their caps. There was extra-loud cheering for the contingent of women marchers, also a certain amount of frivolous comment by the crowd. There was cheering, too, from the sentimental Londoners when they heard the bagpipes, and Dione couldn't get anywhere near the edge of the crowd to shout for the Scottish contingent. So far she hadn't seen the Sallington men, but they might have come another way—the police were constantly moving the spectators about, making them run sometimes, so as to open a different way. " Why are they doing that ? " Dione asked Lambert.

" They don't want to make it seem too important and official, and they want to keep people moving—it's the time-honoured way of dealing with crowds."

" The horses are beginning to get nervous, always being backed into people."

" My dear Mrs. Galton, the whole police force are nervous, and I very strongly advise you—though I don't suppose you'll take my advice—to get out of it before the row. They're much too frightened for a row not to be inevitable. I've seen the police looking like this in Berlin and Prague and New York. Luckily, our fellows aren't armed, so it won't be *that* sort of row. One bit of advice : if they charge, keep away from the railings."

" So as not to be squashed ? "

" Exactly."

Now Dione and Phœbe went through on to the grass, where speeches were going on, and the men were lining up to have tea at a canteen. Here were men from South Wales and Bristol, from the Potteries, from Staffordshire. They were talking and making friends ; small groups collected round a speaker or singer ; the onlookers made friends, too offering cigarettes and joining in the talk.

And here at last was a big banner saying, " Sallington Hunger Marchers."

She felt surprisingly shy of them. Why ? Because they're Sallington, she thought, and they're workers, but they're not Labour. They were most of them standing round one of the speakers, but obviously only the nearest could hear him ; others were talking and lighting cigarettes. Dione went nearer. Phœbe was busy drawing Bristol dockers ; three of them were sitting for her—in fact there'd been a bit of a scrap for the privilege ; they thought she was a journalist, at any rate she'd stood them fags and now she was telling them things about London that made them laugh—not that they believed her !

" Hullo, Harry," Dione said, having at last found someone she knew. " Well, what sort of time have you had ? "

" Oh, not too bad, Mrs. Galton," Harry said, " and fancy seeing you here ! There was a piece by Luton where it rained like—like it was sent by the Government !—but here we are, and we'll get the petition through. Won't we, Mrs. Galton ? "

" I hope so," she said. " Tell me, is Adam Walker here ? "

" Yes," said Harry ; " that's him. Him with the face."

Dione looked in the direction of his thumb and saw the scarred face of the ex-Service man. So this was Adam Walker. And he might have been hanged. And be dead now instead of enjoying the doubtful pleasures of hunger-marching. And he might have been killed sixteen years ago. In any earlier war he would have died of his head wounds, very quickly ; it was only the progress of modern science which had landed him alive and not too disfigured in Hyde Park on November 26th, 1932. There was a man standing with his back to her just beyond Adam Walker, rather better-dressed than the others, with a felt hat. That

hat——? He turned his head and she saw it was Idris Pritchard.

He didn't see her, and her first impulse was to bolt. The sight of him had roused every one of those filthy memories; the muscles of her body and legs jerked and twisted with acute unpleasantness, her heart began to beat chokingly. He turned away again and she contemplated his back with a decreasing distress. Nonsense, she said to herself, Dione Galton, don't be a coward! Why are you frightened—because you got the worst of a bargain? Well, haven't you decided you're not going to care about bargains ever any more? Now then, you heart, you're jumping like a puppy. Get back or I shall smack you! Now then, you knees, straighten up. Now, now, now, don't behave in this ridiculous, defeated way! You're not a cave woman.

The clamour in her body died down; she drove it past Adam Walker and tapped Idris Pritchard on the shoulder. "Well," she said, "what are you doing here?" He turned and looked at her; he was horribly startled and he hated her; she could see that. The fool, he would.

He said: "You know very well the reason why I am here."

"I'm afraid I don't," she said. "I don't really follow all your movements, Idris!" He deserved a little irony.

"Do you not?" he said, and stared at her. "Yes, you do, you bitch! They gave me the sack all right, two days after."

Dione didn't, as a matter of fact, mind being called a bitch; she thought it was rather funny. But she was extremely surprised. "From the rink, do you mean?"

"Yes," he said, "as you know."

"I don't know! If you suppose that I went and complained about you to the rink, you're even more of a fool than I thought."

"*Didn't you?*" He looked at her so hard that she felt most uncomfortable.

"If you don't believe me, ask Agnes Green."

"She said it was not you; but——"

"You told her I had, I suppose! Bloody little idiot you are, aren't you. Naturally I did nothing of the kind."

"I don't believe you," he said, and turned his back on her.

She shrugged her shoulders and walked away. It was very unpleasant, but if he took it like that, there was nothing to be done. She said to Harry: "Idris Pritchard tells me he's got the sack from the ice rink."

"Yes, Mrs. Galton," said Harry, "and it's my belief that rink's going broke. But Pritchard, he gets all worked up about it if one says a thing. He thinks he's been victimised."

At any rate, he hadn't said it was her to the rest of them. "He was just in time to join up with you, I suppose?" she said.

"Well, they give him the sack the day before with a week's notice, but he forfeited a week's pay to come with us. Looked a proper little toff, he did, when we started." She offered him a cigarette. "Thanks, Mrs. Galton, I don't mind if I do. And how's Mr. Galton keeping?"

"Oh, pretty busy. How are you going to vote next election, Harry?"

"Ah," he said, with a large wink, "we'll see!"

Dione went off to find Phœbe; she didn't really want to stay any longer. What a fool the man was, though! But Phœbe was drawing busily and enjoying herself. Dione wandered off towards the speakers, wondering which was Wal Hannington. The police seemed to have gathered into compact bodies, solid islands here and there among the wandering untidy crowd. "A good day for the burglars, officer!" Dione said as she passed one group, but the man didn't even smile. Presumably the joke had already been made rather often and usually with a touch of malice. Someone touched her arm. She looked round; it was Idris Pritchard.

He said: "I do believe you, Dione. Agnes Green was certain it was not you. Yes, indeed! Only—— But I do believe you now, comrade."

"Don't comrade me!" she said. "I'm not a Communist." And then: "Well, so that's all right." She walked on.

He followed her: he said softly in that rather attractive voice: "I am that sorry, Dione. Do you hate me?"

"No," she said, "but you don't interest me much. Which is Wal Hannington?"

He caught hold of her hand: "Oh, please! I've been hating you that much. I had a big thought, I had been done out of my job again."

"In the usual way," Dione said, allowing her hand to stay slack as a dead fish in his. But, oh, she thought, I mustn't be so nasty to him, poor little man. She turned and said: "You know, I believe that rink is going broke. But there must be others." Suddenly a brilliant idea came into her head. "Listen!" she said, "I know two of the instructors at the Oxford rink are down with 'flu, and I believe they'd take you on. I know the chap there—come over to one of those telephone boxes and I'll put through a trunk call now and ask him. It would only be temporary, but they might take you on afterwards." She added, "I'll pay your fare to Oxford."

"You are not really meaning to do that?" asked Idris Pritchard in a curious, remote sort of voice.

"Yes," she said, "come on," and began to walk towards the Marble Arch way out of the Park.

After a moment he said: "No. Stop," and then: "I had a letter from Agnes Green this morning telling she had found a job for me as cinema attendant at the Sallmouth Palace—that is a small one by the docks. I am going there when I get back."

"But isn't that a beastly kind of job and badly paid?"

"I will be showing dock-side tarts to their seats. The smart ones. Bowing to them. In uniform, to show I am their servant. It is worse pay than I've ever had."

"You'd better try Oxford, then. Why not? You might easily get a permanent job there."

He shook his head; he was looking down, at his feet, at the trampled grass. "No, I am going to take the cinema job. You see, Dione, I am not losing touch with the Party this way. I would do that at Oxford. You see, don't you, the Sallington Party want me to stay there. I may be useful to them. You see, don't you?"

"Oh yes," she said, "I see. Idris, I like you much better than I did five minutes ago!"

For a moment the Grocer's Scales swung between them unchecked. He was still wondering whether she could really have got him that job if he'd said yes. It looked like she could have and—there'd been half a minute when he'd nearly taken it. He dreaded that cinema job; he'd been doing something like praying for a way out of it ever since he'd found Agnes Green's letter at the post office this morning. And the way out had come: to Oxford, where he'd always wanted to go—and there'd be the colleges he'd seen photos of—and it was the second biggest rink in England. And she lived there and it meant, anyway, she couldn't be hating him, and she might give him another chance. And they'd surely understand in Sallington; there must be a Party branch at Oxford, undergraduates perhaps, real 'Varsity men that would be comrades with him all the same. A fresh start. But he had not said yes. And he was going back to Sallington and the cinema. And she had not done the dirty by him after all, he was sure of that now, though in a way he'd almost hoped she had ; it would have been a class thing, and he'd kept up on the march, hating her. At the end of twenty miles, with bread and tea for supper, hating her. Well. He shivered a little ; he felt cold and emptied.

She was looking past him. " What's up over there ? " she said.

He looked too, and said : " It is beginning, yes ! You'd better keep out of it."

" Not much ! " said Dione, and plunged into an agitating, puzzled crowd of hunger-marchers and onlookers, nobody knowing exactly what was happening, everyone wanting to see, no one wanting to be hurt. Six mounted police went by at the trot, scattering the crowd from in front of them. " And about time, too ! " said an educated voice from behind Dione. But on the whole the general opinion was against the police, though not violently so.

It was very difficult to see quite where one was in this crowd, but she must, she thought, be pretty close to Marble Arch, though whether inside or outside the inner railings she didn't know at all. She had lost Idris Pritchard completely. " What's happening ? " she asked a man next her. " Blessed if I know ! " he said.

Then someone trod on her toe, and in a moment the crowd was being heaved violently back, swearing a little, saying : " Mind my hat ! " or " Look who you're a-shoving of ! " but definitely not letting loose any Communist or other war cries. It was a case of using one's elbows and not getting carried off one's feet. Dione looked round and was rather alarmed at seeing some railings quite near on her left ; she tried to shove away from them, but couldn't do much. For a moment the crowd blocked, she heard angry voices pretty close in front of her, someone shouting, a whistle, and saw over the heads a mounted policeman with his hand up. From somewhere behind her someone threw a stick which might have been meant for the policeman, but missed him by yards. A voice said : " If only we'd a-got bottles, we'd get that cop ! " and a real Cockney woman's voice answered loudly : " Shime, an' you call yerselves Englishmen ! "

Again the crowd heaved violently ; Dione, right off her feet this time, was really frightened. People were throwing things, shouting. There was a scream from somewhere, the crash of something breaking ; she was horribly near the spiked railings. Then a yell : " They're charging us ! " and above the human voices the primitive whinny of a horse, frightened too. Then to her right the crowd broke and ran. She was knocked down on to her knees, but not right over—she picked herself up extremely indignant and almost under the nose of a police horse. " Look out, my good man ! " she said. The rider swerved : " You clear out, ma'am ! " he said, irritated but still respectful.

Dione, trying to get out of the way, saw past this horse to the next in line, and saw and heard a police baton come down on a man's head. For a moment she was swept on, shoved by the horse's side and the policeman's foot, and then she was dropped behind the line. The police were past her and she was left with the obvious job of picking up the man who'd been knocked over. Thank goodness, he wasn't dead. In fact he was trying to sit up. " Lie down," she said, " it's all right, I'm helping you." He flopped back again with his eyes shut ; she thought he must be one of the marchers, he was thin and big and more raggedly dressed than any Londoner. She felt his head gingerly and decided that the skull wasn't fractured, it was just a scalp-wound. It was very odd being alone in the middle of London—yes, there was the Marble Arch!—with a wounded man. She had a solid handkerchief and a Woolworth tube of iodine in her bag. She proceeded with the iodine; the man opened his eyes and clawed at her with his hands, trying to sit up again. "Quiet!" she said, "Mother's got you." Again he collapsed. But the handkerchief wouldn't quite go round his head; she held it against the bleeding wound, wondering what to do. If only one wore petticoats nowadays!

Then two St. John ambulance men came trotting up. "Now, what's wrong?" they said, and one of them remarked to Dione: "Don't you worry, ma'am, we've had a dozen like him already."

There was now a small crowd gathering round them. Dione, still on her knees, looked up and saw Lambert passing. "Oh!" she called to him, getting to her feet. "You'll report this, won't you, Mr. Lambert?"

"Of course I shan't," said Lambert; "this is stuff for my memoirs, not for my paper!" And he went on.

Then Dione saw a dismounted policeman, who asked the ambulance men: "Is he all right, that chap?"

"So it was you hit him!" Dione said fiercely.

"He was going to kick my horse!" the policeman answered.

For a moment Dione was assailed by overwhelming class-prejudices, horror that someone should have tried to hurt an innocent and valuable animal. Nice horse. Patting nice nursery horses held up to feed carrots velvety-soft snuffling muzzling noses—and then: "You might have killed him!" she said.

"And a good thing, too!" said someone in the interested little crowd.

"I shall report it!" Dione said furiously.

" Well, report away, ma'am," said the policeman and walked off. And someone else said: " Who to ? " and laughed.

Dione looked round for the speakers. There was one couple in good clothes—a lady's face and eyes, but she said, glaring down at the wounded man : " They ought to give him six months' hard ! "

" Ought never to have been allowed," said the man, " the Government was too weak for them. Never trust that fellow Ramsay ! "

" Letting these hulking great brutes into the Park ! "

" I saw a horse down myself ! " That was what had moved them, of course—the horses.

" And you," the lady who had spoken before said suddenly to Dione, " you, madam, you have the voice of a lady, but you behave like one of the criminal classes. You —deserve to be slapped ! "

Dione gasped. Dione was aware of her hat being crooked and her hands blood-stained. Dione slapped, herself, at that lady's face, most ineffectively, and heard the crowd laughing at her.

And the next thing was, the lady's escort had hard hold of her wrists. " Now then," he said, " I'm going to give you in charge. Women like you shouldn't be allowed in public places ! "

Dione struggled to get her wrists loose, silently, furiously, and more and more frightened. And all the time some back part of her mind was trying to place his public-school tie, she knew she'd seen it on one of Tom's pupils quite lately—Harrow—Marlborough ?

" You'd better keep quiet," he said, " or it will be the worse for you. Now madam, your name and address please."

" Oh, go to hell ! " said Dione, choking with misery and

helplessness. She wasn't going to give her name—Tom's name—the constituency—but if the police got her, they'd find out—and oh, what could they *do* to her?

"Don't swear," said the man; his companion and everyone else laughed except one old London woman, who said: "Pore thing!" In wild irritation Dione struggled again—and thought she'd get the skin torn off her wrists.

But the St. John ambulance man intervened: "Now, sir," he said, "this lady was doing a nice piece of first-aid just now, and she's naturally a bit upset-like. You let her go, sir."

The lady whom Dione had tried to slap said: "Yes, let her go, John, don't take her seriously. She's just one of these women who can't help making fools of themselves."

"The squawking sisterhood," suggested someone.

"She ought to be taught not to meddle with Reds," said the man.

"Well, you haven't time to teach her now," said the lady, looking contemptuously at Dione. "She didn't even know how to hit straight!"

The man said to Dione: "If you were a man I should kick you—hard. As it is——" In one movement he let her go and boxed her ears.

Dione ducked and staggered, dropping her bag. When she'd picked it up they had their backs turned and were walking away. The things they'd said were a good deal worse than the immediate pain. You haven't time to teach her now, said the words; you haven't time to rape her now, said the tone. Oh, God! The ambulance man laid a hand on her arm: "Now you just go along home, ma'am, and have a nice lie down." Someone else said it was a bleeding shame, but whether that referred to the treatment of the hunger-marcher, the policeman's horse or herself, she didn't know. She turned and hurried for the Park, for the big crowd, for anonymity, for Phœbe. Oh, where was Phœbe? She got on to grass again, scurried here and there, looking for Phœbe, but couldn't find her. Her ears and cheeks were stinging still. Suddenly she threw herself down at the foot of a tree and burst into horrible, angry, humiliated tears.

She faced against the tree so that no one should see, she didn't let any real yell come out of her howling, twisted mouth, but someone touched her shoulder and said, "What's wrong?"

"Nothing," she said in a loud whisper, "go away!"

"But, Mrs. Galton——"

Oh, who the devil—she looked up and saw Harry, who had spoken, and Idris Pritchard.

Seeing her face, Idris was down on the flattened grass beside her: "Dione, Dione fach—have they hurt you?" He had his arm round her shoulders and was mopping her eyes with his own handkerchief—hers was still on the wounded man.

She shook her head and pushed him away. "It's all right," she said.

"It is blood you have on you!"

"I was looking after a hurt man," she said, "that's all. And—and I've had my ears boxed for being a Red!"

"There now, Mrs. Galton," said Harry soothingly, "the bastards! Was it the cops?"

"No, no," she said. "It was an old public-school man!" And all at once it began to appear admirably funny. The sting had almost gone out of her ears; it was only her wrists that were really sore, where she'd struggled.

"But they've not hurt you really?" Idris was really concerned about her!

"Not a bit," she said, "but look at my wrists! I know what it's like being arrested now. Good practice for the revolution, isn't it?"

Harry laughed and slapped his thigh: "That's a good 'un, Mrs. Galton!"

"You ought to have cold water on them," Idris said. "We'll get some at the canteen. Can you walk, Dione?"

"Of course!" she said, and jumped up, and couldn't help adding: "You ought to know I'm pretty tough!" It was very odd, she didn't seem to mind his touching her at all now, didn't mind reminding him or herself of what had passed. When he came to the canteen he and Harry between them skilfully bathed her wrists and cheeks with cold tea. They seemed to know all about it, and the woman at the canteen was very friendly.

"It ought to be tied up," Idris said, looking at her right wrist, which was very red. "Give me your handkerchief, Dione."

"I can't," she said. "I used it to tie up the wounded man."

"Proper little comrade you are!" said Harry.

And Idris said: "Take mine, Dione fach, do please. Please!"

She hesitated, thought he'd probably only got one or two, thought she didn't want his handkerchief, thought—"thank you, Idris—if I may," she said.

He dipped it in the tea and tied it round her wrist, his curly head bending over it; she thought his hands were shaking a little. Only ten days ago; and it was all washed out, by to-day. Or—was that right? No, it wasn't really so neat and tidy; it wasn't twopence one way and a packet of chocolate the other, all accurately paid for and cancelled out, something for each side. It was simply the succession of events. Things didn't fit together nicely finished and cancelled, they just went on; and the less one thought about justice and a fair deal and all that, the more freely and interestingly and newly they went. " How does that feel now ? " said Idris Pritchard.

Then Phœbe turned up. " My dear, what on earth happened to you ? It's nearly dark." Dione explained and introduced the other two. Phœbe was impatient to get off.

" Well," Dione said, " thank you very much, both of you. I'm sure to see you again some time soon. And best of luck with the petition ! "

" Thanks, Mrs. Galton," said Harry. " So long."

" Good-bye, Dione," said Idris, " will you write to me ? Please ! "

" I'm afraid I've forgotten your address," Dione said, and then—for he looked hurt, the silly goose !—" but I'll ask Agnes Green. Yes, I really will write some time."

They walked out past Marble Arch, where there was still a certain amount of crowd and the railings looked damaged. Phœbe hailed a taxi : " We'll pick your bag up at Paddington, go round by Muriel's, and I'll take it on to Clare's. Then I'll pick you up at seven, and we'll dine at the Café before the party."

" My word ! " Dione said. " You must have got pretty good prices for your pictures."

" I did," said Phœbe, " and I've got a commission since then—did I tell you ? Yes, it's rather fun. By the way, Dione, who's your curly-headed boy-friend ? "

" I'll tell you some day—perhaps."

" So it's like that, is it ? "

" No, it isn't ! He's C.P., anyway. I wonder if they'll ever get their petition as far as Parliament, poor dears."

Muriel was delighted to see Dione, but not very sympathetic about the hunger-marchers. She had just come back from work at her clinic, *viâ* a committee about the exchange of students between provincial Universities and Germany, one of those small and arbitrary and hard-working committees that do get things done. She was conscious at least of having laboriously piled up two and two and made four, but what did Dione and her hunger-marchers think they were going to make? Dione always found Muriel's criticisms the most difficult to answer, because, finally, Muriel had got something to show—*proxis*—and she hadn't. Muriel was driving a steady and honest trade with the universe. And she?

"Do you know," Muriel said suddenly, "that little wretch Jane Ellis has decided that she won't go to Oxford or Cambridge after all? What's the use of our having sweated and strained and been laughed at to get things like University education for the next generation of women, when now they won't take it?"

"What does she want to do?"

"She's got some wild-cat scheme for going and working in a factory."

"What does Nan Ellis say?"

"Well, naturally its against her principles to coerce the girl, but she's very much upset. She thinks it'll be very bad for her, just at this age—she's overgrown her strength a bit—and naturally she feels it's a pity for Jane not to make use of ten years' education."

"If she survives her factory, she'll probably be a much more grown-up and wiser person than any fourth-year Somerville girl. I expect it's the effect of Russia, Muriel."

"Nan thinks it's the effect of your precious Donald! And if she knew he was really a murderer—you know, Dione, you'll get into still more trouble sooner or later over this. Have you considered that some time someone is sure to go asking your mother after her other son in Russia? Or it'll get round to your uncle in Edinburgh, and the cousins, or to Oxford, or something. It's going to be all very awkward."

“ Oh, don’t I know it ! Well, I hope I shall meet Jane Ellis again in five years. I must go and dress, Muriel. Don’t you think Phœbe’s looking well ? ”

“ Amazingly. And she’s making a big name for herself. And for us, for women. I’m rather proud of being a vague kind of relation of hers—and of having a couple of early Bathursts ! ”

Dione got ready for the party, with a bath and some of Muriel’s excellent bath salts. They stung her wrists rather, which was a nuisance, because she didn’t want to have to think about this afternoon. She was ashamed of herself. She oughtn’t to have hit that woman ; it was giving away her perfectly good case, and now she could think of all sorts of telling things she might have said, and probably the man she’d picked up *was* going for the policeman’s horse, anyway—so what else could the policeman have done ? And what else could the man have done ? But she herself, granted that there was such a thing as free will, might have behaved with much more choice—what else is education for ?

And if they had been armed ? But they weren’t. If you aren’t armed you kick, or hit, or box people’s ears instead of shooting them. She hadn’t felt like she had when her wrists were being held since—oh, twenty-five years ago ! Pretty horrid being reduced to childhood. Have I ever made my children suffer like that with rage and helplessness ? I hope to God I haven’t. I suppose it’s like that being a Communist in most countries. Or a Liberal in Italy. Or—what ?—in Russia. Or when they got a witch. Being stripped and searched for witch marks. That must have been remarkably unpleasant, if one considers it in detail. Yes, one has avoided certain things. So far.

She had a blue silk dress with a little coat of printed blue and green velvet ; it had floppy sleeves that would hide her wrist. She had her best silk stockings, and a Sybil Dunlop moonstone on a long silver chain. A bit North Oxfordy? Well, she was North Oxford!

Phœbe picked her up and they went off together to dine at the Café. Dione still found it ridiculously thrilling to go into the big, ugly, exciting room full of little tables and plush seats; it was lovely when Phœbe was greeted in a fatherly way by a grey-haired waiter and shown to the table which he somehow gave the impression of having kept specially for them—and all for *5s. 6d.* each! Phœbe had a new and amusing necklace of small glass balls half filled with water—" or it may be priceless old brandy, and I shall never know till one of them breaks; just like life!" She pointed out the other diners: " Those three are art critics no doubt hatching horrid plots against some masterpiece; that's a poet and some boy friends—no, Dione, I swear it is! There aren't any publishers, they don't come here, anyway lunch is their time, but that very uncommercial-looking man who's arguing about his fish is a dealer. There's the dear little old B.B.C. How do I know? I've been here with all sorts of people and I always ask questions, and if people have special faces I remember them."

Dione was pleased to be able to recognise and bow to Margaret Cole, who was dining with a woman writer of some sort and discussing the hunger-marchers. And, oh dear, it was so nice sitting down to a dinner one hadn't ordered and didn't know only too much about the origins of! They discussed everything and everyone. Alex and his Nellie and Brian—who seemed to be getting along so much better away from his mother and sisters!

Then it was time for the party; Phœbe paid and tipped with admirable calm. It seemed to be a long way and when they got there it was up a lot of stairs. Someone—not, she gathered, the hostess—met them and said: "We've overflowed into Moira's flat, too—we're dancing there, and there are drinks here. Come and have some!" Then they plunged into a pleasurable and idiotic ferment of bubbling voices and laughter, penetrated by gramophoned jazz from an upper storey. Any clothes would do, for some people were in full evening dress and some in very untidy day clothes. A few seemed to be vaguely in fancy dress, or perhaps that was just what they always wore. There was food about, mostly sandwiches on plates in corners of the floor, and beer and coffee and whisky and some rather bad claret-cup. There also seemed to be some pictures, but they had mostly been pushed away behind one another to make more room.

Dione thought it had the makings of a nice party, but was a little frightened of it. For a time she sheltered behind a cheerful but rather expansive woman, who bulged out of her dress rather curiously in places. Already three people had tried vainly to hook her up. Phœbe had been seized on and carried off. A bald man came and sat down beside her, nursing a saucer: "Do you like olives? You don't—good, then I can eat them all."

"What do you do," said Dione. "Besides eating olives, I mean?"

"I'm an architect," the man said; "at least, I am when I've got anything to build. What are you?"

"I'm a Socialist," Dione said.

"Naturally. All sensible people are. Have you been to Russia? You have—good, then you can answer a few questions about their modern buildings." A pleasant but slightly exhausting talk about Russia followed, and then a girl—whom Dione, after she'd left them, suddenly realised must be their hostess—brought them some nice Sauterne.

After that Pussy turned up, and was charming to Dione

for a quarter of an hour, danced with her and found some chocolate almonds. Dione couldn't help wondering whether he wasn't trying to find out something about Phœbe—*why* Phœbe had shot off like this. He's a little jealous, Dione thought, but whether it's of Phœbe's success or of some man he suspects is at the bottom of it, I don't know. She didn't tell him about Phil, in fact she hinted that Phœbe was singularly heart-whole. " How's Cynthia ? " she asked.

" Well, between ourselves," said Pussy, " I'm not seeing so much of Cynthia." That was somewhat verified when Cynthia came in a little later ; Dione saw Pussy pinch her very hard in a corner, and out of maternal habit almost went and scolded them.

Phœbe turned up again with a young man, and asked Dione if she was enjoying it.

" Yes, I think so," Dione said. " But it seems funny after this afternoon."

" What were you doing this afternoon ? " said the young man, a tall fair-haired creature, just a little older than an undergraduate.

" Oh," said Phœbe, " this is Victor. I don't know his other name, but he wants to found a new religion, don't you, darling ? "

" Not really," said the young man, smiling, " I only said I hoped to see it happen."

" Phœbe ! " said Dione, " aren't you a little bit drunk ? "

" Quite possibly," said Phœbe, " but I shan't have a headache to-morrow morning, which shows that the gods don't disapprove. As a matter of fact the gods like me at the moment. Of course they won't go on, but one may as well make the most of it. I'll leave you Victor ; have a dance with him, Dione ; he dances very well and he kisses one's neck while he's dancing, which is so clever of him."

" Phœbe ! "

" Oh yes, and I gather he writes really good poetry, the sort without any capital letters. Good-bye, lassie, and take care of Victor for me. I'm going to find Pussy now."

" Well, Phœbe, all I can say is you almost justify May Bickerden ! "

" Who's May Bickerden ? " said the young man, sitting down on a cushion at Dione's feet.

" You want to know everything, don't you ! Well, she's a respectable married woman, living in Oxford. Like me. I do apologise for my sister, Mr.——? Oh, all right, Victor. Did you mind ? "

" No. One takes these things from genius. It must be very thrilling to be her sister. Are you anyone special yourself ? "

" I told you, I'm a respectable married woman."

" But in your off moments ? Or don't you have any ? What *were* you doing this afternoon ? "

" I was with the hunger-marchers. Tell me about your new religion."

" Do you really want to know ? Shall I get you a drink ? No ? Well, I see civilisation working up for a new religion. The old ones are broken down, and everyone is questing about with their noses in the air, saying : what shall we do to be saved. There's all this business about groups : Oxford and others. We're all living as if we were waiting for something to happen (all this is much better in my poems !) Well, that something's going to burst through the egg any moment."

Dione said, hesitating : " I know what you mean. I used to feel that, but I don't think I do now."

" That's interesting. Since when did you cease feeling it ? "

" I suppose—I ceased feeling it gradually, since becoming

a Socialist. I've stopped worrying about coming to terms with the universe. I'm just encouraging things to happen."

"And you say you're a respectable married woman!"

"Not those sort of things, you silly ass! But just being alive and not being frightened. The worst of that is I shall die in the end."

"Yes, you'll die in the end. And so shall I."

But it's just another thing that's going to happen! Presumably the last thing, but why go adding it up and making a plus and minus account with that as the line at the end? Still, I may be able to live like this just because I've cut out a lot of the kind of things that puzzle people. All the values and standards in this room, for instance. I'm not trying to understand them, still less to make sense of them."

"Shall we dance?" said the young man abruptly. Dione thought she must have bored him, and was sorry; but he kissed her during the dance, just as Phœbe had said he would. "I always do what's expected of me," he said. "Do you like it?"

"Yes, I think so," she said.

"Think, think, and you call yourself a Socialist!" They went back into the other room.

"Don't you want to dance with—someone of your own age?" Dione said.

"No," he said, sitting on the floor at her feet again and leaning back against her. Quite soon, Dione discovered that she was stroking the young man's hair. It was being a nice party. Phœbe no doubt was where she had seen her last, in the top room, sitting in a heap of cushions and more or less on Pussy's knees. They were both a little drunk. But not enough to do anything silly. And she herself? No, she wasn't. She couldn't be. She never was at parties. After all, if the young man liked to have his hair stroked—as he seemed to—why shouldn't she? Even the monkeys at the Zoo do as much for one another. Joyce had come in; she looked tired and older. What was happening to her? What were her values? Still, no doubt, in the commercial stage. Curious how one could know people, and know nothing at all about them. It was a long time since the dance at Auchanarnish.

Abruptly a girl in black began singing Christmas carols. The gramophone kept on against her for a few bars, then was silenced. The room began to fill with the dancers. She sang: "As Joseph was a-walking."

"What's this about?" whispered the young man called Victor.

"It's about what's always happening to women: 'And Mary gathered cherries, While Joseph stood around.' It must be permanently satisfactory to have a voice like that. One wouldn't have to bother about religion."

"Not till it goes. That gives her about another twenty years, doesn't it? What's this?" The girl sang:

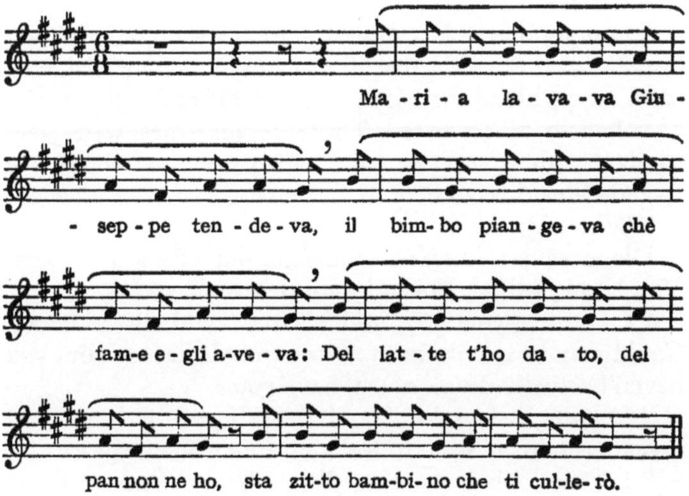
Ma - ri - a la - va - va Giu -
- sep - pe ten - de - va, il bim- bo pian - ge - va chè
fam-e e - gli a-ve - va: Del lat - te t'ho da - to, del
pan non ne ho, sta zit-to bam-bi- no che ti cul-le- rò.

Dione whispered : " It was a man called Joseph who was out of work because of rationalisation in the timber trade, and his wife Mary, and they lived at Marshbrook Bridge."

" Where's that ? "

" Hush ! And they were on the Means Test and only had two shillings a week for her little boy, and you know one can't keep a growing child on that."

The voice went on : " Va là dal gran riccone . . ."

And Dione went on explaining in a low whisper, her head close to Victor's fair head : " And there was a man called Coke-Brown who made a lot of money out of heavy woollens and ran a newspaper, and he wouldn't give Mary and Joseph any more for their little boy. So they thought it was because he hadn't seen for himself. So they sent the little boy, for Daniel Coke-Brown to see he was getting rickets ; but that wasn't any good either, so Daniel Coke-Brown died and went to hell. It was all quite simple, you see. But that was in those days."

" When ? "

" Last summer. No, I mean—what's she going to sing now ?—what I mean is that all that story is commercial, too ; it's a swap, blood for blood—hell hereafter for those who give hell to others here. That's because they were Jews to start with, I suppose, and Italian peasants who wrote it, and Donald was a Scot."

" Who's Donald ? "

Dione gave a jump : " Someone out of another story. You know, I think I must be a little drunk, too."

" Of course you are," said Victor, " and all the better. Could man be drunk for ever—or woman either. But you haven't actually drunk much, have you ? "

" I expect," she said, " it's because I got my ears boxed this afternoon. I seem to feel a bit funny about the ears."

" Let me look at your ears," said Victor, and came and

sat beside her on the sofa and inspected her ears, while the girl at the piano sang " The Twelve Days of Christmas " and " The Seeds of Love," and then started on Campion.

It was a nice party. It went on and on. Dione helped her hostess to mop up beer from the floor. A very eminent painter asked her to be his mistress, and she was very proud of that till she heard him ask someone else the same thing in exactly the same words ten minutes afterwards. She danced with lots of people. They made up dances as they went along, while the gramophone played Stravinsky or Purcell. It was, as she tried to explain to two or three people, in many ways curiously unlike a Labour social; although she had what at any rate appeared to be several very serious and important conversations. It would be nice, she thought, to have a party like this every night. Or at least once a week. Obviously the Athenians had good parties as often as that.

But how the devil to fit it in with Marshbrook Bridge? To have the Taylors and Mason, and that girl Dorothy—yes, she'd do, only could she leave the baby for a whole evening?—and George Grove and Mrs. East and Reuben Goldberg. But they wouldn't enjoy themselves at this party, would they? No, they wouldn't, and they'd be terribly shocked to see her kissing Victor—or even Pussy. And if they did enjoy themselves—if there were enough of them to alter what was being said and done—then it would be a different and less nice party, and somehow—more like North Oxford. Grim thought: perhaps the only way from Sallington to London is through North Oxford. Instead of by Luton and the Great North Road to Hyde Park. Idris might like this party. He'd say he did, anyway. And conceivably Harry would; at any rate, he'd like the sandwiches and beer and he'd feel friendly about the people being drunk. Why? A different Elephant. And Donald? When Donald was still working for the Sallington Communist Party, Donald would have risen up and denounced this party, like Jonah. And so, perhaps, would Mason—and certainly Miss Waterhouse. Yet there's nothing wrong with this party except that it isn't actively getting on with the revolution, and it will not end up by singing the "Red Flag"—or, for that matter, "God Save the King." Well, what about giving the dear old revolution a miss?

She had said that aloud and somebody next her had answered: "I quite agree." And then she had remembered Agnes Green never letting herself rest at all, always with her tired shoulder shoving against the structure of things. It was as though she had harnessed her Elephant to push. And the Labour Elephant pushed too, and when they pushed down the walls of Babylon, no doubt several nice parties were squashed. She turned to her neighbour, who was, she believed, a scientist at London University, but oddly different from an Oxford don, and said: "But what right have we to get drunk?"

"We aren't!" he said aggressively.

"Well, some people here are. I had a beautiful idea that I was."

"Nonsense, let me feel your pulse."

"But supposing we were—just supposing—what right have we to be? It isn't as if we were out of work and terribly anxious and unhappy and perhaps without hope; we'd have some excuse then for taking drugs, but none of us are unhappy——"

"How do you know?"

"Well, we may be crossed in love or something ridiculous, but on the whole we've got interesting jobs and at any rate enough spare cash to get home by Underground."

"But it's stopped running."

"Don't be silly," she said, and wondered what that reminded her of and went on quickly: "Don't you see, we don't deserve to get drunk?"

"The trouble with you is," said her neighbour, "that you've got too much conscience. Weighing things up against one another. The middle-class conscience was invented by Dr. Arnold of Rugby—to whose immortal memory I quaff this glass of whatever it is! Before his time people got drunk honestly, just because they wanted to."

"Weighing things up?" she said. "Then you think the commercial idea comes into that, too. Very probably. In that case we have no business to talk of drunkenness being right or wrong, but we are left with the Marxian criticism that it is another form of opium for the people and stops us from seeing things as they are."

"But at what point can one be said to see things as they are?" said her neighbour, leaning forward and tapping her earnestly on the hand. After that for a long time, or so it seemed, they discussed idealism, in a curious dream-like Berkeleyian atmosphere. And still with half her mind Dione was trying to fit in Marshbrook Bridge with the party and still they wouldn't fit because they would bring their Elephant in with them.

## SALLINGTON 9

DIONE went up to Sallington the next day ; Mason met her at the station with the Ford and took her to Miss Waterhouse's, where she and Tom were to stay this week-end. There were signs of activity about, municipal election posters and posters of meetings where Tom's name figured large as speaker. Ex-Councillor Finch was standing again —Dione had already been to one of his meetings. It was rather difficult to get Labour candidates for the municipals, as very few working people could spare the time for committees and council meetings, and all the odd jobs that a councillor ought to do. The choice was limited to those who had businesses of their own, and could spare the time, those who had retired, and the few high-brows who had sufficient leisure. But the ordinary worker, employed by a commercial firm, by the Synthex works say, or by one of the Coke-Brown mills, was ruled out. There were, of course, women, but it was a little difficult to fit them in ; the Elephant always kept an eye open for them.

Mason was being extremely friendly and nice, making her feel she was really welcome back. On an impulse she told him about the studio party. Mason laughed : " You had a hot time, didn't you, Mrs. Galton ! "

" I don't know that it was exactly hot," she said ; " it was very friendly. I do wonder if you'd have liked it."

" You bet I should ! " Mason said rather surprisingly ; " it sounds a bit livelier than a social ! "

" But—you wouldn't have minded ? "

" Can't tell till I've tried," Mason said. " I dare say I

should have at first, but you'ld have held my hand, wouldn't you, Mrs. Galton ? "

" Yes, especially if you'd call me Dione."

" As a matter of fact the missus and I, we always do at home; it's such a funny sort of name. It sounds like the films."

" Does it ? I'm called Isobel, too."

" That would be a better name for the constituency; still —my name's Stanley, you know, but my friends call me Stan mostly."

" Right-o—Stan."

They had high tea with Miss Waterhouse and then went off to meetings, at each of which Dione spoke for a few minutes. John Collis was speaking at one of them, the Barstone candidate at another. Jo Burrage was a good enough speaker on local affairs, and Mrs. Rivers was all right in the chair. None of the candidates were very thrilling, but what could one expect ? When she came back Miss Waterhouse was waiting to give her coffee and to tell her long stories of old days with William Morris and Hyndman, meetings where stones were thrown at them, the little faithful group of men and women with vision. And now, Dione thought, she is only interested in getting the infant welfare centre on its legs again. That *is* important— Only how to hold the balance ?

She saw various old friends on Saturday, including the girl Dorothy, whose sitting-room was going to be used on the day as one of her father's committee rooms ; it would be darker still with the posters up in the window, but it gave Dorothy the feeling that all her scrubbing was some use. Dione would have liked to ask her what she would have thought of the party, but for shame couldn't; obviously she'd have liked it—if she'd had the clothes. Though almost anything would have done, and she had probably got a thirteen-and-eleven from the Co-op. Suddenly Dione wondered if it would be possible to induce Margaret Coke-Brown to have good parties and to ask people from Marshbrook Bridge. Only where would the other ingredients of the parties come from—the writers and painters and musicians? Were they to be found in Sallington? It seemed very doubtful. Sallington parties no doubt there were, but they'd have a very different atmosphere.

Tom was speaking early on Saturday evening at Sallmouth, exchanging with the Sallmouth Labour candidate, who was speaking for ex-Councillor Finch at River Ward. But he was to join them at eight o'clock at the Barton's End meeting. He wasn't there on time, so Mason whispered to Dione to go on a little longer. She went on, speaking nervously from notes, telling about the wastage in the next generation, who were growing up half-starved, going on to general things, the international situation, China and Japan—remembered that Mason had told her to keep off Russia, and stumbled, repeated herself—talked of disarmament. The clock said eight-fifteen—and there, thank goodness, was Tom.

Tom was obviously extremely upset about something, though he made a particularly good speech to the meeting. The moment he had finished Dione leaned over, whispering: "What's up?" But he only shook his head. She and Mason exchanged glances. Then they were off in the Ford to another meeting, and this time it was Mason who asked what was the matter. "I've mucked up a meeting for them at Sallmouth," said Tom shortly; "you'd better ask them there."

"But how on earth, Tom? I'm sure you didn't!"

He didn't answer for a minute, then he said: "Well, I didn't know much about their local questions there, except unemployment at the dockyards, so I made them a fighting

Socialist speech. It was all right as a speech. But I saw something was wrong when I sat down. Well, apparently they're all out for little-by-little reforms and going slow and not alienating the Liberals, and I've put my foot in it with some of the people they wanted to get hold of! The fools never told me what sort of a fight it was."

"That's my fault," said Mason, thinking of the awkward position he would be in with the other agent; "I ought to have told you. I thought you knew what it was like down there."

"But what *is* the position?" Dione asked.

Mason answered: "It's a three-cornered fight: a Tory, our man, and a Communist. And they're hoping to get the Liberals to vote for our man, so as to keep the Communist out. That's why they're going slow. There was a Tory in for that ward last time, but they're hoping to make a Labour gain of it if only they can get the progressives in general over to our side. See?"

"I don't like speaking against a Communist anyhow," said Tom, "though I suppose I've got to now and again, but to do it and to muck it up like that into the bargain!" He dug his fists into his cheeks like a small boy—like Kenneth.

"Don't you worry about speaking against the C.P.!" said Mason, "they won't worry about speaking against you."

But Tom didn't answer at all. He had two more meetings to speak at, though at one he was so late that he hadn't time for more than a few minutes. It was a pity to let the meetings go on too late in the evening. Mason usually tried to have them over before closing time; chaps deserved a drink after sitting for two hours at a political meeting, especially when it was only the municipals. After the last meeting he suggested that Tom and Dione should come back to his house for a few minutes before going on to Miss Waterhouse's; there were to-morrow's arrangements to discuss, not to speak of the Christmas do's in the various wards.

Mrs. Mason, a fat, smiling woman, rather deaf, made them tea; they discussed arrangements. Tom had got various people to come and speak in the constituency and suitable week-ends were apportioned to them. Dione took notes in her diary. Tom was still very gloomy and unelastic; he sat hunched over the fire in Mason's room; once he dropped his pocket-book, scattering some of the contents; Dione picked it up for him. Suddenly Mason said: "Now, you've got to buck up! We've all of us made mistakes and I ought to have warned you about Sallmouth. But very likely what you've lost 'em in votes one way you've gained the other. And as to the C.P., if they put up candidates against us, that's their look-out."

"Where are they running candidates?"

"Sallmouth. Greenapple. Smedbrook. Oh, and I heard they'd put up one chap in Barstone Central Ward—where even we don't stand a chance. By the way, Oliver of Greenapple is going to give us a meeting in February."

"Is he?" said Tom without warmth.

Mason got up and began to walk about the little room, fingering the plates on his tidy dresser. He said: "Your good lady says I'm to call her Dione, so I suppose I can call you Tom. It's easier so. What's up? What's biting you? Isn't the Labour Movement good enough for you any longer?"

Dione stopped writing. Mrs. Mason stopped darning a sock. Tom got up, too; he looked more cheerful already. He said: "It's not good enough unless it's Socialist through and through, including its councillors. Unless it really means to alter society, not just to add another shilling to the income tax!"

" It is Socialist," said Mason, " but half of it doesn't know it is—yet. It's our job, Tom Galton, yours and mine and all sound men's job, to pinch it and push it and make it think, day in, day out. That's what we're for, that's why I'm agent and you're candidate. And that's plain enough, isn't it ? "

" But how many in the Party think like that ? "

" More than would say so."

" I keep on asking myself, can we wait for the Movement to—begin to move ? We pinch it and push it, as you say, and perhaps it turns in its sleep. The corner-stone of Jerusalem's not laid. If we're to wait for the Labour Party to find out what it's thinking, it'll be too late to act."

" There's been times I've thought that," Mason said, more gently; " I know folks say about me, Old Stan's down in the mouth, old Stan's afraid we shan't win. The League of Youth tell me I don't encourage them. But what else can we do ? "

" There is at least one alternative."

" Meaning the C.P. ? Well, you must make up your mind, and maybe you'll say it's because I'm a Labour Party agent and drawing four pounds ten shillings a week and my expenses out of it, that I speak as I do. They'd say so in the C.P. But it isn't as if I hadn't been a working man and couldn't turn to again if I had to. What I say is, the C.P. aren't practical politics here ; they won't get Socialism in our time or anyone else's. They're not the people ; they're —oddments. They're trying to do it from outside and that's all wrong. There's a lot of chaps at Universities and writers and all that who call themselves Communists ; they're too proud to join the Labour Party. But I didn't think you were one of them, Tom Galton. We thought you were with us, with the people of England that are slow maybe, but solid, and what they do and what they love they'll stick to. Why, Lenin didn't move till he'd got the soldiers and workers behind him. But the soldiers and workers in England—such of them as have thought it out—they're in the Labour Movement. Aren't you with them?"

Tom was leaning against the mantelpiece, one shoulder hunched up a bit; he was poking his forefinger into the damp fibre round Mrs. Mason's crocus bulbs. He said in a low voice: "Quoad respondit Didymus . . ."

"What's that in plain English?"

Dione answered for him: "Lord, I believe, help Thou mine unbelief."

"Well," said Mason, "that's about all I've got to say. Made quite a little speech, I have! You know the arguments against the C.P. as well as I do. And the arguments for it. But—we trust you here as our candidate. We want you to trust us. We trust you enough to give you a lot of rope—you're well enough liked in Marshbrook Bridge, you know, Tom. We'll let you make us as uncomfortable as you can, shove us and jab at us and make us think. We—we want you to do that, that's what you're for. We want you to work at that, we want you to work all out. We're proud of you as a worker. But you belong to us."

"I suppose I do," said Tom, "I suppose I do. And I realise it's an honour. Well, Stan, if you're right about the Labour Movement, I'm yours. Only I'm not going to work like a Turk's donkey for half a dozen reforms that the Liberals would get through as well as we do. But if you're right——"

"I believe I'm right," Mason said; "I wasn't saying it just to get at you." He put his hand on Tom's shoulder: "You're all out." He turned to his wife: "Go and get that drop of brandy from the medicine cupboard, old girl. It's not the best brandy, but we keep a drop in the house against emergencies, and you won't get any from Miss

Waterhouse!" Mrs. Mason brought it. "There now, drink it up, and I'll run you round to Miss Waterhouse's. You're having a hard term at Oxford, aren't you?"

"This is very nice of you," said Tom. "Yes, it's been a stiff term. You see, Oxford's a nice cushy job if you do the same teaching and give the same lectures one term after another. But that's a pleasant habit that's going out a bit. Yes, I've had a spot of work lately."

Mason drove them along to Miss Waterhouse's. Halfway he said: "You didn't mind me speaking a bit rough to you, did you?"

"No," said Tom, "I liked it."

Miss Waterhouse was a little agitated about their not having turned up earlier, but forgave them and insisted on their each drinking a cup of hot soup with thin bread and butter. She told them about the disgraceful state of the school buildings at Little Lumley, where the windows wouldn't open and the closets could not be flushed individually, and were only done twice a day by the caretaker. He made a note of it. After they went up to bed Dione said: "Feeling better, Tom?"

"A bit," he said, "but it was pretty bloody about that meeting at Sallmouth."

"Yes," she said, "and you'd just had a letter from Oksana, hadn't you? I suppose that made it worse."

"It did. But how do you know?"

"I saw it when you dropped your pocket book. Sorry, but a Russian letter's pretty obvious. I suppose they're in for a bad time this winter. Donald seems to think so."

"I'm afraid they are," said Tom, "but they'll get through it all right. They've got faith. At least, enough of them have to keep it going."

"Tom, you feel very differently about Marshbrook

Bridge to how you did, say, at the election last year."

"Do I? How?"

"You aren't a kind of magic person from on top and you've stopped wanting to be an exciting surprise."

"Was I ever that? I don't remember."

"But I do. Now, you're part of them here. You're really a worker, really part of the working-class movement."

"Yes, of course, wasn't I always?"

"No, Tom, you've changed. They've changed you. And me. Or something has."

The rest of the meetings went all right. Tom caught a night train back to Oxford; it was an uncomfortable journey, but he wouldn't be in time for his morning lecture otherwise. Then it was polling day. Someone had lent a Morris, and Dione offered to drive it in River Ward for ex-Councillor Finch. She was down at the central committee rooms at 9.30 on a cold morning, with a little river mist rising off the Sall. Still yawning, she dressed the car in red and green ribbons, and was told about its idiosyncrasies and what to do if the self-starter jammed. As at the general election, there was little to do that morning; most of the women were still in the middle of household chores, though one or two who had small children came with the family, who enjoyed the drive. Dione hoped Finch would get in. She wasn't sure how much high politics he understood, but he had the right instincts. She was glad to be taking people to vote for him.

About one o'clock she drove round to the Carisbrook Road committee room. "Hullo, Dorothy!" she said, "anything to eat?"

"Here you are!" said Dorothy, looking very cheerful in a red stockinette skirt and jumper, and handed her the box packed with solid Co-op. sandwiches and cakes; one like it had been sent round to each of the small committee rooms from Central, with the lists and pencils. Dione and half a dozen other women sat about on chairs or tables, eating sandwiches and drinking tea. " And I've remembered not to give you any sugar ! " said Dorothy, laughing. Then she said : " Now then, you've got to tell us all about the story we've heard—hasn't she ? "

" Yes," said one of the other women, " you promised you'd get it out of her, Dorothy ! "

" Which of my sins is coming home to roost ? " said Dione, a little anxious.

" It's about last Thursday," said Dorothy ; " is it true you were knocked down by a policeman when you were helping a wounded man in Hyde Park ? "

" Not exactly," said Dione, and then, seeing how disappointed they looked, she added : " I did do a little first-aid to a man with a scalp wound, and then afterwards I had my ears boxed by a man in the crowd, but the police were always very decent—to me. How did you hear ? "

" Oh, it came round," Dorothy said ; " my Bill's got pals in the N.U.W.M. What were you doing to get your ears boxed ? Were you cheeking him ? "

" Yes. I expect I deserved it ! But I wonder what's happening to them to-day. They were due to get their petition to Parliament, but I don't suppose they will. They seem to have made rather a muddle of it. Well, I suppose I must be getting off again."

" Come and look at baby first," said Dorothy ; " he's just lovely ! "

Things got brisker in the afternoon and for the last two hours Dione was driving hard. Once the self-starter did jam, but, remembering her instructions, she managed to get it right ; once, suddenly putting on the brakes, which were tighter than her own car's, she bumped the nose of an elector on the back seat. Really, she disapproved of this business of cars, unless people were definitely ill or unable to leave young children. Still, there it was, and she did some amicable racing with a Tory car, which at any rate pleased all the passengers. By eight, though, she was very tired; she took back a load of papers, sandwich boxes and little boys to Central, and then said she'd go off to Miss Waterhouse's for supper.

" The declaration of the poll will be about nine," Mason said; " you'll come along, won't you, Dione ? "

" All right," she said, " if I've got any legs to stand on."

Miss Waterhouse gave her supper and read aloud to her from Walt Whitman while she ate her cutlet. But during the reading Dione kept on thinking of other things: of Dorothy's baby; of a house she'd been to where a quite old couple, one on each side of the fire, had been quarrelling with one another steadily, quite unnoticed by their daughter, who was ironing at a table in the middle of the room; of Lilias asleep in her pram; of the young man Victor—would he send her his poems as he'd promised to? Of Oksana and Neonila and their mother perhaps not having enough to eat; of people being killed in China and South America and Morocco and all the various places where wars were at present happening; of a thousand kinds of death and disease and unhappiness, always going on in spite of human good will.

Good will, that curious product of consciousness, of leisure and energy to spare and share. That thing we put out against the forces of interest. That extra thing. Religions and nations and political parties have taken it and used it as coinage, have said you must only give it in exchange for value. Good will towards other Christians, Moslems, Jews, towards other English, Scots, Allies, Europeans, towards other Monarchists, Republicans, Conservatives, Labour folk, Communists ; hatred and cheating towards heathens, non-Moslems, Gentiles, towards the people across the frontier or with a different-coloured skin, towards all the other political parties. We will give you good will, but you must give us in fair exchange your soul, or your body, or your mind. And lately, since good will has been spoken of more freely, since we have given lip-service to universal good will, distributed free as a kind of advertisement for humanity, we have asked instead that we should be given something to show for it, peace, prosperity, happiness even. If we don't get it we are angry about our bargain and say we have been done. But the whole point of good will is that it is a by-product, a thing we can have too much of for our own immediate surroundings and belongings, as a mother can have too much milk for her baby. We have to give it away, not only in place but in time. We have to give even to the future.

Miss Waterhouse stopped reading. Dione looked up at the clock ; it was nearly nine. " I'd better be going," she said.

" Very well, my dear," said Miss Waterhouse, and saw her into the car. She drove slowly because she was so tired. The car smelt rather badly ; perhaps the exhaust wanted seeing to. But the sour smell of the Synthex works drowned the smell of the car. As she turned the corner towards the committee room she heard shouting, and glanced across and saw people running out of the big, ugly council schools. She checked, not recognising that this was where Finch's count had been held until she heard them singing a wild mixture of the " Red Flag " and the " Internationale," interspersed with much cheerfully triumphant yelling, and a moment afterwards had them all round the car.

She jumped out like a fly into treacle, knowing before

they told her, before friendly arms were thrown round her neck and shoulders, that Finch was Councillor again. They swept her with them along to the War Memorial, on whose steps Councillor Finch, spotlighted by half a dozen electric torches, made a hoarse and much-moved speech to them. Then Dione was spotlighted shaking hands with him, feeling like an imitation film star. Dorothy kissed her, saying: "Oh, this is it beginning, it really is!" But Dione drove on slowly towards the central committee room. So much energy, so much good will, so little to show for it. The mountains of Socialism had given birth among songs and rejoicings to Councillor Finch, much to the happiness of the other mice. And then? But it was the energy, it was the good will, that for the moment mattered.

# PART V

## HILL ERROR AND DELECTABLE MOUNTAINS TO THE ENCHANTED GROUND

" Readers of this strange language,
We have come at last to a country
Where light equal, like the shine from snow, strikes all faces,
Here you may wonder
How it was that works, money, interest, building, could ever hide
The palpable and obvious love of man for man."

STEPHEN SPENDER.

## OXFORD 5

LIKE most of her married friends and contemporaries, Dione would occasionally have two or three days of anxiety, sometimes acute and very oppressive. It was hard to do anything requiring intelligence with that hanging over one; it was difficult not to be cross and snap at Tom and the children. Tom, nearly as well aware of her times as she was, would usually share her anxiety towards the end, but not so immediately or continuously. This time it was five days late. She had already tried a large dose of castor oil; vague pains had resulted, but now she was feeling dreadfully well again. "Perhaps it's this cold weather coming so suddenly after January being so warm," suggested Tom, more to cheer her up than because he thought so. They were sitting in her bedroom before dinner. He had just come back from college hoping to find she had started while he'd been away at work, and would now be feeling happier. But no such luck.

She said: "I've been anxious for a fortnight, Tom. I didn't want to worry you, but the thing is—look here." She went over to the drawer. "You see . . . And I didn't notice it, not till next time, and then, of course, it was too late to do anything. I ought to have been more careful. It was my fault."

"My poor dear," said Tom, "it looks like that, doesn't it. I suppose—well, I suppose if you hadn't subconsciously wanted it to have gone wrong, you'd have been just that much more careful."

"Very likely. But that's not much help now, Tom.

Still, of course it can be dealt with." She spoke rather impersonally: "It's expensive in this country—or else not safe—but I have the name of someone in Paris."

"You're sure that's safe?"

"Oh, quite. I should only be away ten days. I could get Phœbe to come over with me, perhaps."

"I'd come, only it's the middle of term——"

"You certainly shan't. It would be no fun for you."

"It won't be any fun for you, sweetheart."

"No, but—well, I think it's bound to be about twenty pounds. Silly waste of money. Think of the holiday one could have."

"It's more like the price of having slept with one another without its happening all this time. But don't let's think of it as prices."

"I can contribute half. Though it's really all my fault."

"Rot," said Tom, and then suddenly took her into his arms. "Darling, darling," he said, "don't let's have this filthy money business touching us; don't let's price anything. Please, please, don't think like that. Do love me enough not to think of payment and exchange!"

"I do," she said, holding tight on to him; "I do think of you just—with love."

"Marriage has been so hellishly commercialised," Tom said, his arms round her, his cheek against hers; "it's only when one gets out of the proper buying and selling pattern of it that one sees it for the good thing it can be, when it's not bargaining." He was talking partly because he meant it, partly to soothe the tension in himself, and partly to stop her from crying; he knew talk would do that.

"That's *my* idea, Tom!" she said.

"Well, do you want to be paid for it?" He kissed her face turned up towards him.

" No, Tom, it's a good idea, so you must have it, too. Yes, we have got out of the proper Eastern marriage pattern a bit ! " And then she said, half laughing and half very tender : " Tom, this is a funny time to start making love to me ! "

" It's a very good time. You need being made love to. Don't you—just a little ? Don't you, my dear ? "

She thought she would have one more try and took ten five-grain tablets of quinine. Unfortunately they had to dine out that evening—*petit dîner de réconciliation* with the Bickerdens—May showing she was a modern woman and bore no malice to Phœbe's sister. Through a curious curtain of buzz, a constant telephone bell in her head, Dione behaved politely, induced forkfuls of food to find their right way to her mouth, was a perfect lady to May. It was no good, though. Nothing happened. Within a few days Dione began to feel absolutely definite signs of *malaise*, a dislike of certain foods, all the old things. Term went on, the small jobs, the letters to write and answer, bits of Tom's new book to type, things to order, see to, pay for, the children to be looked after properly. Dione wrote to Phœbe asking her if she could come to Paris with her early in March. It wouldn't have been so bad if only she could have done it absolutely at once—next day—while she was still brave, but it was necessary to wait for a bit. Tom asked her if she would mind his telling Oksana.

" Of course not," Dione said. She and Oksana wrote to one another too, less often and perhaps more formally. And twice Tom and Donald had written to one another about a young engineer at Marshbrook Bridge who wanted to go out to the U.S.S.R. Funny this Russian correspondence ! Donald had been furious about Idris Pritchard, but that letter had crossed hers written after the Hyde

Park show. How remote all that was, how curiously unimportant!

"Buck up, old girl," said Tom, watching her, that evening, "it'll all be over in a fortnight."

"I know," Dione said.

"Are you afraid of the actual operation?" Tom asked. "There's no danger if it's properly done."

"Oh, I know. Lots of people have it. I only rather wish I hadn't seen it done in Moscow."

"Looked beastly, did it?"

"Yes, only thousands of women do have it there. And of course I shan't be hurt. They give anæsthetics properly on the Continent. It's only—oh, Tom, I feel like a murderer already!"

"But, my dearest, why? Let's be logical about it. Is it any worse than birth control really?"

"Not really, I suppose. Only—oh, Tom, the little wretch has taken root in me and it's so tough that it won't move for quinine and stuff. It's got the will to live. It's intending to be a man or a woman. And—and then they go and dig about with a great metal forceps and drag him or her out of me. And so—and so it feels like murder."

"Oh, lord, Dione, don't make it so damned personal. It's just a collection of cells growing in you that oughtn't to be there—like a cancer. It's not even a recognisable shape. It's no more a person than the two cells it grew out of were. I don't feel it's possibly personal, and it's half me as well."

"I know," Dione said again.

"But, my darling, you do agree that we don't want to have any more, don't you? Damn it all, we've talked it out and we've agreed not to on all sorts of grounds—I never put pressure on you, did I?"

"No."

"You see the political grounds are more urgent than ever; we can't go giving any more hostages to safety first. And what sort of world is it going to be for the children? If there isn't a revolution it's likely enough that they'll be killed in another war. You don't want to breed sons for that, Dione." She nodded, drawing aimlessly with a pencil on the back of an envelope. "And we don't want to have children growing up like half my best pupils, with plenty of brains and given no chance to use them—eating their hearts out."

"Oh, I know," Dione said; "besides, I haven't the right to when people at Marshbrook Bridge haven't got enough food and clothes for theirs. I *do* know, Tom. I won't bother you with my feelings again. For I know that's all they are."

"Feelings can be damned painful, though," said Tom doubtfully. He wrote to Oksana. "Do you want to put in anything?" he asked Dione. She shook her head. At the moment she didn't want to communicate with anyone.

Phœbe wrote back that she'd come if necessary, though it was the hell of a nuisance at the moment as she was hard at it; still she wasn't going to let Dione do that alone. "The Campbell Women might get you if I wasn't there," she wrote. She went on: "It seems a pity. Of course I'd do it, but I don't want another baby, or if I sometimes think I want one with Phil I paint a picture instead. But when one finds that very rare combination of a husband and wife who are in love with one another—I'm not quite out of date, am I, lassie?—and who both like children, it seems a pity to do this. Aren't you doing it just for the sake of your silly old revolution which won't happen till all of us are dead and buried?" Tom asked across the breakfast table if Phœbe was coming. Dione said yes, but didn't show him the letter.

She wrote to Paris and fixed everything up; it was a businesslike correspondence on both sides. She kept a fortnight of term clear of dates for herself. It meant cutting the Barton's End and Marl social, but that couldn't be helped. She did a good deal of heavy digging in the garden, partly because it distracted her mind and partly because she hoped this way to bring it on—digging Oxford clay was the kind of thing one was strictly forbidden to do in the second month of pregnancy! She was not feeling very well, but was only sick once. She tried to avoid fats, but didn't much like the idea of going on to a regular diet. It would be awful if anyone in the household guessed.

A few nights before she was due to go she woke up crying in the dark. Tom stirred and turned over and said sleepily: "What is it?"

She, still dizzy and soft from her dream, sobbed: "Oh, Tom, I dreamt it was all right."

"I've dreamt that too sometimes," said Tom, kissing her clumsily on the ear.

"Not like I did," said Dione, burrowing away from him, her face into the pillow. "I dreamt it was all right and I could keep him and he was born and he was so lovely——" She began sobbing distractedly again.

Tom turned on the light: "Look here, my dear, if you're going to go and get miserable all the rest of your life, it's not worth it, for your sake—or mine. I know you've been feeling pretty rotten about it all this time, but I can tell you, Dione, I have too! I've not been able to write a word of my book, or that pamphlet, and I've jumped on all my pupils. If you're going to go on feeling wretched it's just going to make everything impossible."

She was wide-awake now. "No, really, Tom, it's all right." Awful, these things happening at night when one was half asleep, hadn't got a grip on oneself—she'd woke up hating him for killing her baby and now he was hating her for ruining his work—in a moment he was going to say he'd never sleep with her again! And neither of them really hated one another—and it was her fault. "No, Tom," she said, "please—I was just being silly. Go to sleep again."

"How can I go to sleep when you're being miserable? Look here, Dione, if you want this other baby as badly as all that, we'd better have it. It's your show primarily. I'll manage over money. I just can't stand your feeling like this."

"But I'm *not*," she said, "and all the reasons we agreed to still hold, and I *will* be reasonable. It's only a beastly pack of chromosomes and I don't care what happens to it."

"But Dione, if you've changed your mind, for God's sake say so *now*. My dear, don't think I'll be angry, but I just must know."

"No," said Dione. "No, no! Don't bother me, Tom!"

The next day Morag came back from school with a headache. By evening her temperature was up to 103° and she had been devastatingly sick. Then, thank goodness, the rash came out. None of the children, including Brian, had yet had measles. Probably they all would, one after the other. They mustn't go back to school, of course. She didn't mind so much about the older ones, but Lilias was a bit young for measles. All the next day Morag's temperature stayed up and she was slightly delirious. Dione got in a nurse from the Ackland, whom Morag unfortunately hated at sight; she had red hair, and Morag, usually so sensible, insisted that she was a tiger and would eat her. Dione stayed with Morag all the time—her own nurse couldn't help because of keeping Lilias out of infection. There were tepid sponges to be given, temperatures to be taken, medicine, everything, and it would be quite an hour between one moment of remembering the other thing and the next. But, disconcertingly, Dione found herself bargaining with some Power: let Morag go and I don't mind what's done to me. No good being Marxist about bargains. At a crisis, centuries and generations of bargainers were too much for her. It would take more than a few years of non-bargaining to drop the instinct, though the practice might go sooner.

By ten o'clock that evening Morag's temperature was nearly 105°. Tom was walking up and down the passage biting his nails, and the doctor was telling Dione to pull herself together, there was no real need for grave anxiety yet. Then Morag dropped off into a hot, panting sleep of exhaustion and Dione went down to the drawing-room, saying to call her at once if Morag woke. There was bad news from Germany in the evening papers. The Reichstag had been set on fire and the Communists, of course, accused; now the Nazis had got busy suppressing and arresting in time for the elections on Sunday. When was that? Oh, to-morrow. The last Sunday in term. And on Wednesday she was due for Paris. She took in the news; it all seemed very appropriate. Suddenly she felt overwhelmingly sleepy and lay down on the sofa, telling Tom to wake her the moment the nurse came for her. He put a rug over her and in three minutes she was deep asleep.

She woke with a jump and glanced at the clock—past two in the morning! How had they let her sleep so long? What had happened? Were they—oh, God, had they let her sleep because—because—there was nothing ever any more to be done for Morag? She ran out into the hall, her hair coming down. Tom looked out of the study. "It's all right," he said, "Nurse says she's still asleep and her temperature's down three points, and probably dropping still. Now, what about going to bed properly ? "

She went into the study : " What were you doing ? "

" Trying to get on with the Heavy Woollens pamphlet." She looked at the waste-paper basket and the floor round it. " Yes, I've scrapped half a dozen drafts. I expect this one'll have to go, too."

For another twelve hours relief asserted itself over everything else, but by Sunday lunch she was worrying again. The fact of her bargain with the Power did not at all alter her point of view about Paris ; she didn't believe in the bargain any longer—obviously it had nothing to do with the fact that Morag, though itchy and blotchy, had now only got ordinary, childish measles, a mere matter of sensible nursing for a few days. Dione was going to Paris, but—the others were almost certain to get it, and supposing Kenneth got ill and frightened like Morag. And Ian, who'd been having earache this winter ; they'd have to be extra careful of him because of the obvious danger. And if Brian got it he'd be pretty sure to get it badly ; it might start some of his old troubles again. Clearly, with this hanging over Brian, Phœbe couldn't leave England. Dione wept with anxiety. Tom had to go over to speak in Gloucestershire that afternoon ; after the meeting they'd motor him in to the junction, and he'd be back by midnight. He was guiltily but definitely thankful to be getting out of the house.

She told Alice she wasn't at home to any undergraduates that Sunday ; the idiots mightn't have had measles. However Teddy turned up on his motor-bike and said firmly that he must have a college document which he had left with Tom to sign—and Tom had promised to let him have it back on Saturday. Dione took him into the study and they routed about for it. When they discovered it finally—

unsigned—she apologised for Tom and explained about the measles. "Old Tom's been on the jump for the last three weeks," said Teddy, "what's been the trouble? You don't look too well, Dione. Affairs of the world a bit depressing, what? All your money invested in dollars?"

She shook her head. It was most annoying, but she was going to cry in a minute if he went on asking questions.

He noticed: "I say, I wish you'd tell me. Perhaps I could help. The trained mind of the biologist and all that. Is it anything biological, Dione?"

"Yes," she said suddenly, "that's just about what it is! I'm pregnant, and I'm going to have an abortion, and I don't want to, and I can't stand it, and—anyway I've got to."

"May I ask one thing?" said Teddy.

"Yes, I suppose now I've said that you may as well."

Teddy most unexpectedly blushed: "Is it by old Tom?"

Dione burst out laughing, which was almost as great a relief as tears. "Yes, rather! I wouldn't mind so much, Teddy, if it was by someone else. And look here, for God's sake don't go and tell Tom I said anything. He wouldn't mind, only—he wouldn't like it."

"Too safe with old Teddy. But look here, Dione; are you sure you've got to if you feel like that about it? You're too much of a lovely, honest-to-God she-woman to let yourself be stampeded into this by the propagandists. Why the devil shouldn't you have twenty children if you want to?"

"It's selfish. Other people can't."

"Lot's of 'em don't want to, the silly bitches."

"Yes, but we'd made up our minds not to have any more. It's partly money, of course, but not mostly. We feel we aren't justified in bringing any more people into such a world as it is. And we feel that the more children we have the more we're bound to cling to safety."

"My dear Dione, I don't see you and Tom turning into . . . little Conservatives—sorry to use biological adjectives! —if you had a hundred infants! Go on, have it, what's one more or less? If you had to think in numbers the way a biologist does you wouldn't fuss so."

"But, Teddy——"

"Now, can't you find a nice girl who'd be willing to bear me half a dozen healthy children and stay intelligent herself? I'd give her every facility. Or shall I have to wait for Morag?"

For a moment Morag's song came back overwhelmingly to Dione: "Ower mony o' ye, little for to gie ye . . ." She shook her head: "Morag won't want a dried-up old professor!"

"Oh, come off it, I'm only twenty-seven! I say, I'm damned glad she's better, anyway." He felt in his pocket: "Will you give her this from me?"

"What on earth is it?"

"It's the skeleton of a kind of African snake. Look, there are its fangs. No, really I don't need it."

"Well, thanks awfully, it's just the kind of thing she adores. She'll probably keep it under her pillow."

"Tell her its from an aged admirer. And—I say, Dione, I must buzz off and get the old Chaplain to sign this: do curse Tom from me—look here, don't you go doing this!"

She shook her head: "No, Teddy, I must be reasonable."

"Don't be reasonable," he said, "be intelligent!"

After he left she wrote to Phœbe, telling her about the measles and the likelihood of Brian's getting it, and that she mustn't come to Paris. Then she remembered it was Sunday and the letter wouldn't get off. She'd have to wire to-morrow. Damn. She wrote out the telegram and asked Alice to send it over the telephone first thing in the morning. And it would be much, much worse in Paris by herself. Or ought she to put it off till after the measles? But she mustn't leave it much longer. Oh, hell. Then she read to Morag and played ludo with her, a game which unfortunately doesn't distract the adult mind much.

She went to bed before Tom got back and didn't wake when he came in. Next morning, when she did wake, he was sitting on the end of the bed reading a letter. She saw it was from Oksana. He saw her waking. "There's an enclosure for you," he said slowly. "I suppose you'd better have it." He flipped it across the bed to her.

"How's Morag?" she said.

"Only 100°, and hungry. But Nurse says she thinks Kenneth is beginning."

"Oh, gosh, I must go and see——"

"He's in bed and quite happy. I've had a look at him. Read that letter, Dione."

"All right. Did you have a good meeting?"

"Pretty fair, but——"

Oh dear, she didn't terribly much want to read a letter from Oksana at the moment!

The letter: "Dione! Tom gives me news of you, and I write back by air this same day. You must, *must* have this child by Tom. He says you have agreed together to have an abort. But Dione, I think from what you have said to me, in Moscow, that you do really want this child, and as you have no profession you can surely have it. I remember also what you say about babies making more difficult your action in a revolution; but, alas! your revolution may be yet long, after Germany and the U.S. You will perhaps afterwards be too old. So I think that you and Tom should have many children now, for after your revolution you too will be able to have big population and join with us. We will then be strong, be helping you. If later it shall be very difficult, the education, the food, as you have said, send me out this child and it shall be to me as though Tom had made me, too, a child. Oh, Dione, do not have this abort.! I know well that you do not want, and I am most glad that you and Tom should so well sleep together; it is proof to me that I was not what Tom says, a bloody nuisance to you. It will be a so good world for Socialists and Socialist children, not perhaps now everywhere, but soon. If it is even a bad world for your children, yet for their children it will be good. Dione, I pray you to bear this child. I have told Tom if he does not give you this letter I will not write to him again ever. I have won a prize for my radio, and I am so much excited. I have told Tom. I love you. Oksana Petrovna."

Dione put the letter down on the bed. "Did you read it, Tom? No? Well, I suppose she said much the same to you. It's sweet of her and she means it, but of course she just doesn't see our problems."

"She doesn't know all the family's getting measles. Otherwise—look here, Dione, hadn't we better reconsider it?"

"There's no new—evidence."

"No, but—it isn't just since this. I was thinking about it all last night at the meeting. Do you believe I love you at all, Dione?"

"But that's nothing to do with this—growth."

"Yes, it is. You see, my dear, you gave your case away when you made the mistake at the beginning. And—oh, I'm not such a fool I haven't seen you wanting it. And you can't go on pretending Lilias is a baby any longer. She'll be four by the time—this one is born."

Dione jammed her head into the pillow: "Tom, don't!"

she said, all muffled. " Do you suppose I don't know the exact date ! "

" Then, my dear, my dearest, let's chuck all this rot about Paris, and have the bloody little nuisance, bless its heart ! After all, you'll have all the bother and pain of it."

" You'll have to support it."

" Didn't I tell you that you weren't to think about me and money in the same breath ? "

" I could always take Oksana's offer," she said, in a curious voice that Tom couldn't quite place, and chucked the letter across to him. His face softened, reading it, differently to the way it softened for her.

" She's a funny kid," said Tom. " Well ? "

" No," said Dione, " the same reasons remain. She doesn't understand. And, damn it all, she oughtn't to want more bourgeois children. I keep on thinking that, too. Properly speaking, we oughtn't to perpetuate our kind. Don't worry, Tom, I've faced up to this, and I shall be all right."

Tom said slowly : " Dione, are you refusing because the final suggestion has come from my—ex-mistress ? "

Dione lay face downwards again, wriggling with distress. At the end she said : " I think I may have had that in my mind, Tom. I've got to think it out. Give me ten minutes." He went away, but she couldn't think it out at all, she couldn't reason. The arguments both ways were solid. She only knew what she wanted—and what she had no right to. Not till it could be the same for everyone. Tom came back. As he shut the door she said : " No, I can't see that it's altered. We've still got no right."

Tom said : " You mean, we've not paid for it. The bargain again ! "

" Oh, don't press me, Tom ! It would keep us from action."

" Action," said Tom, " talking of action, I sent a telegram to Paris saying you weren't coming."

" The devil you did," said Dione, and kept silent for a moment. " You are a he-man, Tom," she said, and then : " You know I shall be ugly and ill and a worry from now till October."

" You exaggerate," said Tom. " I like you that way. At any rate we can have a few months' good honest fun without any of those damned silly ineffective benefits of modern science."

Dione giggled a little : " Yes, I shall like that, too. But, Tom, you're sure you won't hate it ? "

" No, it'll be a baby then, not just—a mistake."

" We'd better call it Oksana to make sure you don't hate it. If it's a she."

" And if it's a he I suppose we shall have to call it Donald, after yet another member of the Communist Party ? Now then, Dione, get up, my lamb, you can tell cook all about it now, and she'll give you your proper food, and you'll be as well and jolly as all those women in Moscow. By the way, Morag wants to see you. I—I went in and told her you were going to have a baby."

" You didn't ! "

" Yes, I thought that would settle it if the telegram hadn't. She's frightfully bucked and longing to be all feminine to you. I know it's a mother's sweet privilege, but I thought I might as well get some fun out of being a father for a change."

## SALLINGTON 10

ALL the children got measles, including Lilias, who got it very mildly. Dione worried about them all, but it wasn't *that* sort of worry. They were delighted about the baby when she told them, though Lilias wept and demanded it at once. At any rate, that was measles done with. . . . All five convalesced together in the nursery rooms with the door open between them, so that they didn't feel gloomy, and were less inclined to scratch. While that was happening Dione went up for the Barton's End and Marl social.

The Taylors had come back, so she and Tom stayed with them this time. Taylor was quite well again and had a job with the municipality. He had put aside some of his prize-money towards building the Labour Hall that he'd had in mind so long, but it was working out very expensive; there wasn't a cheap plot of land anywhere in the division! But it was a much more cheerful household and the mantelpiece was decorated with shells brought back from the seaside. At breakfast Dione refused the eggs and bacon they'd got for her and Tom, and when pressed to take them explained why she couldn't. Mrs. Taylor went pink with pleasure and hugged her, and Bert Taylor shook hands heartily with Tom.

This in general seemed to be how the constituency was going to take it. They went round to the Masons before the social, and Dione told them, as it might have some bearing on future arrangements. Mason at once asked when, and she told him the middle of October.

"Fine," he said. "Now if only we could have the

General then, we'd get Tom in with a couple of thousand to spare."

"But why on earth?"

"The women's vote," said Mason.

"But they've done it themselves; they know there's no question of damned merit about it."

"That's it. They feel you're one of themselves. Some of them feel they want to make it up to you somehow, and some of them feel, well, you must be safe to vote for. You know, there are folks here who're frightened of Socialism; it seems a bit queer to them. But when they see you've done something as ordinary as having a baby, then they aren't frightened. And some of 'em just go all funny when they see a baby—like my missus does, don't you?—and they'll go and vote for you on that."

"Teddy was telling me—he's a biologist at Tom's college—that this soft feeling one gets about babies and puppies is all due to a secretion of the pituitary gland. Funny, isn't it? But, all the same, it's quite real enough to make one act on it."

"They talk a lot of nonsense about glands," Mason said. "I never believe half what they say. Middle of October. Well now, if we arrange a social in November, will you—and it—both come down?"

"All right, Stan!" said Dione, laughing.

At the social she told Dorothy, who kissed her and said: "There, now, isn't that lovely. And he'll just be in time to help build Jerusalem—like Mr. Galton was saying in his speech."

"I feel it's awfully unfair," Dione said, hesitating, "for me to be having a baby so comfortably, with doctors and nurses and all that, and able to stay in bed afterwards, while people here——"

"Oh, get along with you!" said Dorothy, "you have

as good a time as you can, Dione! It's bad enough at the best, anyway. Or so they say. Maybe by the time Bill and me have our next it'll be good times for us all."

She told Edna Boffin, who took her aside and said: "Now, do let me say one thing—don't have it vaccinated, my dear—you've no idea the number it kills!"

"But——"

"Now, we haven't time to go into it now, but I'll send you all the literature and you must promise me to read it. You'll be surprised!"

"I'm sure I shall," said Dione.

She was pleased to see Miss Wills back, though Mrs. East said a little maliciously that she'd only started coming to socials again since she'd got the sack from her Sallington solicitors, who'd had to cut down their staff. She was distinctly more elegant than she'd been two years before, Dione thought—and seemed to have a new, and perhaps preferable, boy-friend.

Mason drove her and the Taylors back, and then he and Tom went on to talk to Councillor Finch about some difficulty he was having with the education people. Mrs. Taylor showed a tendency to fuss over Dione, who accepted a hot-water bottle, but firmly refused a nice drink of Ovaltine. After Dione was in bed with the hot-water bottle but without the Ovaltine, Mrs. Taylor came up, nominally to ask if she'd got everything she wanted, but really to coo over her and allow the pituitary gland to function thoroughly. "Everyone'll be ever so pleased!" was her final verdict.

Dione was suddenly unable not to say: "You know, Mrs. Taylor, this baby that's turning out so important was just an accident."

Mrs. Taylor looked slightly embarrassed: "I could make you a nice hot lemon drink," she said.

Dione, her hands behind her head, and looking definitely rather pretty, added : " There's no form of birth control that's a hundred per cent. safe."

Mrs. Taylor said cautiously, looking away : " I've *heard* of birth control, of course."

" But don't you practise it ? " Mrs. Taylor shook her head. " But, my dear," Dione said, " you're only about thirty-five, aren't you ? Yes, I thought so. And you've been married eleven years ?—and you've only got Emmie. What have you done since ? " Mrs. Taylor was quite silent, reddening, fingering the edge of Dione's folded bed-cover. " But Mrs. Taylor ! Mary ! My dear idiot, you're very fond of your husband, aren't you ? Why don't you go along to the clinic at Sallmouth—haven't you heard of it ? "

" Well, I have heard of it," said Mary Taylor in a low, stifled kind of voice, " but somehow I didn't think—folks like us, who—who can manage without—though it's hard when we're that fond of one another ! It was hard after the accident, when he was sleeping so bad, and we couldn't help wondering—I nearly did ask you then, but——"

" Oh, Mary Taylor, you great goose ! I thought anyone as sensible as you would have known. It's probably very bad for you going on like this."

" Well, I've sometimes thought," said Mary Taylor all in a rush, " that it was that gave me my headaches and sometimes—oh, I just couldn't go talking to the doctor, though he's been ever so kind to us, but him being a man and us on the panel—and Mr. Taylor he's shy-like. Being as he was the only boy in his family and then not going into the army but into prison instead—he hasn't been so much with folks that could tell him. And then, since we was in the Labour Movement—I thought we oughtn't to be thinking of these things. Only I've wondered, with Emmie growing up, and not knowing what to tell her—— But aren't I too old now to go to any clinics ? "

" Of course you aren't," Dione said. " It's really very safe if you're careful—I just wasn't careful enough."

" So now you're going to have a lovely little baby. You'll bring her down, won't you ? And—if you could give me the address of that clinic you were talking about ? "

" Yes, rather," she said, and again Mary Taylor bent down and kissed her.

In a little Tom came in : " What on earth were you and Mrs. Taylor jawing about ? "

" Oh, we were out Elephant-hunting," said Dione sleepily.

The only possible Sunday train was in the afternoon, so they stayed over Sunday morning ; while Tom sat in the Taylors' living-room, working, Dione went over to Greenapple on chance of finding Agnes Green. It was a bore none of their people at Sallington being on the telephone, but inevitable. Anyhow, nothing was much of a nuisance to-day. She walked down the Taylors' street feeling ridiculously happy, waving a hand to a woman at a window, walking lightly and yet securely. The tram magically transported her and her baby, who had been such a little time ago only a nasty unwanted growth of cells, but who was now either Jean Oksana or Donald James, this tough and clever baby who had evaded drugs and knives and was now living and growing like a magic hare among the roots of the fairy hazel tree. You oughtn't to be so happy, Dione Galton ! Stop it, you're only doing the most ordinary, easy thing, there's nothing to be proud about, you fool ! But her smiling mouth gave her away, and the tram conductor, recognising her as Mrs. Galton, grinned back at her.

While she was waiting for her 73 in the Square, Rosalind Coke-Brown got out of her car just in front of her. Dione felt very friendly towards anything or anyone to do with Tom. "Hullo, Rosalind!" she said. But Rosalind looked round, and looked through her, and firmly cut her and Tom's baby. Dione went on waiting for her tram. It was like being swept over by a cloud. But how ridiculous to be depressed by Rosalind! Who cares? It's because she's Tom's sister, the same to Tom as Phœbe is to me. But no, that's wrong, it isn't the physical relationship that matters. Leave father and mother and follow me. . . . All these things very destructive of family life. Leave father and mother. Supposing Morag heard that about—what could it be? What would get at the young in ten years' time? Fascism, perhaps—if you took this almost inevitable road of violent group feeling, how easy to take the right-hand rather than the left-hand fork!—or even old-fashioned religion—that might come again, like Buchmanism. And this baby, so close, so part of herself—but it would be separated, leave father and mother—ah, here's my tram, thank goodness!

Yes, said the little maid, Miss Green was in, but—— Agnes Green's voice called down the stairs: "Who's there?" Dione called up. "Oh, it's you, Dione. Well—come up to my bedroom if you don't mind. We're having—a little meeting."

"But shall I go? Shan't I be a nuisance?"

"You couldn't come back this evening? Oh, well, if you've only got this morning, come up and wait. We shan't be long."

She showed Dione into her bedroom and gave her a current *Daily Worker* and a dozen numbers of the *Labour Monthly* to read. What was going to happen about the United Front, Dione wondered? Both sides suspicious, biting one another. Probably a lot more going on unofficially than any of the publicists would admit. She had rather a romantic feeling about the *Daily Worker*, but if she read it too thoroughly, she had to look through a *Mail* or an *Express* to stop herself going Tory! She turned to the solider stuff. This succeeded in depressing her a good deal more thoroughly than Rosalind had. After two or three articles she began to feel completely worthless. Her own standards and traditions were bourgeois and she didn't really try to defend them, but, still, she couldn't properly sympathise with the new ones; she couldn't help sometimes wondering whether some of the writers weren't perhaps sometimes talking through their hats. But was this just her prejudice? Probably. Oh, it was most uncomfortable. And sometimes she was shocked—and annoyed with herself for being shocked.

Take this question of patriotism, for instance: it always made her a bit uncomfortable to think of soldiers—English soldiers—being encouraged to shoot their officers. And was the Indian problem quite as simple as they always said? And in spite of Merrill and the Tories she had this curious feeling about the Union Jack. It was all very silly, though she could find definite historical grounds for all her prejudices. She remembered suddenly an argument she and Victor had passed on the stairs at that studio party: a young man who had expressed the most violent revolutionary views and who looked quite likely to carry them out, to whom a rather drunken and cheerful Swedish musician had said that the English had been whipped out of Gallipoli—and the revolutionary had turned on him fiercely and explained that this was not so, it was only the Government which had let down the English soldiers—— Yes, we're all one mass of prejudices. Look at this Russian trial business! And I'm bringing another person into it, another mind to be got at and twisted by prejudices, to feel itself irretrievably caught in the sticky spider's web—to beat vainly and miserably against these ideas that still cling, whatever reason one brings to bear against them. A nice look-out for Jean Oksana or Donald James!

Agnes Green came in. "Well, my dear, the business meeting's over, but some of the comrades are still there. They'll probably be gone in a few minutes."

"I suppose—I'd better not come in, had I? They wouldn't like me?"

"That's as you feel, Dione," Agnes Green said, "but Idris Pritchard is there. I don't know whether you want to meet him."

"Oh, we put that right. In Hyde Park. Didn't he tell you at all?"

"Well, he did say something, but I wasn't sure how much I believed him. On personal matters he's so apt to say things happened just because they're what he'd like."

"Yes, I should think he was a bit of a liar. Is he still at the cinema?"

"Yes," said Agnes, and added: "It's not so bad as he likes to make out. He needed discipline. He'd had three times the wages of most of our members all this time. Well, come along in."

There were four men, including Idris Pritchard, and one tough-looking girl, sitting about and smoking. "This is Mrs. Galton, comrades," said Agnes Green.

"How do you do?" said Dione, bowing all round, and shook hands with Idris, who had jumped up, but then sat down again, as though he were rather ashamed of himself. Dione found herself a seat on the divan, beside the girl, who turned to her.

"What, are you Tom Galton's wife from Marshbrook Bridge? What a go!" And she blew out a cloud of smoke. By her voice she came from further south, perhaps London.

"Yes," said Dione, "you don't mind, do you ?—or do you ?"

"I don't mind if you were the Virgin Mary," said the girl, and added : "I work in your brother-in-law's mills."

"What, Reginald Coke-Brown ? He wouldn't like being thought of as my brother-in-law ! I've just been cut by his wife."

"Oh, that bitch. Did you know he's just lengthened our hours ? Tightening up, he calls it, punctuality, the good old Sallington virtue !" She laughed.

"No, I hadn't heard that," Dione said. "What are you going to do about it ?"

"Wouldn't you like to know ?" said the girl. "Gimme another fag, Agnes."

One of the men said : "Well, Comrade Green, we can't discuss any more now, so I'm off." He looked offendedly at Dione.

"I think we'd finished our business, comrade," said Agnes.

"I was looking forward to a bit of a useful talk, but seeing as how you've got company, Comrade Green——"

"I'm sorry," said Dione rising. "I'll go."

"Nonsense," said Agnes. "I asked you here. Sit down." Dione obediently sat down ; the girl beside her laughed—presumably at her.

The man said fiercely : "How can we talk—with her there ? And I don't care if she hears me say it !"

"Oh, come off it, Comrade Hart," said Idris ; "it was she got MacLean away, as you know."

"Yes, after him near breaking the Party !"

One of the other men spoke, across him, to Dione : "Well, how is young Mac ?"

" He's in a metal factory at Kharkov, doing very well," Dione answered. " He's got a nice room and he's married a Russian girl called Anna, and he's on the works committee of his factory."

" Is he, though ! " said the man appreciatively.

" Shall I say you asked after him ? " Dione said. " He's always wanting news of Sallington. Would you let me send him your name ? "

" No," said the man hastily, as though he thought she'd give his name to the police straight-away, and then : " Well, I'm off. So long all ! " He walked out and the other two men after him, the one who had spoken still glaring at Dione, and the other muttering something which she didn't catch, in a very thick accent.

" They're all in the Heavy Woollens," the girl said; adding in a funny aggressive way, " if you want to know ! "

Dione nodded. She couldn't help thinking of Tom's plan for dealing with the Heavy Woollen trade, and wondered (*a*) whether they'd got any plan which was anything like so practical, comprehensive and economically sound as his, and (*b*) whether Tom had sufficiently considered the kind of chaps and girls who were employed in the industry. What were they going to say to his plan ?

Idris said : " Well, Dione, you haven't written to me for a long time."

" No," she said, " I've been very busy. All the children have been having measles for one thing. How's life ? " He made an expressive face. She thought his clothes were distinctly less tidy ; he probably wore his shirts twice as long, too. It was the same felt hat, but—oh, poor Idris.

" Have a fag ? " said the girl suddenly, handing Agnes Green's box.

Dione shook her head : " No, thanks, not now."

" What, too much of a lady for woodbines ? " said the girl, puffing the smoke towards her.

" No," said Dione, " only I'm starting a baby and it makes me feel sick." She saw Idris jump a little as she said it.

" My dear ! " said Agnes, in a funny voice, half affection and half protest.

" A baby ? " said the girl, looking at her hard. " How many have you got already ? "

" Four," Dione said, remembering Oksana.

" You are going it, aren't you ? " said the girl, but she was definitely a little friendly.

" Well, perhaps," said Dione, and then : " Do you think it's wrong of me ? "

" What ? " said the girl. " Bringing another little capitalist into the world ? They'll be wanted in the next war ! "

" I hope it'll be a little Socialist, not a little capitalist," said Dione, rather indignant for Jean Oksana or Donald James.

" Well, it'll be born with a bit of capital behind it, won't it ? " said the girl. " Don't you go telling me you haven't got sixpence laid by—nor a thousand pounds neither ! "

" Yes, it's more than that, I'm afraid," Dione said. " But don't intentions count at all ? "

" Oh, I dare say," said the girl, " and, talking of intentions, come on you, Idris ! " She got up, and Idris got up too, looking rather awkward.

Dione looked him in the eyes and grinned : " Well, good-bye, Idris ! " she said. After they went out she said to Agnes : " It looks as if he'd just about met his match there ! "

" Yes," said Agnes. " You see, since he's had this job at—the usual wages—he hasn't been able to put it across to anyone that he's a little gentleman. Doris there, she's getting twice what he is. It's good for him."

"I'm sure it is," Dione said, and perversely made up her mind to send him a silk tie from Hugh Hall's as soon as she got back to Oxford.

"Are you really going to have a baby?" said Agnes. "Oughtn't you to put your feet up or something? I thought—I thought you'd probably got as many as you were going to have."

"Well," said Dione, "this one was an accident, and at first I meant to have an abortion."

"Oh!" said Agnes, with a kind of gasp, and put her hand up to her face. "How can you talk of it like that?"

"My dear Agnes," Dione said, "thousands of people do—in England."

"But they die!"

"I should have had it properly done. And I wouldn't have died. You see, I didn't think we had the right—as that girl said—to bring another little capitalist into the world. Someone to inherit our standards and values, and—oh, we had plenty of reasons against it."

"But you should have thought of that before!"

"So we did. It wasn't *that* sort of accident, Agnes. We were taking precautions, but the thing didn't work. And then—we decided not to. If it's a boy it's going to be called Donald after Donald MacLean. By the way, he and his wife are going to have a baby this summer, and if it's a girl they'll call it after me. That's rather fun, don't you think?"

Agnes Green suddenly said: "You know, my dear, this is all rather strange to me. I see it going on all round me, of course—but—Dione, I've only once been kissed by a man in my whole life, and he wasn't the right man for me."

"Oh, Agnes!" said Dione, and then: "Why wasn't he?"

"He was a commercial traveller," Agnes said simply. "It was before I took up teaching, when I was still at home. My father kept a public-house, you know. I left home as soon as I could."

"But no one at all since then?"

Agnes shook her head: "No one at all. Once I thought the head master at a school where I was had begun to look at me. So I applied for a transfer. It made me uncomfortable. Sometimes I almost wish I hadn't. The experience—any kind of experience almost—would have been useful to me."

"Agnes," Dione said, "were you—at all fond of Donald?"

"Yes," said Agnes, "but of course neither of us ever thought of—kissing. That was what made me feel so queer when you said you and he had been—doing that—in Russia. But I don't suppose he and I had even been alone in a room together, ever."

"But one doesn't have to be alone in a room to kiss someone!" said Dione, thinking of the studio party. "If you feel very friendly you just kiss. It's not—such a very serious thing."

"Isn't it?" said Agnes; "it would be to me."

"Agnes, you need a holiday," Dione said. "I was awfully sorry you couldn't come at Christmas. Would you come up to Scotland at Easter? That's my mother's house, but I'll arrange it. You'd see Donald's father and mother."

"He told me once his father was gardener to a landowner in Scotland."

"Yes, that's my mother. Sorry, Agnes, but there it is! You'd have to be very careful about politics with the

MacLeans, but they'd love to see anyone who'd known Donald. They're terribly fond of him."

"I couldn't come up to Scotland," said Agnes. "It's too far."

"Well, look here, I'm thinking of driving up with the children. If you didn't mind squeezing in with Morag and Kenneth—yes, and there'd probably be Brian, too—I could come by here and pick you up."

"But surely you oughtn't to drive—just now?"

"I shan't drive fast, and not much more than a hundred miles a day. But if that wouldn't bore you—it's pretty country further along. Oh do, Agnes!" And if you come, she made up her mind, I shall see that Tom kisses you nicely; my poor darling, you're quite kissable, and he jolly well shall!

She went back, as she usually did after seeing any of the Communist Party, with a funny mixture of feelings, to-day even more accentuated than usual. There was the sense of inferiority, that these were the serious people, the ones who didn't compromise, the Bolsheviki, and there was also the sense that it wasn't completely real—as Marshbrook Bridge was real. And this United Front? There wasn't much of it yet, but she'd got to force that girl Doris and those men to let her work with them, and her children with their children. It was up to her. If not—she felt more than ever bewildered by the publicists, more than ever certain about the people. Given good will. Which she had now. So much—and time. That was the difficulty. Before something else happened like in Germany. And some day soon, she thought suddenly, crossing a Barstone 'bus, I must go and see Margaret Coke-Brown—she's kept on asking me to come over and see the perfect baby. Well, I'm going to have a perfect baby, too, and there'll be nothing to be jealous about! Oh, my safe, comfortable baby, warm and growing in my blood-stream, I don't mind how much you take my strength and my life, I shan't ask it back from you ever. Now it will be spring; look, the elm at Canal Corner is reddening for spring; the sap is mounting towards the queer ruddy little flowers that turn so soon to seed. And on the straight towards Henley, where I drove so fast with Donald, the elms will be feeling spring—before the chestnuts, before the primroses, before any flowers, the English elms, rooting into the clay as you root into me, Oxford clay and Sallington clay—

> " In this dead late winter red comes to the elm trees,
> To every high rounded head a bronzy helmet,
> Before bud to the thorn, while mud still chokes cart ways,
> This rud red bloom high above hedges starting,
> Oh, England, we wait, now the great elms have reddened,
> The time is late, in cropped wet Oxford meadows
> I wait Spring and my baby——"

Oh, this spring I shall not see lambs and buttercups and the budding layers of hawthorn without being one of them —I shall be part of this spring. Tom and I will have helped to make this spring. But you must be Sallington's baby, too; you must learn to look at towns. Oh, look, look, there is the Power Station, the beautiful crown of chimneys, the easy purring of the turbines, pouring out power for workers. Oksana would like that, Donald would like that. Donald must have seen the Sallington Power Station often and often; he will come back and see it again, some day, when it is the workers', when England and Scotland are as he wanted them to be. Oh, my baby, the current from the Power Station is taking us along, in this tram which isn't a tram really, because it's got wings, it's a great crow, a great talking crow, and its come back to me. You shall drive tractors, my baby, you shall ride on the crow's wings, you will laugh at seals and kelpies and Campbell Women and all the silly things that frightened your mother. And oh, my baby, you shan't ever be a bargainer, you shall take the world into your good will and throw the grocer's scales into Corryvrechan for ever and ever. Oh, my baby, I'm so glad to have you, so very glad. . . .

## AUCHANARNISH 6

WHEN Dione got back to Oxford she found, besides a family impatient to be read to, played with, and generally de-measled, a letter from Alex and a book of poems from Victor. She had reluctantly to admit that Victor's poems were not very good—or could she be mistaken? Was she just too old to appreciate them? She showed them to several undergraduates, who only confirmed her opinion. Still, that didn't alter the fact that he did kiss very nicely. So few people can kiss while dancing without sooner or later treading on one's toes.

Alex's letter said: "Dear Dione, I haven't written for the last three weeks because there has been rather a fuss at Shields. To begin with, my show there has been got at by these damned politicians of yours, and it's going to turn political, which was the last thing I wanted. Perhaps you'll be pleased; at the moment I've got Labour and I.L.P. and Communists all fighting for my paint-pots, and it's all a beastly nuisance. However, the thing that's made the worst fuss is this. My fool of a girl, Nellie, has gone and started a baby. I told her she ought to deal with it, and so did her brothers, but she wouldn't be sensible, and apparently there's nothing much to be done about it now. I thought you could always go to a chemist's shop nowadays and take some muck, but she says not.

"Anyway, it looks like my having to support a little bastard now. I don't much mind, for I don't feel like marrying. I thought of marrying Nellie, but she'ld obviously be uncomfortable and I don't think there's much point. I shall see the kid's all right and gets decently educated and all that. As a matter of fact, I rather like the idea, and so does Nellie. I hope you aren't shocked, Dione, at the manner of begetting of your future nephew or niece, because I want to ask you if you've got any baby clothes or cradles or whatever it is babies want. I know you say you're finished with yours. I gather my get is due about the end of September. Nellie is pretty well, thank goodness. I'm getting her to go to a welfare centre. I gave her a wedding ring, as I gathered they're fashionable: several of her friends seem to be doing much the same thing, but they've only got Woolworth's—I ran to real gold. It's damned funny, you know. Thank the Lord, Shields is only a couple of hours from Edinburgh by the good trains. Your aff. brother, Alex."

Dione's answer to Alex: "Dear Alex, Congrats. about the baby—is that right? Goodness knows what I think about it. I suppose it's really as sensible as anything else one can do these days. Every kind of social arrangement one makes is so provisional, and this may be as good as St. Giles's or Hanover Square. Give my love to Nellie, and say to eat plenty of oranges and keep off fats, including fried things, especially fried fish—which I seem to remember the family had the day I was there. As to baby clothes, I'm afraid I can't, and why?—because I'm doing the same thing. You are an ass to think one can go to a chemist's shop—I tried a whole shopful on mine without effect, however I'm terribly pleased really. You'd better ask Phœbe; she's definitely finished with hers. And she certainly won't be shocked. Do try and be up at Auchanarnish at Easter. I've asked Mother if I can bring up a friend with me; she's a school-marm called Agnes Green, and such a dear—and she needs a holiday. Do be specially nice to her. She's a fierce Communist, and was a friend of Donald's, but I'm not telling Mother that! I'm sorry about your paint-pots, but I suppose it was inevitable; after all, unemployment *is* a political matter. Thanks, the measles are better. Your aff. sister, Dione."

Mrs. Fraser, delighted at the prospect of another grandchild, said that certainly Dione might bring up her friend Miss Green, but she must be sure to drive carefully—was it really sensible to come by car? She was sure to drive, too, fast on the flat roads, and then there was Rest-and-be-Thankful to cross, unless she came right round. Dione answered that she would be very careful and really Rest-and-be-Thankful was no difficulty with a decent engine.

So when the holidays began—poor Morag very gloomy about its being her last term at school, especially when she'd missed so much of it with those rotten measles!—Dione packed and sent off Nurse and Ian and Lilias, and prepared for the drive up with the three older ones. Tom couldn't come up till just before Easter, but he would be able to drive the car back. It was just about as much as Dione really liked doing, even now.

She picked up Agnes Green, in the same coat and skirt she had worn for last May Day, with a tidy little suit-case. The Midlands were at their loveliest; tender and subtle shades of green had climbed through the great shapes of elms and poplars; there was blackthorn and primroses; but the Lowlands were bare and bleak; spring didn't come there for another month, though there were plenty of March lambs on the hillsides. Agnes sat beside her, while the three children on the back seat played all sorts of make-up games, including great war-cries when they crossed the Border. Dione pointed out the land-marks. Here was Gretna Green, though it didn't look it, and on these dumpy hills Carlyle walked. Wait till you see *my* hills, Agnes!

The Highlands were pretty good. There was plenty of

snow about still, great heartening mouthfuls of cold snow air for Dione and her baby, that brighter, keener than any sea or meadow air, calling to hope and action. They had snow on each side of them on the pass, but the road was clear. Agnes gasped with pleasure, making curiously inadequate and school-mistressish remarks about the lochs and bens. She'll be better before I've done with her, thought Dione. Then they came down by Inverary, and the children booed the Castle. " Campbells," explained Dione. " The MacCallum Mor lives there."

" Who ? "

" The Duke of Argyll. That's our barbaric way of saying it. If you ever want to deal properly with dukes, you'd much better give them names you can put a bit of hate into ! Though I believe the present people are really very nice."

" How much land does he own ? "

Dione told her, adding : " But a good deal couldn't be used, anyway." She went on : " We live on the edge of Campbell country. Of course, you realise, Agnes, that it's nothing to do with the Frasers—they live right on the other side, but my mother was an heiress, so father came and lived on her land. She was a MacLean—like Donald—and Auchanarnish is a MacLean castle. The islands beyond are MacLean and MacIntyre and MacLeod."

" But," said Agnes Green. " You're taking me back into ancient history ! "

" Yes," said Dione, " in some ways. But it explains Donald—and me. And it explains me-and-Donald, if you see what I mean. And also the clansmen—the proletariat—are beginning to want the land. It used to belong to the clan, but that's all over a long time. It's on the cards that there might be a green revolution up here, Agnes. If we could only give this wretched lion a good dig in the ribs ! "

" *What* lion ? "

"The gules lion. Scotland. But it's all right, Agnes; I'm not really a Nationalist. At least—I'm a Socialist first."

They came to Auchanarnish and spring was there before them. The rhododendrons were all massing into blossom; the magnolia was showing waxy-white flames like a Japanese print. The primrose bunches clustered round all tree bases, the violet stalks were long. In the lawn Mrs. Fraser's daffodils held up proud leaves and heads; Agnes quoted Wordsworth at them. There were all sorts of pretties out in the walled garden—Dione took her up there at once after lunch: "Look, these are some of the finest blue primroses in Scotland, though I love the big ringed polyanthuses, and here are little scillas, and hepaticas—they grow wild in Norway, Agnes—and oh, look at the darling ferns beginning to uncurl! This is Donald's father's work—and there he is. Are you ready to meet him, Agnes?"

Agnes nodded: "Yes." For a moment she stooped over the rockery and a group of bulbocodium daffodils, but was she even seeing them?

Dione went ahead of her: "How do you do, MacLean? You've made it too lovely again this year, and I suppose I'm not to be allowed to pick anything? My Oxford garden is still all dead and wintery, and I cannot get my reticulata to do properly."

"No doubt you'll be giving them the wrong soil, Mistress Dione—they need an awful bad soil, you should put some gravel in with them."

"But I did, and it's no good. How's Mrs. MacLean keeping?"

"Ah, well, she wasna so grand over New Year—we missed you this year indeed, there was only Mr. Alex here at all—but she's better the now. We had word from Donald, saying he was married to a Russian woman; he has sent us the photograph of the two of them. Maybe you'll have been hearing as well ? "

" Yes, he sent me a photo, too ; she looks nice, don't you think ? "

" Aye, she's a good, homely-like lassie, and no' my idea of one of they Russians. Now, what will be your opinion on this Russian trial ? "

" The engineers will get a fairer trial than people accused of being Communists in other countries." MacLean shook his head and pulled up a dandelion ; she went on, hastily, to something less controversial. " Donald told me in his last letter that they were going to have a baby in summer, and if it was a little lassie, they'd name it after me."

" Guid sakes, Mistress Dione ! " MacLean stood dumb for a moment in the middle of the path, scratching it uncertainly with his rake. Was Agnes watching him ? " You'll maybe not be liking that, Mistress Dione ? "

" But I shall love it, MacLean, I shall be a kind of god-mother to it. I'm going to have a baby myself in October."

" Your mother was saying something o' the sort to me last week, Mistress Dione. I'm sure I hope ye're keeping well. I was to be sure to send in plenty vegetables."

" Here's someone to see you, MacLean. This is Miss Green, who was a friend of Donald's in England."

" How do you do, ma'am ? I am very interested to be hearing that, indeed I am. I am wondering if you were in the politics."

Dione said quickly : " Miss Green is a schoolmistress. Couldn't we go up to your house and see Mrs. MacLean, too ? "

It was a curious interview, with queer currents going on among them all, each hiding some of her or his thought from the others. Agnes Green was shown the photograph of Donald and his bride, taken outside against snow—Donald with a fur cap down over his ears, and Anna with her fair head bare, but a fur cap in her hands, both laughing. It was a nice photograph—if only Mrs. MacLean would admit that it was—if later on she could have as happy a photograph as that of Morag or Kenneth, she wouldn't care if they'd left her—left Father and Mother to follow—whatever it was. But yes, she *would* mind what they followed. There must be Socialist mothers in Germany whose sons had gone Nazi. Got at. If that happened—She could see the idea of Russia hurting the MacLeans. She wished she could tell them that if her baby was a boy it would be Donald after their Donald—they'd never guess otherwise, for Donald is a common enough Highland name. She wished she could tell them that Donald's hands had been good to feel—did they know that scar on Donald's hand as she did ?—or had that happened since he left home for good ? Most likely it had. She wished she could tell them that before the end she had wanted Donald's kisses. But what was the good ? In spite of Highland democracy there was too much of a barrier up between her and them for that telling. More than democracy was needed to break it down.

As she and Agnes were going back through the garden, Agnes wiped her eyes quickly. " What is it ? " she said.

" It's so terrible," said Agnes, " that they should acquiesce ! "

" In—all this ? Being my mother's gardener and so on ? Yes, I think it is. It's the remains of something that had value once. But we can't unstick them, Agnes. Nor my mother. It's had to be Donald who ceased to acquiesce. And me."

" Yes," said Agnes, " I suppose you don't really acquiesce, Dione, though sometimes I think you do."

" Honestly, I don't, Agnes. Sometimes I get entangled

with certain sorts of beauty—houses and gardens and pictures and old furniture ; I want them to fit in. That's all. But I've ceased to believe in the value that those kind of things have expressed. One can't go back on that. Look, Agnes, look at the lovely smooth trunk of the red-gum, the eucalyptus, and its long leaves hanging like combed hair. Go south from here, and you won't find another till the Riviera. That's the Gulf Stream that just happens to come by here. I suppose without it Scotland would be something quite different."

The next day Phœbe came up with Petronella, who had definitely started training for ballet, and Clemency, still occupied with wireless. Then Alex came, and then Tom, travelling up uncomfortably on Good Friday night. On Easter Sunday the grown-ups hid small chocolate eggs all over the garden, and then all the children, including the Finneys, the little Anderson boy, John MacLean's ten-year-old sister from Lerguligan, and red Peter's wicked and attractive imp of a son, also red-headed, hunted for the eggs. While the hunt went on, the grown-ups sat in the summer-house at the top of the garden and watched. Tom was very sleepy, as he always was the first few days of the holidays, and lay with his eyes shut in the sun ; the others sat on cushions on the stone steps. " Kenneth and Clemency are getting most. They're the practical ones ! " said Phœbe.

" I think Chrissie Finney has got most. She's an intelligent kid."

" Now how, for instance, will that child be educated ? " asked Agnes.

" She and her brother will probably both go to a University. You ought to meet Mr. Finney, Agnes. He knows pretty exactly what he wants politically."

" What is he ? "

" Dissatisfied Labour. Like a lot of us."

“ Look at that imp of Red Peter’s climbing all over the rockery ! MacLean will have his head off ! ”

“ My angel Morag isn’t getting any herself—she’s just trotting Lilias round.”

“ I expect, Dione, she’s too old to want eggs herself. In another three years she’ll have someone else to trot round ! ”

“ Oh, Phœbe, won’t it be lovely—won’t it be such fun to be putting another into the gang ! In another thousand years, when all our art and all our science seem childish and silly, people will just ask about us, were we happy and did we have children, did we continue mankind.”

“ And you’ll be able to say yes.”

“ For this moment, yes. For this hour, in the sun, in this particular place. But something might happen to-morrow ——”

“ But it won’t, lassie. What extraordinarily bright heads Scottish children running in sunlight have ! ”

Alex suddenly said : “ Well, I’m damned if my kid shan’t have it, too ! ”

Dione said, lower—for she hadn’t said anything to Agnes about Alex’s affairs : “ I expect you’ll want to bring him, Alex. I shan’t be surprised if you end by marrying Nellie.”

“ She’d like this better than Edinburgh.”

“ And I suppose it’ll be yours some day. A touch of the Earl of Burghley you know, Alex ! ”

“ Nellie wouldn’t be such a fool as that girl ! But, about Auchanarnish, I’ve no idea if Mother’s made a will, even—have you ? It’ll be the family house anyway. Unless your lot have abolished inheritance by that time.”

“ Yes, I suppose it ought really to be made into a sanatorium or something. A damned inconvenient one, with no electric light and no telephone and no central heating and miles from anywhere! What do you think, Agnes?"

"I don't want to go into political controversy now," said Agnes, "but how much land goes with it?"

"The policy itself is pretty small. The home farm is about forty acres. The rest is let off in small farms. Then there's Ardfeochan—up there—that won't even do for sheep."

"The farms must go to those that use them. What are your labourers like here? Are they—class conscious?"

"These farms are mostly worked by the farmers themselves with very little help—usually relations. Finney at Carse of Easland is the only one who's interested in modern methods. It's difficult enough to get the Andersons at the home farm to keep the cows decently clean. Morag's a cleaner milker than Mrs. Anderson. You'd better have a talk to the plowman, Agnes. That's his cottage, in the rowan patch over there. He's a marvellous dancer. I'm inclined to think the civilisation we want to aim for here is a loose co-operation of small farms; you can't do large-scale farming on land as hilly as this, though there might well be some more afforestation and that should be done centrally—from Edinburgh or Glasgow or wherever the real capital of Scotland will be. This might work best with several families living together as they did on the old Icelandic steadings; they'd get more comfort that way—they could, for instance, have lighting and power plants, run off the burns. But I don't know how much they'd like it. They certainly wouldn't stand for a kolkhoz, at any rate not yet—not till the kolkhoz idea is out of date."

Tom woke up: "Isn't it nearly tea-time?"

"I shouldn't come to the big tea if I were you, Tom. It'll be a frantic bun-fight with all the children. I'll bring you some through to the study."

"All right. I've got some more typing for you to do some time, Dione."

"Well, I can't do anything to-day. We shall have hide-and-seek all over the house after tea. Can you bear to play hide-and-seek, Agnes? It'll be light till quite late, so you won't meet the family ghost!"

"I don't believe in ghosts, you know," Agnes said.

"Nor do I really. Only—this is rather a special one. Well, it looks as if they'd got pretty well all the eggs. Come along."

They played general post in the big drawing-room, and then they played hide-and-seek all over the house, according to old-established rules. James Finney had one side and Morag the other. In a house of this complexity you needed as many seekers as hiders. All the grown-ups played except Tom, and about 6.30, after several children had burst in on the study and then explained that they'd forgotten it was out of bounds, he said he'd play, too. It was still full daylight and the sun was streaming into the western windows, dazzling the eyes of the seekers. "I'll go up to the old schoolroom and look there," said Dione to James Finney, who nodded. She went up slowly, for she had done a good deal of running and it was beginning to tire her. She wondered what would ever be done with the mass of unwanted books up there—she ought to get her mother to let her go through them. Out-of-date history and school books, bound volumes of magazines, all Mrs. Ewing—which the children wouldn't read—all Ainsworth, all Dickens, all Dumas, the poems of Coleridge highly illustrated, three top shelves full of theology, the volume of trials—would Morag be interested to read about Green Jean? She opened the door cautiously and looked in; the room was golden with the late sunlight. There was someone there, sitting on a window-sill, her back to the light; not seeing the face, for a moment she thought it was Phœbe. When she saw who it was she took a few steps nearer, thinking the appearance was bound to fade, afraid it would, hoping it would, hoping, afraid. It remained. Dione said to the figure sitting on the window-sill: "It is you, Green Jean, isn't it?"

"Aye," said the figure softly, and it had a voice something like Donald's. "They call me that. I am Jean MacLean of Auchanarnish."

Dione came nearer: "May I touch you?"

"If you are not feared for me," said Green Jean, and reached out a hand from under the plaid that hung over her shoulders.

Dione took the hand: "You feel like a real woman, Jean."

"Why would I not feel like a real woman? Because I am a witch?"

"No. Because—because——" It was obviously ridiculous to say to this woman, because you are dead. Instead, she said: "How have you come back, Jean?"

"I am never long away from Auchanarnish."

"Why have you shown yourself to me, then?"

"I was thinking maybe you would like to see me, you and your baby. My baby is sleeping. Wheesht, now!"

"I do like seeing you. Is it about anything—special?"

"Aye. I am wanting to help you, Isobel Dione. You have the Campbell Women against you, too. You ken that, maybe?"

"But are they—real?"

"They are as real as ever they were. You and your coven are in danger, Isobel Dione."

"My—coven?"

"Aye. Think, woman, think! Will I help you to see?"

"I wish you would. But, forgive my asking you—is there a price?"

"Na', there's no prices between us. I do it for good will. But maybe you will not like what you will be seeing."

"I want to see, all the same."

Green Jean put her hand in under the lacing of her kirtle and took out a small white stone with a hole pierced through the middle of it: "You have heard tell of this stone, Isobel Dione?"

"I—I thought it was cast into the middle of a loch somewhere."

"That would not be hindering it. Dare you take it until your hand?"

Dione held out her hand and Green Jean laid the stone in it. It felt like—an ordinary stone. "Dare you keek through it?"

"Will I come back safe if I do?"

"I can promise you that, Isobel Dione."

Dione looked through the stone.

# PART VI

## BEULAH

" All you that have a cool head and safe hands
Awaken early, there is much to do ;
Hedges to raze, channels to clear, a true
Reckoning to find. The other side commands
Eternity. We have an hour or two."

DAY LEWIS.

DIZZY and exalted with the rustling of the ballot papers. Dizzy. Looking over the tellers' shoulders. Now it was the final count. One after another, the crosses against Galton. Mason was pale and his eyes very bright. "It's dead sure now," he said, "we're in by three thousand. Barton's End went solid. River Ward went solid. Lumley and Marl voted as we've never known them." His hand gripped her arm. The tens were put into hundreds. The deal of the trestles was clear of loose papers.

Dorothy brought sandwiches: "Here, Dione, have one, I made them myself! Look at father, it's like all his dreams come true. But me—Bill and me, we're young enough to get the good of it all. I'm beginning to let myself make pictures of it. Bill and me working for England, not for anyone's pocket. And knowing the babies'll grow up into it! Oh, Dione, it's been worth messing and scrubbing all these years in Carisbrook Road. This'll make up for it." Dione was hungry, she'd had little to eat and much to do all day; she shared the sandwiches with Dorothy, who was going to get free.

Tom had a pencilled list of names in his hand. "We're getting in, all the Left, enough to swamp the old 'uns. MacCosh is in, Furnace is in, Cobleigh's got Widdecombe, Millman and Codd are in, David's in for Llanglas, Mary Peck's in, Colet's in—we've swept the collieries, we've got three wins already in Birmingham, we've got Manchester, Stockport, Cardiff, Bristol, all but one in Glasgow—they're coming in every minute——" The clerk came up and whispered to him. The Mayor of Sallington was at the head of the table. They took their places round him.

"Reuben," whispered Dione, "do you remember last time?" He nodded and squeezed her hand.

The declaration. Tom's little speech, the formal one to the tellers. How she loved him, the winner! Shaking hands with the Merrills. And now they were going upstairs, across a soft-carpeted official-looking room. Someone drew back a curtain from darkness. They were outside on a balcony. Immediately below was the cleared space, but beyond the ring of police was Sallington Market Square, alive with faces pointing towards them, packed beyond sight, the shouting, yelling crowd, now hushed for a moment as the figures went up, then the waves on waves of cheering, the voices pouring up out of darkness like a reflected waterfall, sending them spinning!

Then Tom speaking, shouting back at the crowd, slowly so that every word should tell, his voice almost broken after these queer, strained days—the election coming on them so suddenly, and then the two weeks' effort, all out. Now the end of the effort—no, what was she saying, the beginning, but what a beginning, who cares if we strain to breaking now!

"It will be Socialism in our time!" Tom shouted down to them, and for a minute could say no more against wild and glorious cheering. "This time—this time we're keeping our promises! England will be made fit for you men and women to live in and work for. The workers' England, Socialist England, working with the great Socialist unions for a Socialist world! Socialist Sallington for the Sallington workers, for you!" She heard him speaking still, but the words passed over her, drowning her in joy and pride and a deep seriousness, a bracing of mind and spirit for the new, the bigger effort.

They were in the soft-carpeted room again. Tom had Mason by one arm and Reuben Goldberg by the other. " It will be the next forty-eight hours ! " he said. " We've got to get the banks fixed before they can get England's money away from us ! We'll do it. That's up to MacCosh and Fox—they'll put it through. We'll get the banks and the big industries, we'll get the Press and the B.B.C., and then, my God, Stan, we'll have England Socialist by next Sunday ! "

Reuben said : " You think you can do it, Tom Galton ? You think you really can ? "

" That's what I'm for—that's what we're all for that you've made into your Executive, your fighting machine, your Labour Government ! "

" Socialist England ! " said Reuben suddenly, and his face and hands quivered, " next May Day——"

" Socialist England," said Tom, " and it's the Labour Movement that's done it ! "

Mason answered that, as deeply excited as the others, but still with the salt of irony behind it : " And you were both of you nearly out of it once. Remember, Tom ? And how you went smelling round the I.L.P., Reuben ? And now—now—there's no looking aside for any of us ! "

They were out of the Town Hall again, out into the workers' night. The shouts caught at them again. They were through the ring of police and into their own people, the Taylors, George Grove, Sam Hall, Mrs. East, old Miss Waterhouse blessing them, trembling with age and excitement, John Collis shaking hands, Jo Burrage, Edna Boffin, the Johnstons, Ed. Palmer, the named and unnamed Labour Movement, the hands, the faces, the ribbons, the green and red, young wheat and roses, faces, faces for a moment under the street lamp, love to them, good will, pride, brotherhood. In this instant of time one had the certainty of all eternity.

They were moving across the Square, towards the old car; they couldn't wait, for all their joy and pride, events wouldn't wait for them—London to-morrow, and action! The crowd round them forming and reforming, opened long enough for her to see across to a group in a car, silent mouths, eyes observing them, and she knew they were Coke-Browns and Campbell Women and she knew they weren't afraid—yet. They knew what power they had behind them. And the kind, the darling crowd was not hurting them, was leaving them to stare and plan evil and cruelty. It carried her and Tom past them, corner-wise across Sallington Market Square, in a great eddy of noise and feeling.

Once more the eddy was pierced, this time by a little dark figure, a woman in a coat and skirt, pushing through, with a plain red ribbon on her breast. "If you really mean this, Tom Galton, if you're really going to carry it out, we're with you. Trust us." Agnes Green. But where had she seen Agnes Green last? In the hall, running through towards the kitchen with Morag, one of the hiders in a game of hide-and-seek.

Dione looked up, not from faces to the starry sky above Sallington Market Square, but from the white pierced stone to the face of Jean MacLean who had been dead more than two hundred years. The excitement and joy shed away from her slowly like rain-water from one coming into the house after an August storm. She said: "Was this true? For if it was—oh, if it was, it is all I need!"

Green Jean said: "It might be true, but how can we be kenning if it is true? The stone, as you will have heard tell, is not a stone of truth but of warning. It means that this might be happening one day, yet maybe it is not even likely."

"Warning?" Dione said, "but there was no warning about that. It was as good as any of us have asked." Still she could hear Tom's voice saying Socialist England.

"Look again," said Green Jean, "if you dare look once yet, Isobel Dione."

Dione looked through the stone.

# PART VII

## THE RIVER

" Enitharmon laugh'd in her sleep to see (O woman's triumph !)
Every house a den, every man bound : the shadows are fill'd
With spectres, and the windows wove over with curses of
iron :
Over the doors 'Thou shalt not,' and over the chimneys 'Fear'
is written :
With bands of iron round the necks fasten'd into the walls
The citizens in leaden gyves, the inhabitants of suburbs
Walk heavy ; soft and bent are the bones of villagers."

William Blake.

"MORAG, Morag, my darling, can't you tell me?"

"Oh, Mother—oh, Mother——"

"There, my lamb, my sweet, Mother's got you—— Oh, Morag, for God's sake tell me what's happened! Where are the littles?"

"Nurse took them—she said she'd get to Scotland somehow——"

"But why did she take them?"

"When Mrs. Crewe telephoned that the Specials were coming—she and Ian took your rucksack and Father's—oh, where's Father?"

"Morag, I don't know. I heard—I heard he'd been seen alive after the gas attack—he said he'd try to get to Sallington. Morag, my darling, he'll get through. Where's Ken?"

"Oh, Mother—oh, Mother——"

"Morag—is he dead?"

"Mother. I don't know. They took him off. Two days ago. I've been alone ever since, waiting for you. Oh, Mother, I thought you'd never come."

"Who took him off—the Specials?"

"Yes, after they shot Teddy."

"Teddy——?"

"Yes. I buried him in the garden, in the hall rug. That was right, wasn't it?"

"Morag, my darling. Tell me something. What did the Specials do to you? Can't you tell me, Morag? Morag! Was it—that?"

" Yes, Mother."

" My darling, my darling, can you tell me at all? It might help you to get it out of your mind. When this is over, we'll get away, we'll go to the U.S.S.R. and you'll forget all about it. I promise you we shall."

" I don't want to go to the U.S.S.R. I want to die. I can't ever forget."

" Oh, my dearest, my dearest. Were you—very badly—hurt?"

" Yes. But I'm better now. It's stopped—bleeding. Mother, if I—if they—if it starts a baby I shall kill myself. I shan't mind killing myself. I nearly did after I'd buried Teddy, only—I wanted to tell you. I didn't want you to come back and find the house—like this. And no one."

" They tried to burn it, didn't they?"

" Yes, that's what the mark is. Only it was raining and it didn't catch. They said once they were going to tie me up and burn me."

" Morag!"

" They didn't. I don't suppose they would have really. Only—Mother, you'd better see what they did in the drawing-room. I tried to tidy it a bit. I didn't want you to see——"

" Don't cry, my pet, my baby——"

" It was when they broke up your little desk, Mother—and they broke the lovely bowl—and my little Chinese man—and look what they've done to the pictures."

" Yes. Yes. I see. But they're only things, Morag, only things. Don't cry about them. They don't matter really."

" Oh, Mother, it made such a beastly noise—breaking the things. And the picture of the unicorns in the wood. Mother, where's Aunt Phœbe?"

" I don't know. And—and I'm afraid Petronella's

dancing school may have been in the gassed area. I don't know. Yes. I suppose they did this all over the house?"

"Yes, Mother. They went up to the nursery and threw Donald's ship and Lilias's dolls' house out of the window. I—I was awfully glad they'd got away."

"Had Nurse any money?"

"Yes, she had some money of her own, and Cook gave her what she had—and I gave her Aunt Muriel's ten shillings, which was all I had. She said she'd try and walk and keep off the main roads. She took the push-cart for Donald."

"I wish you'd gone with her!"

"Ken and I decided we must stay and guard the house, for you and Father and—and Socialism. Cook said she'd stay, but then she got frightened. Oh, Mother, it was so awful seeing them come up the lane. Mother, shall we go and talk in the garden? I don't like staying in the house."

"I suppose they've smashed up the study? I'll just——"

"No, Mother, don't look, don't! That was where—I haven't been in since. Oh, they were such beasts. I just never knew——"

"All right, Morag, come out. There. What's happened to the rose-bed?"

"I buried Teddy there. It was the softest ground."

"But he wasn't a Red! I thought he was on the Reconciliation Council?"

"Yes, but you see he came just after they'd—done with—me. And he got frightfully angry and—and said what he thought of them. And then one of them just shot him with a revolver."

"Tell me about Ken, please, Morag. If you can."

"Well, Mother, we thought when they came we'd better try to be polite, because we couldn't stop them. But Mrs. Crewe had told us to burn Father's papers and we'd burnt a lot and—and I'm *glad* we had !—only they saw the grate full of ashes, and they got terribly angry, and—and they began to knock us about and call us names. They called us dirty little rats, and—and all sorts of horrid, nasty words ! So we said : ' We're Reds and proud of it.' We had to say that, hadn't we ? And they said the most awful things about Father, and they began smashing up his things. The little clock you gave him for Christmas, Mother—and his books—the big Cobbett and his Nonesuch Blake—and we had to look on. They said the most beastly things about Father—and you. And they tried to make us say them—and when we wouldn't they pinched us and pulled our hair. Oh, Mother ! "

" What sort of people were they, Morag ? What sort of voices ? "

" Just ordinary people. One or two of them looked like undergraduates. But they were mostly older. The only man I recognised was the man from the Banbury Road sweet-shop, the one at the 'bus-stop. And he was one of the men who—oh, Mother—oh, Mother——"

" Oh, my God. Morag, we'll get out of Oxford. You need never see it again. Go on, if you can."

" I whispered to Ken not to fight—he wanted to. But I thought—I thought it was our best chance. But they hurt us and teased us till we were both crying and then one of them said—oh, Mother, I *can't* go on ! Two of them tried to stop the others, but they wouldn't. Oh—oh—oh—I wish they'd shot me ! "

" Darling, darling, don't cry like that ! Please, Morag, please ! Try to tell me about Ken."

" That was afterwards. And after they'd smashed up the drawing-room. When Teddy was shot. Two men were holding Ken, but when he saw Teddy still—still twisting a little—he got loose and went for the man with the revolver.

He was nearly as tall as the man. Only the others all got hold of him and pulled him down. Oh, Mother, I thought they were going to shoot him, too! They nearly did. But then one of them said: 'If you're old enough for that you're old enough to be a Special and defend your country!' And he said to Ken: 'Are you coming with us?' And Ken said: 'No, I'm a Socialist.' And the man said to me: 'You'd better tell your brother to join.' And I said: 'I'm still a Socialist and I won't and he won't.' And the man said—and the man said——"

"Yes, Morag?"

"He said: 'Then you'd better say good-bye to one another.' And—and we did. Oh, Mother, Mother, have they shot Ken? We couldn't do anything else, could we?"

"No, my darling, you couldn't. And—and perhaps he's all right. Perhaps we shall find him again quite soon. Morag, we must think what to do now. Is there any food in the house?"

"Only a little rice and sugar and stuff. Nurse took some, and they took the rest. There are beans and peas in the garden, and lettuces. And gooseberries and strawberries still. Where can we go, Mother? Can't we find Father?"

"I think we'd better try. It's no use our trying to get away from a southern port, they'll all be guarded, but if we made our way to Scotland, we might get a boat."

"To the U.S.S.R.?"

"Yes, to Oksana and Donald. I've got hardly any money, though. Did they take my jewel-box?"

"Yes, and they wanted the silver, but I didn't know where the key of the safe was. They twisted my arm to make me tell, but I *really* didn't know!"

"Father's got the key. That's no use. There may be some little things left we can take with us and exchange for food. How far a day can you walk, Morag—twenty miles ?"

"Oh, easily. To Scotland ?"

"The question is, shall I try to go in to Oxford and see what's happening ?"

"No, Mother, don't! I tried to walk in to Oxford. I thought I'd go to Mrs. Crewe. But when I got to the beginning of the Banbury Road houses—that was yesterday —I met the odd-job man and he told me to go back. He said the Specials had got Oxford and I couldn't get across. And they'd know you. The telephone's cut off. Let's go to Scotland."

"Shall we try and go by Sallington ? There's just a chance that they may have held in the Midlands and the North."

"Oh, Mother, if they had——!"

"Let's try. Anyhow, we shall find out what's happened at Sallington and—if—if it's the worst—if we can't find Father there—we'll try for Scotland."

"For Auchanarnish ?"

"Yes. Nurse and the littles might have got to Auchanarnish."

Auchanarnish ? The littles at Auchanarnish. But they were all playing hide-and-seek at Auchanarnish. All over the house, the passages, the old schoolroom, Green Jean. She looked up from Morag's face to Green Jean's, her eyes were still smarting with dreadful unshed tears—unshed so as not to hurt Morag more. "Jean!" she cried, "oh, Jean, do you know what I saw then ?"

"Aye," said Jean, "it was the hunt."

"It was the counter-revolution."

"You will be naming it that, maybe. We had other names. But mind you, woman, mind you, it might not be true. It is a warning against the Campbell Women and all those that follow them. Dare you keek through the pierced stone again ?"

"Must I, Jean ?"

"There is no must to it, but I am thinking you will be wiser to take the full warning that's been got ready for you."

Dione looked through the stone.

# SALLINGTON 12

She got the news from Mrs. Taylor and Dorothy. They were sitting in Dorothy's kitchen. The front blinds were drawn and she had knocked for minutes before Dorothy had pulled the blind a few inches back, and saw her and opened the door and let her and Morag in, and then burst into tears and told them. The kitchen was dark, and Dorothy had taken down and burnt the Socialist posters. No one had dared to keep them up, even inside the houses. After she had been told, Dione said nothing for a minute or two. They stood and watched. Morag had collapsed into the armchair and lay with her eyes shut; it was as though not even this news could touch her any longer. "When have they fixed for the execution?" Dione said.

"This evening," said Dorothy, "my Bill." Her lips went on moving, but no sound came out of them.

"I take it you've both done everything that was in your power?"

"Everything," said Mrs. Taylor, "but they won't listen to us. And him—always so gentle—he wouldn't hurt a fly. After being a pacifist all his life. And now——"

"Don't, don't! You say your father was killed in the fighting, Dorothy?"

"Yes, and Ed. Palmer, and Edna Boffin and Mrs. East's boy, and—oh, it would have been better for Bill if he'd got killed then, when we was still hoping!"

"You say Tom was—wounded?"

"Yes," said Mrs. Taylor. "But it wasn't much. I bandaged it myself. He kept on talking about you, he said——"

" Don't tell me now or I—I shan't be able to do anything. And Mason's wounded ? "

" He broke his arm."

" Listen, Mary Taylor. I'm going to try and see Rosalind Coke-Brown. I don't know what chance I have. Don't hope. But if she's got any decency she ought to listen to me. Keep Morag here. If I don't come back help her to get off to Scotland. But I shall come back. No, I won't have tea or anything. It'll take an hour to walk to Barstone."

She knew the house well enough. Those lunch parties. Before Marshbrook Bridge. It wasn't the parlourmaid who opened the door, but a man in the uniform of a Special, who at first refused to let her in. But when she asked if she might write a note, he let her, grudgingly, and took it through. Dione waited, curiously aware on Rosalind's doorstep of having walked through her stockings and not having washed properly for days. The man came back and told her to follow him. In the hall he turned and looked at her, his arms a-kimbo. He said : " So you're Galton's wife, are you ? " And then he laughed and it was worse than anything he could have said. Rosalind's boy George came out of the dining-room, an officer of the Specials, with a chocolate macaroon in his hand. He looked at Dione and dodged back, dropping the macaroon. Rosalind was in her drawing-room at a desk, in the feminine version of a colonel of the Specials. She was dictating something to a girl with a pad on her knee, and when the girl looked up, with a stiff, scared face, it was Margaret Coke-Brown.

Dione said : " Rosalind, do you know that your brother is going to be shot this evening ? "

Rosalind said in a loud voice : " He is a traitor. He is not my brother any longer. He and his like must be wiped out."

" Rosalind——"

" I forbid you to call me that ! "

" Tom is wounded." Rosalind moved her head uneasily from side to side, then stayed still, frowning. " I believe you will regret these executions. They will make a very bad impression on foreign countries."

" We are not like you rebels. We are not concerned with what the foreigner thinks. We are concerned with our English Empire. These executions are necessary. They are a purging. Our country had gone rotten. Now it will be England again ! "

" Is it English to shoot prisoners ? Wounded men ? "

" It was their doing. They began the revolution. We have to crush them. In a week we shall have order again. We cannot have any false mercy and weakness now ! "

" But——" For some ten minutes by the clock Dione Galton argued with her sister-in-law. She tried to argue in general, not especially for Tom. She thought of Stan Mason and Taylor and Dorothy's Bill. She daren't make Rosalind angry, daren't say what it would have been such a relief to say. She thought of Morag waiting in that kitchen. She had to be very gentle, very patient; if Rosalind thought they were beaten—thought she had them down—as they were down.... She listened patiently when Rosalind suddenly launched off on to a lecture about the other plane. And as the ten minutes went on, she became more and more certain that it was no good. Tom would be dead before night. Tom. Suddenly she noticed that she was crying. The tears were coming down her face on to her dusty, dirty dress. And at the same time Rosalind said sharply : " Go away ! I don't want to see you any longer ! I haven't time. I'm busy ! "

Then Dione took two steps to the edge of the desk and went down on her knees, catching at Rosalind's khaki cloth skirt. She couldn't think of any but the most ordinary words. "Rosalind!" she cried. "Rosalind! For God's sake, don't let them shoot Tom!"

But Rosalind jumped up, twitched her skirt out of Dione's hand, and hurried out of the room, calling: "George! Reginald!"

Dione slipped, fell with both hands on the floor. She picked herself up and faced Margaret Coke-Brown. "What are *you* doing here?" she said.

Margaret Coke-Brown answered in a low, hurried whisper: "I had to, I tried to join the Reconciliation Council, but I couldn't—my husband—at least I'm not in the Specials!"

"You were a Socialist once," Dione said.

Then Rosalind came back and young George with his black moustache, and a riding-whip in his hand instead of a biscuit. "Now!" she said.

"Rosalind!" Dione cried desperately, "think of Muriel! What'll she say when she knows you've killed Tom!"

"I don't care what she says!" Rosalind half shouted. "She's one of the Reconciliation Council—traitors—and stupid traitors, as they'll find out before we're done with them!"

"Oh, Rosalind, you've got us beaten and smashed—we're begging for mercy now——"

"I won't have it! I won't! Now, George."

George tapped nervously with his riding-whip. "Get out," he said, "or—or I'll make you!"

"George!" Dione cried, abasing herself hideously to the boy, "don't you remember summer holidays——"

"No, I don't!" shouted George, and caught hold of her and hauled her out of the room. In the hall the other Special got hold of her.

"What do we do with this one?" he said, and Dione

was frightened as she didn't know she had it in her to be frightened still.

Suddenly George said: "Take her to the prison and bloody well make her look on! That'll teach her!"

Two Specials took her handcuffed at a sharp trot down the road. They saw an empty car with their pennant, and hailed it and shoved her in. She sat between them, her head dropped over the handcuffs, her messed-up hair plastered over one damp cheek. The car stopped with a jerk, and they ran her out of it and into the gaol. They passed a prison official—not one of the Specials—and she went down on her knees and begged to be allowed to see Tom. The official hesitated. "She can, can't she?" he said to one of the Specials, who answered sharply that she couldn't, and then whispered something to the official, who hurried away. She was taken through to a high narrow yard. There was a squad of Specials sitting about, some reading newspapers, others with playing-cards.

"Give her a good view," sniggered one of them, and made her climb up on to a heap of sand and planks. She seemed to be standing there for hours, handcuffed. It was perceptibly darker already. She couldn't think about anything.

Then she heard a sharp order behind her, and the slamming of rifles—the squad was formed up. And then a small door opposite her opened. First three armed Specials came out, and then the prisoners bunched together, their eyes blindfolded already, and their hands tied behind them. They were strung out along the wall. Nearest to her was Taylor, the man who disbelieved in violence. Then Sam Hall, with a scalp wound plastered with dark blood. Then Dorothy's Bill. Then Reuben Goldberg. Then Mason. But they hadn't tied his hands because his arm was broken; his coat was buttoned over it and he shook a little. Then

Tom. With his trouser cut off at the knee and his leg bandaged. Beyond Tom two women. "Tom!" she yelled suddenly. "Tom, we'll remember, we'll——" And then there was a hand over her mouth, she staggered and was shoved back, gagged.

She saw Tom turn, heard him call for her agonisedly: "Dione!" and couldn't answer him. She saw the others turn too, Stan Mason, the women beyond Tom—heard the order to the firing squad, the click of the loading—heard the beginning of the "Red Flag," the voices rising to it raggedly—Tom's voice—and saw that the two women were the Communist mill-hand Doris and Agnes Green.

Agnes! Tom!

The suffocating gag held her, she tossed away from it, tossed her head back, gasping, choking. "Jean—Jean—was that true?"

"You have been warned," Green Jean said in that gentle voice like Donald's, and faded—faded—and the sun had set.

And Agnes Green came hastily into the schoolroom: "Dione, what were you doing? We lost you!"

Still gasping and sobbing, Dione caught hold of her: "I saw," she said; "I saw the counter-revolution happening. And you were all being shot!"

"My dear, my dear, you're over-tired. Shall I get you a glass of water?"

"No—Tom," she gasped.

And then Tom came in, too, and saw her clinging on to Agnes Green, and cried out: "Sweetheart, what is it?" and caught her under the shoulders, his arm by Agnes Green's arm.

"We have been warned," Dione said, and it was as though a steel spring had suddenly loosened and vibrated inside her. The baby was coming alive and moving in her for the first time.

Lightning Source UK Ltd.
Milton Keynes UK
UKHW010630060819
347486UK00002B/404/P

9 781849 210263